Praise for *In a Not S*

"A stellar romance rich in voice, hu
must-read for those who enjoy nove
Meet on Vacation."

—*Library Journal* (starred review)

"Looking for the perfect escape from our not so perfect world? Neely Tubati Alexander's latest is just what we all need right now—warm weather and romance with the author's signature humor and intelligence. I loved this book!"

—Sarah Jio, *New York Times* bestselling author of *With Love from London* and *Blackberry Winter*

"A fantastic mix of smart writing, fun twists, and fate. . . . Neely's voice is just perfect—reading anything she writes feels like listening to a fantastic story from a best friend. . . . A truly fun, thought-provoking, coming-of-age read with nods to feminism, *In a Not So Perfect World* may be the perfect thing to read while inhabiting our own imperfect worlds."

—Zibby Owens, author of *Blank* and *Bookends* and host of the podcast *Moms Don't Have Time to Read Books*

Praise for *Love Buzz*

"For anyone who has ever gritted their teeth through a bachelorette weekend, *Love Buzz* is the perfect escapist read. . . . A journey into identity, love, fate, and determination, *Love Buzz* is absolutely delightful."

—*Good Morning America*

"I loved this book! Neely Tubati Alexander is a writer to watch!"

—Emily Giffin, #1 *New York Times* bestselling author of *Something Borrowed*

"An exciting debut novel."

—*Pure Wow*, "Best Beach Reads of Summer"

"A sparkling debut about grief, love, family, and the road not taken. . . . I can't wait to read whatever she writes next."

—Allison Winn Scotch, *New York Times* bestselling author of *The Rewind* and *Cleo McDougal Regrets Nothing*

"*Love Buzz* is a delightful love potion you'll want to drink in one gulp. . . . Warm, tender, and life-affirming, a reminder that chasing love is the most worthwhile pursuit."

—Taylor Hahn, author of *The Lifestyle*

"*Love Buzz* offers readers a delightful story sure to spark moments of thoughtfulness and joy as Serena seeks a life crafted for—and by—herself, which just might include the very charming man she must find again."

—*Shelf Awareness*

"[An] outstanding debut. . . . Readers will be swept away. . . . Alexander's inclusive representation of diverse backgrounds and sexual identities in lovingly crafted characters with rich and unique personalities is truly impressive. Readers will hope for more from this exciting new romance writer."

—*Booklist* (starred review)

"Funny, thoughtful, original, and romantic, *Love Buzz* is an deftly crafted novel by Neely Tubati Alexander that will have a very special appeal to readers with an interest in rom-com style contemporary romance."

—*Midwest Book Review*

"A charming debut. . . . Endearing side characters that readers won't get enough of round out this moving tale of embracing life's imperfections. Tubati Alexander will win plenty of fans with this."

—*Publishers Weekly*

"Growth, change, and a little bit of luck are at the center of Alexander's romantic debut. . . . Will appeal to romance readers who like their books with a hefty dose of personal growth and women's fiction aficionados seeking a happily-ever-after."

—*Library Journal*

In a Not So Perfect World

Also by Neely Tubati Alexander

Love Buzz

In a Not So Perfect World

A Novel

Neely Tubati Alexander

HARPER PERENNIAL

NEW YORK • LONDON • TORONTO • SYDNEY • NEW DELHI • AUCKLAND

HARPER PERENNIAL

This is a work of fiction. Names, characters, places, and incidents are products of the author's imagination or are used fictitiously and are not to be construed as real. Any resemblance to actual events, locales, organizations, or persons, living or dead, is entirely coincidental.

HarperCollins books may be purchased for educational, business, or sales promotional use. For information, please email the Special Markets Department at SPsales@harpercollins.com.

FIRST EDITION

Designed by Jamie Lynn Kerner

Library of Congress Cataloging-in-Publication Data has been applied for.

ISBN 978-0-06-329294-9 (pbk.)
ISBN 978-0-06-337710-3 (library edition)

24 25 26 27 28 LBC 5 4 3 2 1

For the Pessimists

In a world full of chaos and uncertainty,
love remains our constant anchor.

—Paulo Coelho

In a Not So Perfect World

1.

I ALWAYS THOUGHT MY FIRST REAL LA EARTHQUAKE WOULD BE catastrophic—the Big One that has eluded me my whole California life. Instead, it's a 4.1 on the Richter scale and barely registers with the other patrons of the upscale West Hollywood bar I find myself in on a Monday night. It *is* big enough, however, to cause the already wobbly drinker next to me in the ladies' room to lose her balance. As the earth trembles, she crashes to the floor—her glittery platform heel catching on a loose bathroom tile, causing her to land mouth-first against the unforgiving ceramic.

I hear the crack when her face connects.

"Oh my god," mumbles my best friend, Tess, spinning to face the corner like a kid in time-out to avoid the spectacle.

I bend down closer to the girl on the floor as the earth stops its relatively minor quake. "Are you okay?"

She peers up at me, her face equally stunned and distraught, as I attempt to hide my alarm at the state of her face. Her mouth and chin are swathed in blood, and I'm pretty sure she's missing a front tooth.

I was absolutely looking for a distraction from Tess's plan for the night, but this certainly is not what I had in mind.

"Ith it bad?" the girl asks, swiping her fingertips along her bottom lip. She doesn't wait for me to respond. Instead, she pulls her hand up to her eyeline, takes in the sight of her blood-smeared fingers, then clambers to her feet. In an instant she is staring at herself in the water-marked mirror above the oversize sink, a trough-like basin with three faucets.

"Oh," she whispers at her reflection. Her mascara has smudged under her eyes, her face a canvas of black and red, making the scene all the more unsettling. She turns on all three faucets and begins alternating time at each, lapping handfuls of water against her marred face. Perhaps she believes she's getting more water this way. Perhaps she's in too much of a panic to see the clear lack of efficiency. I'm about to remind her of the drought but decide it's not the best timing.

Tess is still in the corner and has gone to her happy place, humming "Let It Go" with her eyes pressed tightly shut, a pointer finger shoved into each ear. She'd immediately pass out if she were forced to see this girl's bloodstained face. And as the only other person in the bathroom, I don't particularly care to handle both situations at once.

"Why 'th there tho much blood?" the woman pleads as she continues to splash herself with water from all three faucets.

"Facial lacerations bleed heavily. Highly vascular," I say, circling my palm in front of my face to articulate my point. "Don't let that scare you though. It's probably way less serious than it looks."

When the woman has cleared most of the mess from her face, she lets out a yelp of disbelief when she finds that one of her front teeth is in fact missing. She leans in close to the mirror to evaluate, bumping her nose against it, leaving a smudge of fair-colored foundation the size of a nickel. It's not chipped, not loose—that tooth—but completely gone. I'm already on the ground looking for it, running my hands along the black ceramic floor tiles of the heavily trafficked bar bathroom. I push away a wad of disembodied hair, a gum wrapper, and a lime-green press-on nail.

I will bathe in hand sanitizer when I get home.

"Found it!" I declare, picking up the tooth from a grout line (by the crown, never touch the root), and handing it to its owner.

"Whath do I do with ith?" she asks, her left eyelid twitching under the smear of black. Her bluntly bobbed auburn hair has, through it all, impressively maintained its perfect drape.

"Wash it off, then *gently* try to push it back into place."

The girl attempts to do as I've suggested, shoving the tooth mercilessly into her undoubtedly tender gum.

I wince.

"Ith's nod working," she says, her body taking on a jittery bounce.

"No, it's not going to just go back in and stay, but if you can position it in place until you get to an emergency dentist, that would be best."

She tries again to place the tooth.

It looks like a Chiclet shoved into a watermelon wedge.

"It'th thill nod working," she says, panic raising the octave of her voice.

"Stay here. I'm gonna get some milk from the bar."

"What?"

"Milk. We'll put it in a small glass of milk to keep it wet. It's better than water. Water's too harsh for the root," I tell her, heading for the door.

"Are you a denthist?" she asks, turning her attention from her reflection for the first time to evaluate me.

"No, she just knows weird shit!" Tess yells from the corner, still facing the wall.

The girl looks back at me, her desperate raccoon eyes questioning.

"I learned it in a video game. *Immortal Clash.* A right hook to the mouth is my favorite knockout move." I mimic a right hook into the air.

She blinks hard. Clearly not a gamer.

"Sloane! Take me with you," Tess squawks from the corner, hands over her eyes.

I grab her elbow and lead her out of the bathroom toward the bar.

The girl's friends find her and rush her out of the venue, one carrying the cup with her milk-soaked tooth. I hope they can get her to an emergency dentist at this hour without drunkenly losing the tooth. I think of tagging along to ensure the crisis is handled properly, though Tess would not allow it. She's on a mission tonight. And that mission is centered around me.

While I'm certainly glad it wasn't the Big One that hit tonight, it's troubling that nobody else in the bar seemed to notice the earthquake at all. I get it. We're Angelenos. We worry more about reusable straws and gluten than preparedness. Nonetheless, a brief acknowledgment of a natural disaster seems warranted. Perhaps I imagined it, but I swear the crowd may have even cheered like the jerk of the earth was nothing more than the perfect bass drop. It's as if the walls around them would need to be crumbling before they'd grasp the slightest sense of trouble.

Amateurs.

Now that the quake is over, Toothless has been handled, and I have adequately calmed Tess, I rest against the back wall of the swanky bar with two simultaneous thoughts: *My cocktail has far too much sugar*, and *I've got to figure a way out of the plan my best friend has concocted*.

"What about him?" Tess says, pointing to her sixth potential candidate.

"Definitely not." I lean back more against the wall, the mahogany rail pressing into my shoulder blades, evaluating the guy Tess has set her sights on.

"Why?"

"Because . . ." I assess the guy at the bar, looking for something—anything—I can use against him. "He's wearing a sweater with elbow patches. On a scale of one to serial killer, he's like a full 'will wear my skin as a dress.'" I wrap my arms around my waist protectively.

Anticipating my reaction, Tess exhales, then moves on undeterred. "Fine, him?" She points to a guy sitting at the far corner of the coffee-colored bar—potential suitor number seven.

"No way. He's got a man bun. You know I don't do man buns."

"I don't know, I kinda like it," Tess says, biting at the tip of her straw playfully.

I take another sip of the drink Tess paid for—something she's done a lot lately, since I'm currently jobless with a laughable bank balance. This place, with its real copper mugs and upscale hipster customer base, is, as a result, her choice, not mine.

"Him?" she says, pointing in the opposite direction, a clear attempt to disarm me with speed.

"No. Look at him." We both watch as the guy in question runs a hand through his wavy blond mane. His mouth is a thin straight line and in this shadowy light, it's hard to tell if he has lips at all.

"I'm looking. He's cute. What's the problem?"

"I get the feeling he doesn't like animals. People like that can't be trusted." I lean forward and squint to observe him more closely. "Actually, he looks like that guy in Modesto who killed his wife and kids and hid their bodies in the walls."

Tess's right eyebrow, which seems to move of its own volition, arches.

"I listened to a podcast about it."

Her eyebrow reaches higher, threatening to impose on her hairline.

I know I'm being petty, superficial, and downright rude

judging these men. But I can't bring myself to really look at any of them as potentials. It's maddening, more than anything, that my heart is still holding on to a place—a person—that can't properly truss it; fingertips on a crumbling cliff.

I evaluate the possible Modesto murderer. He brandishes a shaved line through his right eyebrow and an ironic mustache.

"There was a picture of him in the show notes, you know. In fact, now that I really look, it could actually be him—"

"Okay, stop!" Tess looks to the ceiling, exasperated. "Maybe Satan Sloane needs to come out to play. Conjure her, please."

I think back to the fall evening during our sophomore year at UCLA that was my first brush with vodka. Freshman year, Tess and I had obtained fake IDs stating home addresses in Spring Lake, New Jersey, purchased for one hundred and fifty dollars from a biomed senior who still lived in the dorms. Tess secured a two-for-one discount because she agreed to dress as the Harley Quinn to his Joker for that year's Comic-Con.

After three vodka sodas, I got us banned from Freddie's, our favorite Westwood bar, for throwing a dart at the guy who grabbed Tess's butt, but not before threatening to castrate him. Thus, Satan Sloane was born. She typically only appears to make bad decisions after a few too many cocktails, which could include anything from overconfident flirtation to dart attacks, though she has been known to occasionally show up during a particularly raucous game night as well.

"Absolutely not. I cannot deal with the ramifications of Satan Sloane tonight. I have an interview tomorrow. *The* interview."

"Okay, I give up." Tess throws her hands up like she's tossing confetti. "You choose, then, since none of my selections seem to live up to your standards."

"Or you could drop this ridiculous game."

"It's not a game, Sloane. You *need* this. You've been pining away over Zane for nearly six months now. You deserve to be free of his hold over you. I promise dropping that dead weight will make you better in *the* interview tomorrow."

A little piece of me wilts inside when she says his name. *Zane.* That baby sprout of hope that I could hear it and not have a physical reaction, trampled. "I hardly see how making out with a random stranger at a bar is going to help with either of those things."

"It'll break the seal, get you comfortable around guys again. Take all the pressure off so you can focus on the *real* next time. And, it'll give you an adrenaline rush that can carry you into tomorrow's interview!" She pauses for a long sip of her cocktail—something a cloudy yellow color with a massive sage sprig sticking out of it. "Besides, we could have died tonight in that quake had it been the actual Big One. Do you want your world to end with *Zane* being the last guy you kissed?" She says his name like it brings up a splash of throw-up in her mouth.

I am inclined to defy Tess and call it an early night; but one, she's paying for the drinks, and two, she's giving me the look that has served her well in getting what she wants in life—eyebrows raised, blue eyes gleaming, and mouth parted in a devious smile that makes people unsure if she's about to scold or compliment them. Half the time, I'm uncertain myself—and we've been best friends since coding camp when we were twelve. It's what makes her a successful attorney, I think—her ability to get what she wants with a look. She doesn't spend her days in courtrooms. Instead, she sifts through financials and angry text messages in messy divorce cases, a line of work that's made her anti-relationship. You'll never hate someone more than the person you once loved, according to Tess.

I can attest to that.

We were an unlikely pair, Tess and I, even back during that

first summer at camp. I was captivated by every bit of knowledge I could gain, greedily exploiting the access to development software and courses on writing code. I convinced my parents to send me after I'd researched and delivered a presentation on the benefits of coding for girls. Although looking back, I think my mom had secret hopes of me meeting future suitors. On the other hand, Tess was only there because her parents booked an impulsive romantic getaway to the Italian countryside, and sleepaway coding camp was the only childcare they could find last-minute. We bonded over our mutual disdain for Sammy Baskin, the fifteen-year-old miscreant who built goblins named Tess and Sloane into the *Ghostbusters* knockoff game he built that summer. Sammy Baskin is now an Indiana congressman.

I look at my phone—9:42 p.m. I've got to wrap this up if I want to be in bed by eleven. I need a solid seven hours of sleep in preparation for what I am resisting calling the most important day of my life so I don't dissolve in panic. Tess had convinced me to come out so I wouldn't sit home alone in my apartment stewing over my interview, but now I'm not so sure it was a good idea.

I'd better get on with it.

"Fine, I'll choose for myself," I tell Tess. "If it'll get you off my back and it means we can leave. God, this night would be so much better if I were at home on my couch in my underwear with Finn." I instinctively pull at the waistband of my jeans.

Tess moans. "How would that be different from any other night of your life?"

A tall, slender guy with a wiry beard standing next to us peeks over his shoulder at me with a sly grin.

"Relax, dude, she's talking about her dog." Tess flicks her hand at him and he turns away.

My annoyance is ballooning and it fuels my search as I scan the crowded bar. I wonder how all these people have the energy, time, and money to be out on a Monday night. Not to mention, every guy in here is so . . . pretty. It may not sound like a problem, but I've never been particularly attracted to in-your-face handsome. And the pants are all so tight. I am genuinely worried for their collective sperm count. In the event of a zombie apocalypse, or a flaming asteroid hitting this spot in West Hollywood, I'm certain they'd all be trapped by their lack of ability to run in those debilitating pants.

I'm about to point and say "what's that?" to Tess to get her to turn away from me so I can bolt for the entrance—

Then I spot him.

He's a few feet away, sharing a table with three other guys. I watch as he rubs his hands together in small circles absentmindedly under the table, the muscles up his arms flexing lightly as he does. There is no man bun. He's wearing a black-on-black Dodgers cap, but under it I clock that his eyebrows are the right amount of unkempt. His jeans are somewhat loose. Because he's facing my direction, I can see he's wearing a white T-shirt with a picture of a cactus that says FREE HUGS. Cute. He raises his left hand, removes his hat, and runs his fingers through his dark hair before replacing it again. I take note of the absence of a ring. There's no potential girlfriend nearby, and he doesn't seem to be romantically attached to any of the men in his group. He smiles at one of his companions across the table, raising his chin into the light, and I see a dimple shadowed along his right cheek. I feel something like attraction. It's a sad, nostalgic feeling.

There's a familiarity about him, though after three sugary cocktails, I can't quite place him.

No matter. I've chosen my mark.

I hand Tess my drink and head over, leaving her staring, mouth agape. She doesn't think I'll do it. I can feel her eyes burning into my back, and I know she's trying to decide if I'm making a run for it. I don't. Instead, I walk right up to Free Hugs Guy's table.

She's right, after all. We could have died tonight had that minor quake been the Big One. And the world *cannot* end with Zane being the last guy I've kissed.

2.

HERE'S WHERE IT GETS AWKWARD—AS IF THIS WHOLE THING ISN'T awkward enough. He's sitting at a table, and I'm now standing behind him. Do I squeeze my way between his chair and his friends, then crouch down in an unattractive squat? Do I tap him on the shoulder and ask if I can take him up on a free hug, as his shirt offers? Do I just stand here and hope he notices me?

I really do suck at this.

I look over at Tess, who flicks her chin skyward, as if to say *Do it now or earn my wrath*.

I'm about to swerve and make my way to the ladies' room to buy some time when Free Hugs Guy shoves his chair back to stand and the rail hits me square in the stomach. I let out a cry, double over, and instinctively wrap my arms around my center.

"Oh shit, I'm sorry." He shoots up from the seat, places a hand on my lower back, and bends down to meet my eyes.

"It's fine," I groan, my voice a stiff baritone. He remains bent, his broad hand pressed firmly against my back, until I change position. Then, slowly, I straighten, and he does the same. My eyes meet his face, and I find a modest grin across his mouth, dimple marking his right cheek.

"It's you," he says, his eyelids constricting a bit.

"What?" I mutter, still reeling from the windless sensation in my gut.

"Nothing, no, I'm sorry," he says, mouth contracting back to its neutral state. "Are you sure you're okay? Do you want to sit?" He extends an arm toward the chair that just attacked me.

"I'm fine. Really."

"Let me get you a drink. As an apology." He holds his hands out in front of him, palms facing the ceiling. I try to think. And physically recover. But his presence is too distracting. Up close and upright, he's taller than expected. His deep brown hair is almost black, the edges of it sticking out the sides of his cap. He's got this universal tan that's indistinguishable and could mean a variety of ethnicities, though his eyes, lightly shadowed beneath the brim of his hat, are a pale blue. The whole combination makes his face rather interesting, though not offensively pretty like the others.

He raises his charmingly mussy eyebrows in what I take as a doubling down of his offer.

"I'm ordering the most expensive tequila in this place," I say, attempting to hide a grin. "Maybe it'll heal the internal bleeding."

"Great. I mean about the drink, not the internal bleeding." He holds his arm out toward the bar as if to say *After you*.

As I lead him to the bar, I steal a glance at Tess in the corner, who is chatting with the guy she pointed out to me earlier, adorned with a man bun, sweater with elbow patches, *and* tight pants (the Tess trifecta). She's momentarily distracted from her mission for me. Nonetheless, I'm in it now. I've got something to prove to myself. Zane doesn't get to keep his hold over me anymore. And I am more than capable of taking this one, silly step toward finally being free of him.

Free Hugs Guy leans against the shiny mahogany bar as he orders our drinks, one stark white canvas sneaker propped on the footrest. It's crowded, and we have pressed in between two barstools, stationed closer than I'd otherwise choose, practically touching. I position my face so the pimple on my right cheek is subdued in a shadow, surprised at the care I'm placing on putting my best foot forward. He says something, but his words are swallowed by the swirl of noise around us and I begin to panic. I can't do this. I don't want to do this. I'm not ready to put myself out there again.

I glance over my shoulder and see Tess is still with Man Bun, though her attention is focused on me, probably because she can sense I'm potentially chickening out. She's likely only a few seconds away from abandoning her own conversation and making her way toward me as fast as her little legs can manage.

Time's up.

The bartender sets down two tequila sodas in front of us. Free Hugs Guy turns to hand me one. I can't help but think I should be pulling a cocktail condom out of my purse to protect my drink from the stranger danger in front of me. But there's no time. I won't be drinking it anyway.

One song ends and another begins—the Uncle Kracker version of "Drift Away" sweeps between us and I take the softer song as a sign to press forward with this questionable plan.

"Can I . . . I mean, would you . . ." I fumble every potential whole sentence that might make its way out of my mouth. "I have a favor to ask."

"What is it?" He takes a sip of his drink, so casually I almost feel bad that I'm about to ambush him.

"See, my friend Tess . . ." I glance over my shoulder at Tess, who has returned her attention to Man Bun, now twisting her body right to left in a flirty sway. If I weren't in the midst of this current situation, I'd pull out my phone and record her acting decidedly un-Tess-like in her clear flirtation. "She has this plan for me tonight," I continue, refocusing. "I'm supposed to kiss someone." My maturity level at this moment feels like that of a preteen. Why did my breakup with Zane launch me so far backward?

He cocks his head to the right and it's reminiscent of Finn when he's trying to understand part of a conversation. "Kiss someone," he repeats, crossing his arms in front of him in observation.

"Yes. It's stupid, I know. It's just . . . I need to do this or she's not gonna let me leave and I need to get home and it's—"

"Yeah, okay."

I stare up at him. "Really?"

"Sure, why not?"

"Don't you even want to know why?" I ask, surprised and somewhat skeptical of his willingness.

"Do you want to tell me why?" he asks.

I shake my head. "Not particularly, no."

"Okay then."

Is it really this easy? He's acting as though mine is a normal, perfectly sound request. Does this kind of thing happen to him a lot? I appraise his objectively handsome face for a moment and believe that perhaps it could be a common occurrence for him.

Then, before I can think better of it, I throw my hand to the back of his head and pull it toward me. Our faces ram into each other, the corner of the brim of his hat nearly catching me in the eye, and the shock causes a bit of a bounce before our mouths land together again. When we do, I suction to him with all the vigor I can muster.

At first, he is rigid. A stunned animal gone stiff in an attempt at self-preservation. Despite voicing his approval of my request, I don't know that he expected me to act so suddenly.

But then . . .

Slowly, he melts, lips parting. I feel his tongue make its way to mine, soft and playful. My hand is still stationed behind his head, though it's no longer pushing, and I run my fingers along the soft spike of his hair that juts out just beneath the bottom edge of his hat. We both tilt our heads to find a deeper, more gratifying angle.

He is kissing back. Definitely kissing back.

I gently tug at the front of his FREE HUGS T-shirt at chest level, my arm pressed between his torso and mine. His heart thrums against the side of my fist, fast and steady. It makes me feel powerful, the beat inside his chest drumming stronger because of me, because of what we're doing. The kiss crescendos to a forceful press, though this time it's his mouth leading the dance.

Kissing him is like being drawn into quicksand, though, and I'm getting sucked in fast. I pull back as abruptly as I leaned in.

It's official, I've accosted a stranger.

He's looking down at me with these half-closed eyes, all pupil, and it sends a pulse from the nape of my neck down to my center. I try to take it all in. Him and his flighty expression. His chest pulsing against his FREE HUGS T-shirt. His dark hair poking out the sides of his hat. Me and whatever dormant thing inside me now alive. For a split second, I contemplate leaning back in for more, but I'm terribly distracted. It's too much, feeling these kinds of feels again.

Then, staring into his post-kiss face, it hits me fully. The familiarity that's been nagging at me since he caught my eye moments ago across the bar. I *do* know him. Okay, I don't *know* him, know him, but I do know *who* he is—

"You," I say. He cocks his head again, seemingly hanging on what I might say next. That perhaps he understands the realization I've just come to. Before I can continue, Tess grabs my arm, shouts a "well done," which I believe is meant mostly for him, then hauls me in the direction of the door. I think I hear him yell "wait"—a distant voice drowning in the sea of noise, though I can't be sure. And I definitely can't look back, too stupefied to do anything other than follow Tess.

As we spill onto the sidewalk, I picture him still standing there at the bar, next to our two expensive drinks, wondering what the hell just happened. I think to go back in, address the situation with him, but embarrassment takes over me. Thank goodness Tess chose a location I'm okay never returning to, because humiliation will keep me from ever revisiting this bar, or maybe even the whole damn street.

"You did it!" She slaps me on the butt in celebration as if I've just accomplished something particularly noteworthy. "Figured you needed some saving."

I'm dazed and confused and can only wish it were a weed-induced state. "I'm going home now. Good night, Tess," I say, starting in the direction of my apartment two blocks north. I don't hear Tess's footsteps behind me, and relief at this realization propels my steps. She knows I'm overwhelmed and need to be alone, that kiss having had a different effect than what she or I had hoped. There are too many competing emotions to reconcile. Humiliation and satisfaction. Thrill and self-loathing. Regret and whatever the opposite of regret is. And, there's the idiocy of three cocktails the night before *The Interview.*

As I position my Mace in my right hand and take on a determined stride, I see Zane's face in my mind. I imagine kissing him, holding him, laughing with him and wonder if I'll ever experience a love like that again. Though the guy at the bar did stir a short charge in me tonight—helped me see signs of life—I'm fairly certain the answer is no.

The farther I walk, the more the nagging feeling in my belly grows as my thoughts shift from Zane back to what just happened at the bar.

How did I not recognize him sooner?

3.

DESPITE MY REALIZATION CONCERNING THE GUY AT THE BAR, I CLIMB into bed thinking of Zane. Of our complicated history. Of the way he seems to have some ownership over me, still. I am, as I have been since we broke up, adrift. What happened tonight made me realize just how much he still affects me. Of how little progress I've made in moving on.

I dream of him in a restless, hallucinatory sleep. Zane and me playing *Elden Ring* on my couch, him congratulating me on a decisive demigod kill rather than claiming it was due to luck, as he normally would. Me actually sharing my game designs with him, instead of being too afraid of his reaction. At his family's house on Thanksgiving, though in this alternate universe, his parents believing I'm good enough for him. Zane with me in my childhood home, wading through the shin-deep water, proclaiming there's nothing to save. This last instance he was never a part of—I met him much later—but in dreamlike states like this he tends to be there with me often, though never particularly helpful.

The enjoyable parts of him are the especially achy ones, though, memories sore like overused muscles. Sure, I know that as many problems as Zane and I had, I've inevitably romanticized parts of us. Of him. No matter what distance does—how it might skew—I do still remember the good.

Like the way his face changed over time, as though he were a shape-shifter.

Zane has a big nose—not prominent in a way that demands respect or denotes importance, just too big for his face. I say this objectively. It's broad and bulbous and long and sits high against his other features, the protrusion starting above his eyebrows instead of just below. It took just two dates for me to stop seeing his nose first. It quickly receded and I saw instead the almond, curved-up-at-the-corners shape of his eyes and the way his smile spread across his face in a flat line instead of upturning. I fell for the way he pressed his bottom lip into his top one when immersed in thought. I was enamored with how he observed the world, reaching for a tree branch to feel its leaves or stopping to stare at the markings of a cloud-smeared sky. I took envious joy in the way he pressed his eyebrows together when concentrating on the designs on his laptop screen that seemed to just pour out of him. And before long, I grew a deep affinity for his nose too.

It's these good parts of Zane that I denote as special. Unique. Fearful that on anyone else, I would find them to be unnoteworthy. Just a big nose and a flat mouth. A tree toucher. A sky starer. I don't know if I'll ever again find these types of mundane details of another human fulfilling.

The sound of banging on my apartment door jolts me awake. Finn pops up from his bed on the floor in the corner and cocks his straw-colored head at me to determine our next move. It's why I chose a Labrador, intelligent though not aggressive.

I turn to the clock on my nightstand. Two a.m. I decide to check things out—if for no other reason than to determine whether I'm still in my dream state or real life.

"Hey, it's your neighbor! You've gotta come out here!" a voice shouts from the hallway. Finn releases one sharp bark, warning our visitor of his presence, then trots close behind me as I fumble my way from the bedroom. Grabbing the canister of Mace from the console table, I look through the peephole, leaning forward with my feet an ample distance behind me so the person knocking won't detect my shadow under the door. All I see are blurry features and tan skin, but my throat instantly burns, knowing who it is on the other side.

I gather myself, say a silent string of curse words for my stupidity at the bar, and fling the door open. "What's going on?"

The man at my door is shirtless, wearing only dark gray joggers and black slides. I wonder again for a split second if it's a dream, because outside of last night's bar debacle, that's the only place I tend to interact with the opposite sex these days, particularly if said male is shirtless.

But then I realize I am too aware of my surroundings and deficits for this to be a fantasy. I'm wearing a MS. PAC-MAN T-shirt and oversize men's boxer briefs. I take in the faint smell of mint and remember I ran out of pimple patches and have a blob of toothpaste on my right cheek over that stubborn zit.

It's real life.

"Hey, sorry, but it's kinda an emergency," he says, thick eyebrows raised.

Our eyes lock and my throat clenches. I was born via emergency C-section after the doctors found the umbilical cord wrapped securely around my neck, about to cut off my post-birth air supply. I'm convinced this is why my throat is the literal choke point for all my bodily stress.

In this situation, *he* is the cause. It's him. Free Hugs Guy from hours ago who I attacked with my mouth, who is also Hot Neighbor Guy. How could I not have made the connection before I kissed him? I am vaguely aware there's a hot guy who lives just across the hall, but I rarely see him, and usually at a distance. So rarely, in fact, that I don't even know his name. And it's been so long since he moved in, and the bar was so dim, and he was wearing a hat last night that apparently obscured his face, and I've been too consumed with Zane and—

"Hello? I said it's an emergency?"

I come to. "What's the emergency?"

"I smell smoke. I think the building's on fire."

"What? Oh shit!" I have a flash of my childhood home, waterline well above the baseboards, photo albums and throw pillows floating along, colliding into waterlogged walls like bumper boats. I shake my head furiously. Not again. I am prepared for this moment. It's sort of a nighttime ritual of mine, lying in bed imagining worst-case scenarios and how I might handle them.

I stride past him into the hallway and pull the fire alarm, wondering why he didn't think to do it. Why he came straight to me instead. There's no time to contemplate. I rush back into my apartment, leaving him standing at the door. In my bedroom, I grab the large duffel bag that's shoved into the back of my closet. It already holds a first-aid kit, a piece of flint, dehydrated meals, and a few water bottles. I throw my phone, laptop, Kindle, and their respective chargers inside. I pull out the drawer of my jewelry box that holds the few small important items. Amma's wedding ring. The bracelet I've added charms to since I was five, which I miraculously found clasped around a dresser drawer handle in my waterlogged room at age eleven, when so much else had been permanently lost. The delicate "I'm sorry" diamond bracelet from Zane. The only diamonds anyone has ever given me. I hesitate for a moment, contemplating if I should let the latter burn.

No.

Despite it being a remnant of our failed relationship, it's undoubtedly an expensive piece. I can always hawk it on eBay should I lose all my other possessions in this fire.

Finn, who's taken his leash in his mouth, follows me around the apartment, his own senses keen and now a bit jumpy with the alarm blazing. He drops the leash only for a second so he can pick up his oatmeal-colored teddy bear from the kitchen floor and place it in the duffel bag.

"Are you coming back?" Hot Neighbor Guy/kiss recipient yells from the doorway.

"Yes, yes, one second!"

The fire alarm continues to rage. Why did it not go off on its own, without my having to pull it, if Hot Neighbor Guy was already smelling smoke? I intend to write a strongly worded letter to building management, should I come away from this unscathed. And if there is any silver lining here, it's that the urgency of a fire supersedes the need to address the kiss.

I throw on a zip-up hoodie despite the sweat forming at my hairline, then collect all the loose sheets of paper scattered across my kitchen table, shoving them into my sketchbook before placing it in my bag. Finally, I take the stack of three-ring binders on my kitchen counter and toss them inside too. I'll be damned if my presentation goes up in flames, literal or figurative. I debate grabbing the gas mask in the hall closet, but I'm already struggling to zip the duffel closed. I get it halfway and decide it's good enough.

"Okay, sorry," I say, breathless when I return to the front door, bag slung over my shoulder. He's still shirtless and holding only his phone. Why is he not more prepared?

"C'mon," he says before starting down the hall.

"Wait!"

"What, do you want to carry your furniture out too? Let's go!"

"No," I say, insulted. "What about Mrs. Crandall?"

He stares blankly at me.

"Mrs. Crandall, 6D?" I point to her door, a few feet behind us, as I secure Finn's leash with my other hand. "She may need help."

I make my way to her door and bang with both fists, surprised when Hot Neighbor Guy starts drumming against it beside me. I assumed he would have given up on me by now and headed for the stairwell.

"Mrs. Crandall, there's a fire!" I yell, then bang some more. Finn gives another rare bark. He lifts to his hind legs and taps his paws against the door to assist.

Nothing.

"How do you know she didn't already get out?" he asks.

"Did you see her while you were waiting for me?"

He shakes his head.

"Well, I doubt she got out before you were in the hallway," I yell over the shrill ring of the alarm. "Mrs. Crandall, open the door. It's an emergency!"

Still nothing. I smell it now too—the scent of something charred, sharp and bitter.

"You should knock the door down," I tell him.

"What? That seems a little over the top, no?"

"It's a fire! She's an old lady. Maybe she can't hear the alarm." When he doesn't move, I raise my eyebrows at him as he rubs at his bare shoulder. "Seriously?"

"I have a bad shoulder."

I'm about to throw my bag down and do it myself when the door finally opens and Mrs. Crandall appears. We're hit with the overwhelming smell, a mix that reminds me of singed hair and vinegar.

"What the fuck," she says, looking back and forth between us. She's wearing full-length light pink silk pajamas that hang on her delicate frame and they seem to give her blue-gray hair a pinkish hue. So taken with her bedtime style, it takes a moment for me to recognize the smear of black soot across her front right side.

"There's a fire. Don't you hear the alarm?" I shout over the shrill drone.

"Of course I hear it. It's deafening. But there's no more fire. I took care of it."

Hot Neighbor Guy, Finn, and I exchange a three-way look.

"What do you mean, you took care of it?" I ask.

She opens her door wider and I see that her kitchen, including the wall she shares with Hot Neighbor Guy, is covered in black soot. It's littering the ground in front of her stove and has traveled halfway across her ceiling. A thin red fire extinguisher sits on the counter, surrounded by a collection of various ashtrays.

"*You* started the fire?" Hot Neighbor Guy asks.

"Oh, it's nothing. Can you tell them to shut these damn sirens off already?"

"Mrs. Crandall, I think we should get out of the building and let the firefighters take a look," I tell her.

She stares at me.

"It can't be healthy to stay here and inhale all these fumes," I try.

"It'll be much quieter outside," Hot Neighbor Guy offers.

"Fine," she says finally, releasing her grip on the door handle. She grabs a coat and purse from the rack by the door and steps into the hallway, her feet clad in white fuzzy slippers. We wait while she fishes around for her keys then locks the door behind her. I want to tell her it's unnecessary and likely problematic for the firefighters, but I bite my tongue to keep her moving.

As we make our way down the hall, two firefighters enter our floor from the stairwell in full yellow uniforms. "What are you still doing in the building?" one asks.

It's too much to explain, so I simply say, "Sorry, we're going."

"The fire was in 6D. It's out now," Hot Neighbor Guy calls after them when we pass. He takes the keys from Mrs. Crandall's hands.

"Hey!" she protests as he tosses them to one of the firefighters.

We make our way down the stairwell in painstaking fashion,

six flights of Mrs. Crandall clinging to the rail with both hands, refusing to let Hot Neighbor Guy carry her despite his multiple offers, seemingly willing to temporarily overlook his bad shoulder for the sake of getting her out of the building safely.

When we finally make it to the ground floor and onto the street, I throw my bag down and maneuver my neck in small circles, breathing deeply, grateful for the crisp early morning air. The rest of the residents of our building have all gathered across the street. We join the huddle, seemingly the last arrivals.

"Why do these things always have to malfunction in the middle of the night?" some lady behind me says. "It's ridiculous."

"It was probably that kid from 7C. He's got crazy eyes," suggests the man standing next to her, though 7C is within earshot. I take a look at the group, all these people who avoid eye contact in the lobby and elevators, standing out here in their pajamas and bathrobes: 5C, a beautiful server/actress, has her hair pulled back in a perfect ponytail and is in a sports bra and tiny shorts. Another resident who looks vaguely familiar offers her his jacket and she accepts—much to the dismay of 7C, who is ogling her. The couple from 2A are in matching navy-blue pajamas with an upside-down pineapple print—his a pair of boxer shorts, hers a two-piece tank top and shorts set.

Upside-down pineapples. I've learned something new about the couple in 2A.

Beside me, Hot Neighbor Guy has helped Mrs. Crandall take a seat on the curb and has his arms wrapped around himself, rubbing his biceps up and down aggressively. His skin is perfectly smooth, minus the goosebumps; no tattoos, no blemishes, not a mole or birthmark to be seen. I'm covered in small moles that look like freckles, so his flawless skin momentarily captures my attention. I take note of the v-cuts from his hip bones that curve forward and dive beneath his sweatpants. Those are hard to ignore, objectively.

"Are you cold?" I ask, because I'm uncertain what is considered appropriate small talk with the neighbor you drive-by kissed a few hours earlier as you wait for the fire department to clear your apartment building at two a.m.

"Freezing. I would have grabbed a shirt if I knew I'd be waiting for you in the hallway for fifteen minutes."

Ouch. "Do you want my sweatshirt?"

He looks over at me and shakes his head, though I can sense his envy.

Of course this happens the night before—or technically, the morning of—my big interview. As I stand on the curb, watching firefighters move in and out of the building with no particular urgency, I succumb to the reality that it's going to be virtually impossible for me to be at my best. The most significant moment of my life to date is happening in a little over five hours, and I'm on the sidewalk waiting for the fire department to find and deal with Mrs. Crandall's kitchen disaster.

All the preparation in the world couldn't have readied me for the predicament I currently find myself in.

4.

I SIGH, RUB MY EYES, AND PLOP DOWN NEXT TO MRS. CRANDALL ON the curb, pressing my shins against a sleeping Finn, whose light snore reminds me that I am missing crucial sleep.

My phone beeps and I take a look, knowing there's only one person who would text me at two a.m.

Mom: Here.

It's a link to an Indeed job post for an entry-level civil engineering position in Chico. When my mom can't sleep, she sends job postings in attempt after futile attempt to drive me back into the "respectable" world of engineering, while simultaneously emphasizing that my unemployment has caused her insomnia. I don't click the link. Instead, I shove my phone deep into my bag.

Several minutes later, we are seemingly no closer to getting back into our building. Mrs. Crandall has fallen asleep leaning against Hot Neighbor Guy's bad shoulder as we sit in a line on the curb. He's still shivering, the gentle movement of his body seemingly keeping Mrs. Crandall in a deep slumber the way a vibrating chair might for a baby. It's a chilly October evening, a time in LA when the weather could go either way. Though our days lately have been light-sweater warm, the evenings have taken on the imminent winter chill.

I unzip my sweatshirt and hold it out to him.

"I'm fine," he says.

"Okay," I say with a shrug and set it on the sidewalk behind us. He eyes it, then me.

"How are you not cold?"

"Adrenaline. Anxiety. All the body heat around us." I point to the rest of the crowd of disgruntled neighbors, some of whom have wandered across the way to lean against the Dunkin' Donuts building we share a parking lot with.

"You're sure you don't want it?" he asks.

"I'm sure."

He gently shifts Mrs. Crandall from his shoulder to mine and presses himself into the zip-up hoodie. I watch amusedly as he shoves his arms in, pulls the hood over his head, and tugs it together in front, stretching it as he does so he can zip it. When he finally gets it on, he sighs.

My pink-and-orange tie-dyed hoodie is now a crop top.

"Don't say it," he says without looking at me.

"I didn't say anything," I respond, my mouth twitching at the corners.

"It seems like we're gonna be out here awhile. I run cold."

"I thought most guys run hot."

"Yeah, well, I guess I'm special."

"Indeed," I say. I want to tell him it's completely illogical for him to sleep shirtless if he runs cold, but I don't know what his bed situation is. Perhaps he has seven down comforters to keep himself warm. Perhaps there's usually a lady friend beside him who radiates body heat.

We both go quiet and I debate whether to bring up what happened at the bar. I didn't know it was the guy from across the hall when I shoved his face into mine. I must have mistaken his familiarity as attraction. Had I consumed three fewer drinks and had more gumption to follow my own free will and not listen to Tess, this wouldn't have happened.

Hot Neighbor Guy is staring straight ahead and I now wonder if perhaps he was too drunk to remember it? Or at least too drunk to realize the stranger from the bar is me? He didn't seem drunk, but a girl can hope. Nonetheless, I accept his lack of bringing it up and raise him a sweep-it-under-the-rug-completely.

And then, as if he can read my anxious thoughts, to ensure my unease, he says, "So is it, like, some weird fetish of yours to kiss relative strangers at bars?"

My breath catches in my throat. The Dunkin' Donuts sign flickers ominously behind him. He looks over at me and his eyes constrict then relax again, everything about him too calm in comparison to my overwhelming discomfort.

"I . . . I didn't realize you were my neighbor," I say, which probably makes it sound even more absurd—that I had thought he was a *complete* stranger when I kissed him.

The corners of his mouth tick upward and his cheek dimple deepens as he watches me struggle for words. "Relax. I thought you might not have recognized me. It's okay."

It's okay. There are a million different ways to interpret those two little words. But he has definitively answered one thing that had been on my mind: he absolutely knew who *I* was. And he kissed me back anyway.

Mrs. Crandall stirs against my shoulder.

Hot Neighbor Guy must see the redness of my face and lack of eye contact and gracefully changes the subject. "What do you think she was doing in the kitchen at two a.m. anyway?" he asks, voice lowered conspiratorially.

"Chain-smoking while heating water for tea, maybe? And then fell asleep? She seems to do that easily." I shrug slightly and she lets out a sort of low growl.

He raises his eyebrow and gives a slight jerk of the head and I understand his offer, gently pushing Mrs. Crandall back to his shoulder. She adjusts her head a bit like a cat curling into itself and settles again.

The heat in my ears dulls, and I'm further thankful we are no longer talking about the kiss.

"Why do you think she has so many ashtrays in a non-smoking building?" he asks over her head.

"Maybe she collects them. People collect all kinds of weird shit."

He nods. "My uncle Bravo collects resin skeletons of small animals."

I have so many questions, but "Your uncle's name is Bravo?" is where I choose to start.

"Yeah. My mom's other brother, the oldest, is Alpha. My grandfather was a weird dude."

"Interesting," I muse. I try to picture what bizarre collection might sit just across the hall behind his apartment door.

"How long have you lived in the building?" he asks, though I'm still assessing the unique family details he's just shared. "I'm pretty sure you moved in before me?"

I stretch my arms above my head, attempting to release the post-adrenaline strain from my shoulders, and sense him watching as I do. "Yes, I believe so." I remember now the first time I saw him in the lobby, six months ago. He'd been dressed in gym shorts, tennis shoes, and a navy UC BERKELEY T-shirt. It was early April, one of the first too-warm days of the year, and I was returning to the building sweaty after an ill-advised mid-afternoon walk with Finn. Zane and I had just broken up and I watched from the lobby corner as Hot Neighbor Guy carried a large box to the elevator. I sent a silent wish into the universe that this might be the person moving into 6A. Some eye candy across the hall could help, I thought. It didn't. I barely saw him after that move-in day, and I couldn't fathom feeling anything for anyone other than Zane anyway.

But recalling that scene, I can't believe I didn't put two and two together last night. I want to smack my forehead with my palm. "I've been here almost two years," I tell him.

"Clearly I've made quite an impression on you," he says with a sarcastic huff. "And how many fire alarms during your time here?"

"Two others. No, wait, three, actually. No actual fires though. This is a first." We both look at Mrs. Crandall. "She's been here ten years, I think," I tell him.

"She made it a decade without committing arson. Impressive."

"That we know of. Perhaps she's been setting fires all across Los Angeles this whole time," I whisper over her head.

He leans forward to get a good look at her sleeping face. Her skin pulls, wrinkled and divoted, reminiscent of fork marks pressed into rolled dough, gravity tugging the loose skin of her face toward his shoulder, and I can't help the bit of fondness I feel as the sight makes me think of my grandmother. A gentle hum accompanies each of Mrs. Crandall's exhales. "There *is* something sinister about her. Should we search her for matches?" he whispers back. He smiles and I notice the slight dimple in his right cheek again, unusually high for a dimple, landing more atop his cheekbone than under.

As I evaluate him, a question I've been attempting to formulate becomes clear. "Why didn't you try to save anything from your apartment, while you were waiting for me?"

We watch as a firefighter exits the building carrying a thin fire extinguisher that looks a lot like the one Mrs. Crandall had sitting on her kitchen counter.

"There's nothing I couldn't live without," he says with lax conviction, then turns to face me. "Besides my fishing pole. In hindsight, I should've grabbed it." He smiles and it pushes the dimple deep into his cheekbone.

I now remember seeing him getting onto the elevator at an early morning hour a few months back, rod and tackle box in hand. Finn was on day four of an antibiotic after a rather unfortunate incident with a possum and his bladder had a five a.m. wake-up call all week. I wondered how many mornings he did this, up and out before I was typically awake.

His forearms rest on his thighs and his hands are together in front of him as he absent-mindedly rubs them in small circles, just as he had under the table last night. I watch his hands, recognizing his undoubtedly solid grip strength. I make a mental note of this particular skill of his—fishing—as a valuable end-of-days competency. It's another habit of mine—placing people into skill categories for post-apocalyptic survival.

I struggle to find a solid trade for Tess.

The kiss from last night shoves its way back into my mind and I wince. I cannot get derailed by a guy, not now. Certainly not today. And certainly not by one who lives across the hall, whom I have the potential to run into every day. One whom I kissed then bolted from. Absolutely not.

I want to wrap caution tape all around him.

"I'm Charlie, by the way." He holds his hand out, the one not trapped under Mrs. Crandall's weight. I give him a nod and knowing smile. Alpha, Bravo, *Charlie*.

I shake his solid hand as he looks into my eyes.

"Sloane. Nice to meet you, officially."

And that's how I meet Free Hugs Guy, also Hot Neighbor Guy from 6A. Officially.

5.

IT'S NEARLY FOUR A.M. WHEN WE ARE ALLOWED BACK INTO THE building. To my relief, Mrs. Crandall's daughter drove from San Fernando to pick her up, despite her mother's objections that she was happy to stay in her soot-filled apartment; I was afraid I'd be tucking her in on my couch, further derailing my focus on today's upcoming events.

I let the heavy duffel bag fall from my shoulder to the floor in my entryway, assessing the mess I made in the frantic sweep of my apartment for things to save from Mrs. Crandall's kitchen fire.

People I meet often ask how I can afford an apartment in West Hollywood without a roommate. But those who have seen it understand how it's possible. The building has no super, the ceiling tiles are discolored from what I can only imagine are mold stains from a long-standing AC leak, and I have to choose between running the microwave or TV, as both won't work at the same time. But they allow dogs. And it's mine. Not to mention the vast basement storage space that could be used as a bunker should the need arise.

At this point, I know it's better to stay up than try to sleep for less than two hours, so I pull the three-ring binders out of my bag and open one to the first page. Finn curls up at my feet, exhausted from the unexpected middle-of-the-night outing.

I could have easily just emailed my presentation to the HR

person at Catapult, but I wanted to do something that would make me stand out. As a largely self-taught programmer, I know I'm likely up against pedigrees I could never compete with—Harvard and MIT virtuosos who've rubbed elbows with the likes of my interviewers since birth. A physical copy to hand to each panel member will help me stand out a little, I hope.

Propping my laptop open, I begin navigating through my online portfolio. I review my character design samples and graphics, though there's truly no need. I designed them and know them inside and out. Besides, it's tough to concentrate. I still can't believe I get to meet *the* Jack Palmer today. I know the complete life history of all three of my interviewers, down to where they grew up and their favorite games, should there be an opportunity for small talk.

"Thank you so much for having me, gentlemen," I say to Finn, whose ears perk, though he doesn't lift his head. "C'mon, Finn, help me prep."

He groans and lifts himself up. "Thank you," I breathe. "You be Jack Palmer."

Finn cocks his head and I take it to mean he's ready to play the part of Catapult's founder.

"Why do I want this job, you ask? What a great question, Mr. Palmer."

Finn juts his chin in the opposite direction.

"You see, I quit my job at Stanton Engineering four months ago and gave myself six months to go full force after this dream of game design. And you, sir"—I clear my throat in correction—"*sirs*, are the pinnacle of that dream. To work here with you at Catapult Games would be the thing I've wanted since I was a kid playing *Super Mario Bros.* in my parents' basement. Not to mention, I'm about to run out of money and promised my mother I'd lean into a career in civil engineering when my timeline expires in a few months. So really, you'd be saving me from that life too." I look down at Finn, who's been listening intently, rotating his chin from side to side in contemplation. "Too much?"

He groans and lays his head back down.

I nod in agreement. "Too much."

I fight off a yawn and shake my head vigorously to shock myself awake. In a few short hours, I may get everything I've ever wanted.

The sound of screeching metal forces me awake. Surveying my apartment hazily, I quickly recognize the shrill noise of the recycling truck from the street just below my kitchen window. I realize two things as I take in my surroundings. The first: I've fallen asleep at my kitchen table, bent forward, face pressed against the cheap manufactured wood. The second, more critical, circumstance: I have no idea what time it is. I jump out of my seat in a panic.

Finn rises in a fit. I can practically see his thoughts: *This again? So soon?* I look at the time on the microwave: 6:42 a.m., forty-two minutes past the time I intended to begin my morning preparations. I've got seventy-eight minutes to get myself presentable, do my final interview prep, then book it the two blocks to my interview.

I have a bit of déjà vu from the fire alarm hours earlier, running around my apartment, slinging items into a bag. I again shove things into my tote: the three presentation binders. My laptop. My phone.

Shower or no shower? It's a difficult call—the ultimate two-horned dilemma. If I shower, I risk showing up late and with semi-wet hair. If I don't, I may look and smell as though I've spent the wee hours of the morning squatting on a dirty west LA curb. No matter my choice, I am confident the decision will haunt me.

I arrive at the Catapult Games offices four minutes late, showered with still-damp hair. Luckily, the front desk in the lobby is empty, so my exact time of entry will be unclear. Unless they check the cameras, in which case I'm screwed. I instinctively look up and smile at the ceiling camera stationed on the front desk.

"Ms. Cooper?"

I turn to find a woman striding toward me from what appears to be the main hallway. "Yes, hello." When she reaches me, I shake her hand with all the false confidence I can muster.

"I'm Anita, Catapult's HR manager." She releases my hand and smooths her mint-green silk shirt, the color of the Easter eggs I dyed as a kid.

"Ah yes, Anita. Thank you so much for coordinating this interview." *Anita. Been here four years. Holds a masters in HR Management from Cornell. Flies cross country each April to run the Boston Marathon, always placing in the fastest twenty-five percent of finishers.* I researched her too.

"I saw the portfolio you sent with your application and insisted the team meet you." She flickers a smile at me that is gone in a flash, replaced by a pleasant but neutral expression.

"Wow, thank you," I say. This woman is decidedly a saint.

"Right this way." She begins leading me down the broad hallway. "The team is ready for you." She takes long, assertive strides, her heels separating from her ballet flats each time her feet lift from the ground. I take on an awkward walk-trot to keep up.

The office's style is "rich nerd chic" and as full of gaming flair as I had hoped. To the right, a gamers' room with lines of TVs and massive beanbag chairs on the floor, where two men are punching the air while wearing virtual reality headsets. Double doors to the left mark a motion sensory room, which I know is for tracking human movement for character authenticity in the games. Vintage posters line the walls: Mario, Pong, Pac-Man. And of course, there are nods everywhere to Catapult's most successful game's star character, Cannon Jack. Cardboard cutouts of Cannon Jack grimacing while pointing an assault rifle, his cartoonishly large arms flexed. Cannon Jack grimacing with his dukes up. Cannon Jack grimacing while holding the severed head of his dystopian rival, Centiant. I never particularly noticed it before, but Cannon Jack, modeled after Jack Palmer, grimaces a lot.

We pass a shelf in the hallway and I almost trip over my own feet. Floor-to-ceiling shelves contain what appears to be every video game ever made. I spot a vintage Atari *Air Raid* case at my eyeline and salivate. There were very few copies ever made of this particular game, and only two known to exist include cartridge and box, one of which is right in front of me. This one game alone is worth over thirty thousand dollars. I am already daydreaming about coming to this office every day, staring at this surreal collection during my breaks.

A preteen version of myself comes vividly to mind—dressed in knockoff Doc Martens (five years past the height of their popularity) and Levi's. My mom would only ever buy me Levi's, probably because the brand was the most wholly American one she knew. I sit in the basement, crammed full of unopened boxes—the last remnants of the move four months earlier—a gray exercise bike found at a garage sale on the neighboring street, and an immense number of fake plants. There's a console shoved into the far corner of the room, attached to a ten-inch TV with a sea of cables collected on the floor beside it. I'm cross-legged against the champagne-colored synthetic carpet, with harshly cut, too-thick bangs and weedlike eyebrows, wholly immersed in *The Sims*.

When I couldn't sleep, when I needed to escape the fear in my head, when I didn't quite fit out in the world, I built the life I wished I had in those characters.

We moved into that house soon after the flood that destroyed our Santa Clara bungalow, the home I grew up in. Santa Clara was, and still is, described as one of the safest places to live in America. But most of those lists only consider man-made travesties, not natural disasters. The storm that took our house, a flash flood after heavy rain, barely made the news. Even after nearly twenty inches in less than twenty-four hours, I never assumed we'd go back to find a house that was uninhabitable.

I was angry at my parents for the longest time, wondering why they hadn't been more prepared. Why did they choose a home positioned at the lowest point of a potential flood zone? Why did they keep our irreplaceable sentimental belongings (like my baby book) in the bottom of the curio cabinet, so low to the ground? Why didn't we take the important things with us when we left for the hotel as a precaution as the storm approached?

I learned quickly that video games are not only a great distraction and escape from the plagues of real life, but that many can teach you how to survive all sorts of possible disasters, regardless of how realistic or obscure.

Today, inside the Catapult offices, twelve-year-old me does a happy dance.

If only my parents could see this is where I belong.

We keep moving and I find the conference rooms are named after the most popular video games of all time. We pass *Portal* and *Kirby* and stop in front of *Zelda*, which sits in the middle of the sea of desks like a barge.

"Thank you so much," I tell Anita when she steps aside. I picture myself as Link, the *Zelda* character, walking into battle against Ganon.

Anita clasps my right hand in both of hers. "Good luck," she says with an intensity that unnerves me. I watch her turn and dash down the hallway, back the way we came, until she's entirely out of sight. Some eyes flicker up across the rows of desks, and I suddenly wish the conference room didn't remind me of a zoo enclosure—me the freshly cleaved meat being tossed to the lions.

I close my eyes, inhale mightily, force out the breath, and then enter the den.

6.

"HELLO, I'M SLOANE COOPER," I SAY TO THE THREE MEN, WHO RISE and greet me, one by one. Jack Palmer, Founder and President. Kenji Sugano, Lead Engineer. Ross Feldman, Vice President of Product. I shake each of their hands firmly, sure to look them in the eye as I do.

My interviewers take their seats and I follow suit. I knew they were all men, of course, which would be no different at any other major player in this space. Especially when most of the games developed at this firm, in particular, center around zombies, aliens, and post-apocalyptic survival. Apparently, I'm one of only a few women who'd sell a kidney to design these types of games at a firm like this. Or if there are more women like me out there, I just haven't found them. And at this firm, the longest-standing game development company in the US, having created many of the top sellers, past and present, it's no surprise that a twenty-eight-year-old, half-Indian woman would stick out. Whether I stand out in a good way is yet to be decided.

"Sloane, thank you for being here. Your online portfolio is intriguing," Jack Palmer says. His thick, back-combed white hair is offset by his gray O'Neill T-shirt and floral board shorts. His tanned skin reminds me of a slice of raspberry fruit leather.

Jack Palmer is the youngest recipient of the Game Developers Choice Awards' Lifetime Achievement Award, has attended the White House Correspondents' Dinner twice, and was featured last year on the cover of *Forbes*. He's been photographed at Dubai rooftop parties, laughing with Jeff Bezos and Elon Musk. He is still highly involved in development and game production, even after twenty-one years heading up the company, and, amazingly, he's done it all while maintaining a relatively small, start-up-like team.

"Thank you for having me, Jack Palmer," I say.

He smirks as he unwraps the tinfoil from a meatball sub. Great. He knows I'm in hero-worship mode. Not a good start.

I expect some small talk—an opportunity to show off my knowledge of the company—but they dive right in. The three of them volley detailed questions about my designs, Jack in between too-large bites of his sandwich. How did I come up with my concepts? Which games do I play myself? What's my high score on *Immortal Clash*? With every answer, I know they are impressed. Or perhaps surprised. I can feel it as the discussion grows deeper with each question. It's only as we approach the end of the interview that they successfully put me back on my sensible black heels.

"Tell us, Sloane," Jack Palmer says, wiping marinara from his chin with a crumpled napkin, then leaning forward and clasping his hands together in front of him against the table. "What's your . . . life situation?"

"What do you mean, exactly?"

"Are you married? Do you have kids?"

"Oh, no, I am alone. All by myself. Alone." *Stop talking.*

"That's good news," Kenji Sugano says, and for a split second I wonder if there's a sexual-favors component to this interview and, perhaps, the job itself. I've heard stories of this type of behavior in the gaming world, of course. Of women being limited to low-impact positions like debugging and testing instead of design and development. Of endless sexual invitation. Of having to sit quietly by while that misogyny makes its way into the games in the form of sexually charged female heroines who have intercourse with every creature they encounter. The Reddit threads are endless on this topic.

Just as I'm assessing how to decline their advances tactfully, Kenji adds, "The last girl we hired—"

Jack Palmer clears his throat.

"Woman," Kenji corrects himself. "The last woman we hired had a lot of . . ." His eyes dart to Jack's then back to me. "Personal issues. Relationship stuff, mostly, but it bled into her work."

Jack Palmer's eyes pulse wide as he nods. Kenji Sugano scrunches his face in what I assume to be disgust. Ross Feldman lets out a yelping laugh, then quickly looks down at his chair, as if it made the noise instead of him.

Ah. Kenji isn't being suggestive. They just don't want to hire a "troublesome girl-woman." Or what they deem as such. Which, as I'm quickly gathering, means one with a romantic life. I look up at the framed poster of Princess Zelda on the wall across from me and silently ask her for some help here.

"I'm as low-maintenance as they come, gentlemen. So incredibly low-maintenance. And I'm happily, resolutely, forever single." I wince at the fact that I'm discussing my lack of a romantic life in a job interview with Jack Palmer.

They all nod in approval, which keeps me talking. "I would be fully dedicated to this job. You don't have to worry about that."

"Well, that's a relief. Anita urged us to hire that last one and it didn't work out. Like at all. She had . . ."

"Too many personal issues." I nod, finishing Jack Palmer's sentence, so he knows I'm listening. He points his pen at me and winks in approval.

"Yes. Exactly. So, if you were to get this job, you would . . ."

They all raise their chins, eyes questioning. I unconsciously mimic them as I gain an understanding of what's supposed to come next.

". . . have no personal life whatsoever," I state slowly as my chin comes down.

They all nod again.

I think of my mom, how urgently she's trying to push me back into engineering. And how I have no solid counterargument as long as I'm unemployed. I think of my bank balance—how, despite saving enough to get me through six months of job searching, I am about to be two months past due on my rent thanks to my car's recent demand for a new transmission. Mostly, though, I think about how this job, this career, is the only thing I've ever wanted with every fiber of my being.

"And do you *want* kids?" Kenji Sugano asks. The topic has come up twice now. "Children are great and all, but you know, difficult for someone trying to build their way up in a company like this. Taking months off to have a baby, leaving early to relieve the sitter, stuff like that is hard with a team like ours, with our demanding schedules and tight release dates and such." He leans back in his chair, bouncing forward and back a bit, arms crossed against his chest. "Could you imagine a new hire taking months off at a time? That could delay game rollouts."

I swallow hard, wondering if this is a joke everyone else is in on, if someone is about to jump out with a camera and yell "gotcha!"

Instead, they all just stare at me.

I look around the room, recalling all I know about these three. Jack Palmer is in his early fifties, on his third marriage, with one child from each. Kenji Sugano is, by all accounts, one of the biggest fuckboys of the greater Los Angeles area. And Ross Feldman, well, not much about his personal life came up in my research, but evaluating him now with his wet lips and watchful eyes, questionable porn fetishes seem like a safe bet.

Do I want kids? I think about my parents and our lives as a formidable trio. How they are celebrating their thirtieth wedding anniversary next month with a vow renewal. How they exude this chasmic care for each other that I know comes from time spent and deep knowledge of the person you share consistent space with. How my quiet, passive father still looks up and smiles when my mom enters a room. How he saves her the last bite of every good meal. All things considered, outside of the ruin of our onetime home, my life with them was good. Is good. If only my mom would see me for who I am instead of who she wants me to be. She's a woman who left her homeland, came to the States, built a solid life she couldn't have even dreamed of when she was little. Mothers like mine are inevitably disappointed by their daughters. We grew up on opposite ends of privilege.

The truth is, I do want a family. I'm embarrassed to admit it at times, because I want a career—this career—so badly, and I'm meant to believe I can't have both. That I have to choose. But I'm brazen enough to admit only to myself that I do want it—my parents' deep partnership, a husband, kids, his-and-hers closets, a double toaster. I do want it. But I don't know if I'll ever be brave enough to have it. Not after Zane, and certainly not when it would mean more people to care for and keep safe in this far from perfect world. And perhaps this is Jack Palmer's profound wisdom showing through, trying to tell me what I've already come to believe. I can't have both.

I need this job, I remind myself, rising slightly in my chair.

Perhaps they are just being hard-asses to see if I can hang. That's it. I need to prove my ability to hang. "No kids, currently," I say, and they all nod again. "And look, I hear you. I have absolutely no plans of dating or marrying or procreating anytime soon. Not for like five"—they all raise their eyebrows at me in unison—"fifteen years. Not for, like, fifteen years, at least. I plan on being married to my job. This job, if I were to get it." They all nod in approval again, and I feel like a puppy they've taught a new trick to.

"That's great. Love to hear these are your plans . . . self-proclaimed, of course, we just so happen to align in thinking," Jack says. "Can we get that in writing?"

They all laugh heartily and I'm unsure if it's actually a joke.

"But really," Jack says, leaning in. He crumples the foil from his sandwich into a ball and rolls it back and forth between his hands. "None of this is required, of course. We're merely . . . exposing you to the Catapult culture and how to thrive here. We want our next hire to be set up for success. We would never tell an employee what they are and are not allowed to do in their personal lives," he offers.

Anita's face flashes in my mind and I wonder how much of a scolding these three received to ensure Jack's last statement.

I nod. "Of course, Mr. Palmer. I understand." I make eye contact with each of them. "Completely."

"Well, if there's nothing else," Kenji Sugano says, hands clasping the sides of his chair, elbows pointed behind him, ready to scoot his way out of the room.

"Actually, there is one more thing, if I may," I say, and he releases. I pull the three binders from my tote and hand them across the table, one to each of them.

"What's this?" Kenji asks as he flips open the cover to reveal my design portfolio.

"This," I tell them as I lean in, "is the potential future of Catapult Games."

I proceed to walk the three of them through my portfolio for as long as they allow me to speak. And they allow it for longer than I anticipate. Their eyes are stationed to the binders, flipping the plastic sleeve-protected pages carefully—Jack Palmer consistently three or so pages ahead of where I'm at in my presentation. I tell them about each character, the type of game they might suit. How Layla, the *Tomb Raider*–esque hero with pixie-cut fiery red hair, standing next to an arsenal of weapons, would fit into any number of their existing dystopian games as a nice alternative to the one existing female player option in each game. I don't point out that her chest isn't disproportionately large and her waist isn't disproportionately small, as most of their female characters, though I hope they notice her more realistic shape. I tell them about Finn, the hero golden retriever who carries around a teddy bear and looks like a cute, harmless companion until he activates the laser eyes of said bear, capable of severing limbs, heads.

When I'm done, the room falls silent and I await their feedback, growing more distracted by my heartbeat with each brutal second that clicks by.

Jack Palmer is the first to speak. "This is impressive," he says, closing the binder and clasping his hands atop it. He assesses me for a moment, seemingly wrestling with a thought. Finally, he says, "Here's what you can do next."

At this, Kenji and Ross both close their own binders and clasp their hands atop them, mimicking Jack's position. Kenji's eyebrows come to a point. Ross's mouth is open, though I can't tell if he is confused or just a chronic mouth breather.

"There will be a final interview, but it's not a meeting," Jack says. He has a spot of marinara on the right corner of his mouth and the room smells like a pizzeria. "Build a game sample. It should have the potential for commercial success and be something that could fit well within our existing brand portfolio. We'll make a final hiring decision based on the game designs of the final candidates."

My mouth is now also open, wider than Ross's. I'm a final candidate?

I'm a final candidate.

My throat constricts.

Jack stands abruptly, taking my binder to his armpit but leaving the foil and crumbs of his meatball sub. "You've got ten days," he says without looking back as he strides purposefully out the conference room door, Kenji and Ross scurrying out in tow.

7.

AS I EXIT MY BUILDING ELEVATOR AND HEAD TO MY APARTMENT, MY mind is somewhere else. Two blocks away, specifically, still in the *Zelda* conference room at Catapult Games.

What exactly happened back there?

As I approach my apartment, I'm pulled back to the present when the door across from mine opens. It's Free Hugs Guy's apartment. Who is actually Hot Neighbor Guy. Who has a name: Charlie. I've lived a few feet away from this guy for nearly six months and have barely seen him, but now, after all the awkwardness of last night, we are about to get a hallway run-in. Excellent.

I am prepared to give him a pleasant but non-committal nod of acknowledgment when, it's not Charlie who steps out into the hallway, but instead, a woman. For a moment, I wonder if I've made a mistake. Did I get off the elevator on the wrong floor? Am I somehow confused about where my door is? No, that *is* Charlie's door.

And the woman is gorgeous—beautiful in that classic way that is universally, undeniably attractive. Brunette, slim, in possession of remarkably poreless skin with the kind of dewy glow that would look slimy on me if I attempted it. She slings a large leather tote over her shoulder and turns back to the door, where Charlie leans against the frame.

Charlie—who I kissed last night, who gave me some small flutter of feeling, who *kissed back*—now, just a handful of hours later, has a girl leaving his apartment. They stand and stare at each other a moment, and I can almost see a wave of unspoken words rushing between them. It's evident this is not someone he just met.

Stepping closer to my door and them, I find she smells of jasmine. I likely smell of Jack Palmer's meatball sub.

"Goodbye, Charlie," she says, her voice narrow and possibly a bit sad.

"Bye then," he says, his voice clipped, but with a ripple of emotion brimming in its delicate sternness. I look up to find his expression firm and fragile at once.

I make brief eye contact with her, then him. They watch as I fumble with my keys and step into my apartment. I glance back at my door after I've closed it, wondering what I just stumbled into.

I haven't yet changed out of my interview clothes when there's a knock at my door. I can't help but groan. I've left the rest of my day open, my first priority sleep to recuperate from the emotional roller coaster of the last several hours.

When I open the door, Charlie stands in the hall. He's wearing a gray T-shirt and jeans that are, once again, the perfect amount of loose. His tee has three periodic table elements: bromine, uranium, hydrogen. They spell out BRUH.

"Here's your sweatshirt," he says, arm outstretched.

"Thanks," I say, holding it up against myself. "Although it's probably too stretched out for me to wear again." I don't mean it as a compliment, but his smirk tells me he takes it as one.

We stare at each other for a moment, but he makes no motion to leave.

"Do you want to come in?" I'm not exactly sure why I offer. Perhaps my inhibitions are lowered from lack of sleep. Or maybe it's sheer curiosity about who Charlie actually is.

He enters and stands in the center of the room, scanning

the space before turning to face me again. "It's the same layout as mine, just reversed," he says. This notion feels somehow more personal than it likely should.

Charlie leans forward and jiggles both sides of Finn's face, who has planted himself at his feet. "Hey again, buddy." Finn smiles and grunts happily. Most people would stop there. But then Charlie gets down on one knee, bends to eye level, and lets Finn lick his nostrils without hesitation.

"His name is Finn," I say.

"Yeah, I caught that. Last night."

It occurs to me that there are two versions of last night. One where we sat as neighbors on the curb until four a.m. because of a fire alarm. The other where I kissed him at the bar. The thought of the latter makes my skin prickle with embarrassment.

"Who's he named after?" Charlie asks, now flipping my dog's ears back and forth, to Finn's moans of delight.

"What makes you think he's named after someone?"

Charlie gives me a look that reads like *stop it*.

"Fine." I fiddle with a lock of hair. "He's named after a character on an old TV show I used to watch as a kid."

"What was the show?" Charlie's face takes on a sort of wayward grin, his dimple sinking deeply into his cheek, somehow knowing there's an embarrassment factor associated with the answer. "What was the show?" he repeats, this time in a lower, slower tone. He stares at me and I'm the first to look away.

My right eyebrow twitches. "*Buffy the Vampire Slayer*," I say in defeat. "Riley Finn."

"There it is," he says, clearly proud of himself. His mood is noticeably lifted from a few minutes ago, with the brunette in the hallway. He rises from the floor. "You look . . . put together," he says, giving me a once-over. "Why are you home instead of"—he looks me over again—"assisting customers with their banking transactions?"

I look down. I suppose I do look like a teller in my black pantsuit.

"I had an interview. I'm in between jobs right now, if you must know."

"Ah. Did you lose your last one for taking too long to react to a fire?"

"Very funny. Actually, I figured out quickly that engineering is not my thing. Quitting was the only way to force myself to pursue my dream."

"Which is?"

"Video game design."

Perhaps I imagine it, but he seems to be holding back a compliment.

I glance at the specks of white paint across the front of his jeans and Bruh T-shirt. "And what about you? Are you an artist? Or is the paint splatter just some new LA hipster look?"

He looks down at his jeans, then back up at me, and smiles.

Don't do that, I want to tell him. *Don't try to disarm me.*

"I was actually painting Mrs. Crandall's kitchen."

Right before or after you had a visit from the mystery brunette? I want to ask.

"What, are you trying to swindle her out of the insurance money by charging her to paint?" I say instead.

"Are you always like this?"

"Like what?"

"Negative. Hostile. Impulsive." He says the words flatly as if stating facts.

Impulsive. I can't help but assume it's a reference to the kiss. The heat rises to the tips of my ears and my palm instinctively cups my tightening neck.

"You look stressed. Do you need an adult coloring book?" he asks, in a faux-sympathetic tone.

It would do me no good to tell him I have a drawer in my nightstand dedicated to this particular hobby.

What I want to say, what I should say, is *I'm just trying to make sure you know I have absolutely no interest in you. I can't. Oh, and that kiss was a one-time thing, and had I realized you lived across the hall and had a mystery woman-friend, I would have chosen my target more wisely.* Though given he just called me negative, hostile, and impulsive, I doubt he's particularly fond of me either. "I'm simply a realist."

He squints at me and then stares for a moment as if his eyes are an x-ray machine, scanning for an image that computes. "For the record," he says finally, "I went over there to check on Mrs. Crandall when she got back from her daughter's, and the guys who were painting—the professional, paid-by-the-hour painters she somehow found within hours—they were taking their sweet-ass time and being sloppy at that, so I grabbed a brush."

"You did?"

He nods, while I catalog his survival instincts. Care for others could be his downfall at the world's end. "Oh, well, that was . . ."

He crosses his arms, presses his lips together. "You can't do it, can you?"

"Do what?"

"Give me a compliment."

I bite the inside of my cheek. He's razzing me like he's known me long enough to know I'm not particularly easy to earn a compliment from.

"Okay, well, thanks for returning the sweatshirt."

"There's something else too," he says with some newfound urgency. He pulls out a folded piece of paper from the front right pocket of his jeans. Despite his generally calm demeanor, there's a slight tightness that overtakes his jaw. Is Charlie nervous?

"What's this?"

"It's a ticket," he says as I scan the document. "For a weeklong trip to an all-inclusive resort in Turks and Caicos."

I examine the creased receipt in my hand for another moment, then regard him again. "These words mean nothing to me."

He feigns annoyance. "Let's go to Turks and Caicos." He says it as if he has just suggested we go to the mailbox or to paint Mrs. Crandall's kitchen.

Finn, disloyally, has stationed himself against Charlie's right side, his errant golden hairs pressing into Charlie's pant leg.

"You're inviting me on a trip to Turks and Caicos?" I ask in my most questioning tone.

"Yes."

My throat constricts in response to the emotions wrestling one another inside me. Intrigue. Excitement. Fear. Confusion. Ultimately, skepticism wins out, pinning all other feelings to the mat. "Why? We barely know each other. And you basically just told me you don't even like me."

"I didn't say that."

I consciously blink at him.

He raises himself onto my kitchen counter with barely any effort, the action both distracting and impressive. Finn follows, shamelessly licking one of Charlie's dangling ankles.

"This seems like about the right time to get a restraining order," I say.

"Which would be difficult because I live across the hall—"

"Okay, come on. What's this about? Is this some kind of dare? Did Mrs. Crandall put you up to this? Is she gonna burn down my apartment while I'm gone?"

He cocks his head. "Is that a 'yes'?"

"No part of what I just said insinuated a yes. Explain yourself."

He slides off the counter and makes his way over to my couch and plops down, seemingly unable to stay in one spot for long. Finn joins him, placing his face in Charlie's lap, and Charlie begins circling between Finn's ears with his fingers. Finn's eyes roll back in satisfaction. "My girlfriend dumped me. Two days ago. The day before the fire alarm, actually. So yeah, it's been a great forty-eight hours all around. That was her." He points lazily at the front door. "She stopped by to get her curling iron and sleep retainer."

I raise my eyebrows, and he offers a meek smile.

"It feels really good to tell you about her retainer."

I can't imagine someone like Charlie—objectively attractive and so seemingly confident—finding himself dumped. And his willingness to admit it so freely catches me by surprise. There's also a weird sense of satisfaction that the brunette is a former versus current flame, which nags at me. "I'm sorry."

He stares at me with weakened resolve.

"Can I ask what happened?"

He shrugs. "Basically, I asked her if she'd started packing for our trip and she said 'I can't do this' and I thought she meant the trip—like there was an issue at work and she couldn't take the days or something—but then she was sure to clarify that the 'this' in 'I can't do this' was us. She couldn't do *us* anymore."

I watch as he runs his pointer finger along the seam of my couch cushion.

"That's heavy," I say, joining him on the couch. That traitor Finn remains with Charlie instead of shifting to my lap. I can't help but think about Zane and the disastrous way our relationship ended, and I feel a pang of empathy for Charlie.

"Yeah. So anyway, I've paid for this trip and can't get my money back, so I figured I should still go. At first, I thought I'd take a buddy and drink, hook up—"

"I'm certainly not—"

"No, not you. I don't mean hook up with you."

"You don't have to sound so disgusted." I think of the kiss and imagine him wiping his mouth in revulsion as soon as Tess hauled me away.

"I just meant I was gonna take a guy friend, meet girls there. That was the original plan."

"Charming."

"Okay, you're missing the point here." He pulls his phone from his jeans pocket, taps at the screen then holds it up for me to take a look.

"Brooke Brady," I say, reading the name on the social media page. The profile picture is of the beautiful brunette from the hallway, her ample chest clad in a crocheted bikini top, and a gorgeous sunset behind her. She's holding a drink with a neon yellow straw in a giant fishbowl glass, smiling generously at the camera.

"Yeah, but look at the most recent picture," he says.

This one is a close-up selfie of her and a handsome older man, who looks to be in his late forties, his salt-and-pepper hair gelled back in a suave pouf reminiscent of Jack Palmer's. Charlie speaks the caption aloud. "The best love grows with time. I didn't know the love of my life was here all along."

Oh dear, he's memorized it.

I'm grateful that I surreptitiously blocked Zane on all social media within hours of our breakup.

"Her coworker, Spencer. The guy she'd go to happy hours with and work late with and insisted for our entire *two years* together that she didn't have feelings for. She waited exactly one day after our breakup to post this."

"Ouch. Do you think they were sleeping together while you two—" His eyes narrow and I stop talking. "Sorry."

He clears his throat. "Right, so I saw this, and I thought, what would piss her off more than if I took another girl on the trip that was meant for her? If she saw me posting happy vacation pics with a new woman? And then just now she saw you in the hall, so she knows you're my neighbor, which would make her wonder if I was cheating on her the whole time too—" He springs from the couch, clearly amped as he relives it all.

"Wait, you want me to go on this trip with you so you can make your ex-girlfriend jealous?"

"Yes."

"For what purpose? Do you want her back?"

"Hell no. Not after this bullshit." He raises his phone into the air. "She wasn't a great girlfriend, now that I look back on it. I should have seen the red flags."

"Tell me the red flags."

"Why?"

"So I can gauge if they're legit or if you're simply bitter."

"I'm not bitter."

I cross my arms and he concedes. "Fine. For starters, she could never just stay home. We always had to be out, doing something 'exciting.' Like, can't you ever get takeout and watch a movie on a Tuesday night?"

He waits for me to confirm this as a neutral assessment. When I don't, he continues, his face reddening a bit. "She's lactose intolerant. Did I really think I was going to live the rest of my life with someone who can't eat *cheese*?"

"That's not her fault," I say.

He releases a breath in concession.

I note that he had thought about spending the remainder of his days with her, but try not to linger on it. I allowed myself to feel that way, just once. I'd watch Zane play "getcha" with Finn at the park across the street, moving back and forth like a receiver juking their defender, thinking he'd make a good father. Look where that got me.

Now Charlie is pacing my apartment, the list spewing out of him. "She never came fishing with me. Not once in two years.

Despite the fact that I went out to so many 'hot new clubs' and 'it' restaurants for her." As soon as he reaches the front door, he turns and walks back. "And she doesn't read. Like, ever. I don't trust people who don't read." We both instinctively look over at my bookshelf, full from top to bottom, which, if he stepped closer and really examined, he would see is organized by category, then color, with two full shelves dedicated to post-apocalyptic romance.

Now he steps over to study the lineup more closely. My chest tightens. It's oddly intimate, having someone scour my bookshelves, like they're viewing my DNA under a microscope. He settles on a hardcover, presses his index finger into the top edge of the spine, and pulls it back at an angle. A recent commercial fiction bestseller, not in my post-apocalyptic romance section.

"The ending of this one sucked," he says, then presses the book back into place.

I open my mouth to argue the review I hadn't asked for but find I can't. He's right. The ending did suck.

I envision his nightstand covered in a messy stack of novels and it's . . . intriguing.

He sits back down on the couch, sighs in defeat. "Fine. I want her back. There, I said it. Does that make you more inclined to come?"

"Why would you want someone back who cheated on you?"

The words ring hollow though. I know why.

Because ninety-nine percent of him knows he deserves better. That it's not healthy or logical or at all intelligent to want to go back to someone capable of such disregard. That in his head, he knows this person isn't right for him. That he should have more self-worth. But the other, nagging one percent tells him what they had was so special—too special—that he will never find a love like that again. And that one percent is a tiny eyelash stuck in his eye that leaves the other ninety-nine percent forsaken.

That inside your feeling receptors, the need to be chosen is a cloud cover over all rational thoughts.

Charlie, as I expect, does not answer.

These are not things easily articulated to a virtual stranger.

8.

"WHY ME?" I ASK INTO THE SILENCE. "DON'T YOU HAVE OTHER OPtions? People you know?"

He sighs. "Anyone I know, she knows too. They either wouldn't go for it, or Brooke wouldn't believe it. But you—you live across the hall. Imagine all the sordid details she'll conjure up once she sees it's you."

I cross my arms, furrow my brow in scrutiny of him. "And why would I do this, exactly?"

"For starters? A free beachfront, all-inclusive seven-day trip to paradise. One I spent most of my savings on."

Ouch. He really saw a future with this girl. "With a stranger who could easily murder me and hide my body on foreign soil? Or under it. Technically," I say. I make a mental note to google the island's extradition laws later.

He squints at me for a moment before responding. "You're one of those girls who falls asleep watching true crime shows, aren't you?"

I see no point in providing confirmation. When I don't respond, he continues, "And second, I'd be forever indebted to you. Think of all the neighborly things I'd be obligated to do for you. Carry groceries, change light bulbs, serve as a pretend boyfriend for any of your needs."

"That's incredibly sexist, you know, assuming I need a guy

to do those things. And what makes you think I don't have potentials to do that stuff?"

His mouth takes on a humble frown, his bottom lip pressed tightly into the top one. "You're right. Sorry. I've just never seen a guy coming or going. I never see anyone, really." He looks around my apartment and I can't help but think he's looking for a cat. Or six.

His eyes linger on the row of kerosene lanterns lined along the console table against the back of my couch. It's become a bit of a hobby, adding new lanterns to the collection.

I shake my head. "I can't possibly go on this trip with you. I have ten days until this hiring decision is made, and I have cleared my schedule to do nothing but work on a final interview game proposal. And even if I wanted to go, I can't afford a ticket right now." I look down at Finn, who's now lying on the floor between us, his head volleying back and forth as we talk. I'm tempted to use him as an additional excuse, but I know he'd be thrilled to have a week with Tess.

Charlie stops moving, stands before me. "You can use my miles. And what better place to get work done with no distractions than on a beach in paradise?"

"I have my own miles. Even so, I could *not* fly three thousand miles away and work right here in my apartment, which also has no distractions."

"Except if Arsonist Betty down the hall starts another fire. And there's that bakery delivery truck that drives by at six every morning. And what about the barking goldendoodle in 6F?"

"Betty?"

"Mrs. Crandall. Her first name is Betty."

I realize he knows more about the people in this building than I do, which is embarrassing. I should be much more observant of my neighbors, the evidence of which is standing right in front of me.

"But you never bark, do you, Finny?" Charlie is kneeling again, his lips practically touching Finn's snout. "How is he so well-behaved?"

I shrug. "Wish I could take credit, but he has always been like this. He's a rescue, so I don't know his full story. He's basically the dog from the movie *Up*."

"I was hiding under your porch because I love you?"

"Exactly." I can't quite tell if who Charlie is is becoming clearer or more confused in my mind as this conversation continues.

"If I were to go on this trip with you, how do I know you won't murder me in my sleep?"

Charlie's now at my kitchen table, flipping through the stack of character drawings from my sketch pad. Zombies with human flesh hanging from their lips. Aliens wielding shimmering swords. Body-armored warlords. He holds up a drawing of a young girl in a floral bib dress holding a chain saw. "It kind of seems like, between the two of us, *you* are the scarier one."

"Regardless, I'm not the kind of person who jumps on a plane with a complete stranger on a mystery trip." I fold my arms across my chest for emphasis just as the goldendoodle from 6F bursts into a barking fit, his muffled yelps invading my apartment as if to voice his support of Charlie's points.

He shrugs and starts for the door. "Okay, suit yourself. I just thought . . ." He pauses as he approaches, then turns to face me again. His face is close to mine, and my breath catches as I peer up at him, his pale eyes an almost unfathomable color—like the blue of a gas flame. I want to study his family tree in photos to discern how these eyes made their way to him—based on objective genetic interest, of course.

"You thought what?" I ask, maintaining my position.

He looks over my head, breaking our gaze, then shoves his

hands into his front jean pockets. He leans in as if what he's about to say is a secret, though we are in the privacy of my apartment. When he opens his mouth to speak, his lips are so close they practically graze my ear. "I just thought the girl who kissed me last night at the bar would be the kind of girl who'd take a chance or two." He turns to leave, but not before I catch the hint of a daring smirk across his lips. He exits into the hallway and closes the door behind him, leaving me standing in the middle of my apartment with a light but pleasant ache in my belly.

9.

THE DAY AFTER THE INTERVIEW AND CHARLIE'S UNEXPECTED INVITA- tion, I've come up with a solid nine-day plan to tackle my game design. The first thing I need is a firm concept. I stayed up well into the night scouring my archives, looking over game samples and character drawings, even revisiting my list of idea concepts that are not yet developed. Though they were enough to get me to this point in the interview process, none are memorable enough to submit as my final impression. Not for Jack Palmer and Catapult. I'm giving myself twenty-four hours to come up with something new, which will leave me just over a week for design and run quality assurance of a reasonably put together prototype. But ever since Charlie mentioned it, all I can seem to hear in my apartment is the damn yapping goldendoodle from 6F.

So, notepads and laptop in hand, in need of massive inspiration, I head to the deli next door—the place where some of my best gaming ideas have been shaped.

"Sloane!" Marv, the shop owner, waves from behind the counter as soon as I walk in. "A Cubano for my favorite customer?"

"You say that to everyone." I drop my stuff onto the table closest to him. Marv's is a long and narrow space reminiscent of an alleyway converted into a deli. With its sourdough scent and mustard-yellow walls adorned with black-and-white framed photos of C-list celebrities biting into hoagies, Marv's feels like a hug from my favorite uncle.

"Not true, not true. My other favorite customers order ham and Swiss on rye!" He laughs heartily at his own joke.

As I'm setting up my workstation at the front window two-top, seat facing the door, Marv comes over with a Cubano and a stack of chocolate chip cookies.

"Marv, if I ate everything you try to feed me, I'd keel over in a food coma."

"And I'd find you a pillow and a comfy spot in the back to lie," he says. "Whatcha workin' on this time? Zombies or werewolves or aliens?" He points his rag at my sketchbook.

"To be determined."

"Ah well, if you need some inspiration, let me know." He crosses his eyes, sticks his tongue out to one side, and wraps his hands around his throat like he's choking himself.

The bell on the door chimes and a man who looks to be in his late fifties enters. "Angelo! Long time no see! Ham and Swiss on rye for my guy, uh?" Marv is off.

I open my laptop. Concepts. I need a game concept. One unique enough that Jack Palmer and his team will find compelling, but not so out there it doesn't fit into their post-apocalyptic fantasy brand. Developing the concept alone could typically take months, and now I have a little over a week to figure out the concept *and* prototype and I've already lost almost twenty-four hours charting out options that I inevitably deemed unviable. I take another scroll through the many game ideas I've accumulated over the years, all in various stages of conceptualization, just to be sure there isn't something I overlooked last night.

Nothing with zombies—too overdone.

Same goes for landmark cities in alien-generated ruin.

I could create a post-apocalyptic world where rising temperatures have created resource scarcity. No, too much world-building required for just nine days.

There's no time for design documents or a formal blueprint

of any kind. They likely expect a game that was already at least partially constructed in my previous work, as it's incredibly unrealistic to assume someone could build a full game in ten days. But everything in my portfolio is insufficient for one reason or another—it either doesn't fit Catapult's niche, the graphics are too weak and require complicated fixes, or the premise is not interesting enough. Though it's a much harder road, I must push myself to create something completely fresh.

The bells chime again and I instinctively look up. When I do, everything inside of me stops. My heart, my breath. I even feel the blood in my veins come up against tiny, invisible dams. I know who it is in my bones before my brain can fully register the sight.

"Zane, Zane, Zane, whatcha doin' here, my guy?" Marv speaks slowly and he can't help but glance in my direction. I'm trapped in this corner with nowhere to go. I grip the table's edges and go statue-still, hoping Zane won't notice me. No such luck, though, because Marv's constant skittery looks in my direction cause him to glance over. We make eye contact and it's like a bullet to the throat when our eyes meet. It's the first time I've seen Zane since the evening six months ago when I left his apartment in tears. He looks exactly the same as I remember, and I feel just the same as the day I met him. Gripped. That feeling used to be akin to the draw of a magnet. Now it's like a vise.

"Lo, hi," he says, only a few steps into the small space and standing right across the table from me.

The sound of his pet name for me, mixed with the sound of his deep, familiar voice, sends a pang through me. He might as well whisper something dirty in my ear—it would feel far less intimate.

He's wearing the black CHRIS STAPLETON tee from the concert I took him to for his birthday last year at the Hollywood Bowl.

My mouth goes desert dry. "What are you doing here?" I ask. It's a fair question. Marv's is *my* place. It's right next door to *my* apartment. *I* introduced Zane to it, to Marv.

We used to split a Cubano and eat it on the way back to my apartment, the walk just long enough to finish the last bites as we rode the elevator up to the sixth floor, finish chewing by the time we got to my apartment door, finish crumpling the paper by the time we got into my apartment and to the waste bin under the kitchen sink. He'd open up the paper wrapping before we stepped outside of Marv's, hold the two sides up next to each other, then hand me the larger half. There was always a larger half. And when Marv figured out our ritual, he started dividing it more and more unevenly. Toward the end, my "halves" were nearly double the size of Zane's. Still, Zane gave me the larger half without even so much as a good-natured protest. He was good at that—small measures of selflessness. Only small ones, though.

It should have been an unspoken agreement that he was never to come back here after our breakup. I didn't realize I had to spell that out for him. The anger starts to rise from so deep in my belly that it feels like my lower back.

"We just moved into the neighborhood. Into that new building on Fairfax." He points in the general direction of Fairfax, but I'm stuck on *we*.

Who the fuck is *we*?

It's then I notice the woman who's appeared by Zane's side. "This is Jenna."

Of course. Jenna.

She smiles. I take in her perfect white teeth and too-red lips and white silk tank top. Who wears white silk to a deli? I hope she drips mustard all over it.

Jenna bends across the table and reaches out her hand. Do I have to shake this person's hand? I begrudgingly take it and almost wince at its infirmness.

I look over to Marv and his face betrays him. He already knew this bit of information and chose to keep it from me. I should probably speak. "Jenna, I'm Sloane."

"Oh right, Sloane! I've heard so much about you!"

Yeah, I bet.

Jenna's raven-colored hair is sheet straight and silky (like her stupid shirt) and it sways luxuriously back and forth when she moves, like the smoke releasing from a cigarette.

As I'm focused on watering the drought in my mouth, Jenna lifts her left hand, tucks a line of hair behind her ear, and I am blinded by the rock on *that* finger. I have a *Mean Girls*–esque hallucination of leaping across the table, wrapping my hands around her throat, watching her eyes bulge from under their ambitiously shimmery lids. Zane and I broke up six months ago, and somehow he's already engaged and he moved in with her . . . into *my* neighborhood.

She smiles at me and her nostrils flare.

Flaring nostrils. I imagine Zane eyeing her flaring nostrils during an argument, knowing how much he usually despises facial tics like this in others. The vision causes me a fleeting moment of delight.

Because I can't show Zane or Jenna how upset I am, I turn and glare at Marv. He drops the spatula in his hand and it clangs against a metal cookie sheet before he bolts through the plastic divider to the back of the deli.

Never let your guard down. It's been my motto for as long as I can remember. It's the way I survive, apocalypse or not. Being with Zane was only the second time in my life I felt truly out of control, and it certainly didn't serve me well. I mentally slap my own cheek to remind myself of my impenetrable armor.

"Oh, look at that," I say with saccharine adoration, pulling Jenna's hand toward me. I place my palm under hers to admire the ring. Her hand is so delicate and thin that mine feels like a catcher's mitt in comparison. The ring is stunning—princess cut, gold band, more than I know Zane can afford. I have a brief fantasy of shoving her hand into her face, that rock likely to gouge her eye. I think better of it, of course. It's not her fault. None of this is. I refuse to be a woman who blames the other woman. I cannot blame bubbly, silky Jenna for everything that happened with Zane.

Zane is engaged. To Jenna, of all people. And they are here at Marv's. *My* Marv's.

Before I can ask why they chose *this* neighborhood, he answers the question barreling around in my brain. "I'm interviewing for a job two blocks from here, so it'll be perfect if it works out."

"*When* it works out," Jenna says, placing her hand, the one with the ring, on his chest and looking up at him. She's blinking too much.

"Where?" I ask, though I'm afraid I know the answer.

"Over at Catapult," he says. "They're hiring a new—"

"Game designer."

"Yeah . . . wait, are you interviewing for it too?" He's smiling, but his expression isn't friendly. His right eyebrow twitches in its tell that he's amused. He doesn't view me as a threat. In fact, he finds it comical that I believe I could get the job.

I think back on my time with Zane. When we met, it felt like kismet, serendipity, whatever the hell you call it when the universe puts someone in front of you and it feels meant to be because of some odd connection. What were the chances that two video game designers would meet randomly as we had? One of the main reasons I thought he was my perfect match. It was clearly a more misguided idea than white silk in a deli.

I get a flash of Zane and me sitting on a bench at the West Hollywood Dog Park, watching Finn, tennis ball in his mouth, play keep-away with a black Corgi. I feel Zane's arm wrapped around the back of the bench, his fingers aimlessly twirling a lock of my hair.

"I'm so incredibly proud of you," I told him, my hand clutching his knee.

"Thank you, babe. It's really exciting."

"Triton. It's a dream come true. I can't believe you'll be working as a game designer at Triton Media."

He cupped his chin and rubbed at the stubble. "It's pretty insane."

"Maybe I'll be there someday too. That'd be pretty cool, wouldn't it? Both of us designing at one of the biggest game development firms in the world?"

He squeezed my shoulder then and jumped up. "Finn! C'mere, boy. Time to go!"

"Yes, I am interviewing for it." I force my eyes to stay tracked on his instead of flicking down to the ground as they demand.

"Isn't that something!" Jenna says in what I've quickly identified as her standardly upbeat way.

"It is. Good luck, Sloane. May the best man, or woman, win." He holds out his hand. I look down at it. I don't want to touch it. I don't want to touch him. I'm afraid of what it will do to me.

It's just a handshake, I tell myself. My hand moves in slow motion toward his. And when we make contact, it's worse than I imagined. I was afraid I'd feel attraction, longing, loss. Instead, there's nothing but blind pain, like his fingers are knives carving their way under my skin as he grips. I pull away quickly.

He's already a designer at Triton. Why does he need to butt his way into *my* dream job?

"Well, I better go. Lots to do. I'm so busy . . . in demand . . . all the things." I gather my items scattered across the table as they look on, then I rush out the door. I need to get a million miles away from them. Away from Marv's, which used to be my sanctuary. Away from Zane and Jenna. I can't think of anything

I need more than to be on the flip side of the earth from Zane and Jenna. Away from the crushing walls of what is now *our* neighborhood.

My heart is throbbing and my breath is short by the time I make my way to Charlie's door and bang my fist upon it.

Then, against my better judgment, despite my true crime-built logic, and in contempt of every survivalist instinct within me, when he opens the door, I blurt, "Fine, I'll do it. I'll go on the trip." I turn toward my door and then pivot on my heels to face him again. "But if you try anything, I'll murder you. I'm quite knowledgeable about how to hide a body."

He leans against the doorframe, a sly smirk across his full lips. "History tells me I'm not the one to worry about when it comes to keeping my hands, or lips, to myself," he says, the smirk of his mouth growing to a full-blown grin.

10.

"YOU DID *WHAT*?" TESS SHOVES HER PALM INTO HER TRAINING DUMMY with a lackluster shove, then turns to face me, pressing her hand to her brow like a visor to block the afternoon sun.

I leap forward and sweep my dummy to the sidewalk as she watches me, mouth agape. The inflatable dummy—which I've monikered Zane—rises, wobbly, to face me again.

"Yep," I say through a heavy breath. My best friend's reaction doesn't help quell my anxiety about joining a virtual stranger on a trip out of the country. I try to play it cool nonetheless, pretend I'm someone who does unreasonable things like joining a guy on a trip to the Caribbean on a whim of fancy. Or that I'm someone who says things like *whim of fancy*.

"It's so . . ."

"Unlike me?" I give Dummy Zane a front kick to the midsection, then smile at a passing Pomeranian because it appears to be smiling at me. Finn lifts his head from the sidewalk beside me to acknowledge the pup with fur a half-shade darker than his.

"Yes. Completely, wholly unlike you." Tess gives her dummy an inconsequential jab with her fist. Unsurprisingly, her self-defense efforts are less than impressive. "What is this class, anyway? I thought in self-defense you get to take your aggression out on a real guy, like kick him in the groin and scream 'NO!' over and over as loud as you can. Was this a Groupon?"

I shrug. "Thought it would teach us some good skills. Maybe I can bank some moves for my game characters. And, because it's outside, they allow dogs!"

Finn's ears perk, knowing he has entered the conversation.

"And being typical me hasn't been working out so well lately," I add.

"How did this happen? Does this guy have some kind of dirt on you? Is he blackmailing you? Or are you just sleeping with him and hooked on the D?"

"Tess, my god. I'm not sleeping with him." I was contemplating telling her Free Hugs Guy is also Hot Neighbor Guy, aka Charlie, but I don't want to give her the satisfaction of knowing this is all the result of her ill-advised mission at the bar.

"Well, explain then! I don't want to be interviewed on *Dateline* defending why I didn't do enough to stop you from going on the trip that ultimately led to your demise."

Tess is also a true crime fan.

"For starters, I'll be able to work on my game concept for Catapult. What better place to get work done with no distractions than on a beach in paradise?" I wince a little inside as I use Charlie's argument to convince her. "And I *have* to get this job. I'm running out of money . . ."

Tess exhales and shakes her head. "You've been so consumed with preparing for the end of the world, you neglected to prepare for the basics of your actual life."

I choose to ignore her and give Dummy Zane another kick, this one a roundhouse to the face. "And did you know Turks is the gem of the Caribbean?" I say, undeterred, regurgitating what I read in my online research last night. "And Rihanna visits often? I could be partying with Rihanna all week. I can't deprive myself of that opportunity."

"The chances of you running into Rihanna—"

"Providenciales is a small island! Only twenty-three thousand people. So really, the chances aren't that unrealistic. And he'll owe me. I can make Charlie go with me to my parents' vow renewal next month. It'll get them off my back about not having anyone." Though the last part hadn't occurred to me until this minute, I might as well leverage the situation to my benefit.

Our instructor approaches Tess and places his hands on her hips to correct her poor form. She bites her bottom lip and scrunches her nose raunchily at me when he's not looking as if it's some form of foreplay.

"But *I* was gonna go and fake-announce myself as your lover," she says when the instructor has given up.

"It was a solid plan, but then I'd have to explain, at some point down the line, why you are no longer my lover and still my best friend."

"Fair," she concedes. "Why don't you just finally tell your family what really happened with Zane?"

I shake my head. "I can't."

"Why not? Wouldn't the truth be better than them thinking you let this amazing guy go? Tell them what a dickhead he really is."

I shake my head again, this time more firmly. "If I tell them the truth, everything they believe about me will also be true. That I couldn't make a good decision for myself if my life depended on it." I say *they*, though we both know I'm only referring to my mother. My father's love is simple, unyielding, and unconditional, sort of like Finn's. I realize I'm comparing my father to a dog, but I do mean it in the best possible way.

"So you'd rather them think you walked away from something they believe was perfect?"

"Yes, because then at least they might have some faith in me that I can find perfect again." Though I informed Tess of the Zane and Jenna update, I don't care to discuss it further.

"I still don't understand how Zane got your parents to love him so much."

"They didn't love *him.* They loved that I might finally get married. My mom's standards lowered considerably when she thought there was a ring in my near future."

According to my mother, I need a man but, equally, should be self-sufficient. She focuses her efforts on one versus the other depending on her mood on a particular day, or on which she believes I am currently failing at most.

Tess shakes her head. Conversations trying to make sense of my mother's logic never seem to go anywhere. "I still can't believe you're doing this," she says. "You know you'll probably fall in love with this guy, right? Or sleep with him, at least. It's inevitable."

"Not going to happen."

"Right."

"No. Really. It cannot happen. I sort of promised the team at Catapult I'd stay single."

"I'm sorry, what?"

"Yeah. It's an all-dude creative team and they're wary of hiring a woman. So, I promised I would have no distractions. That I would be fully dedicated to the company. No boyfriends, no babies, no problems."

"Is that their recruiting slogan?" She crosses her arms. "You realize there are about a hundred HR violations in what you just said, right? They can't expect that of you."

"Yet—that's how it goes if I want to get my foot in the door. This is the career I want. The only thing I'm good at. I can handle a little misogyny to get it."

"How would they even know you had a boyfriend anyway?"

"I'm sure they would keep tabs somehow—they seem to care about it too much not to pay attention. Besides, now that Zane's living in my neighborhood, I bet he'd rat me out if he ever saw me with someone."

"You think he'd do that?"

"If I got this job over him? Psht. One thousand percent. I'm sure they bro'd it up in his interview, even mentioning that there was a lonely girl final candidate, in the running as long as she is single. And now he knows that girl is me. And the gaming world is small. I can't become known as the other girl with boyfriend issues. It would ruin me, professionally speaking. And besides, who wants to constantly sneak around and act like they are ashamed of their own relationship? No guy would sign up for that."

"A married guy might."

"Hmm, tempting. But I'll opt for singledom over mistressing."

Tess takes a long sip of water, then pours some into Finn's mouth from the bottle. I feel a strong opinion coming. "Why don't you find another company—or better yet, build one yourself? That's the *ultimate* dream, isn't it?"

I sigh. "It's not that easy. Catapult is the number one—"

"Number one game design company in the world, right in our backyard. Yeah, I know. But it's pretty shitty that they can all have multiple marriages and booty calls and whatever else they're into, and even Zane can be *engaged*, yet they expect *you* to promise a life of spinsterhood to even be considered."

"I can play the game."

"Pun intended?" She kicks her dummy with the toe of her purple sneaker.

"Yes. Besides, it's not like I'm looking for a relationship anyway. After Zane, a life dedicated to work and Finn is fine by me. Delightfully fine." I kneel to give him a top-of-the-head scratch.

"If you say so," she says with a sigh. "Okay, if you plan on selling your soul for this job, I suppose I can get behind you having this little adventure first. I hope you sleep with this guy. And anyone else you cross paths with. Maybe one guy each day. Like the twelve days of Christmas, but as a countdown to your vagina being closed off for good."

"You need help," I say.

"Not as much help as your vagina."

"Can we please stop talking about my vagina?"

Finn groans at my feet.

"Ladies, less vagina, more balls!" our instructor calls out from the front of the group.

"Excuse me?" Tess and I say in unison.

"Balls," he says, pointing to the medicine balls stacked against the side of the building.

"This class makes no sense to me," Tess says, grabbing one and setting it at her feet. "Am I supposed to have a medicine ball with me at all times to throw at potential assailants?"

"Maybe it's for building core strength so we can *fight off* an assailant."

She shrugs. "If you insist on going on this trip, please don't get murdered. I really don't have time to organize candlelight vigils. I know how you feel about candles."

"Full of arsenic."

The other class participants have broken off into pairs and are throwing the medicine balls back and forth. I throw my ball at Tess, who steps aside and lets it hit the cracked sidewalk. I won't be bringing her to this class again.

"You are so not disaster-ready," I tell her.

"I don't need to be. I have you," she says. "So act like the responsible human you are, please."

"I'll take my Mace on the trip."

"Great. Now can we please go get a proud-of-ourselves-for-working-out cocktail?"

"Can't." I grab Finn's leash. "Interview game design." Finn and I say our goodbyes to Tess before she can argue.

As we begin the walk home, I wonder why I've pushed so hard to convince Tess this escapade is a good idea when I'm not particularly convinced myself.

11.

ON THE TREK HOME FROM SELF-DEFENSE CLASS, I PLAY THE CATAPULT interview over again in my head, remembering how I felt distinctly like lion feed walking into the *Zelda* conference room. A block from home, I'm struck with the spark of a game idea and spend the rest of the day scoping out a plan for the prospective concept. I map out a *Groundhog Day*–style time loop where the playable characters are trapped in a zoo in which all the animals have been released from their exhibits and are running wild. Ultimately I scrap it, though, because I find once the escaped animals are sedated, the game becomes a bit anti-climactic. Though wandering around eating churros and hot dogs from abandoned food carts is potentially appealing in real life, it wouldn't sell as a game. I've wasted almost two of my ten days and still have nothing.

All I can seem to think about is Zane. Then Charlie. My mind oscillates between them, and I can't help comparing the two. I was afraid Zane had killed my ability to trust or feel attraction, that I am, still, just one big deadened nerve. Charlie is the only guy I have been remotely attracted to since Zane, and that feeling is equally reassuring and unsettling.

When I reach my apartment, there's a sheet of paper stuck to my door. I rip it off, already anticipating what it might say. RENT PAST DUE, it reads in aggressive all caps, bolded font that looks too much like a ransom note. My hand goes to my neck, mound bulging in my throat. I'm appalled by the public call-out. Couldn't building management just continue to email me? Is it the public humiliation factor they're going for? A bullying tactic? *You've been so consumed with preparing for the end of the world, you neglected to prepare for the basics of your actual life.* Tess's words nag at me. It's unnerving when she's right. I crumple the sheet into a ball as I enter the apartment and toss it to Finn, who promptly collects it and brings it back to me.

"We're not playing fetch with my harassment letter," I tell him.

He looks up at me woefully and places his chin against my leg.

I sigh. "Fine, but at least drool all over it." I throw the letter across the room and watch Finn do as I asked, the quickly wet paper clinging to his snout.

I am twenty-eight years old and can't pay my rent. This isn't just my mom thinking I make bad choices anymore. This is me possibly losing my home. The distress of my life failures spreads across my insides like dry rot.

My phone vibrates just as I've set up my laptop at the kitchen table. "Hi, Mom." She has a knack for calling when I'm at my lowest.

"Sloane, ah, what are you up to?"

"Just, you know, getting ready for this trip with Tess." Yes, I lied to my mother about going on a trip to a foreign country with a guy I've barely met. Tell me you wouldn't do the same.

"How is Zane?"

"Mom, you know Zane and I broke up six months ago. So you can stop asking about him anytime."

"I just wondered if you two had figured things out yet."

"No, and we won't be."

I feel her eyes rolling on the other end of the line. "Anyone else, then? Have you gotten on that India Match dating application yet? Lots of doctors there."

As I inch closer to thirty, my mother reminds me more and more often that my "best eggs" have died.

"How do you know that?"

"Jaya's mom told me."

I picture her head moving in a slight figure-eight motion, gold earrings waggling as she does. The Indian head bobble I've never been able to master.

"I'll check it out," I lie. I'm grateful I'll at least have Tess by my side at the vow renewal to help distract my mother from Zane talk. Charlie flashes in my mind, then my conversation with Tess earlier. Perhaps *he* could serve as a reasonable solution too. A date, even a fake one, could be enough to keep my mom on her best behavior for the night.

She moves on to her next item of concern. "Tell me when you get back from this trip you will get serious about your job search. Ah, it's been weeks since you left that secretary position."

I think once again to correct her, that I wasn't a secretary, rather an assistant at an engineering firm, and also, people don't say secretary anymore. But trying to politely educate an elder Indian woman is a lost cause. Especially if that woman is your mother.

"I'm looking. In fact, I had an interview two days ago," I say and immediately regret it, preparing for the inevitable blow.

"What is the job?"

"Actually, it's a game design position with Catapult Games. They're the number one—"

"Really, Sloane? When will you take your career seriously, use your engineering degree? You must earn your own way and take care of yourself. Nobody else will do that."

I sigh. Obviously I know that. I spend most of my time preparing in some way or another.

She's been married to my father for almost thirty years and

still has a separate bank account so she can "fend for herself" should the need arise. She is prepared for surviving people, just not natural disasters. Although now, at my urging, my parents live on a hilltop.

I picture her expression when we went back to face our post-storm home, three days after we had left for what we thought would be an overnight escapade to a hotel, armed with exclusively non-valuable basics that could be easily replaced—pajamas, toothbrushes. My dad's "good pillow" he couldn't sleep without and my mom's silicone earplugs to drown out his snoring. At least I had thought to bring my frayed copy of Judy Blume's *It's Not the End of the World.*

But more than anything, I remember my mom's face when we saw our house again, the flood damage so fresh the reservoir inside had not yet fully receded and still days away from the decomposing smell of water rot. In contrast to the shock on my dad's face, she looked . . . resigned. Like she knew her life had been too smooth for too long and this was the thing that was lying in wait, ready to level her.

Everything was new after that, largely paid for by insurance. Clothes, furniture, books, things. New meant not yet messed or waning, but also, void of story or sentiment.

I want to remind her—as I have so many times before—that the gaming industry is bigger than Hollywood and the music business *combined*, but again, there is no reason to argue.

"I'm looking at other jobs as well." Another lie.

"You've promised me, if no job by end of the year, you will find an engineering position. Not a secretary one."

"Yes. I'm aware."

"So, better hurry up. Say hi to Dad." I hear her rustle around and hand the phone over.

"Hi, honey," he says. I picture him on the couch, remote in hand as he flips channels, never settling on any one program for more than two minutes, unless it's a Bob Ross rerun. I imagine him wearing the HAPPY LITTLE TREES T-shirt I got him several birthdays ago that's become a weekly staple.

"Hi, Dad." I see his smile, the thin, even slats of space between each sharply rectangular tooth. I think about how tonight the two of them will cuddle into the same corner of the couch, used so much it sinks lower than the rest of the barely touched cushions. I picture his arm around her neck, her hand resting on his knee. How he'll sweep her hair to the side and rub small circles into the back of her neck. How she'll get up to make a tea for them to share, knowing he'll refuse his own and opt for sips of hers. How easy they make love seem.

Mom takes the phone back. "I'll reach out to Jaya's mom, ask her about the firm she works at. Good benefits, I hear. Also, don't forget to put a chair under the doorknob of your hotel room. I saw a story on it. Hotel rooms, not safe."

We hang up and I try to picture myself working at another engineering firm, sitting at a desk all day, clicking around on CAD software, hating life.

Catapult has to work out.

It has to work out so I can pay my rent. So I can show my mom game design is a promising, lucrative career. It has to work out so I can beat Zane. So I can prove I am a damn good designer. And most importantly, it has to work out because I have no backup plan.

After another hour of staring at my computer screen, no closer to identifying a viable game concept, I give up and close my laptop. I can only hope this trip offers me some creative juice. Finn lifts from his spot at my feet under the table, walks groggily to the bedroom door, stops, and looks over his backside at me with a lazy expectancy.

"All right, buddy, I'm coming." I follow him into the bedroom to pack. It's an early flight to paradise tomorrow.

12.

TESS INSISTS ON DRIVING ME TO THE AIRPORT IN WHAT SHE DEEMS AN added measure of security, though I hardly see her logic when I'm about to be alone with Charlie for seven days.

"What are you doing? Just drop me at the curb," I tell her when she drives past the departures lane toward the parking garage.

She shakes her head. "He needs to see my face."

"And what will that do, exactly?"

"It will remind him there are people who know you are with him, people who love you. Maybe it'll make him think twice before he tries anything."

"You *are* rather intimidating," I say, looking her up and down from the passenger seat. She comes across particularly juvenile today in a floral sundress and flip-flops, her blond hair pulled together in a loose braid at the nape of her neck.

We find Charlie leaning on the side of the ticketing counter. He smiles when he sees me, pushes himself up from the counter's edge. He's wearing a dark gray T-shirt that says CAN I GET A WATT WATT with a pair of yellow light bulbs and dark gray joggers that look a lot like the ones from the night of the fire alarm.

Tess steps in front of me when we reach his side and shakes his hand aggressively. "Charlie Sawyer Watters. Born December fourth, nineteen ninety-four, to Sheila and Corbin Watters in Santa Fe, New Mexico. Full-time waiter at The Wexley on Santa Monica in West Hollywood, part-time actor whose most notable role is as the guy in the muscle spray commercial where you spray on fake abs then cannonball into a pool." She shakes his hand aggressively, stares him down as she does.

Yes. I've seen those commercials. But once again, I haven't put two and two together. So incredibly disappointing that I keep missing things when it comes to Charlie, given I pride myself on preparedness. And preparedness, at its heart, requires observation.

The ridiculousness of the situation hits me. I'm about to get on a plane and spend seven days sharing a suite in paradise with the spray-on abs guy.

"I had to show that the product is waterproof. Their sales went up thirty-five percent after that commercial." He looks to me for answers.

"My best friend, Tess."

"Nice to meet you, best friend Tess. I'm sorry, I haven't online stalked you."

"All you need to know about me is that I excel at finding things on the internet, I have a slew of legal resources at my fingertips, and my uncle is a retired Green Beret sharpshooter. Can hit a target from over twenty-three hundred miles away." She squints. "He never misses. And I may be small, but I practice Krav Maga." This last bit is entirely made up.

"Okay then," he says, taking the handle of my roller suitcase. All he has with him is a duffel bag.

I hug Tess goodbye, but her eyes are still on Charlie.

"Wait, aren't you . . ."

"Okay, bye, Tess!" I stiff-arm her in the stomach.

"You are! Oh my god, you're the guy from the bar!" She's undeterred by my hand in her gut. The small ones are always surprisingly strong.

Charlie looks to me and raises his eyebrows with a sheepish grin.

"We're leaving," I say, shoving him since the tactic didn't work on Tess. He turns and begins walking with his arms up in surrender. I grab the handle to my bag and press my palm into his back to keep him moving.

The last thing I hear is Tess yelling "Make good choices!" as we head toward the security line.

"Let's take a picture," Charlie says soon after we board the plane. He's given me the window seat, despite the all-limbs guy in the aisle seat to his left. As the plane fills with the remaining passengers, I can't help but notice how many passing women sweep a gaze over him. Charlie returns any eye contact with non-committal though polite smiles, but appears otherwise oblivious.

"What? Now?"

"Yes, we're *so* excited for our romantic adventure to begin," he says, deadpan.

He leans in, pressing the side of his head into mine, our temples touching. He smells like some sort of silky bar soap and it's surprising yet pleasant.

"Just don't tag me in anything," I warn. I can't have word of any of this getting back to Jack Palmer.

"Deal. Now, smile like you love me," he says. I smile, the pressure to get it right leaving me feeling like a grinning sloth (and not in the adorable way).

"Wait, let me see it." I reach for the phone before he can place it back into his pocket.

"Why?"

"Because I want to see the picture that's going to introduce us into your world as lovers." I cringe. Why did I say *lovers*?

Charlie hands me the phone. If I didn't know better, I'd say we make a cute couple. Our skin tone is virtually the same and we carry matching wide grins. His piercing, pale blue eyes are easily the most captivating part of him. And if I really didn't know any better, I'd say he looks happily in love.

"Seems believable," I say as I hand the phone back to him.

He pauses to evaluate the picture himself. "You look great, if that's what you're worried about."

"That's not, I'm not—"

"Relax," he says, putting the phone away.

"You relax," I whisper, mostly to myself as I begin to feel the weight of what I've agreed to. "We need to set some ground rules for your posts."

He wriggles his body into his seat and shifts to face me. "Let's hear 'em," he says in an amused tone.

"First, you need to make all your socials private. I don't need anyone in my life coming across your posts. Second—reminder that you cannot tag me in anything."

He nods. "Done. What else?"

I feel like there should be more, but I can't seem to think of anything. "That's it. For now."

He holds out his hand and I shake it, our agreement for this trip official.

When the engine begins to hum in preparation for takeoff, Charlie goes quiet. I soon see that his hands are curled around both armrests and he's bouncing his knee aggressively.

"You okay?" I ask.

"Yeah, fine. Not a great flyer."

"You're afraid of flying?"

"I'm not afraid. I'm just realistic. Planes are not natural." He glances toward the cockpit.

"Birds are natural. And planes are shaped like birds."

He doesn't acknowledge the comment, so I keep trying. "The chances of dying in a plane crash—"

"One in eleven million. Yeah, I know." His grip on the armrests tightens.

Interesting that he knows the survival rates. "Would you like my tie-dyed hoodie? As, like, a comfort item? I think I have it here somewhere. Or an adult coloring book, maybe?"

"You're not funny."

"C'mon, it's pretty much your emotional support hoodie by now, isn't it?"

His jaw is stern and I imagine he's questioning his decision to bring me on this trip, albeit as his beard.

I soften a bit when he presses his eyes shut. "Quick—tell me your pet peeves. What about people drives you crazy?" I ask.

"What, why?" He opens his eyes and shifts them toward me but doesn't move his head from its press against the headrest.

"Because you can't be scared if you're annoyed. Annoyed is better than scared."

"I'm not—"

"You're not scared. Nervous. I got it. Now come on. Share. I promise it'll work."

The plane accelerates.

He exhales sharply.

"Fine, I'll go first," I say when he doesn't respond. "I can't stand when people don't return grocery carts. People who are rude to servers, that's a big one. Drivers who creep way past the end of the merge zone to enter into traffic—"

"How long is your list, exactly?"

"Long. People do a lot of annoying things."

"That last one, creeping past the merge zone? I do that occasionally." He jerks the right corner of his mouth into some semblance of a fleeting grin at my look of dismay. "What else?" he asks, the tension in his neck softening.

"Replying All on emails. If you say you do that, I might have to get up and leave. And we're on a plane, so that says something."

"You're safe there. I totally agree on that one," he says, easing a bit more.

"Your turn."

"Okay," he says, moving his hands from the armrests to his lap. "I hate, like really hate, eating sounds. Chewing, slurping. And tapping. Nails, pens. It drives me crazy." He shudders.

"Misophonia," I tell him.

"Miso-what?"

"It's called misophonia. Your strong distaste for chewing, slurping, et cetera." I grin.

"It's not funny. It's a real problem. You'd be surprised by how many people are loud, open-mouth chewers. And they all seem to be in LA. Just watch. Now you're going to notice it all the time."

"Well, thanks for ruining every future meal for me."

I think I see a slight smile, then the plane lurches once more as we climb and his knuckles are chalk-white again.

I pull my massive carry-on from under the seat in front of me into my lap and start digging through it, holding up items. "Would a snack help? I have almonds, granola bars?"

He shakes his head.

"A book? I have three." I hold up the stack of paperback romances, a shirtless hard-bodied male adorning each cover. He takes a look, then shakes his head again.

"What I need is the drink cart." He looks ahead to the flight attendants who are still strapped into their seats.

"I should have brought alcohol," I muse, more to myself than him.

"I didn't think your doomsday plans would involve booze," he says, returning his attention to me.

"It's multifunctional. Can be poured on wounds or consumed to help you forget it's the end of days."

"It can also kill poison ivy," he says. "Should Earth become overrun by it when most of the humans are gone."

It's perhaps the most attractive thing anyone has ever said to me.

"We'd just need apple cider vinegar, for the rashes after exposure," I say, practically giddy at the turn in our conversation.

"What else have you got in that Mary Poppins bag?"

One by one, I pull out the remaining contents and place them between my lap and his. A packet of baby wipes. Mini first aid kit. Eye mask and earplug set. A freezer-size bag of rolled-up chargers. Flint, which accompanies me most everywhere. A pocket survival kit, which causes him to raise his eyebrows.

"Why do you need three ChapSticks?" he says, referencing the next items in my palm.

"As you said, I like to be prepared." I leave the pack of toilet seat covers and extra pairs of underwear at the bottom of the bag.

"For what, extensively cracked lips?"

"That, and ChapStick actually has several potential uses in an emergency. It can fix a zipper, patch holes, even stop a small bleed."

"Why are you like this?" he asks, his arched brow and twitching eyelid indicating what I believe to be genuine interest.

I shrug. "There's so much that's out of our hands, you know? Being prepared for any situation helps me feel more in control."

"What made you feel so out of control that you needed to gain it back?"

The question comes out as if it's no big deal. As if he's not asking me to bare the rawest parts of myself. I clear my throat, thinking of my childhood home. Of Zane. "I don't know. Do you always ask this many questions?"

Seemingly out of nowhere, the plane lurches and he grabs my knee with a white-knuckle grip. He leaves it there for a moment and we make eye contact, his pale blue eyes seemingly cataloging me once again. I break the gaze, looking down at his hand. He retracts, moving it back to the armrest.

The flight attendants, barely affected by the turbulence, arrive at our row with the drink cart and we both order rum and Cokes.

Charlie eyes me as I take the Coke but toss the mini rum bottle into my bag. "If you're not going to drink that . . ."

"Oh, so now you appreciate my Mary Poppins bag."

The plane lurches again and he squeezes his eyes shut until it settles.

"Yes, I do. Very much so."

"Yes what?" I cock my head and urge him along like a schoolteacher with a student who's got the correct answer on the tip of their tongue.

The plane shifts again and he succumbs. "Yes. I appreciate you and your Mary Poppins bag."

I reward him with the mini rum bottle.

"Now, handle yourself, please," I tell him as I pull my laptop out of the bag and lower my tray table. "I have to figure this game out."

He shrugs. As I place the other items back inside my bag, he touches my wrist.

"Wait," he says when I lift the books.

First my leg, now my wrist. Despite his claim that he runs cold, his hand feels burning hot against my skin. Or maybe it's just me.

"I'll take that," he says, pulling one of the romance novels from the stack.

"*The Burning Locke* is a personal favorite," I tell him.

"Yeah, well, I don't have anything else to do. I guess this'll help me fall asleep." He opens it and flips to the first chapter. "You know, I didn't take you for a romance kind of girl."

"Oh, and why is that?"

"Doomsday prep and apocalyptic gaming don't really go

hand in hand with romance, do they? I would have taken you for more of a how-to guide reader."

"Well, I'm a multifaceted human," I say.

His mouth takes a downward curve and I can't tell if he is frowning or contemplating.

After he downs his double rum and Coke, it only takes a few minutes for Charlie to stop gripping the armrests completely. I glance over to see his eyes are closed, chin pointed to the flight attendant call button, full lips slightly parted, and *The Burning Locke* spread open across his lap. My eyes linger. I can observe him freely now, in close proximity. His dark brown hair curves perfectly to the right. I notice for the first time how long his eyelashes are, silky and naturally curled. I also see the dimple that sits atop his right cheekbone leaves a faint trace, even when his face is at rest.

I force my attention away from him. With Charlie sedated, I should focus fully on my design. Jack Palmer only provided light direction, but I imagine they will rate the game demo on playability, graphics, mechanics, and, most importantly, the potential for commercial appeal. None of this is possible without a concept, of course, and I have to come up with an idea, fast.

I stare at the blank screen, but all I can seem to think about is Charlie, this trip, and his plot for revenge on his ex. I wonder if I'm breaking some sort of girl code by being complicit in his deceit. I know I'm only hearing one side of things—Charlie's—and I don't even know if what he has shared with me is true. At best, his take is muddied by a broken heart.

I'm using him too, I remind myself. For this trip. For the opportunity to potentially tap into some creative brain flow that may only open when I'm thrust into entirely different, tropical surroundings. And of course, to get as far away from my neighborhood—and Zane and Jenna—as quickly as possible.

I sigh and stare out the window, wondering if this is a good idea. Perhaps my temporary impulsivity has led me too far in the opposite direction of who I am. I continue to watch as we rise above the remaining cloud layer to a level glide.

There's no going back now.

13.

AS WE BEGIN OUR DESCENT, THE SUN IS SETTING AND MUCH OF THE SKY is the color of peach sorbet. Charlie slept for most of the flight while I worked, but as the plane bumps along on its way back down, he awakens with a slight jerk.

"We made it," I say when Charlie turns to me.

"We almost have," he says with a sleepy grin.

There's something intimate about seeing him just as he has awoken, eyes soft and the skin of his neck and cheeks tinged pink. I look away.

We both lean toward the window for the final descent, Charlie's arm pressed against mine. The sky is now a mischievous orange and the water a brilliant turquoise blue. There's an endless number of cays and inlets as far as we can see, most appearing uninhabited. Each its own truly unspoiled tropical paradise. The sight causes a twinge of excitement to ripple through me. I'm almost convinced we are about to have a water landing for how close we are to the still sea until, at the last moment, a runway emerges.

When we land, the plane halts and we both go straight to our phones. There are three missed calls in a row from a number I don't recognize, so I ignore them. Next, I navigate to my texts.

Mom: Enjoy your trip. I hope you and Tess have a lovely time. Text when you land.

Me: Landed!

Tess: Our code word is J.D. Text it if there's trouble this week. And remember, daily check-ins!

I get her reference, of course. J.D., as in Brad Pitt's character in *Thelma and Louise*, our favorite old movie. Her implication is clear: falling for J.D. did not end well for Thelma.

Me: Landed. So far, still alive. No J.D. in sight.

Tess: We miss you already!

She immediately replies, followed by a selfie of her and Finn, their faces pressed together, Finn's mouth open, tongue hanging out to one side. I already miss that adorable grin (Finn's, that is).

I glance over at Charlie, who's staring at his screen, eyebrows knitted together and eyes narrowed. He senses me observing him and turns his phone toward me without a word. There on his screen is Brooke, and her new beau—Spencer, I think his name is—sitting at a high-top table in a restaurant, an exquisite living wall of greenery behind them.

"Olive House," he says. "Our favorite spot. She's with *him* at Olive House."

I think of my run-in with Zane at Marv's and I empathize with Charlie deeply at this moment. I can't help but feel the ache of it all again through him. The tug from his core that threatens to swallow him into himself. The feeling of longing and deep desire for someone who hurt him more than he thought possible. The nagging I-wasn't-good-enough mantra likely stampeding through his mind. The frustration that he should be better than someone who could be overtaken by *them*.

"You know, the part of your brain that lights up when going through emotional pain is the same part that lights up from physical pain. That's why heartbreak feels like an actual punch to the stomach," I tell him.

His eyes remain stationed on his phone, but he acknowledges my words with a long blink.

"Why don't you just block her?" I ask. "Or unfollow her altogether? Why torture yourself like this?"

He shakes his head. "I told you. I'm not gonna slink away. She cared about me once. I know she still does."

I deflate, as absurd as it is. I know my role here. Still, hearing him talk about her, seeing him hurt, sends a pang through me. One I wish wasn't there.

He stares at the picture a few seconds longer before the plane arrives at the gate and people rise and begin crowding the narrow aisle. Charlie is still immersed in his phone, having switched screens. I don't intentionally read his text, though my brain registers the words nonetheless.

Jacob: Hope you make it through this fake romantic week. Who's the girl you roped into going, anyway?

Charlie: She's nobody.

Ouch. Perhaps Charlie is just like Zane—careless, treating women as disposable. *I don't know him*, I remind myself. Charlie could very well be just like Zane, though something in me immediately wrestles the idea. Regardless, seeing his text is a solid reminder that I've got a bad picker. I send a silent thank-you to the heavens for reminding me to keep my distance from Charlie. Staying away from him this week will be a breeze.

We deplane, make it through customs, and collect our bags

from one of the two carousels at the humble airport. When the doors open, we are met with a blast of warm, wet air.

"Wow," he says, wearing a teasing smile as we wait for the resort shuttle on the curb.

"What?"

"Nothing, it's just . . . your hair. You look like Monica from *Friends*. The one with Monica's island hair."

"Yeah, I know the one." My hair is a moisture meter, and, by the look on his face, we are at a solid ten out of ten. I grab a hair tie from my tote and pull my hair into a high bun, noticing how his eyes linger for a beat on my neck as I do.

We hop on a shuttle and catch our initial glimpses of the island by night, heading to our resort in Grace Bay on the northeast coast of the island of Providenciales—Provo for short. As we make our way, there are small strip malls at equal intervals, intersected by spreads of trees and foliage. It reminds me of an LA suburb, but with more turnabouts and open space. Though it's dark, there's a distinct island-ness to it all: happy, unhurried. The air is thick and sauna-like even within the confines of the shuttle.

"Are you feeling better now that we're on land?" I ask as we make our way along a now dark road. We are tourists on an unlit trek on a foreign island in a stranger-driven shuttle. For a brief moment, I wonder if this excursion ends with a robbery. What would I do? Am I prepared? I clasp my phone in my hand, ready to go live on social media should things go awry and signs begin pointing to Charlie and me being left on the side of this winding island street in our underwear.

I try not to picture Charlie in his underwear.

Unsuccessfully.

Our driver has far too kind eyes to do such a thing, I decide. And Provo has one of the lowest crime rates of any island in the Caribbean, or so I read.

"Much better, thanks," Charlie says. "So are you really gonna spend this whole trip working?" He flicks his chin at the laptop poking out of my carry-on bag on the floor between us.

"I need to. This interview—this job—could be my big break."

He shifts his body to face me. "Oh yeah?"

I nod. "That's why when they said in the interview they expect me to be single in order to work there, I didn't flinch."

I make brief eye contact with our driver in the rearview mirror. His eyes flicker wide at me then promptly move back to the road. Even he knows how absurd my situation is.

"What? They really asked that of you? You can't be serious."

"Oh, I'm serious. And it wasn't so much of an ask as a prerequisite. Though they didn't say those exact words, it was heavily implied." I shake my head in an attempt to downplay. "It's not a big deal. I have no relationship plans in my future anyway."

"Aren't there other options? Companies that aren't so . . . horrendous?"

"No," I say flatly. "They're the number one game design company in the world, and right in our backyard. And, truthfully, the only one open to considering applicants without a certain kind of résumé and pedigree. If I close this door, there's no other door. They're it."

He looks contemplative. "Why game design?" he eventually asks. "How'd you figure out it's your dream?"

I stare out my window at the darkened sky. "When life gets hard, I've always turned to gaming. It's sort of my safe space, I suppose." I picture our home after the flood, then the hours I spent immersed in *Tomb Raider* right after Zane. Then, I picture the girl gang that made my early adolescence miserable, particularly during my unibrow stage, aka grades four through eight. The three of them all carbon copies of L.O.L. dolls, with Disney princess eyes and hair to their butts. Olivia, the one with the unreasonable confidence and crafty charm, once smeared a jar of tikka masala along the underside of my desk, ensuring I'd carry the scent all day. She was creative in her maltreatment, that one. Two years ago, Olivia went viral for a Serena Williams Halloween costume that included blackface.

"I want to create that escape for someone else." I pause for a moment. "I used to play *Super Mario Bros.* so much I'd walk through the halls at school picturing Yoshi sticking his tongue out and swallowing up all the people who tormented me."

Charlie huffs amiably.

I go on, unable to contain my enthusiasm. "You get to create an entire world of your own making. One you can escape into whenever you need to flee real life. The release of knowing there's another world—one that people I don't even know might come together in, all momentarily unified . . . it's the deepest form of connection I can imagine."

I think of my mom, who has always held a scarcity mentality from having grown up with so little. I imagine there's a bit of her in there too. In my need to be prepared for anything, even pre-flood. That by building my own worlds in games, I have that preparation and control; it's an easy thing to accomplish in a world in which you know the ending.

Charlie and I catch each other's gaze in the darkened car interior and the sternness of his jaw draws my full attention. He looks at me so intently I feel myself blush.

"I get that," he says, though he doesn't elaborate. I can't particularly imagine him having been teased in school, but perhaps there have been other challenges that have made him feel alone. I appreciate the camaraderie nonetheless. "Being an actor isn't exactly cool and respected until or unless you get that big breakout role. We moved around a lot when I was a kid. I played Gomez in three different productions of *The Addams Family* at three different schools. So that escape you're talking about? I guess I found it onstage. I never really thought about it that way though. Until now."

He stares out the window as I envision sitting in a high school auditorium, watching him perform in a pin-striped suit and center-parted hair.

"I've seen you before, you know," he says after a bit, eyes still stationed out the window.

I stretch the shoulder strap of my seat belt so I can turn to face him.

"I've seen you collecting gaming magazines from your mailbox. And hunkered down at Marv's. I saw those sketches on your table. I wish I had a passion like that. One I couldn't ignore." He leans in as if the next part is a secret. "I hope you get the job."

There's a hum of something up my spine.

"Even if those guys are royal assholes," he adds.

Sitting next to him in the dark of the shuttle, as our legs lightly connect with each bounce of the road, I can't help but think of our kiss at the bar. My belly tics and I send it a silent warning to stop misbehaving. *But we are on vacation, away from real life*, suggests Satan Sloane. I envision punching Satan Sloane between the eyes, refocusing on Charlie when she goes down.

As the drive continues, we begin to pass more buildings in what looks like a modest suburb, and I notice that many are cement, which I assume helps them withstand the hurricane-force winds Caribbean islands regularly face. I have a vision of an actual hurricane hitting while we are here, but quickly shake it out of my head.

When the breeze from the driver's open window has grown even damper and dense to the point of raindrop-like dew, we pull through the gates of the Turquoise Point Resort and along a stretch of narrow road, lit only by roadside lanterns, serving both an eerie and romantic feel. That is, until we turn the corner and the full resort comes into view. One, two, three . . .

six stories of softly lit archways. The glowing light illuminates the gentle yellow of the building framed by bright blue shutters outlining every window. If the resort looks like this, I can only imagine the view just behind it.

We step out of the shuttle and I breathe in the balmy sea air. For the first time, albeit briefly, I feel like this trip is inarguably a good idea.

Even before we walk inside, it's evident to me that this resort is pricey. Not just thoughtful-romantic-getaway pricey, but beachfront-Caribbean-island pricey. Charlie can't make much between his part-time acting and waiting tables at The Wexley, and my heart pinches a bit thinking he could have lost his girlfriend *and* all the money he spent on this trip. Much of his savings, he told me just three days ago when he first invited me, back in my apartment thousands of miles away. I'm glad he still got to come, even if the circumstances are far different than planned.

We make our way through the grand lobby, complete with white marble floors and two-story ceilings.

"Wow," I say aloud, mostly to hear the echo.

A bellman escorts us up a mirrored elevator with elaborately etched wood railings and crown molding to the sixth floor. At the end of the tiled hall, he opens the double doors of our suite to a grand living room. I'm taken first with the suite's size. The ample space opens to a massive terrace that spans the length of the suite. Beside us, there's a kitchenette with a full-size fridge, and to the left, a bedroom door. This place is irrefutably larger and better maintained than my apartment. The room is adorned with ornate mahogany tables (dining, coffee, end) with sexy, curved legs that bring to mind someone sitting back with their feet kicked up. Even the furniture here is on vacation.

Charlie tips the bellman before he leaves and we are, for the first time, officially alone on this trip.

My attention is drawn to the kitchenette's counter, where an enormous bouquet of red roses is placed. *For Brooke*, I think. The girl I replaced on this trip. The residue of her hangs in the air like a thick cloud of smoke. Charlie steps beside me and we observe the flowers in loaded silence as if they are placed above a cemetery plot.

"I prefer black," I eventually say.

He turns to me in question.

"Black roses. Red is so traditional."

"You're dark," he says with no eye contact, but his expression softens a bit.

I decide to explore, stepping first into the bedroom, but as soon as I open the door, I regret it. There's a trail of red rose petals leading to the bed, where they flow into the shape of a heart.

They really love roses around here.

And, it's one bed. The king-size, turned-down bed is covered in rose petals placed inside the flower heart with a tray holding a chilled champagne bottle, two glasses, and a platter of chocolate-covered strawberries with white drizzle.

In my haste to distance myself from Zane and Jenna, I never confirmed with Charlie that he'd changed the reservation to ensure we had two separate, adequately spaced beds.

I feel Charlie's presence close behind me and goosebumps rise across the back of my neck.

"I paid extra for the romance package," he says flatly, looking over my shoulder. He squeezes past me to grab the champagne and then swivels to head for the terrace.

I'm not quite sure what to do. Arriving here and seeing this spread must be soul-crushing. I don't know Charlie well enough to know whether he prefers company or to be left alone when he's upset. I don't know him well enough to know if he is angry or sad. Or both. And I certainly don't know him well enough to be on a trip with him halfway across the world in a suite with a rose-petal-covered bed. Yet here we are. I sigh, grab my computer and the two champagne flutes he's left behind, and head to the terrace.

He's standing against the rail, looking out at what I imagine to be a beautiful view. Though I know there is nothing but sand and shoreline ahead of us, the moon is positioned behind a cloud and we stare at a vast canvas of deep gray. Still, I can practically see the calmness of the waves, the sound more of a hum than the crash of the Pacific back home. I take a deep breath. The air here feels different, constantly replaced with each sea breeze and gentle push of water toward the shore. I may just be convinced that I can, in fact, be more creative here than at my nicked-up kitchen table. The goldendoodle from 6F feels every inch of those three thousand miles away.

"It's beautiful," I say.

"It's practically pitch-black," he responds.

"The sound, I mean." I too stare in the direction of the water. Of the lulling whir.

He's still holding the champagne bottle by the neck, though he hasn't opened it. I hand him a glass.

"You can have the bedroom," he says, taking the glass. "I'll sleep on the couch tonight. I tried to trade the suite for two separate rooms before we left, but with everything going on, I forgot to follow up to confirm. I'll call down in the morning if that's okay with you."

"It's fine. But you paid for this trip. I insist you take the bedroom tonight."

"I really don't want it." He eases the cork from the bottle with precision. No spray. No pomp. He fills my glass and hands it over. "Not after seeing that red rose murder scene in there."

"I can get rid of all that stuff."

"Really, it's fine." He fills his glass and plops down, a slight swish of champagne escaping, landing on his sweatpants at his thigh. He doesn't seem to notice. I want to clink his glass, but am at a loss for an appropriate toast. Cheers to us and this misfit trip? Cheers to Brooke Brady, may she grow jealous and remorseful as a result of this week's worth of photos you post online? Neither seems right, so I say nothing.

I quietly sip my champagne. It's good. And though this trip is already riddled with potential pitfalls and will likely consist of Charlie moping and me working, for the moment I am content staring into the gray. The sound of the ocean before me releases the pressure from my neck, my shoulders with every swaying motion.

There is, however, one thing that continues to nag at me. I am, at least for tonight, staying in a rose-petal-covered, beachfront suite with Charlie, having wholly underestimated the romantic nature of it all.

14.

WHEN I ROLL OVER THE NEXT MORNING AND GLANCE AT THE ALARM clock on the bedside table, it's a little after seven. Even in paradise, despite the well-stuffed feather pillows and high thread count sheets, I can't manage to sleep in. Forgetting to close the curtains last night before I collapsed into bed surely didn't help. I spin toward the wall of glass and am overwhelmed by the view awaiting me in the crisp morning light. Captivated, I rise from the bed, walk to the bedroom terrace door, and slide it open. A blast of damp air hits me. The balmy feel is reminiscent of being lathered in lotion that's not fully rubbed in and I anticipate messy buns and swamp ass for the next seven days, though I surely can't complain. We are closer to the water than I had realized, our terrace hovering above the chalky sand. It's a cloudless morning, and there's endless blue reaching to the shore where our building sits, the line where the sky meets the sea unclear.

"Morning."

I flinch in surprise.

In the same seat from the night before, Charlie is already awake, one leg propped up against the rail. I wonder for a moment if he ever left. He's shirtless. Sipping coffee shirtless.

I look down at what I slept in. It's the second time he has caught me unexpectedly in pajamas. This time I'm in an oversize ZOMBIELAND T-shirt (complete with Woody Harrelson's and

Emma Stone's faces) and black boy shorts. He takes in my outfit, eyes catching at the ruffled hem of my shorts, and I tug at my T-shirt. He turns his attention to the water.

"I didn't realize you were up," I say, heading back inside the bedroom.

"Couldn't sleep," he calls after me from the terrace.

I grab a pair of jean shorts from my suitcase and throw them on before heading back outside.

"Didn't mean to scare you," he says. "I couldn't sleep," he repeats.

"Same."

"Busy working on your game?"

"Kind of."

He waits for me to elaborate, and when I don't, he says, "I called downstairs. There are no single rooms available, just a suite double this size and triple the price. I'm sorry."

Correction—I *am* staying in a rose-petal-covered romantic beachfront suite with Charlie for the next week. Somehow, though, the daylight and serenity of the early morning make it seem less of an issue than it did last night.

"It's okay," I tell him. "But I insist—"

"I'm not taking the bedroom," he says. "It's my fault we're stuck in this situation. Please just take it."

I throw my hands up in defeat, attempting to avoid the disappointment I feel when he references being stuck sharing a suite with me.

"Wanna order some breakfast?" he asks, clearly wanting to move on from the logistics of it all.

"Yes. Absolutely."

It turns out the romance package is in fact all-inclusive, complete with bottomless mimosas alongside breakfast, so we order generously.

When the waiter leaves our room after delivering our order,

we immediately wheel the carts to the terrace, the spot we've silently agreed holds our best chances, both individually and combined, at vacation bliss. I take in the pullout couch and rumpled blankets in the living room and am a bit relieved to see he did at least make an attempt at sleep.

We each man a cart and begin removing plate covers. It's more food than we could possibly eat in an entire day and my joy is fleeting as it feels wasteful. It seems Charlie reads my mind because he says, "Maybe just one item each tomorrow."

"Definitely."

We both fill heaping plates from the buffet of food we've ordered. I scoop scrambled eggs, bacon, boiled fish, grits; our first experience with authentic island food, the resort version at least.

We sit side by side, overflowing plates in our laps, observing the beach below. The sand is lined with bright yellow umbrellas shielding matching chairs, though most sit empty at this hour.

It's an exceptional start to the week, considering the circumstances that brought us here. I feel an overwhelming sense of gratitude toward Charlie for allowing me this experience.

I watch him pour a mimosa from the carafes on the cart. Though I don't know the appropriate proportions of a mimosa, I'm fairly certain his recipe—ninety-eight percent champagne, two percent OJ—is likely not it. He offers me the glass, and when I shake my head, he downs it before taking a single bite of food. He pours himself another. I think to suggest he slow down; it's not even nine o'clock on our first morning. But also, I get it. I can't say I didn't turn to mimosas after my breakup with Zane, though mine were in the form of whiskey neats consumed on my living room floor, Tess by my side.

"This place is incredible," I say, captivated by the view and our proximity to the water. "I feel like I'm in a Bob Ross painting."

Charlie shakes his head. "There aren't enough happy trees for it to be a Bob Ross painting."

I cock my head at him the way Finn does when taking in something new. I'm surprised Charlie even knows who Bob Ross is, given my knowledge of him only exists because falling asleep to his videos has long been one of my father's favorite pastimes.

"So what's your story?" he asks through a mouthful of chocolate chip muffin. "Tell me more about the woman I'm madly in love with." He grins, his cheeks bulging.

I feel a bit of empathetic relief at his temperament. Perhaps a piled-high breakfast plate and a good night's sleep have improved his mood. The mimosas can't be hurting either.

"What do you mean?"

"All I know about you is that you live across the hall, you carry a Mary Poppins bag, you're a video game designer, which is very cool, by the way, you have an awesome dog, and you're the person I'd want next to me if the world was ending."

I raise my eyebrows at the last bit.

"Because of your clear survival instincts," he adds.

I take a bite of mango and my eyes instinctively close as I savor its freshness. Mango every day—new vacation rule. "You've gotta try this," I tell him.

"Way to change the subject," he says.

"What specifically do you want to know?"

"Okay, where'd you grow up?"

"California, my whole life. Never far from LA," I tell him.

"What's your favorite color?"

"Sage green."

"Why do you keep a bug-out bag in your apartment?"

I note and appreciate that he even knows the term *bug-out bag*. "I like to be prepared."

"Are you prepared or scared?" he asks, then takes another bite of muffin.

"We're rhyming now? Are you Dr. Seuss? Or just obtuse?"

"You're impossible."

"But also responsible."

"That doesn't even rhyme."

"Give it time. Okay, I'm done."

He squints at me and I can see he's about to double down, unwilling to let me deflect with childish wit. "Who's the guy that broke your heart?" he asks, double-down voiced.

I eye him, holding a bite of mango in my cheek. "Why do you assume some guy broke my heart?"

"Because you've got that look."

"What look?"

"The one like you want to be left alone but also don't want to be left alone." His gaze makes my throat burn. "I know it well," he says, shifting his focus to the water.

"There's no guy that broke my heart," I say. Zane is the part of me I can't manage to share. Even though Charlie might relate, my heartbreak feels like weakness and I can't share weakness. Not with a guy I barely know. And not when I'm trying to convince myself—and Jack Palmer—that I am capable, strong, focused.

We look out at the water, chewing slowly.

"It's not fair, you know," he says after some time.

"What's not fair?"

"You know all about my breakup, this embarrassing, painful thing that's just happened to me, and you won't tell me anything about yourself."

We both stare at the water again. He's right, of course. I'm being guarded in my interactions with Charlie. There's a mile-long list of reasons I need to keep him at arm's length. But still, I have empathy for him that is too specific.

I have a flash of Zane and me on Terramar Beach in Carlsbad, watching the afternoon surfers as we sat upright against the rocks, sharing a pepperoni pie from Pizza Port. Zane spotted one of his dorm suitemates from UCLA and trotted a few yards down the beach to say hello, leaving his phone face up on the blanket beside me. The screen buzzed and lit up so, naturally, I looked.

J: Tomorrow 🩶

I didn't even ask him about it, just silently explained it away. There were so many possible explanations. And there was nothing that bothered Zane more than signs of distrust. Instead, when he returned, I lifted his arm and placed it around me, nestled into his side.

Now I say, "You shouldn't be embarrassed, Charlie. Relationships don't work out. And sometimes, people do things we assume they'd never do. It's not a reflection of who you are."

I can feel him observing me, but I keep my gaze on the water.

"Are you speaking from experience?" he asks, eyes still fused to the side of my face. It burns, the left side of my face.

"I told you my favorite color is sage green," I say after a beat.

"What?"

"You said I didn't tell you anything. My favorite color is sage green." I lift the plate from my lap and set it on the small side table between us. "The color of the succulents my mom keeps a row of along the windowsill in our kitchen. She's done that in every home we've had."

"Every home?" he asks.

I go quiet, wishing I hadn't added that last detail.

After a moment, he shakes his head. "Maybe I'll earn your trust eventually," he says, pouring another mimosa.

Trust. Such a brittle thing. Capable of flaking away with one wrong touch. I try not to read too much into his words, but they stay with me long after he's said them. Does Charlie care about me trusting him? Is my trust something he desires?

I try to shake the questions. I shouldn't care what he thinks. Furthermore, I can't allow him to take up brain space that should be dedicated to Catapult.

Charlie holds the champagne bottle up in another offer when he finishes refilling his glass.

I shake my head. "Can't. I've got work to do."

As I retreat to the bedroom and close the door behind me, I wonder if I've imagined the twinge of disappointment in Charlie's eyes just now.

15.

IT'S THREE IN THE AFTERNOON BEFORE I HEAR A PEEP FROM CHARLIE, and it's far more than a peep. The sudden music blaring from the terrace causes me to jerk, almost dropping my laptop from the bed. Hitting save on my work, I head to the scene of the noise.

I find Charlie, barefoot and still shirtless, dancing to Taylor Swift's "Blank Space" blaring from his phone. He's singing along, though yelling may be a more appropriate description. If the phrase "dance like no one's watching" were a person, it would be Charlie. He's hopping around while crossing his arms back and forth in front of him like some cross between a rhythmic gymnast and a hacky-sacker and it's bad. So, so bad.

"Hey!" he shouts over the music when he sees me. He grabs my hand, circles my waist with his other arm, and twirls me around the terrace. When he releases me on the opposite end of the small space, I stumble to regain my footing, pressing my hand against the stucco wall that separates our terrace from the next for support. I take note of a second almost empty champagne bottle.

Charlie's been busy.

"Have some water," I say, handing him the untouched glass from the table beside us.

"Water's lame," he yells, swaying slightly offbeat.

"It's not lame, it's important. Here." I hold the glass in front of him and turn down the volume on his phone. He shows his dismay in the furrow of his brow but drinks it in its entirety. While I'm happy to see Charlie in some state of bliss, I know it's misleading. He's mostly just numb.

"I think I brought charcoal pills. I'll grab some for you."

"Of course you did. That's so Sloane." He shakes his head as he picks up his water glass to take a sip. He holds it to his lips and, when nothing comes out, pulls it in front of him to observe it. Empty. He nods and sets the glass down, as if he's just remembered he finished it a few seconds ago. "Do you believe in fate?" he asks, his tone suddenly serious.

"What?"

"Fate. Like two people are meant to be."

His words immediately conjure Zane's face in my mind, and I promptly shove it out. "What are you talking about, Charlie?"

"I read it in that book you gave me on the plane." He pauses for a moment to brush the hair from his forehead, slightly damp with sweat. "I thought Brooke and me, I thought we were soulmates. That she was The One. Isn't that just . . ." He plops down into a chair, breathing hard. "Ridiculous."

"I'm sorry," I offer, because I don't quite know how to console him.

"I know you are," he says, pulling gently at my wrist so I fall into the chair beside his. "You're so great. Thank you for being here. I don't know what I'd do without you and your Mary Poppins bag of romance novels." He looks like he's tearing up. Something I've learned about Charlie today: he turns into a sap when he drinks.

We sit quiet for a moment as he leans his head against the reclined chaise. His breath steadies.

"Why do you read romance novels anyway?" he asks just as a shoreline breeze finds us, spinning my hair in small pirouettes against my cheek. Charlie watches as I tuck the loose strands behind my ear and twist the gather of it at the nape of my neck.

"When you think about it," I say, "love and the apocalypse are not all that dissimilar."

"Is that what you want written on your tombstone? Or printed on a T-shirt maybe?"

I slap his arm playfully. "Seriously. Think about it. In romance novels, it's all about the grand gesture. The guy comes to the girl's door holding a stack of poster boards that profess his love. A rush to the airport to stop him from getting on the plane. A flash mob at a train station before she gets on that train and leaves forever. We swoon over the big, grand gesture because it's so hard to find in real life. But really, if it *were* the end of days, you want the person who will make the grand gesture by your side. They'll be the one who'd step in front of a swarm of zombies for you. The grand gesture of all grand gestures."

Charlie looks at me with a slender grin, and I can't help but smile at his disheveled state—hair a mess, eyes a little glassy, breathing still slightly elevated from all the dancing. I have to consciously look away from his reddened lips. I think he will respond with something like, *You need help*. It's what Zane would have said.

But instead, he nods ever so slightly and stares at me when he says, "I get it."

Who are you? I want to ask. I squint as if it might help me see his insides.

"And why are you a doomsday prepper?" he asks, his whole body curving toward me. "Do you have some secret government knowledge about an impending catastrophic event?"

It's not lost on me that Charlie keeps asking different versions of the same questions.

"I wish," I say, leaning back in the lounger and folding my

arms across my chest. "But no. I guess it just comes with the territory if you love gaming."

He shakes his head. "I don't buy that. There're lots of gamers who don't carry three tubes of ChapStick in case there's a hole to patch or cut to salve."

"Look at you, already picking up tips from me," I say mock-proudly.

He taps at my forearm. "C'mon."

"Fine," I say, and his face further softens. Somehow, it's easier to talk to drunk Charlie than sober Charlie. Perhaps he'll forget it all anyway. "I guess it's because . . . because I grew up with a mom who always felt like the world was out of control. Like, coming to the States from India, she saw everything as new and scary and every precaution needed to be taken at all times. And then when I was eleven, our home was ruined after a flash flood. None of us were hurt, but we lost our house and virtually everything in it."

"I'm so sorry. Losing everything like that . . ." He leans toward me and lays a hand across my forearm. "I'm sorry that happened," he says again, his eyes so pale they look faded by the sun.

I clear my throat and attempt to shrug it off. People say they're sorry, they always do. They say losing your home "must have been so awful" and "that really sucks." No shit. I rarely mention it anymore, because it creates this weird moment in conversations. I see it in the straight line of people's eyebrows and the clench of their jaw. How much sorry is the right amount of sorry to offer before moving on? Typically, I take pity on them and change the subject myself.

Charlie's "I'm sorry," though, feels genuine. Like he'd listen to every detail, should I choose to share. "Right, so I didn't want to live my life scared like my mom. She was always uncertain of the world around her, and then after we lost our house, her anxiety grew tenfold," I tell Charlie. I think of how much my mom worries about me. "So I guess I went in the extreme opposite direction to ensure I'm prepared, rather than scared."

"Are we rhyming again? 'Cause I'm ready if and when."

"Please, no."

The corners of his mouth pull and release and he runs a hand through his already tousled hair. "Seriously though." His tone grows heavy. "Thank you for telling me that."

There's an unease that begins to rise from my belly. Did I just share with Charlie, whom I've known for a mere few days, what it took me six years of therapy to learn about myself?

He leans back in his chair, seemingly sensing my discomfort with this topic. "So what did your mom think of you coming on this trip with a virtual stranger? She must've loved that."

"I told her I was coming with Tess," I confess.

"Bad Sloane," he says. It rings of a frisky scolding, sending a slight shudder through me.

"What about you?" I ask. "Why are you not prepared for anything, like, ever? And impulsive. Why are you so impulsive?"

"Oh, now I'm the one that's impulsive."

"You invited a girl you barely know on this trip."

He raises a conspiratorial eyebrow at me. "And she came. Besides, you live across the hall and have a cute dog. Serial killers don't have cute dogs, do they?"

"The ones who use them to lure strangers into unmarked white vans do."

"Shoot. Do you own a white van?"

I shake my head. "A blue Kia."

"Safe then," he says, pretending to wipe his brow.

"You're really gonna leave me out here on the sharing limb all by myself?"

"No, I guess I won't." He tilts to his side to face me again, propping up his head with his elbow. "I was born in Ohio—Columbus. My dad grew up there too. He worked for a refugee resettlement agency there after college before going to Panama, where he met my mom. That's where she's from."

"How'd he end up in Panama?"

"He thought he could do more from Central America. So he joined a refugee organization that was hiring Americans. We moved around a lot—my dad followed the need—so I never really latched on anywhere. They intended to settle in Ohio, but they couldn't sit still there. LA's the longest I've stayed anywhere. So I guess, where you went the opposite way, I clung to my nomadic roots." He absent-mindedly slides his fingers up and down the woven material of the chair.

"I think it's why I spent so much time and energy trying to create a future with Brooke. I thought if I had someone, a long-term someone, it would show my parents not everything in my life is . . . unsettled. A love like theirs, though, it's hard to find. I don't know if they realize it."

I clear my throat, trying to reconcile my feelings about what he just said. Empathy, pain, jealousy, kinship—it's all there, in a blender in my stomach. I thought it was just me who felt pressure to deliver on a "perfect" relationship like the one my parents have.

People look at my mother and father and say, *You're so lucky to have parents who love each other like that*. The truth is, it also puts a ton of pressure on me. Like, how can I be such a fuck-up in relationships when I had such a healthy model? I think of Zane again and how hard I worked to make us fit. To give myself a shot at something like what they have. How far I would have gone to keep the ruse going. "Sometimes the only way to know something's not right for you is to do it and feel regret," I say.

I stare forward because I might crack if I look at Charlie,

especially as his gaze continues to burn like a laser into my left cheek. He's bringing out a vulnerability in me that I'm unaccustomed to, especially with someone I'm just getting to know.

"You don't have any siblings?" I ask.

He shakes his head. "You?"

I shake my head back. As an only child, it often seems as though every other person on the planet has at least one sibling. I can't remember the last time I met someone who was like me. I wonder if he is also close to his parents in that "just us three" way. I wonder if he, like me, carries a small bit of resentment that they didn't give him a peer.

"Well, it all sounds pretty amazing," I say.

"Which part?"

"Your dad's work, mostly."

"I thought for a minute you were going to say *me*. That I'm pretty amazing."

I shake my head as his mouth twists. "You don't need the compliments, Charlie. I assume you receive plenty of praise." At the gym, from many a female suitor.

When he gazes at me with a merciless smile, I turn back to the water, clear my throat. "This really is heaven." I abruptly face him again. "I don't think I've said it, but thank you."

"I'm glad you came," he says, holding my gaze. "The only thing that'd make it better is if Finn were here." He reaches down between us and mimics scratching the top of Finn's head.

"I've never been anywhere like this. I've never been anywhere, really."

"Not to India?"

I shake my head. "My parents have always footed the bill to have family come to the States to visit us instead. I think so much time passed that eventually my mom thought it would be too different from what she remembered and that scared her. Plus, it's a big trip to plan."

He nods. "Makes sense."

"What about you? Have you been to Panama? Still have family there?"

His cheeks lift and I instantly know I've hit on something special. "I go with my parents each summer," he says. "Best two weeks of the year. I sneak a bag full of my grandmother's fry bread home every time."

I nod. "Being here makes me want to do the same, to India. It makes me want to travel in general." I stare out at the water again, with its soft green tint and almost eerie calm. "It's far too rare to look around and be in awe of what you see."

He leans in and it catches me off guard. He runs his fingertips along my forearm and I can't tell if he's even aware he's doing it. Regardless, I erupt in goosebumps. I'm about to suggest he drink more water but he speaks before I can. "Thank you for being here. For helping me. I know it's a shitty position to have put you in." His face is incredibly close to mine.

"I can think of worse places to be," I say, though the words come out breathier than I mean them to.

He wraps his hand around the edge of my chair to brace himself as he leans in even closer. "You're pretty incredible, Sloane. I just—I want you to know that."

"You're drunk, Charlie."

"I wasn't drunk when we kissed the other night at the bar." His voice has gone soft and he licks his lips and I'm focused on his now wet mouth. "What was that, exactly?"

"It was . . . I don't know, a stupid bet with Tess. I'm sorry about it."

"I'm not," he says in immediate response.

I look down and he ducks his head to catch my eyes again.

"I'm not complaining about it. Not at all," he says quietly. "I've thought about it. A lot."

I want to argue. Tell him that's not possible when he's consumed with wanting Brooke back. That he said himself, I'm nobody to him.

He raises his free hand and cups the side of my face. "You're so . . ." He doesn't finish the thought.

My brain tells me to pull away. To break this . . . this thing between us. But I don't listen. I focus instead on Charlie. Just Charlie.

As if he has heard my internal battle and final relent, he leans in and presses his lips to mine.

I know I should rip myself away. He's hung up on another girl. He's drunk. So drunk. But his kiss . . . it doesn't feel drunk. It's not sloppy or aggressive or overindulgent. It's soft, gentle, and full of intention.

I'm instantly taken back to the moment in the bar, the way he slowly gave in to me. It feels like we're traveling in time, back and forth, between that moment and this one, flecks of desire pricking at my skin.

He moves his hand to the back of my head and his fingers graze my hairline, his thumb running slowly up and down the back of my neck, sending a shiver down my spine. He cradles my head toward him as he presses his tongue against mine. His taste has a familiarity, and not just because we've kissed before. No, it's something else. It's like the first bite of my favorite oatmeal raisin cookie after not having one for months. Like the splash of cool raindrops hitting my bare skin on a sweaty summer day. It's anticipation and nostalgia all rolled into the softness of his lips and the slick of his tongue.

On the precipice of giving in completely, I come to my senses.

I pull back and he stares at me, looking a bit like a stunned animal. Again.

"I'm sorry," he says. "I—"

I can see that he is about to explain it away. To tell me he's drunk and not thinking clearly. That he doesn't know what he's doing. I don't want to hear any of his words. Because I already know.

He kissed me to get over *her.*

He thinks I'm nobody.

"Don't do that again," I say, before standing up and walking into the bedroom, closing the terrace door behind me. But I don't finish my explanation either. *Don't do that again unless you mean it* is what I would say, if I had the guts.

Me: J.D. J.D. J.D.!

I type to Tess when I'm in the safety of the bedroom, then delete the comment before I can hit send. There's nothing she can do to help me. I suddenly feel like I'm on a collision course with faulty brakes, Charlie the freight train at the other end of the line.

16.

TWO HOURS LATER, THERE'S A LIGHT KNOCK ON THE BEDROOM DOOR.

"Sloane, can we talk?" I close my laptop and take in the shadow of his feet under the door. It's only the first full day of our trip, and I can't avoid him all week. We're sharing the same suite. And I'm not prepared to jump on a flight back home because of one impulsive kiss. Or two.

I open the door and try not to be amused that we're wearing matching plush black robes, the Turquoise Point Resort sunshine logo positioned just above his right pec.

"Hi," he says delicately, and I see the sober remorse all over his face. "Look, I want you to know how sorry I am. That was totally inappropriate of me and it won't happen again."

I think of the way his lips felt on my mouth, the way his thumb sent goosebumps down my neck. "Good." And then, so I'm not a total hypocrite, I add, "Same here."

He smiles at my admission, tucks his hands into the robe's pockets. "We've both spent the entire day cooped up in this suite and I thought it would be good to get out. I don't know about you, but the seventeen pounds of breakfast have worn off and I'm starving. Wanna go down to the restaurant and have dinner?"

"I don't know . . ." I lean against the doorframe. "Will there be mimosas involved?"

He presses his lips together. "No more mimosas for me. Probably ever again."

I cross my arms and evaluate him, pretending to contemplate. I like having this power over him.

"I'll get dressed," I say finally, and his face promptly softens.

Fifteen minutes later, I step out of the bedroom pushing the last bobby pin into my topknot. I notice his eyes rake over me, so subtly I could have easily missed it.

"You look great," he says.

"You can stop sucking up now. I forgive you."

"I'm not sucking up. It's just a compliment."

"Thank you," I say, one eyebrow raised.

I don't own many clothing items that fit a tropical theme. Luckily, Tess does. This dress, a blush-colored high-low impractical floral wrap, purchased from her favorite online boutique, The Flatterie, is something I would never buy for myself. Once I put it on, though, I could see the appeal of adding some color to my wardrobe. My tanned skin pops against it in a way that makes it look like I have doused myself in cocoa butter. And though Tess is tiny, the wrap silhouette allows it to fit me, though the high part of the high-low skirt does hit quite scandalously at my upper thigh.

Charlie heads into the bathroom and I step out onto the terrace. The evening temperature is not much different than the daytime hours, but I'm grateful for the light breeze that grazes my bare skin. It catches the thin fabric of my dress and waves it around playfully. On the beach below, a couple walks hand in hand along the shoreline, the right side of her body pressed into his left. Every few steps, they stop to point at something noteworthy or examine an item in the sand. On the terrace to the right, I hear a woman laugh, though I can't see her because of the privacy wall.

It's easy to feel windswept here. To be overtaken by the tropical vibes and indulgent meals and romance package. All it takes is a single breath of the viscid, sodden air to remind me how contentedly far I am from home.

The bathroom door opens and when I turn, I can't help but regard him. Charlie is dressed in a white button-down shirt and loose tan pants, looking as though he belongs on the cover of a resort brochure. I've only ever seen him dressed casually: joggers, T-shirts, or no shirt at all. This island-chic look is a close second to shirtless.

I press my eyelids together so tightly they hurt. I am not here to play house with my heartbroken neighbor who's using me to make his ex jealous.

"Are you planning on working through dinner?" he asks, pointing to the laptop poking out the top of my tote as we make our way out of the suite.

"Maybe." I know I likely won't work while we eat; nonetheless, bringing my laptop at least indicates the intent to work and thus makes me feel better about the small break.

We make our way along the winding path to the restaurant, dimly lit every few feet by the romantic glow of tiki torches, and as we encounter the other resort guests for the first time, I notice another thing I hadn't considered when agreeing to this trip. Virtually all are couples. Couple after couple hold hands, smile longingly at each other, stop to kiss. Couples so wrapped together in a tangle of limbs I'm impressed they can walk. Charlie and I avoid eye contact the entire way, our discomfort growing with every touchy-feely pair that passes.

That is, until Charlie suddenly halts, his arm instantly stretched out in front of me in a protective stance.

"Stop!" His warning is so loud I close one eye and stick a finger in my ear retroactively. When I comply, he steps in front of me, using his body as a shield. For what, I'm still not sure.

He turns his head so his mouth is close to the side of my

head, though his eyes don't leave the path. "What the fuck is that," he says, more statement than question, into the same damaged ear he just yelled into. My chest presses into his back as my heart thumps in reaction to the tumult.

I lean to look around him and follow the direction of his pointed finger. Several feet in front of us, half on, half off the walkway, I see it.

Scolopendra gigantea.

An Amazonian giant centipede.

I know from my research of all things Turks that they are local to the islands, but rarely seen by tourists, and even more rarely seen on the walkway of a five-star resort. It's a truly extraordinary moment.

I get Charlie's reaction. This isn't any ol' bug. It's monstrous. Like, the length of my arm, thickness of a hot dog. I rush to pull my phone from my tote and snap some pictures.

"Don't," Charlie says, still shielding me.

"It's fine, Charlie." I brush past him, his hand grazing along the length of my arm as I do.

As I approach, its yellow toothpick-length legs scurry it quickly out of sight into the dark brush, but not before I get the satisfaction of a few photos.

A few feet behind me, Charlie stands in the middle of the walkway, moonlight serving as a spotlight. His chest rises and falls with resolve and I'm oddly taken by the intensity of his stance, his adrenaline.

I make my way back over to him.

"You took pictures of it," he says, eyebrows pressed together in perplexity like I'm some kind of freak.

"Yeah, it's not every day you get to see something like that. Could be good in a game. Imagine seeing one of those suckers crawling across the screen." I scuttle my fingertips up his forearm and he retracts in a jerk. "Don't worry. Venomous—yes. But it wouldn't kill you." I place my hand on his upper arm. "Are you gonna be okay? Or do you need my—"

"I do not need your hoodie," he says emphatically.

"Or—"

"Or an adult coloring book." He smiles, ever so slightly. "Get me out of here," he says, scratching at his neck then his forearm. "I can feel that thing all over me."

"Charlie, the chances of seeing one again—"

"Please don't talk about it," he says.

I take his arm and he leans into me the rest of the walk, his eyes shooting around the pavers and brush as we go. Now we too look like lovers wrapped together, and I find my body fits dangerously well beside his.

A host greets us when we arrive at the restaurant and ushers us to a table, which I deem as one of the best in the place because of its proximity to the water. The restaurant is open-air, waterfront, and lit by the velvety glow of bamboo torches. Every detail of it is . . . wait for it . . . romantic.

Despite being here with Charlie post-drunken kiss and despite the terms of our trip, I can't help but relax a little as we take our seats. Seeing Charlie terrified of an arthropod makes all of it seem a bit silly. And silly is hardly threatening.

The evening air is the perfect temperature, perfumed with the desert rose and cordyline that line the restaurant entrance. In my right ear, low, slow dinner music emanates from the restaurant and in my left, the light ocean waves. A perfect combination. And there's something about this torchlight—everything, including Charlie across from me, looks softer, more inviting. I kick off my sandals and dig my feet into the impossibly soft sand.

We order drinks and I bite at the inside of my cheek when Charlie informs the waiter he'll stick with water.

"You're allowed a cocktail," I say.

He shakes his head. "I'll pass. But I would like to order a cheese plate," he says, shifting his focus to the waiter. After we've ordered, he leans in conspiratorially. "I might as well eat all the cheese I want while I can, right?" He smiles and it's like too much sunshine on a delicate bud. *While I can.* Meaning, when his plan works and he's back together with lactose intolerant Brooke, he won't be able to eat cheese anymore. I'm annoyed with myself that this innocuous comment causes me to deflate. But it confirms to me that the drunken kiss earlier was a mistake he'd rather move on from.

Agreed.

17.

MY RUM PUNCH ARRIVES AND IT'S DIVINE, LIKE SOMETHING I WOULD have consumed in a dorm room at UCLA, in the best possible way—plummy and sweet. On the waiter's suggestion, we've both ordered the jerk chicken, which arrives plated with three large, bone-in pieces of blackened chicken, shoestring fries, and a condiment bowl filled with a spicy sauce so delicious I want to drink it. Before I've swallowed the first bite, I decide to order this food and drink combination as many times as possible on this trip. Watching Charlie's eyes close in delight upon his own first bite confirms it.

We clear our plates in haste, and as we wet-wipe our fingers, Charlie asks the waiter refilling our water glasses, "Excuse me, would you mind taking our picture?" He hands the server his phone and we lean in from either end of the table, producing photo-worthy smiles. As the waiter positions the phone, Charlie reaches across the table, places his hand atop mine, and pulls it gently toward him. We are holding hands across the splatters of jerk chicken sauce and I force myself to remember, it isn't real.

He thanks the waiter then focuses on his screen.

"What?"

"Nothing. It's just kind of fun, posting pictures of us on this trip." He evaluates the photo a little longer before replacing the phone in his pocket.

Every table is now full, and I see there *are* some families in addition to all the couples, though they are sparse. Despite the restaurant's full capacity, there's ample distance between tables and we might as well be in a private room that contains a private ocean. The temperature has dropped slightly and a playful breeze bounces across the space. I wrap my arms around my center. "Do you want me to run up to the suite and grab a sweater?" he asks.

"No, I'm okay. I like it," I tell him.

"How's the game going?" Charlie asks when the waiter has cleared our plates.

I sigh. "I haven't even chosen my concept yet."

"But you worked on it the whole plane ride yesterday and all day today, I thought."

"I did . . . I mean I thought I was building something workable, but it turned out to be just a distraction."

"I'm sure you'll come up with something great." He says it so matter-of-factly that I almost believe him. "Your family must be incredibly proud of you, the way you're pursuing your dreams."

"Video games are a hobby, not a career, my mom says. Or at least, certainly not a career that seems promising to her. I want to prove her wrong. Prove everyone wrong."

He listens intently and I keep talking, hoping the uncorking will allow some game-related creativity to escape me too.

"The only careers my mother would respect for me are as a doctor or engineer. Everything else will lead to me ending up with a sign on the side of the road begging for money, she thinks." I shrug. "Luckily, Finn's cute. I may get some sympathy side-of-the-road bucks because of him."

"You've clearly thought about this."

"I have."

I reflect on the call with my mom the other night. Every day that goes by without a job in game design is another day closer to Plan B—the version of my reality where I work in engineering and marry a guy of my mother's choosing, knowing I failed at building the life I actually desired.

"So you really think your parents wouldn't help you out, if it came to that?"

"There's no way I'd admit to my parents if this doesn't work out. My mom's got a whole horrible plan for me . . ."

"One that involves an office and no video games."

I point at him. "Right."

Charlie leans forward with his hands clasped, resting his forearms on the table. My eyes linger on the blond hairs against the tanned skin of his forearms. "I can relate," he says. "For my parents, having their only child pursue acting isn't exactly something they rush to tell the neighbors about. Especially when they've spent their lives doing humanitarian work. And *especially* when the biggest thing I've done is a spray-on abs commercial."

I warm, realizing Charlie and I do have some things in common after all, besides recent heartbreak.

"So acting is the dream, then," I say.

"Yeah. It is." He presses his lips together thoughtfully. "I don't know if I've ever been willing to admit that out loud since it hasn't worked out yet, not in any real way. But perhaps you've inspired me a little." Charlie lifts his water glass, hoists it into the air. "To pursuing our passions, regardless of whether it disappoints our parents."

I clink his glass and can't help but laugh a little at how in one brief conversation, Charlie has supported my dreams more than most of the people in my life.

Charlie takes a long sip of his water, sets the glass on the table, hand still wrapped around it. "You said what you've been working on was a distraction—what did you mean?"

He watches as I mentally debate whether to share what I've spent my time on these last two days. The time that should have been dedicated to choosing and starting on a viable concept for Catapult. Before I can overthink it, I pull out the laptop from my bag and open it. He watches as I navigate to the right screen and then turn it to face him.

"*Revenge Cheese*," he reads from my screen, eyelids narrowed in a question.

"You were so . . ." I want to say *sad*, but feel as though that description might poke at him. "So preoccupied yesterday and today. I set out to create the game for Catapult, but it turned into this and then I just kind of went down a rabbit hole."

I click to the next screen and hand him the laptop, the avatar I created staring back at him. "Oh, wow!" he declares. "How'd you get it to look so much like her?"

"I stalked her social media last night, then built the avatar as close as I could get it."

Before Charlie on the screen is an image that bears a strong resemblance to his ex. She's wearing a crocheted bikini top, inspired by the one Brooke is wearing in the picture he showed me the other day. Her chestnut hair hangs in a wavy pile against her back. Though I couldn't see the rest of her outfit in that profile picture, I've taken the liberty of adding a blue-and-green floral wrap tied around her waist and a pink plumeria tucked behind one ear to go with the beach-themed outfit.

"You made this?" He looks at me with regard, jaw slack, and it feels like a profoundly personal compliment.

"I did."

"Wow," he says quietly, eyes fluttering around the screen, taking in every detail. "You did make one mistake." He shifts the screen to me. "Her eyes don't look diabolical enough."

I laugh awkwardly. *Then why do you want her back? Why*

would you want to be with someone you have such animosity for? I want to ask, again and again. But again, I know the answer.

He begins to follow the prompts on the screen and soon realizes the game's goal. He laughs—a real, crowing laugh I've never heard from him before.

I stand behind him now, leaning over his shoulder. "I figured, sure, you could walk around with a machete or a gun or something, but there are already so many violent video games like that, and when you're building a prototype of a real person . . ."

He nods. "But cheese?" He laughs again. "How'd you come up with that?"

"You told me she was lactose intolerant."

I watch intently as he navigates the prototype, leading his own avatar through the cityscape, looking for Brooke. He's smiling the entire time, dimple etched deep into his cheek, as he navigates LA—walking south on Vine, past the Capitol Records Building, down the middle of an abandoned Hollywood Boulevard, across from El Capitan. When he eventually finds her, exiting a party bus in front of Larry Edmunds Bookshop, he yells "There!" then pushes the button to release her punishment. His avatar winds up, leans forward, and slings a slice of cheese, which lands squarely on her face. A direct hit. On my computer screen, she squeals in disbelief, her one visible eye wide and blinky.

"Nice!" I say over his shoulder, and we high-five.

He's still staring at the screen, at Brooke's avatar—a slice of yellow cheddar covering most of her face. "That was surprisingly satisfying," he says on an exhale. "You did this all in the last twenty-four hours?"

"Some on the plane too. While you were sleeping. But yes, I stayed up most of the night, couldn't seem to stop myself."

He twists to look back at me. "How could you possibly build this so fast?"

"Concept prototyping can be done on existing platforms,

so really it was just a matter of making some key decisions . . . the look of the avatar, replacing a gun with a slice of cheese, et cetera. And I figured I'd put her in front of a bookstore to throw you off."

He shakes his head and smiles. "The music is my favorite part."

I don't tell him it's one of my favorite parts too. Something I created for a previous design—an upbeat percussion ensemble reminiscent of the intro music of *Sex in the City*, which oddly fits the hunt.

"Sloane, this is incredible."

Shocks of electricity bolt in my stomach as I realize the magnitude of the moment. I hadn't thought about it before I showed him, but this is the first time I've shared any game creation, silly or otherwise, with someone other than the interviewing panel at Catapult. Tess hasn't even seen any, despite her multiple requests, which I've held off with a "when they're ready." Even Zane never saw anything I had worked on. I was afraid he'd think my games were juvenile, underdeveloped and unsophisticated compared to his master designs.

"It's throwing cheese at someone's face in a video game. A rip-off of an old TikTok trend. I'd hardly call it incredible. And it's not much more than a mock-up."

He shakes his head and hands me the computer. "Don't do that."

"Do what?"

"Downplay what you've done here. It's brilliant. You're really talented, Sloane." He takes a sip of water, holding my gaze. "Can I play it every night before bed while we're here? I think it'll help me sleep."

I cannot contain my delight. "Absolutely."

He smiles at me, a sincere, tender smile that makes my throat burn.

"Thank you," he says, and I truly feel as though I've given him some kind of gift.

This. This divine, tactile sense of satisfaction is why I have to work in game design. I didn't fully realize until now how desperately I crave the acceptance Charlie has just given me.

Throughout my relationship with Zane, I sought validation from him that I could be even a fraction as good as him at game design.

"Everyone thinks they can do this," he told me once over eggs Benedict in his apartment after I had worked up the nerve to tell him I wanted to be serious about game design too. "Like, just because you might be able to come up with a decent game idea, that you can actually execute on it. Those are two *very* different things." I remember looking down at my plate, realizing the ham rounds I'd used might be expired. I silently watched him take another bite as I pushed my own plate away.

I replace the laptop in my bag and look at Charlie. "Yeah, well, now I have you to blame if I have nothing to show the team at Catapult except a game of throwing slices of revenge cheese."

"I think if you show them you can come up with something like that in forty-eight hours, then hiring you should be a no-brainer." The right side of his mouth twitches into a half smile.

The rum punch begins to settle and so do I. I'm a bit euphoric from having shared my design—any design—and having it met with an overwhelmingly positive response.

Over the next thirty minutes we laugh a lot, recounting the ridiculousness of the fire alarm and Mrs. Crandall's antics. He even ribs me about the fact that I didn't immediately recognize him that first night at the bar, which I accept affably. I sway to the island music, still riding the *Revenge Cheese* high.

"You okay?" Charlie asks amusedly from across the table that seems to be shrinking us closer with each minute that passes.

"Yes, fine, just enjoying this delectable punch."

"We're switching places from earlier, I see."

I lean forward. "No. No, we are not. Because I don't plan to drunkenly kiss you later."

Been there, done that.

He leans forward and rests his arms on the table, our faces inches apart. "Is that what happened?" he asks, his eyes constricting. He's so close I feel the warmth of his breath.

"What would you call it?"

He shrugs. "From what I remember, you kissed me back," he says, and I'm suddenly unsure which kiss we are talking about. The fact that there are now multiple kisses with this man is the definition of dangerous.

"I'm surprised you remember it at all."

"Oh, I remember it. And I don't hear you denying it."

We sit for a moment, staring at each other across the table. I don't know what to say. He's not wrong, but I certainly can't admit it.

I wince as Zane shoves his way into my thoughts. I think of how he made me feel about my career dreams, how I stayed in my assistant position at the engineering firm way longer than I should have, afraid to pursue anything more significant.

I can't get distracted from this opportunity at Catapult, I remind myself again. And I certainly cannot fall for the guy across the table who's staring at me with an intensity that makes my stomach feel like it's trying to escape me. Especially when I know he's in love with someone else. There's no scenario where this ends well for me.

He leans in again. "What are you thinking about?" His voice is softer, deeper than usual.

I tilt further into the table. "I'm thinking . . ." I say slowly as he grins at me, his eyelashes shadowing the tops of his cheeks thanks to the torchlight beside us. "I'm thinking I really, really love this punch."

I lean back in my chair and grab my glass to accompany me as I do. I take a long sip, holding the pink straw between my thumb and forefinger. He clasps his hands in front of him, rubbing them absent-mindedly, and I keep drinking—one long, endless suck—until I hear the slurping of air.

"I'll take another, please," I tell the waiter, who is standing a few feet away. I feel Satan Sloane lurking and mentally elbow her in the gut.

"You sure that's a good idea?" Charlie asks, his lips still curved up at their corners.

"I'm not sure any of this is a good idea," I say, licking the sweet punch residue from my lips.

18.

I WAKE THE NEXT MORNING FEELING THE ACHE AT MY TEMPLES BEfore I open my eyes. I roll over and immediately regret it. The movement makes my head feel like it's being flattened in a juice press. In addition to the physical torment, there is a lightness in my belly I can't quite place yet, something akin to a cocktail of embarrassment and regret, though it's too soon to understand it. The last time I woke up with that intuitive remorse in my belly was the morning after the dart-throwing incident in college.

Desperate for water, I force myself out of bed. Once upright, I look down at my pitiful self. I'm still adorned in the floral wrap dress from last night, but the tie has come undone and it's now more of a robe, exposing my black bra and Spanx.

I quickly tie the dress and walk out of the bedroom toward the kitchenette in search of water, the five or so steps feeling like an eternity. I'm certain my body is at least twenty-five percent drained of its liquid and I'm sputtering forward like a car whose gas tank is quickly approaching empty.

"Hey."

I scream. "What the hell are you doing?"

"Sorry, I was just lying here." Charlie pushes the throw blanket covering his legs to the side and sits up on the couch, the pullout already tucked away.

"Sorry," I say as I catch my breath. "I forgot you were here for a minute. Don't you ever sleep? What are you, a vampire or something?"

"Why, did you bring a stake in your Mary Poppins bag that you plan on driving through my heart?"

I shake my head. "It's too early for your intended wit." I raise my fingertips to my throbbing temple. "What happened last night?"

"You don't remember?" he asks, lips pursed in clear amusement.

"I remember dinner. Punch, lots of rum punch. I remember . . . dancing? After that, it's all a blur." I rub my forehead with my thumb and index finger. "Tell me everything."

He smiles wickedly, his mouth taking on the shape of a half circle.

"First, you may want to fix your dress. It's a little distracting." I look down to find the front of my dress tucked into the waistline of my Spanx.

I tug it loose and give him a stern look. "Speak!"

"Okay! Well, for starters, you're surprisingly skilled at getting strangers to dance with you. You danced with our waiter. You danced with the older couple at the table beside us. And with this dude on vacation with his parents. Actually, you told his mom he's a SILF."

"A SILF?" I say, rubbing my eye with my palm.

"Apparently it means a Son I'd Like to—"

"Oh dear god."

"Or at least that's what you told his mom. But don't worry, he's eighteen. He made sure to tell you that." He's grinning again.

My skin begins to tingle as if trying to rise away in embarrassment of its association to me. "What were *you* doing during this time? Not helping, clearly."

"Watching. You were quite entertaining." He crosses his arms and observes me with too much pleasure.

"Thanks for the support."

He stands and I take in his yet-again-shirtless torso and black jersey shorts. "Oh, believe me, I tried. But you're incredibly strong. You called me Zane, told me you didn't need a man rescuing you and that you could take care of yourself. And you kept insisting we fill the bathtubs with water in case of emergency? Your urgency to fill the bathtubs is what finally got you to head back to the room. But not before you threw up in a bush. Then you fell into another bush. It was not a good night for you and bushes."

"That would explain the little leaves in the bed," I mutter, grabbing a glass from the cabinet and filling it to the brim at the sink.

"All I could think about was you landing on one of those Amazonian bugs." He wiggles in disgust. "And why water in the bathtubs?"

"A water reserve should the supply be cut off. First thing you should do in an emergency, ensure you have water."

That amused look again.

I glance down, then at the wall. Anywhere but at him. "I don't know what happened to me last night."

"I think we've established that punch happened. Lots of rum punch."

It's not like me to lose control like this. But the stress of designing the perfect game for Catapult, the run-in with Zane and his now-fiancée, this situation with Charlie—apparently they all led me to an unfortunate amount of rum punch.

My mind strains, trying to focus on the last thing I remember from the night before. The two of us, staring at each other across the table, our faces inches apart. A warmth in my belly. "Please tell me we didn't do anything," I say.

"No, we didn't. You weren't exactly in the right state of mind."

Is he insinuating that if I *had* been in the right state of mind, perhaps we would have?

Would *I* have?

Charlie stretches, pushing his arms up and out over his head. I've never actually seen this guy work out, so now I'm wondering how his firm shape is possible. I find myself annoyed, wanting to yell at him to put on a damn shirt.

He begins folding the blanket on the couch and I chug a second glass of water before heading back to the bedroom and closing the door. After a cheeseburger and fries from room service to grant my hangover the grease it craves, I end up sleeping off the aftereffects of my ill-advised night for most of the day. I awake in the late afternoon feeling better physically, but at a low point mentally. We've been here for almost forty-eight hours and I have made no progress toward building a game concept for Catapult that will convince them to hire me. And I'm in paradise and have barely left the suite.

The sun is setting when I exit the bedroom to once again find Charlie sitting on the terrace. Though tonight's sky doesn't rival the blanket of orange we saw from the plane, it has taken on a magnificent arrangement of colors, pink leading the symphony.

"She lives," he says, closing my romance novel and placing it in his lap.

"Barely. No more rum punch for me." I fight back a grin at his vintage TLC T-shirt that reads DON'T GO CHASING WATERFALLS, complete with T-Boz's, Left Eye's, and Chilli's faces.

"No mimosas or rum punch. I wonder if there'll be any safe alcohol left by the time we leave here."

I take the seat beside him. "No kamikaze shots for me either," I say. "Since we're listing banned alcohol. I went to Rocky Point in Mexico for spring break my junior year of college and passed out in the bathroom after too many of those. But not before dancing on the bar with the tip jar between my knees." There's a wave of nausea I have to swallow back down.

"Drunken dancing seems to be a theme with you," he muses. "I would have liked to have seen that. Before the pass-out, I mean." He lifts one eyebrow so quickly it's likely unintentional. "It's cheap tequila for me. Also college. Grad night. I woke up in my underwear on a park bench. To this day, I have no idea what happened to my clothes."

"Well, you do seem to have a lack of enthusiasm for shirts, so my guess is you derobed voluntarily."

He responds with a contemplative look, as if he hadn't previously considered this version of events.

We settle into a comfortable silence and I let the fresh air do its healing.

"You know, your game is really special," he says after we both track a cormorant gliding across our sightline.

"You mean the cheese-throwing thing? That was silly. I have to do more. I need something huge that's gonna leave no question in their minds that Catapult has to have me." I stare at the sky, now overtaken by an impossible spray of purple and yellow, and I can feel him looking at me. "What?" I ask.

"Nothing. It's just cool that you're so passionate. You've figured out what you want to be when you grow up." He lies back and stares up at the sky. "I certainly didn't think I'd be turning thirty and my claim to fame would be as the guy who sells fake abs in a muscle spray commercial."

"It's a tough business, right?"

He shrugs. "Yeah, it is. You don't realize how lucky you are though. To know what you want to do and be talented enough to actually do it and be balls to the wall about pursuing it. The stars don't align like that for most people."

"I guess you're right," I say, wishing his validation didn't make me warm.

"Tell me more about how you got into acting," I say, wanting to know all the parts he's played, down to the costumes and lines.

"I was in drama all through middle school and high school. Since we moved around a lot, I liked becoming someone else. Someone better. More interesting than who I actually was. Life's a little easier if you get to be someone else."

I have a hard time picturing an awkward, teenage Charlie. The laid-back, easygoing cool seems to encircle him like an aura. But it's the second time he's referenced it.

"I haven't always been so go-with-the-flow," he says. "It used to give me a ton of anxiety each time we set up in a new place. Joining the drama club helped."

A feeling of empathy presses on me. I would have never pictured Charlie as a loner. "I dunno, I think you're pretty . . . okay," I tell him.

"What a compliment."

I turn to face him. "Maybe you could be a voice actor, voice the characters in my games."

"Now, that sounds like a promising future." He raises his water glass in a cheers-ing motion.

"Say, 'The zombies are coming! To the arsenal!'"

He clears his throat, steadies his gaze to show me he's serious. His eyes narrow and he tilts his chin to the ground. "The zombies are coming! To the arsenal!" he proclaims in a deep, guttural bellow.

I laugh. "No, that was bad. So bad."

"What? I thought it was great."

I laugh again and he smiles in observance before we return to staring at the sky, the color becoming more and more magnificent, now a smear of mostly purple.

"For what it's worth, I didn't always know game design was what I wanted to do. I mean, I always thought about it, but not necessarily as a career. I've definitely fumbled my way around a bit. Less than a year ago, I was working at an engineering firm doing photography as a side hustle."

He shifts to face me. "Really?"

I nod. "I figured it could be a useful skill for game design."

"Why'd you stop?" He props his head in his hand, elbow against the headrest of the lounge chair.

"It was fun when it was a hobby. I loved it. I still do, when it's on my own time. When I get to be creative." I silently scold myself for failing to bring my camera on this trip. "But once it turned into a business, all the fun got sucked out of it. Especially when I shot weddings."

"What? But you're such a romantic." He picks up *The Burning Locke* from his lap and wags it at me. I notice the bent page corner to hold his spot and flinch internally at his tarnishing of the crisp page.

"There's a lot of pressure shooting weddings. I once had a bride shove the proofs at me, yelling 'Look at these! Look at my face!' "

"What was wrong with them?" he asks.

"Nothing. It was just her face."

He grins and it shoves his dimple deep into his cheekbone.

"There's also the abomination that is missing a key moment at a wedding. The groom's first look. The first kiss. The first bite of cake. The father-daughter dance. One time I was so engrossed by the flower girl bouncing up and down to 'Gold Digger' that I missed a bridal party entrance completely. I felt so awful about it. That bride raged and threw a Big Gulp at my head when I dropped off the proofs."

"What was in the Big Gulp?"

"Sprite."

He shrugs. "Could have been worse. Cherry Coke, for example."

"Anyway, that was my last wedding."

"So that's why you've put this off until now. You've spent your time pursuing other things to avoid the one thing you really wanted to do." He says it as more of a statement than a question, as if he has just marked a fact about me on a checklist.

I open my mouth to counter, but no words come out. Is that what I was doing?

"So is Zane the guy who broke your heart?" he says after some time.

"What?"

"You called me Zane last night. When you were insistent on your drunken independence. So I'm assuming it's him."

"Why do you insist someone must've broken my heart?"

"I told you why. It's in your eyes." He stares at me, brief and intense, before turning back to the water. "Same as mine, remember?"

I shed a breath, shake my head slightly. "He's nobody."

"Whatever you say."

I don't know why I can't seem to share this part of me. The part that is so similar to him and what he is going through with Brooke. Perhaps it's because I'm terrified of the weakness he'll see in me as a result. But then again, maybe sharing my past with him could help him move on and realize he deserves to be with someone who sees how great he is. Someone he doesn't have to deceive to be with. I want that for him.

"Charlie, I—" I stop as he stares into my eyes. He clenches his jaw and it feels like a dare. A dare to spill all. A dare to be vulnerable with him. A dare to stop thinking and act.

I have a brief flash of a different version of last night—one where we did end up in bed together. Where his touch made me forget Zane and Brooke exist.

His phone beeps on the table beside him, but his attention remains focused on me.

"You should get that," I tell him, that little ding returning me to reality.

He holds firm for a long beat, then, when he sees the moment, my contemplation of going there with him, is gone, he hangs his head and reaches for his phone.

I watch as he reads, eyebrows narrowing closer together with each millisecond that passes. I'm about to ask if everything is okay, but he launches to his feet before I can. "What the fuck?"

"What is it?"

"What the fuck," he repeats, still staring at the screen.

"Are you okay?" There's that feeling again. The lightness in my belly of proactive regret.

Finally, he looks at me, brows still pressed together so tightly they're practically touching. "Did you . . ." He shakes his head as if he can't comprehend what he's about to ask. "Did you message Brooke last night?"

I stand to face him. "What?"

"Did you message Brooke last night?" He enunciates each word.

"No, of course not. Why would I . . . do . . . that." It all comes rushing back as my words limp their way out. Stumbling across the resort back to our suite, phone in hand, typing. Charlie several yards behind yelling "hang on" as he trotted to keep up. I was typing. Then I fell in the bush, but apparently not before hitting send.

He sees my face change as I remember, and his does too, the wide round of his eyes telling a story of fiery disbelief.

"I didn't mean to. I mean, I was drunk. It was an accident."

"Where's your phone?" he asks quietly. He follows me to the bedroom where we find it lying on the bed. I enter the passcode. He taps his foot against the tile floor as I strain to remember just how bad this is.

I find the message. It's bad.

"I'm so sorry," I say.

"Lemme see," he says, holding out his hand. I place my phone in his palm and close my eyes, mortified by what he's about to see. I open them, in time to watch his eyes grow wide as he reads. "*To Brooke with the big chest.* That's how you addressed it?" He's looking through me with a scowl.

"I think I was thinking it was, like, Becky with the good hair?" I say, trying to help us both understand my choices. I press my lips together, waiting for him to keep reading, because it gets worse.

So much worse.

"Charlie and I are having a great time on this trip, having all the sexxx." He stops reading long enough to scowl at me again. "I just wanted you to know, he's happlier than hiss ever been. With me. And I let him do butt stuff."

I cringe as Charlie throws my phone onto the bed.

"Dammit, Satan Sloane," I mumble under my breath.

"What?"

"Nothing. Look, I'm so sorry, I don't know why I did that. I think I thought I was helping . . . What did she say to you?"

"Oh, yes, let me share that with you." He holds his phone up and begins reading in a disdainful tone. "Hi Charlie, not exactly sure what to make of the message your new girlfriend sent me last night. Glad you're happy but perhaps you could ask her to focus on your relationship and leave me out of it?"

I cower, a storm in my stomach as flashes of lightness streak across my insides.

"I'm so sorry," I say again.

He doesn't respond and instead stalks out of the room, leaving me standing there in my own self-loathing.

19.

THE NEXT DAY, MY GOALS ARE CLEAR: WORK ON THE GAME AND FIND A way to make things up to Charlie. When I head out of the bedroom a little after eight a.m., I find the couch intact, blanket slung over the arm. I look out to the terrace, and he's not there either. Sullen, I throw on a black one-piece and purple ombré cover-up, place my laptop in my bag, and head down to the beach.

The damp air accosts me as soon as I step outside but I don't mind it because for as far as I can see it's white sand and turquoise water, as if I'm inside an Instagram filter. I stroll across the whitewashed planked walkway, adorned with white ropes and matching wood posts that escort me to the sand.

I spot Charlie easily on the beach, as there are very few chairs occupied at this early hour. We may be the only two people who can't sleep in while in paradise. He sits in a chair in the row closest to the water, shaded by one of the yellow umbrellas. As I make my way toward him, I see he's wearing blue-and-white-striped board shorts and a blue Dodgers baseball cap, once again reading the romance novel he started on the plane. He's more than halfway through. I glance at him only briefly, but it's enough to notice the sheen of sweat across his bare stomach.

I cautiously take the seat beside him. He doesn't look up, though he doesn't ask me to leave, either, so I consider it a win. I silently apply sunscreen and then settle into the chair. We sit this way for a while, him reading my romance novel and me trying to concept out my interview game.

At the hour mark, I haven't made much progress, but I do have a disturbing realization as I can't help but steal glances in his direction: Charlie looks strikingly similar to the shirtless man on the cover of *The Burning Locke*. Same dark brown hair, same square jaw, same affable face, same sculpted torso. I reposition myself in the lounge chair, uncomfortable with the uncanny resemblance. Is this why I'm attracted to Charlie? Because subconsciously, he's the physical representation of every fictional man I've ever read about? I think of Tess, how incredibly ridiculous she would find this detail.

My phone buzzes in my bag and I fish it out. Three more missed calls from a mystery number. Checking my call history, I see it's the same number from the plane. I ignore it again, figuring if it's important, they'll leave a message.

Eventually, Charlie sets the book on the chair and heads to the water to swim. He does this a few more times, vacillating between lounging and cooling off in the water. I watch him walk away each time.

When Charlie is in the water for the fourth time, my phone buzzes with the same mystery number. I decide to answer this time, if for no other reason than to put an end to the incessant calls. Tess would have insisted I just block the number, but I feel bad doing so without verifying if it's a valid caller first. "Hello?"

"Is this Slo-Anne Copper?"

I press my eyes shut in annoyance. "This is *Sloane Cooper*, yes."

"Ms. Copper, this is Jeffrey calling from Jarmin Financial Services. I'm calling about your past due rental fees to Sampson Building Management."

I lean forward. "Are you a collector?" I say, my raised voice doing little to hide my distress, grateful Charlie is in the water and can't overhear this mortifying conversation.

"Indeed, ma'am. Your building management has submitted your account to us to collect on your past-due rent."

"But I'm only two months late! It's a little aggressive to engage a collections agency, isn't it?"

"I can't be the judge of that, ma'am."

I take a deep breath, trying to avoid an angry exchange with Jeffrey, who is just trying to do his job. Besides, I remind myself, I did this. "I understand. Look, I'm working on it, okay? I should have the money. Soon." These last few words make me feel like I'm begging a loan shark not to rip off one of my fingernails with a pair of pliers in exchange for an extension. I wince as I hang up on poor Jeffrey. I know it's impolite and I'm disgusted with myself for it, but I don't have the energy to get into a back-and-forth that will still inevitably end with me not having the money.

Catapult has to work out. It's my only viable option of getting a large enough paycheck, and soon enough, that I can somehow keep my apartment. I quickly run through the options of what I will do if I am indeed kicked out, a list I've explored many times in the last few months. I could move in with Tess. Her building is insanely strict with their couch-surfing rules, though, and she's got too many nosy, tattletale neighbors. I couldn't risk getting her thrown out. The other alternative is to go crawling back to my parents, having to admit I've failed at my attempt at living life my way, and at adulting, generally. I can't believe I have built my life around preparation, only to be somehow completely unprepared for the basics of life, as Tess pointed out.

Catapult *has* to work out.

When Charlie has returned from his swim, I make my way to the water, hoping it might help relieve my mental constipation. I take one cautious step in, bracing myself for the cold, as the Pacific has conditioned, but instead it feels like bathwater, warm and perfectly still. In this mid-morning heat, it's equal parts lovely and unrefreshing.

When I'm several yards in, feet still touching the ground, I turn to face the shore. There's Charlie, my book in his lap. He has put on a T-shirt, and I'm both relieved and disappointed. He's looking at . . . me? We're too far away from each other to make eye contact, so I can't be sure. But then, he picks up the book from his lap, face soon hidden behind it. I dip my head underwater and hope the mini baptism will wash away all my Charlie-related sins before I head back to the sand and the work ahead of me.

A little over two hours later, back in my lounge chair next to Charlie, I think I've had a game breakthrough.

"This is it," I say, only realizing I've spoken the words aloud when Charlie looks up. "I think I figured out the game concept," I tell him. Today his selection of T-shirt is white with a picture of Albert Einstein's face. Below it, black print that says IT'S ALL RELATIVE.

"Oh?" he says, one syllable that doesn't allow me to gauge how upset he still is. "Tell me."

"Really?"

"Yes. I'm invested," he says, laying the book across his lap.

His tone is a bit clipped. Still, I'm immensely grateful for the truce flag, even temporarily. "I've been researching the games Catapult has put out over the last ten years, and they've focused largely on post-apocalyptic events and survival, like their recent release *Shelf Life*," I say, voicing the information I largely already knew well before today.

"I've played it," Charlie says.

"You have? You didn't tell me you're a gamer."

He shakes his head, arms folded across his chest. "I'm not, but my buddy Jacob is, and sometimes he ropes me in. It's a decent one, as far as end-of-days, alien invasion survival games go." He gives me a glimmer of a smile, though his face is still sullen.

"Jacob." I nod in understanding. The friend whom he texted *she's nobody*.

I shake my head to void the reminder, clear my throat, and continue. "Catapult has dominated the market in the space, but take a look at this." I turn my computer to him, watch his eyes scan the Reddit thread. "Recent gamer buzz is that they are unable to penetrate other genres. Their biggest competitor, Triton, has the top sellers in virtually every other space. But for the last few years, Catapult's concepts are largely recycled, with new games released that don't differ much from their previous ones."

I'm talking fast, in full geek-out mode. Usually, this is the part where people's eyes glaze over. But Charlie leans in a bit. His arms are still crossed, his face still stone, but he's listening. Really listening.

"They need something sinister, apocalypse-adjacent, if you will, but fresh and new." I close my eyes, take a deep breath, and say a silent thank-you to this beach, and Charlie, for helping me finally flesh out a viable concept.

"Like what? What do you have in mind?" he asks.

I maneuver away from Reddit and once again turn my computer screen toward him, and he smiles. He doesn't try to hide it.

"Meet *Arsonist Betty*," I announce, and his grin grows into that familiar wicked half circle, as though he's in on a masterful joke. "An elderly arsonist who sets fires all across town. Catch her before she sets the entire world ablaze." I say the last part with as much mischief as I can muster.

He clicks through the rough designs and stops on the page with her fire-starting tool kit. "Why chocolate and a soda can? For low blood sugar moments? All that fire starting gets her famished?"

"Sometimes she has to get creative. Chocolate can be used to polish the bottom of a soda can, then you focus a beam of sunlight with it and—" I throw my arms in the air.

"Fire," he says. "I'm starting to wonder if *you* are the real arsonist in our building."

I shake my head. "I do not condone or glorify arson. That's why the player view is trying to *catch* Arsonist Betty. To stop her. A vigilante, civilian hero." I scratch at my forearm absent-mindedly. "And I'm thinking, perhaps there's an underlying love story. She's wreaking havoc because of a lost love whom she believes died in a fire, but at the end of the game, you find out he's actually still alive and they're reunited. Maybe as a player, if you complete the entire game, you find out *you* are her long-lost love."

Charlie takes on that rascally grin again, dimple sinking deep.

"What?" I feel a twinge of embarrassment about telling him this last part. "Arsonists deserve love too."

"Nothing, I just like how you can't help but root for a happy ending." He rubs his hands together as he continues to survey my screen. "It's great, Sloane. Really great. They're gonna eat it up."

He hands the laptop back to me and, as he does, looks at me with something deep, something like admiration. The only time I ever saw a look like that from Zane was when he was assessing his own game designs.

We both linger a bit too long, each holding one side of the laptop between us to avoid the end of the transfer.

"It's brilliant," he says, letting go. He runs his hand through his damp hair. "I can't wait to see what you come up with in the design."

I know he means it. I want nothing more in this moment than for things to be good between us. "Charlie, I—"

"Hey, aren't you the guy from that muscle spray commercial?" I look up to find a woman standing over Charlie's lounge chair. She's younger than us, early twenties maybe, and has gotten all dolled up for her beach day, in a bright yellow bikini and matching duster cover-up that are an impressive shade match to the umbrellas and chairs. Large-barrel brown curls cascade down her back and her heavy foundation is perfectly smooth despite the humidity. I instinctively swipe at my damp brow.

I can't wear yellow. With my skin tone, I'd look jaundiced.

Charlie presses the side of his hand to his forehead like a visor as he looks up at her. "Yeah, that's me," he says, sounding a little embarrassed, though he has no reason to be.

"I thought so! Wow, so cool. I'm Maddie," she says, extending a hand.

He swings his legs to the side and stands, instantly towering over her. "Charlie," he says, shaking her hand.

"Your eyes are stunning, Charlie," she says, still shaking his hand, though with the midday sun bearing down on them now that he's out of the umbrella's shade, I doubt she can appreciate their full beauty.

He offers his thanks.

Maddie looks down at his Einstein T-shirt. "Cool shirt," she says. "Is that your grandpa or dad or something?"

I clear my throat.

Charlie, without missing a scientific beat, responds, "Yes. Yes, it is."

"Well, it's nice to meet you, Charlie. I hope I'll see you around?" She pushes her oversize tortoiseshell sunglasses up to make eye contact with him. In the bright sun, she closes one eye, squinting up at him, which comes across as unmistakably flirtatious.

"Yeah, sure," he says politely, though his tone is decidedly non-committal. He sits back down on the lounge chair and places his sunglasses back over his eyes. I watch her walk away, alternating butt cheeks rising cheerfully with each bouncy step.

I feel it then. Jealousy. A tad bit of ownership over Charlie. I clench my jaw at the absurdity, angry at myself for allowing it.

"Let's get food," he says out of nowhere.

I swing my feet onto the sand, sit up to face him. "Charlie, I just want to say again—"

"Let's just forget it," he says. "Come on, I'm starving."

I look down at my computer. Now that I've really got something going here for the game, it's an excellent time to pause. To think on the design. Charlie has given me an opening, some semblance of forgiveness, and I want to grab on to it. He points to a shack up the beach with tables set in the sand.

"Perfect," I say, closing my laptop.

We order shrimp tacos and bottles of Turk's Head lager from the lone man working in the tattered wood shack and grab the table closest to the water. I insist on paying. Though the bill isn't much and there's an uneasy feeling in my stomach as I pass a twenty through the splintered wood window, it feels good to be able to treat Charlie in return in some small way.

A few feet ahead on the beach, there's a woman with a stand set up selling anything and everything conch: whole shells, necklaces, bracelets, picture frames. A little past her, a boy in a diaper plays with a bucket at the water's edge. I take a sip of beer, watching the woman shout a warning to the boy, who inches a few steps away from the water and plops down on the wet sand.

"Does that happen a lot?" I ask after my first bite of the ridiculously fresh shrimp taco. "Getting recognized as the spray-on abs guy?"

He raises his left eyebrow at me and the corners of his

mouth twitch ever so slightly. "Every once in a while," he says, then takes a sip of his beer. "They play that damn commercial every five minutes. Everywhere."

I try to fight a full smile but it wins me over. He grins too then shakes his head.

"What would your life look like, perfect world?" I ask him.

"You're not exactly a perfect world kinda gal," he says.

"That's not true. You've gotta know what's good in the world before you can create the agony of losing it."

He squints for a beat and I wonder if it's the sun or something I've said.

"So, c'mon. Perfect world, what would you be doing?" I repeat. "Avenger-style action movies? War stories? Space musicals?"

He takes a sip of his beer and it's evident in the shift of his eyes and the way he fidgets with his napkin that he already knows the answer.

He sets down the beer and leans in. "Honestly?"

I nod.

"I don't know. I thought I'd want to be a regular on a comedy series of some kind, for the character development and stability and all, but now . . ." He holds up *The Burning Locke*. "I kinda think romance might suit me better. That is, if I can ever get it right, in real life." He sets down the book, picks up his beer, and points it at me in an invitation to cheers, as if what he's just said is some twisted form of a toast.

"Charlie, I really am sorry," I say as I clink the neck of my beer against his.

"It's bad luck if you don't make eye contact," he says, slouching to meet my downcast eyes.

I feel the pull again, and do what I can to ignore it as I look up. "Seven years bad sex, as the superstition goes."

"Not possible, especially when I'm having all the sexxx and doing butt stuff." He furrows his brow.

"Oh god, please don't remind me," I say, equal parts mortified and relieved that he's seemingly forgiven me enough to make jokes about it.

"Seriously, though, what were you thinking?"

I scrunch my eyes shut. "I don't know. I think I thought I was helping? Like, what would really get me, you know, if I was in her shoes. And if I had to picture my ex having incredible sex with someone else right after we broke up . . . it would gut me."

I did picture this. It did gut me.

I'm grateful the sun is beating down on us. I was likely already a tinge red before I responded.

"Were you thinking about Zane just now?"

"Geez, what is your obsession with Zane? I was drunk and called you some random guy's name. What's the big deal?"

He observes me for a moment before leaning back in his chair. I can see he's attempting not to be annoyed, pretending to focus his attention on an older man rubbing sunscreen onto his chest just beyond our table.

"You should track that girl down," I say into the silence.

"What?"

"The girl that came over to you." I point in the direction of the lounge chairs we were just occupying several yards down the beach. "You should get her number, have dinner with her, grab a drink, hook up, as you said was your goal here."

He's staring at me and I cannot decode his expression. "I should, huh?"

"Yeah, why not?" It's not a test, I tell myself. It's the practical solution to this whole thing. He can have his much-anticipated post-Brooke fling and get it out of his system. I can put some distance between the two of us and whatever these budding feelings are and, most importantly, focus on the game.

He takes a sip of beer and diverts his attention to the water. "Yeah, I guess I should," he says.

I pull the sunglasses from the top of my head and down over my eyes.

"I think I'll go for another swim," he says, already shedding his shirt.

I'm about to suggest he wait twenty minutes, let the shrimp and beer settle, but he's already gone.

Watching Charlie slide deeper into the water, needing a tie to my real life, I rifle through my bag and pull out my phone to text Tess.

Me: How's Finn??? All good here. Have my game concept. Feeling good about it.

I stare at the screen, debating, then add

Me: Nothing going on with Charlie.

I cannot validate the kiss, or our brokenhearted kinship, or how my initial perceptions of Charlie grow more off base each minute I spend with him. Sharing these things with Tess would make them real.

I watch the screen, waiting for Tess, who is notoriously glued to her phone. A few minutes pass, no typing bubbles. No response within a few minutes is questionable behavior. When I'm about to call her in alarm, my phone dings with a response.

Tess: Sorry, on a hike before work. That's great on the game, don't believe you on Charlie. Finny's living his best life.

A photo follows, taken from behind Finn, Runyon Canyon by the looks of the dusty upward trail and cityscape beyond. I notice the shadows of feet behind Finn from where the picture is being taken, presumably by Tess. But there are two sets of shadows, one pair noticeably larger than the other. Tess is on a hike with someone.

Me: Who are you with?

I watch as the text is marked read. Typing bubbles emerge then disappear, not to reemerge again.

What is she up to?

I look up to find Charlie surfacing from the water. The toddler nearby waddles over to Charlie at the water's edge and hands him a shell. Charlie crouches down, accepts the offering, then turns it this way and that to admire it, to the delight of the boy, before placing it in his pocket.

I look on as the two of them kick water at each other at the shoreline, the pudgy little guy squealing in delight each time his foot makes contact with the water. With every splash, Charlie acts as though the contact is painful, wincing in feigned, dramatic pain. The toddler eats it up, his squeals growing sharper, higher with each kick of water.

Good with dogs *and* babies. Goddammit, Charlie is dead set on making this hard.

20.

"TELL ME AGAIN WHY WE'RE DOING THIS?" I ASK LATER THAT AFTERnoon as we make our way back down to the beach. We stop at the sidewalk's edge to remove our flip-flops before stepping onto the hot sand. Post-lunch, I've thrown a pair of pink linen shorts over my black one-piece. Charlie has put on a fresh pair of gray swim trunks and a hunter-green shirt with dark gray lettering that reads SURELY NOT EVERYONE WAS KUNG FU FIGHTING.

"Because it gets us out of the suite. And it's already paid for."

I raise my eyebrows at him to make it clear these are not good enough reasons. Yes, I've worked on my game most of the day. Even so, a break requires significant justification.

"Paid for," he reiterates. "In full. And it includes drinks."

I sigh.

Sand stinging the bottom of our feet, we scurry toward the group, likely giving the impression that we are particularly excited to be here.

"Yeah! Two more! Welcome, welcome!" a man with short, thin dreadlocks calls out as we approach. His shirtless torso is deep brown and glistening, and his turquoise cargo shorts are so blue they make the water behind him look drab. His waist is the size of my ankle, but somehow he's one of the most toned humans I've ever seen. "You must be . . ." He looks down at the clipboard in his hands while still flicking his hips to the beat of the Jay-Z song that's playing on the boom box beside him. ". . . Ah, Charlie and Brooke. Welcome, welcome!"

The bullet of her name hits Charlie first, then ricochets into me.

"Sloane," we both say in unison.

"Charlie and Sloane," Charlie says, pointing to himself, then me.

Please don't make it more awkward, please don't make it more awkward.

I stare at the thin-waisted man, silently begging him to understand and retreat. He looks at his clipboard, then back at us again, and says, "Ah yes, of course! Charlie and *Sloane*! Come, come!" He puts his arm around my shoulder and escorts me to the rest of the group. "Andres," he says, pointing to his chest.

We join the group, which now consists of eight resort guests in total, and from the looks of the handsy duos around us, it appears we are the only pair that has not had sex in the last twenty-four hours.

I'm about to suggest to Charlie that we duck out and head back to the safety of our suite and the room service menu, but our host must sense my hesitation because he grabs my hand, places his other arm around Charlie's shoulder, and pulls us to the front of the group.

"You two will be my team captains!" he says, placing us in front of the six others, and I'm more confused than ever. Team captains for what? All Charlie has told me is this is some sort of resort contest that previous guests raved about online. Right now, my gut tells me all those supposed praise-filled reviews were posted by Andres.

"Charlie and Sloane, it's time to choose your teams for our first event, water balloon dodgeball! And choose wisely. You never know what may come of the day." Andres releases a maniacal laugh toward the sky, and Charlie and I exchange a glance.

"Are we in *Squid Game* right now?" he whispers.

"I think it's a cross between that and a horrible adult summer camp."

I have so many questions: What are the rules of water balloon dodgeball? What do we win if we do, you know, win? Will I regret having just washed my hair? How much would it cost to adjust my plane ticket home for *right now*?

Just as I open my mouth to suggest we make a break for it, in an unexpected turn of events, Charlie shouts, "I'll take that guy!"

He points to the man on the far right, who must be at least six five. With his too-wide stance to avoid his thigh muscles rubbing together, he looks a lot like Catapult's game character Cannon Jack. I go ahead and assume he is an avid CrossFitter.

The group is now standing at attention facing Charlie and me.

"Sweet," CrossFit Guy says, then jogs over to Charlie's side without a word to his significant other—a toned, perky woman he's left standing on the beach.

I shoot Charlie a look. He shrugs his shoulders at me like I'm the ridiculous one here.

We are very much not on the same page.

"Okay! Yes! And now you, Sloane." The more Andres says my name, the more it sounds like a moan. "Who do you want for your team?"

I feel the sweat trickle down the small of my back. "What are we doing, exactly? I'm not sure I understand the situation here."

"Don't worry. It's fun! Just fun. Choose your team!" Andres says, still bopping to the music and seemingly unburdened by my stress. I play video games. I don't do team sports. I'd much prefer being annihilated on a screen in the safety of my apartment to an in-person competition with the Mount Rushmore of a man that is CrossFit Guy.

"But it really depends on—"

"No, no, Sloane." Andres steps toward me and gives me a look of pity. The poor American who can't cut loose. "Just go with it, huh?" He bends his knees and runs his hand out in front of me like he's petting a dog while surfing.

I look over at Charlie, but he's no help at all. His and CrossFit guy's hands are clasped together between their faces, like they've just decided who to kill first as soon as the whistle blows. Now I'm afraid we're in *The Hunger Games*, and Charlie and CrossFit Guy are career tributes.

It's evident to me now that whatever resentment Charlie is still holding about my drunken message to Brooke, he plans to channel into beating me during this field day from hell. A burst of adrenaline washes through me. I'm going to have to harness all the power of Satan Sloane. I can have rage. I most certainly have rage too. Charlie and his stupid shirtless torso and kiss and charm clouding my ability to work. Zane and his audacity moving into *my* neighborhood, going to *my* deli, and interviewing for *my* job. My mom and her engineering connections. The owners of my apartment building expecting me to pay rent on time. Oh yes, I have rage. And I can certainly channel it all toward Charlie today. The idea of him beating me is unconscionable.

"I'll take her!" I yell. Charlie and CrossFit Guy look over to find I am pointing at CrossFit Guy's partner. CrossFit Girl. She's also built like a steel pylon, her quads roughly the same thickness of about ten Amazonian centipedes. She clasps her hands together excitedly like a cheerleader and rushes over to my side.

"Don't worry, I know his weaknesses," she says in a thick Australian accent, twitching her chin in the direction of Cross-

Fit Guy and then looking me square in the eye. I nod in solidarity, confident I've made a sensible choice. I'm a little afraid of her, but also assured. Now I'm in this. I widen my stance, bend forward, and shift my weight from side to side. I can think of nothing but beating Charlie and wiping that smug expression off his face.

It's his turn to pick.

Charlie and CrossFit Guy are huddled together, whispering wildly, evaluating the remaining four options. Finally, they nod and Charlie straightens. In a voice at least three octaves deeper than usual, he says, "Him. The guy in blue."

I deflate. The thirtysomething guy was going to be my next pick. He doesn't look particularly strong, and I've already overheard him and his partner refer to each other with the pet name Bacon Bit with obscene repetition, but his face turned snarly when we started picking teams and I can see he'll do what it takes to win.

Everyone shifts their focus back to me. I'm up.

"What about that one?" CrossFit Girl says, pointing with no attempt at discretion. It's Bacon Bit's Boyfriend. Or the man whom I presume to be Bacon Bit's boyfriend because they're not wearing rings. He's also wearing blue and I want to say no simply because of their matching outfits, but he's staring at us with an eager expression.

"Him!" I yell, pointing at Bacon Bit II. His face lights up and he executes a perfectly round cartwheel over to us. Yes, okay, we may be able to use those skills.

There's one man and woman left and it's Charlie's turn to pick. They are the oldest among us, probably in their early fifties, and have matching heft. Her frizzy curls remind me of my own in this damp air. The guy has a pretty epic mustache with thin hairs sprouting in all directions. Charlie's going to pick the guy. I know it.

I look over to find Charlie grinning at me, a villainous glimmer in his eyes. "Come on over and join the winning team, sir," he says, attention still fixed on me. Mr. Mustache gives the woman I presume to be his wife (given their matching gold bands) a kiss on the cheek and walks calmly over to Charlie's team. Mrs. Mustache is standing there alone, and I immediately run over and sling an arm around her shoulder. "Don't worry, we've got this!" I tell her with my most convincing pep.

She smiles at me graciously. "I'm not sure how much help I'll be, but I'll sure try," she says.

As we huddle together, I look around at my team: CrossFit Girl, Bacon Bit II, and Mrs. Mustache. We are a spectacle. Not the good kind. I glance over at Charlie's team and it's hard not to feel outmatched. I take in Charlie's arrogant smirk and try to get my head in the game. I'm about to suggest introductions, but Andres blows the whistle and we all obediently make our way back to him.

"Water balloon dodgeball is *on*!" he proclaims, mostly to the sky.

Charlie finds his way to my side as Andres explains the rules. "Care to make it interesting?" he says, his mouth close to my ear. We stand shoulder to shoulder, though my shoulder hits at about the middle of his upper arm. We've both taken on a similar stance—legs far apart, hands locked behind us.

"What did you have in mind?" I look up at him and try to ignore his face's proximity to mine.

"If you lose, I get to send that guy Zane a cringeworthy message, even worse than what you sent Brooke," he says, his face positively exhilarated. Or exhilarating. Both, actually.

"What? No way! And I told you, Zane is nobody."

"Yeah, okay. If he's nobody, why would it matter if I send him a message?"

I break eye contact and look to the ground, desperate for a comeback, but nothing comes to me.

"Oh yes. In fact, it's already coming together." He circles his finger at his temple. "Dear Zane with the big . . ." He looks at me, eyebrows raised.

I shake my head in vigorous disagreement.

"No? Shame. I'll have to work on the opening then. But moving on, Zane, man, thanks for being an idiot and letting a girl like Sloane go. What the hell were you thinking? She can be a pain in the ass, but speaking of asses . . ."

My mind betrays me. When Charlie says *asses*, I briefly fantasize about his open palm swatting my bare behind.

"It's not the same thing," I say, annoyed by his certainty that Zane is the ex who broke my heart, though I've still shared no such information with him. And as much as it mortifies me to think of Zane reading a message like the one I sent to Brooke, I can't help but worry it would somehow make its way back to the team at Catapult and my candidacy for the job would be dead in the Caribbean water. I'd like to think Zane wouldn't do that to me. But he's certainly capable of hurt. I can't argue with Charlie, though, as doing so would mean admitting how much Zane actually meant to me.

"Oh, and I get the bed for the night. You get the couch. My neck is killing me after three nights on that cement pullout. A disappointing pullout."

"That's what she said."

"You're twelve."

I ignore his comment. "Fine," I say, acting as though the thought of him sending that message to Zane wouldn't shove me into a complete spiral. "And if I win, you have to be my servant for the day tomorrow."

"Servant? Like feed you grapes and fan you on the terrace all day?"

"Yes. That and, you know, order me breakfast, foot rubs, generally wait on me hand and foot while I work."

"Sure, that's fine. It's not gonna happen anyway."

"So cocky. What makes you so certain you'll win?"

He shrugs. "The odds are ever in my favor. Look at your team."

He points past the sand to the grass where CrossFit Girl is doing high knees with perfect form. Bacon Bit II is yawning. Mrs. Mustache is sitting in the grass, swatting at a fly.

"May the best man win." He squares up and extends his hand.

"She will," I say, squeezing his hand as tightly as I can manage and shaking it vigorously, knowing a loss to Charlie is simply *not* an option.

Andres finishes giving the instructions (which I've missed completely) and passes out T-shirts. Our team gets red, Charlie's team is blue.

"Okay, here's what we're gonna do." CrossFit Girl huddles us after we've put on our shirts, rubbing her hands together in anticipation. "My husband over there may look tough and be putting on a brave show, but he's terrified of water balloons. Absolutely petrified. A neighborhood boy used to hide in the bushes and throw them at him on his way to school. I guarantee as soon as the game starts, he'll be cowering in the corner like a scared puppy. All we've got to do is pummel him first, then the rest will be outnumbered."

She's vicious. I love it. "Yes, become your enemy. Rule number one on the battlefield. I like it," I say, running through the tactics I've gleaned from every war game I've ever played. "We should also employ a concealment strategy. Perhaps we all start in a line and then break away once we have water balloons, that way the person in front can provide cover to the rest."

My team seems pleased, their eyes coming alive with a glimmer of possible victory. Even Mrs. Mustache is nodding through gritted teeth. I would have expected her to say something about feeling sorry for CrossFit Guy after that sad story, but no. She's in it. At this moment, I'm glad Charlie chose her husband instead.

I think again to ask my team members for their names, but there's no time. Andres blows his whistle and we all take our spots in the grass next to the beach on opposing sides of the grid. He's marked the court with sand and there's a large tub of already-filled water balloons at the centerline. A small crowd of resort guests has gathered in anticipation.

Great, an audience. The pressure gathers in my neck.

"Okay, okay, everyone! Welcome to the first game!" Andres is still swaying his hips. "Blue team, what is your team name?" he asks, focused on Charlie.

Team name? When were we supposed to come up with a team name?

Apparently Charlie heard the instructions because without missing a beat, he steps forward and says, "We're team Good Hair."

I look around their group, none of whom has particularly exceptional hair, and I know it's a dig at me. At my message to Brooke.

I must beat this man-child.

"Ah, indeed!" Andres says. "And red, what is your team name?"

I open my mouth, hoping my brain will toss out an equally thinly veiled dig at Charlie. Perhaps something about his fear of airplanes or wearing my sweatshirt or—

"Team Kick 'Em in the Nuts!"

I turn to find that sweet Mrs. Mustache is the one who yelled it. She steps forward, glaring at the other team, shifting her focus to each of them.

"Okay, okay! Team Good Hair versus Team Kick 'Em in the Nuts! Let's do this!" Andres says the last bit in that slow, lithy drawl.

He blows his whistle again and just like that, the game is in play.

CrossFit Girl and I run to the bucket at the centerline while Mrs. Mustache and Bacon Bit II hang back, our concealment strategy entirely out the window the moment the adrenaline of battle takes over. Charlie and I reach the bucket at the same time and the look he gives me is nothing short of diabolical.

He really wants to get even.

21.

AS CROSSFIT GIRL AND I BACK UP FROM THE BUCKET, WATER BALLOONS in hand, I see CrossFit Guy doing precisely what we expected: hanging back in the far corner of the field, attempting but failing to mask his terror. CrossFit Girl and I exchange a knowing look, then we each throw two balloons at him. He does little to defend himself, flinging a gigantic arm and leg over the rest of his body and turning to the side to lessen the blow. He takes three direct hits and squeals in shame and what I can only imagine as deep-rooted trauma.

"YEAH!" CrossFit Girl releases a guttural scream that makes me worry momentarily about their relationship dynamic. Across the centerline, CrossFit Guy stands, hangs his head, and joins Andres at the grid's edge. I've got two balloons left. As I look around the field, I'm just in time to catch Bacon Bit II taking a balloon to the chest. Charlie is the assailant.

Shit.

We need to regroup. CrossFit Girl is taking care of herself, refilling her arms with balloons, scooping them into her elbow, throwing with her other hand in spiraling succession like a windmill. I find Mrs. Mustache running in chaotic circles at the back end of the field. Initially, I wonder if she is having some sort of episode, but then I realize it's her strategy to avoid getting hit.

I accept her purely defensive tactics.

Across the line, Bacon Bit I is making his way to the balloon bucket empty-handed and I see an opportunity. I strike, throwing both my balloons at him one after another, and the second one lands at his ankle. He snarls at me before stomping off the field to join Andres and the others on the sideline.

I'm surprised at how good I am at this—perhaps all those hours upon hours I've spent with a controller in hand have built some kind of superhuman hand-eye coordination—but the reason isn't important now. I need to refocus. Mrs. Mustache is still running in random sequence, cutting hard turns at uneven intervals, her arms tucked tight and chugging at her sides, and I'm impressed with her endurance. Until, seemingly out of nowhere, Charlie launches a balloon that connects square in her chest. Mrs. Mustache lets out a wail and falls to the ground. She flaps a bit like she's making a snow angel, then slowly rises to her knees and crawls to the sideline, one hand clutching her right boob.

Now it's just CrossFit Girl and me against Charlie and Mr. Mustache, and I'm even more enraged at Charlie for his tit hit. I glare at him from across the field. He grins back.

Mr. Mustache is surprisingly agile, though I observe that his throwing arm is weak. So, while Charlie mimics CrossFit Girl's movements from the other side of the field, following her back and forth, both stalling for the perfect opportunity to strike, I wait for Mr. Mustache to line up his shot at me and await its release. Before he can get his shot off, I hear two splashes then moans and Charlie and CrossFit Girl have landed balloons on each other simultaneously, both out of the game.

My team has now assembled in a row next to Andres, all staring at me with desperation. CrossFit Girl nods slowly, telepathically telling me to show no mercy. Bacon Bit II is yelling so aggressively there's a line of saliva hanging from the right corner of his mouth. Mrs. Mustache is wagging tight fists in front of her as she jumps up and down.

Mr. Mustache and I look at each other, lone soldiers on the field. The only hope for our respective teams. We are in no-man's-land, between our opposing armies, thrust into single combat. There are no landmarks to hide behind, just the open, grassy field. No opportunity for the element of surprise.

I could employ a strategy of exhaustion—wait as he wears his arm out with attempt after weak attempt. But as I glance at my team on the sideline again, it's evident they insist upon a grand finale. Our team intimidation seems to be working as a tactic in and of itself—Mr. Mustache's eyes are shifting back and forth between me and our screaming sideline. Particularly at his wife, who is now yelling "Kill him!"

Ultimately, I know what I need to do. Waiting for Mr. Mustache to throw first, I step backward into a defensive stance. He takes the bait. The second the balloon leaves his hand, I launch mine. True to his poor form, his balloon lands about five yards away from me and splatters in the grass. But mine is a direct hit, square in the face. I see it happen in slow motion. The contact as the balloon snaps against his right cheek, its force knocking his thickly rimmed glasses sideways. His eyes close and his mouth opens, the loose skin of his cheek vibrating from the force like the ripple of a wave.

I've just won the game.

I've just won the motherfucking game.

I fall to my knees and look to the same heavens that are shining down on me as the victor over Charlie.

Andres blows his whistle. "Blue team, Team Good Hair, are the winners!" he proclaims.

"Wait, what? No." I climb to my feet to face Andres. "I got him. I never got hit. *We* win. The red team."

"Noooo," he sings. "The rules state, you cannot hit a player in the face. So team Kick 'Em in the Nuts is disqualified, which means Team Good Hair are our winners!"

Charlie's standing behind Andres, fighting off a laugh. "Nice work," he yells, loud enough for the entire group to hear. He shrugs, holds his hands out in front of him. "Guess you should've listened to the rules."

He removes his wet shirt and his left pec twitches once while I continue to glare at him.

"Uh-oh, lovers' quarrel," CrossFit Guy says. I don't bother correcting him in thinking Charlie and I are together. It's too much to explain in the heat of battle.

"It's okay. We'll get 'em on the next one," Mrs. Mustache says, patting my shoulder. I try to shake off the loss, having momentarily forgotten there is another game, and potentially a third should there be a tie. We're down, but not out. I feel something like malice roiling in my belly, then spreading out through me, hot and thick like magma. I try to muster all the vengeance I can toward Charlie. He called me a nobody. He's using me to make his ex-girlfriend jealous.

I must beat him.

Andres blows the whistle again and we all gather around him for our next assignment. We've barely caught our collective breath, and I haven't fully gotten over my almost-win from the first game. Mr. Mustache is still wiping down his face. I take note that I am the only one who is not wet. I try not to read too much into the fact that Charlie didn't throw a single balloon in my direction, despite ample opportunity to do so.

Charlie stands next to me but I duck to the other side of Mrs. Mustache, placing her between us. I've got to focus.

"Okay, great play, ever-y bod-y," Andres says as he pulls two manila envelopes from his clipboard. "Here"—he hands one to me and one to Charlie—"is your next game." He puts his whistle to his lips. "Go!" he yells, then blows. Wait, what? There were no instructions. Go do what?

"Open it! Open it!" Mrs. Mustache demands. I do as she says and find one sheet of paper with a list, each item covered with red tape except the first.

"Scavenger hunt," Bacon Bit II and I announce in unison.

"The first item is . . . a conch shell," I read to the team, then scan the instructions at the top of the page. "We've got to go in order and only reveal the next item once the one above it is retrieved. I guess it's some kind of sexy scavenger hunt—all the items have something to do with romance."

"I know where to find a conch shell, come on!" Mrs. Mustache takes off in the direction of the water.

Sure enough, at the far end of the beach, off the back of the kitchen of the resort's main restaurant, are a pile of discarded shells, piled high in the water like some kind of shell graveyard.

"Yes!" I yell as CrossFit Girl splashes into the water to retrieve one. The blue team is nowhere to be found.

"What's a conch shell got to do with romance?" Bacon Bit II asks as we wait for CrossFit Girl to return.

"Conch is an aphrodisiac," I say, remembering this detail from my pre-trip research.

"The hubby and I have eaten it every day we've been here," Mrs. Mustache muses as CrossFit Girl returns from the water, shell tucked into her armpit. "Okay, what's the next one?"

I tear the tape to reveal item number two. "Flint," Mrs. Mustache reads over my shoulder. "Where on earth are we going to find flint?"

"I have some!" I yell, and the others look at me. "It's in my suite, come on!" We start in the direction of the resort elevators.

"Why do you have flint?" Bacon Bit II asks as we await the elevator. I'd prefer to bolt up the stairs, though I don't think it would be fair to Mrs. Mustache.

"In case of emergency."

"You brought a piece of flint with you on vacation in case of emergency?" CrossFit Girl asks, pacing back and forth on the small concrete patch at the elevator entrance. "Why wouldn't you just bring matches? Doesn't that make more sense?"

"Matches run out," I tell her as the elevator doors open and we all clamber inside. "Flint can be reused. It's a long-term play. Besides, you can't take matches on a plane." She looks at me with a blank expression, and I can't decide if she's impressed or worried.

"This is a weird list. What does flint have to do with romance?" Bacon Bit II asks. *Winning* should be his focus, I think to tell him, not the relevance of the items on our list.

"Fires are romantic," Mrs. Mustache says. "But they probably don't want us playing with matches all around the resort."

I wonder if she's got a little *Arsonist Betty* in her.

When the elevator doors open on the sixth floor, I rush to our suite to find the door ajar. We all step in and see the blue team rummaging around. Charlie bursts out of the bedroom, my romance novel in hand, and then bolts past us.

"Later, suckas!" he cries as he does, his team on his tail.

22.

THERE'S NO TIME TO CONTEMPLATE WHAT CHARLIE AND HIS TEAM are up to. I head to the bedroom, grab my tote, and dig around for the flint.

"Nice room," muses Bacon Bit II as he admires the view.

"I've got the flint." I hold it up for my team to behold.

"Give it to me," Mrs. Mustache says, grabbing it and tucking it into the opening of the conch shell that is now under her arm. "Rip the next one!" she screams with impressive spirit.

"Right." I rip off the next piece of tape and immediately understand. A romance novel, it reads. Charlie swiped one of *my* books to try to beat me. And it means they are ahead of us. I grab another of my novels and tear off the tape covering the fourth item, the next to last one on the list. We've got to make up time. And fast.

"Chocolate hearts. Where are we supposed to find chocolate hearts?"

"I know this one!" Bacon Bit II takes off and we follow, fumbling behind him down six flights of stairs. By the time Mrs. Mustache reaches the ground floor, he's nowhere in sight. I think to call after him, but I don't know his actual name. It seems the rest of the team is having the same problem, as they look around, uncertain.

"Where'd he go?" CrossFit Girl asks.

"Where was that speed during the water balloon game?" adds Mrs. Mustache.

Before I can answer, Team Good Hair tears around the corner of the building, running by us with barely any acknowledgment. It happens so fast I can't determine if they are holding chocolate hearts, but I do make eye contact with Charlie, who has his mouth open wide, tongue pressed fully out, and bent down to his chin in a taunt. It's the last thing I see before they disappear around the opposite corner.

I CANNOT LOSE TO HIM. I CANNOT!

I'm about to suggest we split up to look for Bacon Bit II when—

"There he is!" CrossFit Girl yells, pointing. I follow her finger to find Bacon Bit II has returned, a bag of heart-shaped chocolates wrapped in red foil in hand.

"Where'd you find those?" I ask.

"Gift shop. My boyfriend browsed there yesterday for over an hour." He pulls a small package from his cargo shorts pocket. "Got this too," he says, holding up a small "survival" kit, though from the looks of it, it's more touristy gimmick than actual disaster-readiness. "It was the last one. It's got flint in it." He shrugs. "Figured it may be the only flint the other team could find."

"Smart," Mrs. Mustache says. "They got us to buy things from the gift shop."

"What's the last item?" CrossFit Girl snaps, tiny red veins like cracks in her bulging eyeballs.

I pull the tape. "Rum punch," she reads over my shoulder.

"That's not a good one for a romance list. Rum punch sex can get a little sloppy," Mrs. Mustache muses.

"Follow me," I say. I've definitely got this one. I lead my team back to the resort's beach side and over to the open-air restaurant, which is packed full of vacationers taking full advantage of their all-inclusive packages.

We find Andres standing next to the maître d', the same one who seated Charlie and me for dinner on our first night, now holding a tray with four glasses of punch. I grab a drink and take a swig, so grateful to have completed the second game that I don't feel a revolt in my stomach from the reintroduction of rum punch.

"Congrats to our winners!" Andres announces, and we all squeal and hug one another in delight. I was certain we'd lost. CrossFit Girl is so excited she shakes her glass above our heads, dousing us all in sticky punch, before throwing it at the brick wall. We all watch as it shatters into shards in the sand.

"I'll pay for that," she says to Andres with a grin, then squats to pick up the pieces.

As we catch our breath, I see Charlie and his team round the corner, running desperately toward the restaurant. Before they can spot us, I usher my team to the side of the building, along a line of feathery bushes, and listen as Team Good Hair arrives on the mat and the maître d' offers them a fresh tray of rum punch. I have to stifle my laugh when they cheer, clinking glasses and patting one another's shoulders.

Mrs. Mustache takes a step forward, but I stop her. "Not yet," I whisper, and she smiles and nods, a look upon her face that's just as devious as I feel. Andres has not pronounced them winners, yet they are war whooping as if they have indeed won since we are nowhere to be seen. Finally, as they finish their punch and start joking about how we must have gotten really tripped up, I lead my team out. We round the building, slow-clapping as we do. All of us except CrossFit Girl have our empty glasses tucked under our arms, specifically to show them we've been here awhile.

As we approach, I look only at Charlie, the mischievous smile wiped from his smug face.

"Team Kick 'Em in the Nuts are the winners!" Andres proclaims, raising my arm in the air as if I've just won the heavyweight belt. "Oh, this is so good!" he continues, swaying his hips to the beat projecting from the boom box that never seems to leave his side. It's Taylor Swift's "Look What You Made Me Do" that plays, and I can't think of a more apropos soundtrack. "I was hoping we'd make it to game three, and indeed we have!" He rubs his hands together excitedly. "Please, everyone. Follow me to learn what the next game will be. The one that will determine our final winners!"

Still grinning, Andres leads us across the beach toward the front of the resort.

"Having fun?" Charlie asks, bumping his shoulder into mine as we walk.

"Fun? No, this is a special kind of hell," I tell him. I can't admit that I am, in fact, having fun. I'll only be able to admit it when my team wins.

"I've been thinking. Perhaps a message to Zane is too unfair. Maybe we should renegotiate terms for tomorrow." He's stepped ahead and is now trotting backward to face me.

"Oh, are you scared now?"

"Not scared, just trying to do you a favor."

"I don't need a favor." I rub my shoulder and wince. "What I think I need is a back rub after all this exertion. Or maybe six. Tomorrow. When you're my servant. And in case you've forgotten, we just won the last game."

Charlie shakes his head, his dimple pressed deep into his cheek from the upturn of his mouth, his pale blue eyes glinting in the sun, before turning and jogging to catch up with the rest of his team, placing his arm around CrossFit Guy's shoulder when he reaches them.

Andres's destination is the resort pool, a massive rectangle, the size of at least seven backyard LA pools laid together. Several people are sunbathing around it, virtually all of the lounge chairs full, most of those vacationers' attention now fixed on our group.

"This is where the final competition will be held. The one that will determine the ultimate Turquoise Point Resort Games winners!" Andres says, his arms outstretched toward the water. Additional resort staff ask those in the pool to exit for our "event," which only adds to the onlookers' intrigue. Our audience is now several dozen people. "And to make it worthwhile," Andres says, "I have a little surprise."

He steps behind a palm tree and picks up a crate the size of a shoebox.

"What's in the box?" Bacon Bit II whispers behind me, adding an ominous air to the spectacle.

"This, my friends, goes to the winning team." He pulls the lid open and tips the crate toward us so we can see its contents.

There are oohs and aahs all around me. As I stare at the crate's shiny load, all I can seem to picture is Charlie and me duking it out to the bitter end in this pool until one of us drowns.

23.

"WHAT A LOVELY MORNING, WOULDN'T YOU SAY?" I STAND BESIDE THE couch pullout, hovering over Charlie as he slowly gains awareness.

"Why?" is all he can manage as he rubs his eyes and laboriously swings his legs to the ground.

"Why is it a lovely morning, you mean?" I open the curtains and he moans as light tramples his face. "Just take a look at our beautiful surroundings."

"No, why are you so damn perky? What time is it?" He rubs his face some more, squinting.

"I'm so damn perky because it's a special, special day. Also known as Charlie the Servant Day, in case you forgot. And it's a little after seven. I want to ensure we get a full day in. Lots to do!" I clap my palms together twice.

He groans and I have to turn away to hide the amusement on my face.

As it turns out, Mrs. Mustache used to coach cheer at her local high school in Michigan, skills that came in particularly handy yesterday when the final challenge was to choreograph and execute a synchronized swimming routine.

"You're actually gonna make me go through with this?" Charlie squints up at me with a drowsy, pained expression.

"Oh, of course I am. I won. A bet is a bet. Now, please go make me some coffee."

"Seriously, Sloane?"

"Deadly. Oh, and please refer to me as Your Highness."

"Yeah, right, I'm not—"

"Well, then I guess I'll have to send another note to Brooke, this one about how Charlie and I aren't actually dating and his sole purpose in inviting me on this trip was . . ."

He rises to his feet, surely attempting to intimidate me with his height. "Okay, fine. How would you like that coffee, Your Highness? Black like your heart?" He says "Your Highness" like it's the name of a communicable disease.

"Oh no, no. There will be no insults today. Only compliments. In fact, I suggest you set a timer so that every hour, on the hour, you are reminded to compliment me. And it seems as though you missed your seven a.m. so . . ."

He presses his eyebrows together, his sharp blue eyes barely slits. I almost feel bad for him. Almost.

"You are incredibly prepared should there be a zombie apocalypse," he says through gritted teeth. "It's rather impressive."

"Wow, thank you, Charlie!" I say in not-totally-feigned delight. "I'll take my coffee on the couch here. And yes, black, please. Black like this lovely plush robe." I tug at the ties around the waist.

Not only did we get the benefit of Mrs. Mustache's choreography skills yesterday, but Bacon Bit II was so dedicated to the win that he provided each of us with one of his collection of vacation swim caps *and* was even willing to cut up his floral robe to create matching sashes (tied around our waists with a bow on the right hip), a look that was met with spectacular applause from the crowd of onlookers.

I turn at the terrace door and traipse back over to Charlie. "Oh, and I almost forgot. I made this for you." I pick up the item I've hidden behind the couch and hand it to him.

"You've got to be kidding me," he says.

The grand prize, the items we four members of the winning team received, were plastic gold statues of a goat. Because we are, in fact, the Greatest of All Time. And being the crafty person I am, I've attached two strands of twine—one from the goat's neck, the other from the tail—to turn it into a necklace. So Charlie can wear it throughout servant day.

The sun sure shines bright today.

I rise onto my tiptoes to place the makeshift goat trophy necklace around his head, my forearms grazing the tops of his bare shoulders as I do.

"Well, that looks even more wonderful than I had anticipated," I say as I straighten the goat, then press it firmly into his chest. "Nothing worse than a crooked goat hanging from one's neck."

"Its ear is poking me," he says, shoving his fingers between the goat and his bare pec. He rubs his chest gently, and I swallow hard.

"No complaining, Charlie. Not today," I say with the raise of my left eyebrow.

"I still can't believe we lost," he mutters, shaking his head as he looks at the ground. "I thought we had it with our routine."

I have to admit, their routine was on point. I knew we had them beat on looks when they showed up to the pool to perform in mismatched suits (as would be expected from a group of strangers thrown together to build a synchronized swimming routine while on vacation). They lined up at the pool's edge, and when the music began, I pressed my lips together and shook my head. Charlie winked at me as "Drift Away" began wafting from Andres's speaker. The song that was playing when we kissed at the bar.

Their routine consisted of sideways dives into the pool, each a half second behind the last, before they formed a line in the water to execute various viral dance moves. The song seemed far too slow for them to possibly dance to, but their moves matched the music, unhurried and even a bit sultry, and it worked. Except CrossFit Guy has little rhythm and was consistently a half step behind.

I think of Charlie's furrowed brow of concentration in the water. He wanted to beat me as badly as I wanted to beat him.

But our routine was on a different level. We started underwater with a dramatic burst into the sky (gasping for air after miscalculating the length of the intro to our song). There were perfectly timed scissor kicks into the air and arms bending forward and back in perfect unison. Our only misstep was when Bacon Bit II faced the wrong direction in our mid-performance lineup, but I grabbed his shoulders and quickly spun him around.

And my instincts told me we needed that one thing that would imprint us in the minds of the onlookers and ensure victory. Like that moment in a game when the other player might think they've won, but then *Arsonist Betty* pulls out her soda can and chocolate or flint and shocks them with her final, fantastic effort.

"What about a lift?" I said in Mrs. Mustache's room as we finalized our costumes. "I know Charlie can't do it because of his bad shoulder—it might give us the edge we need."

Halfway through our routine, I completed a backward flip, which was met with a roaring cheer from the jam-packed crowd. I can take no credit for it, because Bacon Bit II and CrossFit Girl flung me into the air with little effort and I simply had to not flail.

I'll never forget Charlie's face afterward, eyes narrowing in frustration while an amused grin infiltrated his mouth.

With the crowd still cheering as we climbed out of the pool, I removed my swim cap and grabbed a towel, sure to shake it so it whacked Charlie in the spray-on abs.

I'm sure it didn't help that our song was Taylor Swift's "Blank Space." He isn't the only one who can take jabs whenever an opportunity presents itself.

Today, in our room, he peers down at me. The goat bounces against him with his movement. "I feel like I'm going to need a safe word today. I'm afraid," he says, taking a step closer so we are practically touching.

There's a flutter somewhere down there, one I try to ignore. "Afraid?" I say archly. "There is no bumpy airplane, no Amazonian centipede to be seen. What else scares you?"

Somehow we've inched even closer, my breath uneven.

"You definitely scare me," he says in almost a whisper.

I see his tactic. Trying to unnerve me with vulnerable charm in hopes I will go easy on him. I tell myself not to take the bait, though my body seems to disagree. "Kumquat," I say, my face inches from his.

He crumples his brow. "What?"

"Kumquat. That can be your safe word. Should things get too . . . intense for you today."

He fights the smile that's winning control of his face. "*That's* the first thing that came to mind?" He strokes his stubbled chin with his thumb and forefinger. "Wait. Is that, like, your *real* safe word?"

"Wouldn't you like to know." I give him a closed-mouth smile and head for the bedroom, feeling his eyes on me as I do. I don't tell him I only said it because my juvenile self finds the word silly and it was the first thing that came to mind. His reason is far more salacious.

In the bathroom, my phone dings.

Tess: Finn is good, as am I.

Tess: Great, actually. How goes it?

Why did she add *great, actually*? I shake my head, too consumed with my present situation to pick apart Tess's cryptic message.

Me: Great here as well

I text back, but can't stop staring at the screen. Tess is my best friend, yet we are both clearly tiptoeing around each other. The succinct exchange of pleasantries with my best friend makes me feel a million miles from home, the realization that Charlie and I are alone on an island all the more palpable.

I regard myself in the mirror. I got a bit of a tan yesterday, my skin tinged pink at its high points and generally glowing. There's an aliveness in my eyes I haven't seen in months, perhaps years. Yesterday was invigorating in a way I didn't realize I was missing, like I've been buffed clean of a layer of dust. "Playing" with Charlie made for a nearly perfect day.

Nearly perfect because my delight in watching Charlie dance in the water was cut short when I spotted Maddie, the girl from the beach, standing at the far edge of the pool, clapping and bouncing. She was still perfectly put together, despite the afternoon heat, and eyed Charlie like I regard the fresh mango slices at breakfast. I watched as Maddie rushed over to Charlie, her hands clasped in front of her, singing his praises when he climbed out of the pool.

But today, I remind my reflection, Charlie is all mine.

24.

CHARLIE BRINGS ME COFFEE ON THE COUCH WHEN I REEMERGE FROM the bedroom. Today, he wears a black T-shirt with a teal bike, the word CYCLOPATH written above it in bold retro print, and I can't help but presume he's trying to send me a message. After handing over the mug, he turns on his heel to make his escape.

"Not so fast," I say, finger in the air. Man, do I intend to milk this day. There's certainly a part of me that sees the bratty nature of my behavior, but it's payback, I remind myself, for my generosity in supporting this Brooke ruse. Besides, the bet was *his* idea. "I'm thinking of getting a massage today."

"Okay, so you want me to call down to the resort spa?"

"No, I was thinking of something more convenient. Right here on the terrace." I blink at him with doe eyes until a look of recognition crosses his face.

"You want *me* to do it."

"Yes. What else do you have to do today other than attend to my needs?"

"I have a bad shoulder," he tries, and it's equally adorable and immaterial. I know from his offer to carry Mrs. Crandall down six flights of stairs during the fire, from his easy lift of my suitcase onto the resort shuttle at the airport—it's an attempted out rather than an actual concern.

"Consider it physical therapy."

He glares at me and I have to relocate so I don't laugh.

A few minutes later, I emerge from the bedroom, wrapped in the same resort robe. To my surprise, I find Charlie has curated quite a setup outside. He has laid one of the chaise lounges flat and covered it with white resort logo-embossed towels. Soft music plays—something symphonic—and there are even half a dozen or so lit candles placed around the chair on the terrace floor. Where did he find candles?

"Wow," I remark, stepping onto the terrace.

"I aim to please. Now lie down."

"Are you gonna smother me with one of those towels when I do?"

"To be determined," he says, ensuring his face is unreadable.

I reach for the tie of the robe but my hands waver.

Did I really coordinate a one-on-one rubdown? From Charlie, who I'm supposed to avoid becoming attracted to and who is not attracted to me? The same Charlie who's using me as bait to get his girlfriend back? I thought he'd find it torturous, having to pamper me. But now I'm debating a change of plan.

To make matters worse, as the sun has shuffled to its morning spot directly above our terrace, Charlie has removed his shirt. No spray-on abs needed.

Excellent work, Sloane.

"You coming?" he asks, and it's more inviting than I expect.

Before I can think about it further, I pull at the tie on the robe. I can't help but notice Charlie's eyes lingering for a beat as the robe falls to the floor. Apparently, my bathing suit selection is more interesting than my sleepwear. The red bikini I've only worn a handful of times is also inarguably the skimpiest thing I own. A gift from Tess, in her size, so it hugs a little too closely in all the areas.

The timer on Charlie's phone beeps softly. He shuts it off, looks back at me.

I glance at the clock on the wall inside. Eight a.m. on the hour. He actually set a compliment timer.

I'm growing more than slightly annoyed with myself, so I'm sure he's much further along on his annoyance journey. Just when I'm sure he's about to throw a lit candle in my direction, he flips his eyes over me again and says, "You look good in red."

"Thanks," I say, wondering if he can see the flush on my skin. I'm certain I'm as tomato red as this barely there bikini.

Charlie clears his throat and shifts his eyes to the beach as I lie face down on the chaise. I think to ask for a sheet, but before I can, my shoulders are struck by what feels like two Popsicles and I shudder instinctively.

He pulls back. "Are my hands cold?"

"Freezing!"

"I told you, I run cold," he says, now on his knees beside me. I hear the squirt of a bottle, then he's rubbing his hands together aggressively.

He makes contact again, and this time it's softer, warmer. He's even come up with lotion or oil of some kind. It smells like chemicals and cherries, but it does the job, his fingers running slick against the tops of my shoulders. Charlie's thumbs press in on either side of my spine and immediately my concerns about whether this was a good idea subside.

"I thought there'd be some cold-blooded joke in there," he says as his hands find a rhythm.

"I . . . it's . . . yeah."

Despite his claims of a bad shoulder, his grip is firm and intense and . . . what was I saying? I can't remember because all I feel is pure bliss. Okay, not *all*. I feel it growing, something else at the base of me. A swell of warmth, tiny bolts of fire quickly gaining frequency under his touch.

A flash of our kiss on this very spot on the terrace nudges into my mind.

Charlie is crouched so close I can feel his warm, damp breath behind my right ear. With each press of his hands up my back to my neck, my whole right side tingles in fantasized anticipation that he might gently nibble at the tip of my ear.

His hands fan out against my flanks, fingers wrapped firmly around my sides. I lose my breath each time his fingertips barely graze the edge of my bikini bottoms, then again when they slide up and run along the hem of my top. It is by far the most physical contact we've ever had and it feels disturbingly good.

"Where do you see yourself in five years?" Charlie asks out of nowhere as he presses his hands into me, drowning the tension.

"Huh?" I say, opening my eyes. "Is this a job interview?"

He keeps rubbing quietly, and I wonder if he's thinking what I'm thinking—he needs something to distract him from what is happening with his hands. "It's just a question. To pass the time so I don't have to focus on my aching shoulder."

I accept his stated reason. "In five years . . ." I say, then fade away. My reflex is to respond that I hope to be in a meaningful relationship, perhaps thinking about marriage and kids. I'm assailed by an image of Charlie playing at the water's edge with that toddler. But then I remember my promise to Jack Palmer and the team at Catapult.

I can't have it all, and I've made my choice.

"Working at Catapult. Maybe a promotion or two by then. I want Kenji Sugano's job one day."

"Who's that?"

"He's the head of game design. Lead developer of their last three games, all top sellers."

"I could see you running the show there," he says in a voice that reflects a smile.

"So can I," I say, realizing I mean it.

"And what else?"

"What else?"

"Yeah, what about the other parts of your life?" When I don't answer, he adds, "Your personal life."

"I don't know. Right now, I'm only focused on getting this job and proving myself there. What about you?"

The pressure of his hands wanes. "I thought I'd be married by now, or soon. My mom already talks about 'grandbabies.' I'd like to think marriage and kids are still in my future."

It feels like my spine caves at his touch. Even though Charlie and I are not a thing, even though we've known each other such a short time, my thoughts betray me. Because the thing I think in response is, *I cannot give you what you want*. And that thought is like a brick in my stomach.

"Besides, I've gotta use my baby name."

I lift the front half of my body to my elbows and twist to look at him. "You have a baby name?"

He shrugs and nods casually. I think of Zane, who would have run away in a zigzag line screaming "stalker" if I had ever told him I had kids' names picked out.

"I'm waiting," I say.

He leans back, pulls his legs in front of him, and grabs his wrist around his bent knees. "I don't think I want to share it with you. This feels like an unsupportive environment."

My mouth opens wider. "Charlie, you cannot tell me you have a baby name picked out and then not tell me what it is."

He grins. "Oh, I think I can."

Charlie has somehow managed to get the upper hand on this day that is supposed to be mine. I sit all the way up and turn around to face him. I'm on the chair and he's on the concrete, and I appreciate the rare height advantage. "As my servant, I demand you tell me."

He bites his bottom lip, and I force my eyes not to look at his mouth. Finally, he opens that perfectly full-lipped mouth and slowly, emphatically, says, "Kum-quat."

25.

I COCK MY HEAD. "YOU NEED A SAFE WORD FROM THIS CONVERSATION, really?"

He nods, smirking.

I could threaten to message Brooke again, find another way to terrorize him into telling me, but I can't show him how badly I want to know.

"Whatever." I lie back down. "Can we get back to my massage or are you scared of that too among the many other things on that list?"

I hear him shuffle closer. "As you wish," he whispers into my ear as his hands make contact with my neck.

I want to tell Charlie I know what he's doing. That he's trying to gain some power back after losing to me, however playfully. But I won't fall for any of it, I think—though, my body isn't listening.

His thumbs run down the edges of my spine, fingertips brushing along my sides.

I think about his words. His desire to start a family. "If I'm being completely honest," I say, my voice more fragile than intended, "part of me can't imagine bringing kids into this world, with all its imperfections. All its hurt."

"Yeah, but who'd be more prepared than your kids?" He states this so plainly, it's as if even all the world's problems and shortcomings have manageable solutions.

His hands edge deeper into the rub, his movements determined, methodical, and I wonder if he can feel my heartbeat quickening through my back. His hands shift down, slowly, from my shoulders to my shoulder blades, circle there for a bit, then continue to my lower back. It's here that my insides clench. My breath is shallow but hard into the mat of the chaise, and I want to make it stop. Okay, that's not true. I *should* make it stop.

"Tell me about Brooke," I say after a moment, looking for an excuse to level the playing field. Thinking about him and Brooke should adequately douse the heat rising from my base.

"What?" he asks, an edge of surprise in his voice.

"How did you know she was The One?"

His press lightens so slightly it would have been easy to miss the change, and he goes silent for a long while. I'm about to repeat myself when he finally speaks. "I thought she was. Now I'm not so sure."

"Oh?"

"Yeah, I mean, if you asked me a few days ago, I would have told you I wanted nothing more than to get her back. But now? I think I only wanted her back because she caught me off guard. She had all the power in our breakup. I wanted some of that power back, I think."

"What changed?"

He's silent again for a long, brimming moment as he runs his hand into my hair and against the back of my head. I stave off a moan. "I don't know. Time. Being here, away from normal life, away from the places and things that remind me of her." His grip grows tighter and he runs his fingers down around my sides again, sidling up from my hips to just below my chest. Slowly. "And being with you."

My skin grows hot under his touch and my breath ragged. In addition to the intense pull at my base, there's something else. An anxious buzz, almost like fear. "Aren't you terrified you can't trust your picker anymore? After getting it so wrong?"

His hands halt for a second before proceeding. "Yeah. I am. How do you get over that?"

"I guess . . . you meet someone who makes you even more sure than before. And you take the leap, knowing it could still all end disastrously again."

His hands stop once more, for a split second, before continuing along my spine. He's released most of the pressure in his fingers. Now he grazes his fingertips gently across my skin like the sweep of a feather. I immediately erupt into goosebumps. This soft version of his touch is electric, every millimeter of skin he grazes becoming my new center point of feeling, like one of those magnet fragment statues, collecting sensation from all my nerves as they follow and collect at his fingertips. The pulse between my legs grows to a throb.

There's a powder keg between us, his hands the spark of heat that could light the whole thing up. I've fought a quickly growing force this whole time, one drawing me to him. Whether it's pushing or pulling, I'm not quite sure.

"Yes, well, I'm glad I've been able to be a distraction for you this week. Help you see things differently," I say in what sounds too much like a moan.

"You're not a distraction," he says, gripping my sides again and now moving back down toward my hips. The way his hands wrap around my hips has the earmarks of something primal, making me feel under his control. Submissive. It's not something I care to feel often. But with Charlie, there's a call I find myself wanting to relent to. I can't help but imagine he may grab me by the haunches and pull me in.

He doesn't.

"Well, this also isn't real life," I say.

"It's not?"

"No, in real life you wouldn't be my servant for the day, we wouldn't be in this incredible suite in paradise, and you wouldn't be touching me."

He is quiet once more, and again my breathing goes shallow in anticipation of his reply.

He doesn't respond. Instead, he presses into my neck more intensely, and I wonder if I've said something wrong.

"Where'd you find this lotion?" I ask, attempting to ground myself. Even if he might be changing his mind about wanting Brooke back, he's still using me to *get back at her*, so either way, he's using me. And the artificial cherry smell of the lotion is growing disturbing.

"Under the sink in the bathroom," he says.

I lift my head slightly to inspect the little red bottle he has set down on the side table. I pick it up and hold it out in front of his face. "This is lube, Charlie."

He gives me that viciously sexy, mischievous grin, and it's clear he's well aware of this detail. "Is it?"

"Charlie! I'm going to have to shower for an hour to get the smell of edible underwear off me."

His face says it all. Evidently, he will continue to find small ways to entertain himself through his servitude. I can't even say I'm mad, mostly just impressed. As I take in his proud face, all I can seem to think about are his formidable hands cleansing cherry lube off my skin in the shower.

I give Charlie a slight reprieve after the massage and my subsequent shower so I can work on the game. Just as I'm hitting my stride, building the individual components of *Arsonist Betty*'s tool kit into the graphics, my phone hums beside me.

"Ah, there's a hurricane near you," my mom says when I've picked up. She doesn't waste time on formal hellos or goodbyes. More often than not she just hangs up when she has determined the conversation is complete and I have to say hello a few times to verify she is no longer there.

I shake my head, confused. "What?"

"Hurricane. The Big One. Her name is Sheila. Why do they always name catastrophes after women?"

I put my mom on speaker and navigate to Google on my computer, refraining from informing her that they stopped giving tropical storms historically female names in the 1970s, because there is no point in going down that road. "Mom, it's a tropical storm off the coast of Trinidad and Tobago," I tell her, skimming the article on my screen. "That's like, a thousand miles away. Literally. And this article says it likely won't even make landfall."

"Oh, okay. Be careful then. Are you spending this time away to look for jobs? Anything good?"

Did my mom research Caribbean-adjacent natural disasters to have an excuse to call me and ask about my job search? I tell myself no, because it's the more digestible answer. When I don't immediately reply, she adds, "I look forward to hearing about a new engineering job when you get back. Maybe you'll meet someone there you can bring to the vow renewal."

I hear the faint sound of Charlie's phone buzzer from the other side of the slightly ajar bedroom door. Before I can stop him, he knocks once, then pushes the door open fully. "It's noon. I owe you a compliment," he says.

"Who is that?" My mom's voice fills the room.

Sorry, Charlie mouths.

"Nobody, Mom. Just the . . . a waiter. Tess and I are at the resort restaurant so I'd better—"

"What about the job updates?"

"Yes, yes, it's going great. I have another interview." I shut my eyes, but not before I see Charlie's eyebrows rise.

"Oh, great. Is it—"

"I'll tell you all about it when I get back, okay? Talk soon!"

This time, I'm the one to hang up without saying goodbye, feeling awful about it.

"You really shouldn't lie to your mother," Charlie says, arms folded in front of him, wicked smirk back across his mouth.

"That's not a compliment," I tell him.

The afternoon is spent at the beach with Charlie carrying my things and fetching me cocktails while I continue my work on the game. It's particularly satisfying when other guests do a double take at the goat statue around his neck. It's even more satisfying when Andres can't stop laughing and takes a selfie with him, pointing with pride at the repurposed trophy.

We return to the suite in the late afternoon, both collapsing into our loungers on the terrace. I look over at Charlie, who seems downright exhausted. Now I do feel bad. He has taken his punishment like a champ.

"I have one more request," I say, just as his eyes shut.

He opens them, looks over at me with a painful wince.

"It's not something you have to do today. It would be later."

"Later?"

"Yes. A few weeks after we get back." My pulse quickens and I immediately regret bringing it up. Why does what I'm about to ask feel intimate? But the call from my mom today—it was an invasive reminder that there's yet another problem in my life I need to solve for. "I have this thing in a few weeks. My parents' vow renewal. It's local, Van Nuys. It'd be just for that day . . ."

"Are you asking me to be your date?"

"Not a date. A fake date. Like you suggested when I agreed to come on this trip. I need to get my parents off my back after . . ."

He sits up. "After what?"

"I just need them off my back about finding a man."

"So you want to introduce me to your parents." Now he's grinning fully.

"Not like that. It. Would. Be. A. Fake. Date."

"Yeah, but what you're saying is, you think I'm the kind of guy that would impress your parents."

"I'm saying you're my only option," I say, attempting to avoid my own grin.

"I find that hard to believe. That I would be your only option."

I run a hand through my humidity-ravaged hair and focus in on the paddleboarder on the water ahead, trying not to read into his words.

Before I can come up with a response, he says casually, "Sure, I'll go."

"Really?"

"Yeah, why not. It's part of our deal, right?"

I'm happy that I can tell my mom I'm bringing someone besides Tess to the vow renewal, but something nags at me nonetheless. Charlie referencing our deal takes me back to the notion that everything between us is fake.

As I thank Charlie, a thought that's been poking at me since yesterday afternoon leaps to the front of my mind.

"You knew I had flint in my bag."

He opens one eye and turns his head toward me, but he doesn't speak.

"You knew I had flint. I pulled it out on the plane when I offered you comfort items when you were scared."

"Nervous, not scared," he says, one eye still closed.

I open my mouth to speak, but nothing comes out. There's no way Charlie would've let me win. Why would he choose to endure the level of torment I've smothered him with today? And he knew I'd never let him live it down. Why would he possibly?

Ninety-nine percent of me is bothered by the notion that my team might not have won fair and square. But the other one percent, that nagging eyelash, causes a rumble of heat between my legs.

"I'm gonna take a nap," I tell him. "Sleep off the daytime cocktails."

He perks up. "Really?"

"Yes. You're off the hook for a while."

"Thank god," he says, crossing his feet on the chaise with his hands behind his head.

"I'm sorry the day's been so awful for you."

"Yeah, well, it's not real life, right?" he says without looking at me, and a flash of his hands pressing into my back sends a wave of longing through me.

Perhaps if it's not real life, I can allow myself to make decisions I otherwise wouldn't. And probably shouldn't.

26.

LATE THAT EVENING, THERE'S A QUIET RAP AT THE BEDROOM DOOR.

"Sloane, you still up?" I hear him call softly from the other side.

A strike of adrenaline punches through me at the sound of his voice. I sit up in bed, save my game updates, and close my laptop. "Yeah, come in."

Charlie enters, and again we are in matching resort robes. The room is dim, aside from the lamp on the bedside table, and it casts a shadowy glow across us both.

He holds up my romance novel. "I'm just returning this. I finished it."

I hold out my hand. "And what did you think?"

"I get it," he says, handing me the book.

"What do you get?"

"I get why you read this stuff." A sly curve overtakes his lips. "It's end-of-the-world smut."

I move my laptop to the nightstand. "Smut?"

"But really, that sex scene in it? Fire. I didn't know a locksmith could be so good with his hands. Or then again, I guess I should have." He tilts his chin sideways in an indecipherable gesture.

"Yeah, yeah," I say, stacking the book on top of my own on the nightstand.

He turns to leave.

"Wait," I say before I can stop myself. I should let him go. Of course I should. But something about it being late into the evening, about him having just finished reading my romance novel, about being in bed . . . I *really* don't want him to leave.

He shifts at the door and watches as I pick up the book he's just returned.

I glance at the clock. "It's 11:47."

He takes a step closer. "And?"

"And that means you're still my servant for another thirteen minutes."

Charlie shakes his head, acknowledging his mistake. "Now it's twelve minutes," he says, nodding toward the clock. "So what do you want?"

"Is that any way to speak to Your Highness?"

"What can I get you, Your Highness?" he says dismissively.

"I want . . ." I open the book and start flipping through its pages. When I find what I'm looking for, I hold it out to him. "I want you to read it to me."

He takes the book from my hands. "You want me to read this book to you? In twelve minutes?"

"No, you're misunderstanding me. I want you to read one particular scene." My eyebrow arches instinctively.

He looks down at the page I've opened it to and recognition spreads across his face.

"You've got to be kidding."

I shimmy deeper into the pillows behind me. "Do I look like I'm kidding?"

He opens his mouth slightly, seemingly contemplating an argument. Or perhaps an attempt to charm his way out of the request.

"A bet is a bet," I say. "And wasn't this bet, in particular, *your* idea?"

His eyes intensify and I see his surrender coming. "Fine," he says, then sits on the edge of the bed, his robe spreading just above his knees as he does. As I catch sight of his bare thighs, I'm momentarily distracted with whether or not he is naked under there. He clears his throat and turns toward me, book in hand. "For the record, I will never make another bet with you. Ever."

"Perfectly fine. Nothing could top this day, anyway."

He looks down at the page again, shakes his head, and sighs before finally, he begins. "He slid his finger under the delicate strap of her rose-colored pink silk camisole, letting the tip of his finger graze her bare skin as he moved it down her arm." He stops, looks at me, his face a question.

"Please continue," I tell him.

He glances at the clock. "You've got ten minutes left."

"Then I suggest you get to it."

He shakes his head, then clears his throat again as if all his annoyance has clogged his airway. "First one strap, then the other, until the camisole fell like a prize curtain to her waist, revealing her . . ." He presses his lips together.

"Her what?"

He clears his throat again.

"Her what?" I repeat.

"Her ample breasts."

"Lovely, then what?"

He stares at me, lips parted.

"You're wasting time, Charlie. Then what happens?"

He serves me a scowl that looks a bit like a sinful grin and begins reading again. "He raised his hands to her chest. She threw her head back and closed her eyes as he . . . as he took one of her breasts into his mouth, gently flicking his tongue across her erect nipple. He watched as her eyes rolled back, her jaw clenched. His hand instinctively reached up and sheathed gently around her bare neck. He wrapped his other hand around her left breast and tilted it upward, so he could take more of her against his tongue."

Somewhere along the way, Charlie's tone has shifted and his voice has grown deeper and more resolute. There is little hesitation as he continues. "Just as she allowed her first moan, he pulled away, leaving her brooding in dissatisfaction at the separation. Enjoying her discontent, he tugged the camisole from around her waist to her feet, crouching to guide it. Then, from the floor, he pulled the matching silk shorts down in a surprising swoop, taking her panties with it. She stood naked before him, her long ash-colored hair messed, her eyes sharp with singular focus. He observed her from his crouch, finding the angle intoxicating. When he could take it no longer, he rose and reached for her, his mouth making hard contact with hers, her breasts pushed up against his bare chest. His tongue found hers and pressed into her with the force of undeniable chemistry that had been building between them, day after tense day."

I shift in my spot in the bed, unable to keep my seat from moving, distracted by the lines of heat between my legs. Because Charlie is not only reading these words with his deep, now-raspy voice, but now he's making eye contact with me after every few words, ensuring I can't focus my attention anywhere but on him.

He continues, this time without any prompting. "He pushed her down onto the bed behind them and kneeled, grabbing each thigh and pulling her close. From this new vantage point, he admired her for a moment, appreciating that despite the world crumbling to the epidemic of greed and warfare around them—evidence that people inevitably destroy everything they forge—there was still room for something beautiful. He ran his tongue along her inner thigh, and she moaned in approval. Her goosebumps built against his tongue, reaching for more. He pulled away for a moment, appreciating these rarely seen parts of her.

As she questioned his next move, he made full contact, his mouth attaching to her most sensitive part with the force of a—"

"Time's up," I say when I hear the slight tick of the clock beside me striking midnight. The words escape me in a squawk that is also somehow breathy.

He methodically lowers the book to his lap, looks at the clock, then back at me. The dense island air invades the room, my breath forced as he eyes me from the edge of the bed. We remain this way for what feels like several minutes, a silent, questioning stalemate of sorts, both unsure of what comes next, an unlimited range of options at our fingertips.

"It's twelve exactly," he says finally. "How about one more compliment? I'll throw this one in for free." His eyes beat through me, his voice still rich and rough.

Since I cannot speak, I nod.

"I'm in awe of you," he says. "Of all your talent and drive and just *you*. You're . . ." His eyes narrow, and I see him searching for a word. "You're Kix," he says finally, his speech slow, deliberate.

"Kix?"

"Yeah, like the cereal."

"I prefer Fruity Pebbles."

We both speak, delicately, like it's perfectly normal bedroom talk.

"You're Kix," he repeats. "It's the only way I know to describe you. My favorite cereal from when I was a kid. It's, like, all the good things. The smell. The security. The goodness. You're the same feeling. The same . . . flavor."

I can't breathe.

I think I know what he is saying. Charlie is safe. And not safe in a way that one might describe a partner who is boring or prescribed. He's safe like a net below, like a harness, like a life preserver. I've rarely felt safe in my life. Prepared, yes. But not particularly safe. Charlie, he is safety.

He looks at the clock again, which makes me turn to it. 12:01. "What if I gave you ten more minutes?" he asks. I'm in a trance, Charlie my hypnotist. I can't look away, can't manage to break whatever is holding us together.

"Ten more minutes," I repeat in acceptance, unconsciously rubbing my palm against the plush down comforter.

"What do you want from me next then, Your Highness?" He is so calm and soft it's almost as though he's another person entirely. Not the Charlie I've come to know these last few days. But also, deeply the Charlie I've come to know. The Charlie with the sexy abs and sexier face. The funny, kind, supportive Charlie who doesn't make me feel ashamed for who I am and what I want.

I can't seem to formulate a thought other than to imagine him on top of me.

I speak in almost a whisper. "Kiss me."

My invitation is like the opening of a dam. He flings the book to the floor and rushes to me. He sits beside me, cups my chin with his hand. His eyes chase mine before he leans in and barely grazes my lips with torturous finesse. This, our third kiss, is nothing like the first two. This one is like the imprint of a kiss rather than a kiss itself, so achingly soft I may very well be imagining it. It leaves my whole body pulsing for more. He pulls back only slightly, and his eyes align with mine again.

"What next, Your Highness?" he whispers, and the words fall directly into my mouth.

"Take off your robe."

He stands at the side of the bed, eyes me fiercely as he unties the robe and lets it hit the floor. His navy boxer briefs are pretty much at my eyeline, and it's impossible not to notice his erection through the thin cotton. I have to exhale forcibly. He stands there, hands clasped behind his back, obediently awaiting my next instruction.

I push the blanket off my legs. "Take off mine."

He sits on the side of the bed again and unhurriedly tugs at one end of the tie on my robe, letting it come undone. When the robe remains mostly closed, he takes both hands and pulls it apart, inch by delicate inch, his fingertips grazing my bare belly as he does. His eyes sweep downward and he smiles when he sees I'm wearing a shockingly similar pair of men's navy boxer briefs. His eyes stroke upward to my sleep bra, a worn tan cotton thing that resembles a sports bra. My attire is the opposite of sexy, but you wouldn't know it from the look in his eyes.

"What's next?" he asks, his hand still at the edge of the robe, positioned so his palm is touching the bare skin of my lower belly. His pinkie flicks gently at the waistband of my briefs. We are both breathing in short, delicate puffs and the room hangs heavy with a dense, wet heat similar to the one that has assaulted us all week. A million thoughts swirl within me, but it's hard to focus on anything other than the pulsing in my core and the pale blue of his eyes.

His pinkie finger dips below the waistband of my briefs and we both look down, watch as it runs a slow line, steady and unhurried, back and forth against the skin of my lower abdomen. I impulsively, reflexively lift my hips toward him. I need to feel those hands, and his divine mouth, across every part of me.

A knock at the suite's front door makes me jump, and Charlie wraps his hand around my waist in reaction. His grip is firm, and I am practically panting, most definitely in heat, ready to dry hump him just to keep things going.

I'm inclined to ignore whoever our midnight visitor is. Charlie is too it seems, based on his lack of movement. Our eyes lock together once more, and I think I may combust if one of us doesn't look away soon.

27.

THE KNOCK COMES AGAIN, THIS TIME MORE FIRMLY, AND CHARLIE hangs his head.

"Shit, I forgot. I ordered room service," he says, breath warm on my chest.

"At midnight?"

His eyes lift to mine. "I wanted that chocolate soufflé thing."

There's a third knock. He huffs in dismay, then leans in close, his stubbled cheek against mine. "I will be . . ." He tugs at my right earlobe with his teeth and quickly releases. "Right back." He's off the bed in an instant, grabbing his robe from the floor and heading to the door.

When he is gone, I throw my head into the pillow, trying to catch my breath. My body is pulsing and I can't focus on much else besides the slick of desire between my legs. I press my knees together.

I hear Charlie's muffled interaction with the waiter just steps away and I'm certain our visitor can feel the heavy residue of our want in the air upon entering the suite.

As Charlie handles the situation at the door, I burst out of bed and into the bathroom, begin frantically opening cabinets. They're all either empty or contain products that don't help me. Extra towels. A hair dryer. Q-tips. Individually wrapped soaps the size of dinner mints. I swing open the doors under the sink, the last stop in my search. The romance package offered champagne, chocolate-covered strawberries with white drizzle, rose petals. If Charlie found lube in here, then maybe, just maybe—

A triumphant cry escapes me when I see the basket with a stack of gold squares. I tear one from the strand, but not before noticing it's cherry scented. Whoever at the resort is responsible for the romance package clearly has a cherry fetish.

By the time Charlie closes the suite door and turns around, I'm standing in the living room. We stare at each other across the space, his back pressed against the front door, room service cart pushed to the side. He rubs his hands in that circular motion of his in front of him. The smell of burnt sugar invades the space, and it's as if we are baking in an oven alongside the chocolate soufflé.

I'm panting.

Is it possible to crave something you've never had? Because I crave him with such force it seems implausible to want something this much without having previously devoured and revered it.

Charlie's eyes flicker down and he sees the condom wrapper pressed between my fingers. His chest heaves. We've had seventeen hours of unintended dom/sub foreplay—a long few days of rapidly mounting attraction—and have reached the unignorable climax.

There is nothing soft, hesitant, or subservient about his actions this time. He takes one giant step toward me and the force pushes us both onto the couch, all his glorious weight atop me. He sits up, discards his robe, and hastily removes mine in complete opposition from how he did just a few moments ago. I pull my bra over my head as he removes his boxer briefs and then heads for mine. We claw at each other with sublime carelessness. His hands are everywhere, so quick and effectual that I almost believe he's got another pair. They run through my hair, down my back, across my stomach and thighs—as though his gluttonous fingers have hungered for the feel of my skin in every second since we first met.

When I am certain I cannot take it any longer, I impart one final order for his extended day of servitude. "Fuck me," I say, barely audible through a sharp breath.

He exhales forcefully and sits up, unwrapping the condom with his teeth. I throw my head back in anticipation and arousal. When he doesn't immediately make contact, I pull my head forward to find out why. He's looking down at me, a seriousness across his face. He's gentle again, slowly pressing down on top of me.

"You're everything," he murmurs, his lips touching my ear before he enters me with his full length. My hips lift in response. His whispered declaration could mean a variety of things. That I'm everything he has been missing. That I'm everything he's ever wanted. As I look into his vast blue eyes, I believe he means I'm everything he wants—needs—in this moment. This belief serves me the confidence to fuck him without insecurity.

He thrusts forcibly just a handful of times then pulls away. Before I can question why, he has shifted his body downward, his eyes locked on mine as his mouth makes contact between my legs. My immediate instinct is to dissuade him—to allow in the unreasonable discomfort that has urged me to prioritize my partner's pleasure over my own in the past. But something about being with Charlie is different. I'm not in my head.

"You taste like cherries," he says, lifting slightly to look up at me.

"It's the condom," I manage to say. "Weird. Cherry. Fetish. Here." I force each word out on its own exhale. He grins and gets back to work.

Charlie pleasures me in a way I hadn't thought possible. At least not for me. And when I am on the brink of orgasm, without my having to voice it, he spreads back out on top of me and enters me again. This time, he does not stop.

The rest of the night is a dizzying blur of competing sensations. His breath on my neck. My hands cuffing his flexing biceps. His length pressed inside me tightly. The shudder of his body upon its release.

It's not until we are back in our robes eating chocolate soufflé on the scene-of-the-crime couch that I begin to feel something like worry.

28.

SOMEWHERE IN THE EARLY MORNING HOURS, POST—CHOCOLATE soufflé and a second exploit, we made our way to the bed, but not before creeping out to the terrace to watch the stars as it turned further into tomorrow. I forced the flecks of worry out of my brain, wanting to savor the time with him. So long as the sun hadn't yet risen on another day, I could keep the fantasy of us going.

I fell asleep with him curled around me, his weight and cool body like the crisp air of a fan. He found a way to touch me throughout the night—his arm draped across my hip, cheek pressed to the back of my head. If I unconsciously rolled away, he inevitably scooted closer to find me again. And there were the kisses. The way he pressed his lips to my hair or shoulder hazily—his actions so drenched in tender care I couldn't help but give in.

As the early morning light creeps in, I open my eyes to find Charlie still beside me, sheet strung just below his belly button, his bare chest rising and falling in a delicate balance. I observe him unabashedly, as I had on the plane, taking in his perfection at this close proximity. His eyelashes curled upward in a perfect *C* shape. The divot of his cheek. The light hairs on his arms and belly glinting like gold. I have to look away, knowing I could grow to really want this—need it even—waking up to Charlie beside me.

Carefully climbing out of bed, so as not to disturb him, I rummage quietly around the room for my laptop. As I do, I bury *The Burning Locke* deep in my Mary Poppins bag. In the chair in the corner, I open my laptop, not yet wanting to leave his proximity.

I almost drop the laptop when I see the first email in my inbox is from Jack Palmer at Catapult Games.

> Hello,
>
> After careful consideration of our many candidates, I am pleased to inform you that you are one of two final contenders for the game designer position with Catapult. The team looks forward to reviewing your game to make our final decision. When your prototype is complete, follow the instructions below to submit.
>
> Best,
> Jack

I scroll down the email to the referenced instructions, stating that finalists should submit final game prototypes via email to Jack, Kenji, Ross, and Anita, along with their respective email addresses. They must have been reviewing my candidacy, along with the other candidates, over these last few days, secretly narrowing it down.

A glorious thrill shoots through me. I, Sloane Cooper, am a final candidate, one of two, for my dream job at Catapult Games. The job that will let me into the club of the gaming future I've always wanted but was afraid I might never get. It's the validation I've secretly hoped for since I was a preteen, and in the grandest of fashions. From *the* Jack Palmer. I think of Jeffrey, the debt collector, whose additional seven calls I've ignored, and my anxiety dips. I feel closer than I ever have to a solution to all my problems. A real one. Just as I'm about to scream with pride, Charlie's sleep be damned, my exhilaration is quickly smothered. In the To field of the email, my address and one other: nopainnozane@zanecullins.com.

Zane is the other finalist.

Really? Jack Palmer couldn't be bothered to send two separate emails? Or BCC us, at a bare minimum? I wish he'd assigned this particular task to Anita. I think of Zane's entitled face reading this same message and seeing my address as the other candidate, thinking he has it in the bag.

This opportunity can change everything. I recall my words from the interview. *I would be fully dedicated to this job . . . have no personal life whatsoever.* I look at Charlie, still sleeping peacefully in the bed inches away. I contemplate jumping back in with him, snuggling into his side, and letting the pressures of my real life float away, but the weight of Jack Palmer's email holds me back.

I close my laptop and head for the terrace.

"Morning," Charlie says, joining me outside about fifteen minutes later. There's a heavy gray cast over the water, and the air holds the soil-like smell of impending rain. I lean against the rail, looking out at the view I've grown too accustomed to, glancing at him and offering a tight smile. Charlie's dressed in board shorts and a sweatshirt, hood flipped up, which serves me a flash of disappointment that I can't see what undoubtedly punny T-shirt he has on underneath. I instinctively pull the cord of my robe tighter, wishing we could have stayed knotted together in the suite's bed.

"How'd you sleep?" he asks, a still-drowsy smile etched on his face as he draws closer. For a moment, I think he will keep moving forward until he is wrapped around me again, just as he was in bed. I take a step back and continue to stare at the water, unable to make eye contact. At this, he halts.

"Good. You?"

"Fine." He flips down his hood and runs his hand through his hair. "Look, Sloane, last night was . . ."

I turn to face him. "A stupid, silly, drunken mistake."

His face goes stiff, all remnants of sleep cleared. "We weren't drinking."

He's right. These were sober, full mental capacity decisions we cannot dismiss away.

The email from Jack Palmer burns in my brain. "Look, we can forget it happened, okay?" I chuckle awkwardly. "Nothing has changed. We'll continue to post pictures, make Brooke jealous, and I'll keep working on my game. Then we can get home and back to our lives."

His face hardens and it makes my insides liquefy. I want to curl up in his lap like a cat. I want to tell him last night meant a lot to me. More than I expected. But I can't. There's too much to lose. Even if I do give in to my desires for the rest of this week, there's still the nagging thought that Charlie isn't fully over his ex. Even if he thinks he is, it could just be the distractions of paradise blinding him.

"Sloane, I'm sorry," he says. The words pinch my skin like a clamp. He's sorry. He regrets last night. It made him realize how much he misses Brooke, and now he's afraid he's led me on.

"I'm sorry too," I say, because I don't want to give him all the power over last night and now, the aftermath.

"For what?" he asks. He takes a half step closer. His wrist flicks forward, and for a moment I believe he will take my hand in his.

"For letting this place cloud my judgment last night . . ."

His face drops before I can continue. As soon as I've said the words, I know they were too cold. And untrue.

He clears his throat. "Right, well, I'm gonna head down to the beach."

"Charlie," I say. He stops and looks at me with a pleading stare, his eyes practically begging me not to do this. Nothing comes. I'm afraid, I realize. Fearful of letting someone in again. I can come up with all the excuses in the world about Catapult and Brooke and this not being real life, but if I strip all of that away, immobilizing fear is all I'm left with.

I watch in silence as he grabs a towel from the basket by the entrance and lets the door clang behind him. Perhaps I've been too harsh. Perhaps it was just the right amount. Either way, I know last night cannot bleed into today.

I grab my tote and head to the lobby to borrow one of the resort bikes. More than half of our trip is over and I have yet to leave the resort. With the help of Andres's directions, I take the considerable ride along the island's main road to Da Conch Shack, a tucked-away restaurant with bench tables set in the sand under the shade of widespread palms, just a few feet from the water. The building is white with the same bright blue shutters as the resort and cotton candy pink accents across the buildings and signs. It's still a bit before eleven, and the place is virtually empty, except for a small group drinking bottles of Turk's Head while playing Ringing the Bull on a center post.

A perfect spot to spend the day.

I choose the two-top closest to the water and set up my laptop, removing my sandals and digging my feet into the powdery-light sand. *It's pretty magical working on something I love in a place like this*, I tell myself, attempting to ignore my nagging unease.

Once I decided on *Arsonist Betty* as the game concept, things have come together pretty quickly on my design. I can't help but feel thankful for Charlie. Without him, without the fire alarm, without this trip, I wonder if any of it would have materialized the way it has.

Charlie.

Only a few hours have passed since our tryst—or *trysts*, two, technically—and I can't think about him without hearing his voice, soft in my ear as he lay atop me. Feeling his lips all over me. The pressure of his hips against mine, pressing fully into me . . .

Stop.

Focus.

This is precisely why something with Charlie was not supposed to happen. I won't lose this opportunity with Catapult because I let a guy get in the way of my dreams. Even if he is as handsome and supportive and kissable as Charlie. I'll never forgive myself if I do.

Four hours later, with a small break for an equally savory plate of jerk chicken as from the resort, I've made decent progress on the game, particularly the world-building. I've constructed a once-vibrant but now-ashen cityscape, defiled by the elderly arsonist on her reign of terror. I've added many devices to her pyro tool kit: matches, gas can, an array of lighters, and, for the very end, when it seems she's run out of materials and might be done for, a piece of flint she can use to fuel her reign of terror indefinitely.

It's my favorite part: just when you think *Arsonist Betty* is down and out, she pulls out the flint to prove she's an underestimated, formidable opponent. It's certainly not commercial quality, far from it. It's more of the outline of a game than a game itself, but I'm quite proud of what I've produced so far.

Confident about my game design, I pack up and ride back to the resort, my anxiety building as I get closer to seeing Charlie again. Instead of heading to the suite, I detour down to the beach. Perhaps a little more time will help push last night further back into my memory. So far, no such luck. I'm still thinking about his hands gripping the sides of my hips . . .

Before I can round the corner of the building to the sand, my phone rings. I fish it out of my bag and practically squeal in delight when I see it's a FaceTime from Tess.

"How's my baby?" I ask her.

"I'm great, baby," Tess says when the screen connects.

"Where's Finn?"

"Well, hello to you too. He's right here." She leans down from her seat at her kitchen table, and Finn is positioned in his usual spot, pressed up against her leg.

I rub at the pang of longing in my chest. "Finn! How's my boy? I miss you so much!"

Finn rises to a stand, wags the back half of his body, smiles into the screen with a floppy tongue.

Tess's face fills the screen again before I'm ready. "How are things going with J.D.?" she asks.

Now I regret answering. My face always gives me away to my best friend since middle school.

"You slept with him!" she yells, right on cue. A couple passing by on the path give me a curious look, the woman nodding in approval. I nod back, appreciating this stranger's sex positivity.

"Don't be ridiculous. Of course I didn't."

"Don't try to deny it. I can practically smell the sex on you through the phone. Did it, like, just happen? Tell me everything!"

Finn whine-barks in the background.

"It's okay, Finny. Mama got laid," Tess says to him, scratching his head. "Tell me everything."

I sigh. "It was . . . mind-blowing, intense, doubly orgasmic."

Tess shrieks.

"But it was a mistake. I can't let Charlie derail my opportunity at Catapult."

"Why did you promise a life of spinsterhood to a room full of dudes who can't keep their dicks in their pants?"

Tess, as crass as ever. Not wrong, but crass nonetheless. I can't deal with her telling me this situation with Charlie is okay when it is very much *not* okay. As I'm about to make another attempt at explaining why this job has to work out, I spy something in the corner of the frame.

"Tess, what's that behind you?" I ask, and point to my screen as if it gives her any sort of reference.

Tess turns to see the pair of men's loafers lined up next to her couch. I glance at the time on my phone. Three p.m. It's three hours earlier in Los Angeles, which means the owner of those shoes is in her apartment at noon on a Wednesday. Or, was comfortable enough leaving a pair of shoes at her place mid-week. Perhaps there's a non-romantic explanation, but my mind won't acknowledge any of those possibilities. Either way, this is not one-night-stand behavior, certainly not by Tess's rules. Tess—who has not had a serious boyfriend since high school—prides herself on sleepovers she ensures end before the sun comes up.

Tess positions her body to fill the screen so the shoes disappear.

"Tess Carly Hubbard, is there a *man* in your apartment? One who wears loafers?"

"Oh my, I think the connection is cutting ou—" she says before fake-freezing her face and ending the call. I stare at the blank screen. I think how I pulled a similar move yesterday with my mom and feel a twinge of guilt.

Tess has (or recently had) a man in her apartment—in her life—who she's hiding from me! All the more reason to make it through the rest of this trip and get back home as soon as possible.

When I finally round the corner of the building to the beach, there's a crowd of people gathered at the water's edge, some pointing, all facing the same specific plot of sea. I make my way down to the group, unable to identify what has drawn the crowd.

"What's going on?" I ask a woman in the back. She turns to face me and I'm comforted to see Mrs. Mustache, though embarrassed I still don't know her real name.

"There's a girl who's drowning!" she tells me. "Your boyfriend ran in to help her."

"He's not my boyfr—" I start reflexively, before understanding settles in. "Wait. Charlie?" I push my way to the front of the crowd, a lead weight in my stomach, needing him to be okay.

29.

I SPOT HIM SEVERAL FEET FROM SHORE. HIS ARM IS WRAPPED AROUND a woman who is slung upon him, head bobbing languidly against his neck. When the water is waist-deep, Charlie sweeps the woman into his arms, high-kicking his way through the water to the shore.

I calm when I see he's okay—a relief so deep it surprises me a bit.

When Charlie reaches the beach, he lays the woman down. She's conscious, though looks dazed as she coughs with her fingertips pressed to her chest. She moves to all fours and Charlie crouches beside her, his arm on her lower back. If I didn't know any better, I'd say she's a yogi doing a perfect cat pose. Charlie's chest is slick and heaving, skin clinging to each muscle as his body constricts then releases, over and over again. Once again, I have a flash of him on top of me last night.

Not the time.

As she catches her breath, she rocks back and sits on the wet sand, and I see her face. It's Maddie. The girl from the beach, then by the pool on competition day, now this.

A couple whom I assume to be her parents push through the crowd and kneel beside her. The man wraps an arm around her while the woman gently moves the clumps of wet hair from her face. They help her to stand, and when she does, the crowd bursts into applause. They are cheering for her safe return to land, yes, but they are also cheering for Charlie. Some of the onlookers are even filming the encounter. Andres emerges from the group to slap hands with Charlie, who has now risen to his feet.

Maddie has seemingly regained her breath, because as the cheering dies down and the crowd begins to disperse, she rises on her tiptoes to throw her arms around Charlie's neck.

"Thank you so much! I would have drowned without you!"

"It's no problem. I'm glad you're okay," he says when she lets go. I can't help but notice that as she releases him, her hands slide along his neck and down the top of his chest before she pulls them away. He runs his hand through his hair, sending flecks of water into the air, and somehow, as I watch, it appears to happen in slow motion.

"Please join us for dinner tonight. As a thank-you," Maddie's father says, approaching them.

"Oh no, that's okay." Charlie slides his hands into his pockets, fumbling a bit as the wet fabric clings to his skin.

"Really, I insist. It's the least we can do."

I watch as Charlie looks to Maddie, who has brushed all her hair back in what now resembles a slicked-back red-carpet look. I realize she's wearing thong bikini bottoms, which make me want to pick at a non-existent wedgie.

Charlie relents. "Sure, that'd be great. Thank you."

"No, thank *you*," Maddie says, now clinging to his arm.

They make their arrangements and she hugs him a final, lingering time. He looks over her shoulder and sees me, the lone remaining member of the crowd. Maddie and her grateful parents head off, leaving Charlie and me standing a few feet apart on the sand.

"Hey," he says, closing the distance between us.

"I leave you alone for five minutes and you're off saving lives."

He rolls his eyes, pinching at his bad shoulder. "It's all a bit silly."

"Mmmmmm," I say. "So, how exactly does one almost drown in such calm waters?" I make a show of looking out at the perfectly still sea before us—so serene and shallow there's no need for a lifeguard.

He bites the inside of his cheek through a grin he fails to hide.

"Well, enjoy your dinner," I tell him before heading back toward the room. The beach doesn't seem so appealing anymore.

When he returns to the room an hour later, Charlie finds me on the terrace, building in details of the *Arsonist Betty* cityscape. "Hey," he says, leaning against the rail. He has his hat on backward, the same black-on-black Dodgers cap he was wearing the night we met, and it makes him exponentially more attractive. Something I didn't think was possible. With the aquamarine water sparkling behind him, I'm tempted to snap a picture, it's such a photo-worthy sight.

I rub my lips together and look down at my computer. "Hey."

"Can I . . ." He stops talking until I look up at him again.

"Can you what?"

"I just . . . I need to shower. Before dinner. I wanted to check if you needed to get in there before I do."

I can't help but deflate. Part of me thought he was going to say he changed his mind and wants to stay in with me on the terrace instead of having dinner with Maddie and her family.

I sigh. I want to tell him I can't stop thinking about last night. That the relief I felt seeing he was okay at the beach earlier was a lot more than worry over a friend. That in the short time we've known each other, he is proving to be built in a way I didn't know a man could be. I want to apologize for being so callous this morning. But I can't. This whole thing is set up to fail. "Nope, it's all yours" is all I manage.

I type *idiot* into the document open on my laptop, trying to decide if I mean him or me.

He kicks himself off the rail and takes a step toward me. "Are we good?"

"Yes, of course. Why wouldn't we be?"

Because we had incredible, mind-blowing sex less than twenty-four hours ago and my vagina is pissed it can't happen again and if I'm being brutally honest, so is my heart, and now you're off to dinner with another girl.

"Should we talk about last night?" he asks, an uncertainty in the round of his eyes.

I swallow hard. Of course we should talk about it. But I don't see how anything either of us might say will change the set of circumstances that make him and me a bad idea. "No need. Enjoy your shower." I keep my words as light as I can manage, not looking up from my screen, because I don't know if I can offer him a convincing face.

He folds his arms and surveys me a bit longer while I try to will him away. Eventually, he sighs and makes his way to the bathroom, and all I can picture is Maddie wrapped around him, clinging to his arm and beaming up at him through her fake eyelashes, which somehow managed to stay perfectly intact as she almost drowned.

As it nears eleven, my patience is wearing thin. Charlie left for dinner three hours ago and has yet to return to the suite. I've checked the time every four minutes. Sometimes three. I picture Maddie giggling at his gray T-shirt—this one reads SO MUCH PANIC, SO LITTLE DISCO—stroking his arm as she does. When I can't take it anymore, I down the remaining wine in my glass, remove my resort robe, hit save on my game progress—pleased, as I am quickly approaching a reasonable finish—and head downstairs.

It's a chilly evening, the coldest we've had since we've been here. The earlier barely there breeze is now a vicious gust that chills my insides. I wrap my duster tightly around my center as I make my way beachside.

At the restaurant, most of the tables have emptied and I spot them almost immediately. Her parents have gone, so it's just Charlie and Maddie, sitting together on a ledge outside the dining area, facing the dark sea. They both have drinks in hand, which I believe to be rum punch from the tangerine color. As I step closer, Maddie laughs. It's this huge, snorty laugh, and she presses her palm into his forearm, just as I imagined.

I'm about to brush it off, the whole thing—her fangirling over him, her supposed almost drowning, her snorty laugh—but then he turns and looks at her and he's smiling. This genuine, gorgeous smile that pushes his dimple deep into his cheekbone, and my stomach drops. I've walked into an intimate moment.

I silently curse biology, the higher levels of oxytocin in women released after sex, blaming it for my unwelcome feelings of attachment.

In our little bubble over the last few days, away from all the things that have dulled us both, Charlie and I have built something. What, I'm not quite sure—but seeing him look at another woman that way, it makes whatever we have a little less . . . Kix.

As I trek back to the suite, I build a whole picture of a life between Charlie and Maddie, these two beautiful, charmed people. I picture a summer beach wedding, him in a navy blue suit and barefoot, her in a silky slip dress. I imagine them with perfectly tanned kids with names like River and Lake and Stream and Puddle. Summers in Hawaii. Sunday dinners with her parents.

Back inside, I crawl into bed, missing Finn, counting the minutes until I can be back with him. The bedside clock strikes midnight and I half expect to see Charlie standing at the bedroom door in his robe, ready to pounce on me again.

Or was that simply some tropical fever dream?

It doesn't matter. I just have to get through one more day of this trip.

30.

THE NEXT MORNING, I CAN FEEL THE END OF MY TIME WITH CHARLIE looming. I'm confident about the game, poised to earn the job at Catapult and start this new chapter, should they choose me. But I'm also disheartened that this bubble of time with him is just about over. Yes, Charlie lives just across the hall. But he and I aren't a thing. And, across the hall is a world apart when we've been sharing a suite for the last six days.

I throw on denim cutoffs and a cream JOSHUA TREE NATIONAL PARK tee. I already know where to find Charlie. On the terrace, he's in his usual spot, right foot propped up against the rail.

"Morning," I say, more cautiously than intended.

"Hi. Look, I'm glad you're up." He stands. He's wearing a white T-shirt with Nicolas Cage's face on it, JOHN TRAVOLTA written above. "I just want you to know, there's nothing going on with that Maddie girl. She's nobody."

I flinch, remembering his message to his friend Jacob on the plane. "It's whatever, Charlie. You can and should do what you want."

He looks at me with impossibly big eyes and I turn away so I don't get sucked in.

"Let's just enjoy our last day here. Can we, please?" I plead. "Unless you have other plans."

His eyes forcibly find mine again and it's a reservoir of things unsaid. I'm just not sure speaking will help.

"Don't you have to work on the game?"

"I've finished it."

"You did?"

"Yes, last night." *While you were at dinner laughing and drinking with Maddie.*

"How could you possibly build the whole thing so fast?"

I decide to spare him the details—the use of a prebuilt engine, graphics pulled from my existing portfolio, knowledge accumulated from six years of coding camp, and all the games I've built that no one else has ever seen. My general lack of sleep over the last few nights, working a few times until the first winks of sunrise. Instead, I say, "I leveraged a lot of research and work I've done over the years."

I know I could stay sequestered in the suite today, toying with it some more, second-guessing my choices. Though I feel the impending deadline with Catapult, I trust my designs, perhaps for the first time. And I feel this time with Charlie ending. For today, I want to choose him.

"That's fantastic. Congrats, Sloane. Really. Is it weird to say I'm proud of you?"

"Yes," I say, but I can't avoid the small semblance of a smile.

"We should celebrate. What do you have in mind?"

Relief overtakes me. For one more day, life can be paradise. We can, the two of us together, suspend reality for the next twenty-four hours.

"Well, for starters, it's our last morning, so . . ."

"I'll call room service."

"We are the reason all-inclusives increase their fees," he says as he holds the phone to his ear.

When the food arrives, we eat on the terrace. It's a cloudless morning, as if the downbeat weather of yesterday never happened.

"How'd you get your bad shoulder?" I ask him through a mouthful of mango.

"What made you think of that?" he responds through a bite of chocolate chip muffin. Despite the array of options, we've both gone back to our favorites.

"I don't know. I've just been wondering." I wonder about a lot of things concerning Charlie. I still want to know all the roles he's ever played. I want to flip through his T-shirt drawer and evaluate each one, like an old record collection. I want to know if Brooke was his first heartbreak. We are barreling toward our impending end, and I've got to immerse myself in all things Charlie before we get there.

"I tore it during a baseball game in college."

"I didn't know you played baseball." I picture him in his helmet, cleats, jersey tucked into crisp pin-striped pants.

He nods. "Center field. I caught a fly ball in the seventh, threw it to third. Got the out, but it ended my season."

"Did you play again?"

He shakes his head. "Can't really anymore." He presses his fingers into his shoulder absent-mindedly.

"I'm sorry that happened."

I watch as his face takes on a stoic expression. There's a lot more to Charlie than spray-on abs. So much more. He's lost things too. Not just a relationship, but other things that were important to him.

I wonder if his love of fishing grew out of a desire to find something else that fulfilled him, to fill the void after baseball was gone. I picture him, out at dawn, tranquil on the water. It's a dying skill, being quiet. One Charlie has seemingly mastered.

His features are sharp. Not sad, not angry, but thoughtful with a sort of longing that makes something in my stomach sting. I'm desperate to lift his mood. "What was your walk-up song?"

"What?" he asks, and I watch as he reemerges from his internal retreat.

"Your walk-up song. When you played baseball. What was it?"

His face softens and I'm immediately warmed by the change in his demeanor.

"'I Did Something Bad,'" he says through a prideful smile, taking another bite of his muffin. "Taylor Swift."

I press my lips together, charmed. Now that I've gotten to know him, its endearingly on brand. Perfectly Charlie.

We grow quiet, the calm and beauty of this last day washing over us. The scene below us is largely quiet. I imagine beach-goers still lazily waking up, ordering breakfast, lackadaisically changing into swimsuits before heading down to the water as they embrace the island's unhurried luxury.

"I've always been almost good enough," he says after some time. His words fall onto my chest, an added layer onto the same feeling that already exists in me. "I played baseball and thought I might have a shot at going pro, but my shoulder kept me from doing that. I thought acting would be my backup plan, but now I spend far more time serving platters of truffle fries at The Wexley than auditioning."

"I've had those truffle fries. They're excellent." I lean in. "But your big break could come anytime, right? Isn't that how the industry works?"

He nods. "An acting coach once told me that talent and skill aren't the things that determine whether you'll make it. It's stamina. Being willing to do the work past the point where others might give up."

I think about my own situation. "Gaming is sort of the same. Being a game designer may seem cool, and it is, but it's also tedious work. I think a lot of people aren't willing to do the work."

"I can see that," he says. "And then I thought, maybe if I settle down, I'd finally succeed at *something*. It's idiotic, now that I think about it. That I was so wrong about Brooke."

"It's not idiotic, Charlie. It's just human."

"I guess. I just don't know how I could have gotten it all so wrong."

We stare in comfortable but weighted silence at the tranquil setting below. I think about Zane, how far I've come since officially meeting Charlie less than two weeks ago.

Sex with Charlie was unabashed. It was as much about me—my pleasure—as it was his. Actually, no. It was even *more* about my pleasure than his, and the two were directly intertwined. I think back to my sex life with Zane. How it was mostly doggie on the bedroom floor, his favorite combination. How, despite my knees growing raw, I never suggested we change it up. How the only times he said I love you first were when coaxing me down to the scratchy, straw-like carpeting of his apartment.

Sex with Zane was transactional. A morning quickie before he'd jet to the shower to get ready for work. An end-of-day romp to help him sleep. It was my fault too, not just his, that this was our sex life. I rarely initiated, so felt beholden to oblige when he was interested. When we got back together, I tried to sexualize myself, so he'd have so much sex he couldn't imagine looking elsewhere. That he'd be so satiated the thought of new vaginas would disgust him. It didn't work out that way though.

I never thought my pleasure—my dreams, my needs—mattered as much as my partner's. But with Charlie, my wants and needs are at the forefront of myself like they have never been before.

"Do you still believe in love?" I ask Charlie. My voice comes out unintentionally childlike.

He turns to face me, his eyes filled with the intensity of two nights ago when he told me I was *everything*. "Absolutely."

"Really?"

"Yes." I watch his chest rise and fall. "I can't imagine a world where we don't still fight for love," he continues. "Even in your post-apocalyptic worlds, isn't love the driving theme? Even *Arsonist Betty* is setting fires as a result of her broken heart. Without it, we'd just be passionless zombies."

I chew the inside of my cheek, wondering if he can feel the heat radiating off me.

"What's next?" he asks after we've gorged ourselves full of mango and chocolate chip muffins. We've also downed mimosas, Charlie having gotten over his day one aversion. Somewhere inside I know I'll regret it, but another, louder part of me wants to keep the buzz going. The complication of everything Charlie-related melts away with each drink and slowly gets replaced with fun. It's hard to argue with pure fun.

"I have an idea," I tell him as we enjoy mid-morning rum punches at the restaurant bar. It's eleven a.m., and they've barely opened, so we have the place largely to ourselves.

"Please tell me your idea involves more rum punch," Charlie says, the bright pink straw from his drink never leaving his mouth. His mouth . . . on my neck . . .

I clear my throat.

"Obviously more rum punch, yes. But also something else. Do you trust me?" His eyes are even paler than usual against the aquamarine sea behind him.

"I feel like that's a trick question."

"How so?"

"Because if I say yes, you're not gonna tell me what you've got in mind."

"True."

"And if I say no, I don't trust you?"

I smile coyly and take a sip of my drink. "And you'd never know what brilliant thing you've missed."

He takes half a second to contemplate, conviction derived from rum punch. "Fine. Yes, I trust you."

I knew he'd say yes, of course. It's classic psychology and a key component in game theory. If given the option to take a chance or miss out, there's a statistically higher probability of saying yes. FOMO is a real bitch.

"Great, give me five minutes." I jump from my seat and make my way to the concierge before Charlie can change his mind.

Before I can.

31.

FIFTEEN MINUTES LATER, WE'RE IN A SHUTTLE DRIVEN BY ANDRES.

"Are you going to tell me where we're going?" Charlie asks, though he's sipping his third rum punch and doesn't particularly seem to care.

"It's a surprise," I say, then suck at the straw in my own glass. I wonder if drinking in a resort shuttle is legal here, and then contemplate why I'm only asking myself this question now.

"Do you want to take a picture? To post?" I ask.

He shakes his head. "I told you, I've come to my senses. I don't want to get back together with her. It's over, as it should be."

I cross my legs in his direction as I evaluate him. I also realize we haven't taken a picture together for him to post since that first dinner, which feels like ages ago.

Andres turns up the radio and is bopping along, his head and the shuttle bouncing in unison. And then, in a moment of proof that the universe has a truly twisted sense of humor, the first notes of a familiar song fill the shuttle.

To my surprise, Charlie closes his eyes, presses his brows together, and sings.

"Give me the Beach Boys and free my soul, I wanna get lost in your rock 'n' roll and drift away . . ." His hand sways his rum punch back and forth.

I tilt my chin toward him. "What did you say?"

He opens his eyes. "What?"

"What did you just say?" I repeat, the smile across my mouth unavoidable.

"I'm singing the song."

"Yeah, but you said, 'give me the Beach Boys.'"

"And?"

"It's 'give me the *beat*, boys,' not Beach Boys."

He considers for a moment, then shakes his head. "No, I'm pretty sure it's Beach Boys."

"Charlie, no," I say, now in a full-on laugh.

We both listen intently as the next chorus hits.

". . . Give me the Beach Boys," he belts as I simultaneously sing, "Give me the beat, boys" with equal fervor. It's evident we both believe whoever sings louder is right.

"Andres, please, set him straight."

"Ah no, no lovers' quarrels for me."

I don't even think to argue Andres's comment.

Charlie looks at me with faux indignation, but the curl at the corners of his mouth gives him away. He doubles down. "It's Beach Boys."

"That doesn't even make sense."

"Yeah, it does." He stops to take a long sip from his straw, his wet lips curled tightly around the tip, like—

STOP.

"How does that possibly make sense?"

"Because, it's like, listening to the Beach Boys frees your soul." He speaks with such gravitas I almost believe he might be right.

I give him an exaggerated frown. "Are you willing to die on this hill?"

"I'm googling it," he says, grabbing his phone from his lap.

I lean back in the seat, making a show of getting comfortable.

I eye him intently as he types into his phone, scrolls, reads. Then, after a moment, he places his phone on his lap and looks out his window at the ocean.

"Well, fuck."

"At least you're pretty," I say, equal parts consoling and mocking. I pat the side of his face with my open palm the way I might Finn.

He glares at me, but once again, the upturned corners of his mouth give him away.

A few minutes later, Andres alerts me our destination is close, and I pull a scarf from my tote. Technically, it's the sash I wore during our winning synchronized swimming routine—made of fabric from Bacon Bit II's floral robe. I figure I should take every opportunity at a dig I can.

"Turn, please." I hold the scarf out in front of me, taut from one hand to the other.

"A blindfold, really? What kind of kink is this?"

"I told you, it's a surprise. No kink."

"Where was this during my servant day?" he says in a sunken proclamation that makes my skin tingle. "Just don't cover my mouth. I need my punch."

"Deal."

I tie the scarf around his eyes and as my hand grazes the back of his head, I'm reminded of the feel of it against my inner thighs. I feel like a preteen rewinding a sex scene in a movie to watch it over and over again.

When we pull up to the building, Andres opens the door and I climb out of the shuttle, grabbing ahold of Charlie's hand to lead him inside. Holding hands with him out in the world is a first, and I can't help but pay attention to the sensation of his long, thick fingers clasping mine. Then, with seeming ease that causes a rise of heat at the base of me, Charlie interlaces his fingers with mine and squeezes.

When we open the door, a bell jingles, and a man with a now-familiar Caribbean lilt welcomes us. I lead Charlie to the center of the room and remove his blindfold. He squints, then assesses our surroundings. First the art on the walls. Then the man in front of us. Finally, the line of three dental-like chairs at the far end of the room.

Once he's taken it all in, his attention settles on me. "Tattoos? I don't do needles." His eyes are narrowed and there's a slight slur in his *s*'s.

I face him. "Hear me out."

"I'll give you two a moment," our greeter says and then steps behind a curtain. There's only one other customer, in the far chair, the buzz of the needle sounding like a saw on his wrist. The tattoo artist looks up and gives us a Joker-like smile, teeth to his ears and distinctive eyebrows highly arched.

"Nope, not doing it," Charlie says, turning toward the door.

"Wait." I cuff his forearm with my hand. I can't explain why exactly, but I know being here will help him. I know, because I feel like it'll help me too.

Through an exhale, I begin to tell him the things he's wanted to know that I haven't been able to share. The things I *want* to share with him because I trust him. "Zane is my ex-boyfriend. Almost fiancé, actually. At least that's what he led me to believe." Charlie leans his shoulder into the column beside him as if the weight of my words has pushed him over. He has wanted this information, assumed it was there, since we met.

And I want him to know it. To know me.

32.

I CONTINUE BEFORE I CAN STOP MYSELF. "WE WERE TOGETHER ALMOST four years. We met at puppy adoption day at the animal shelter on my street. Our street." I point back and forth between us and swallow my saliva that has grown thick. "We were both sitting on the linoleum floor, covered in dog hair, leaning over the makeshift fence trying to get the attention of this adorable puppy that looked a lot like a yellow Lab." Charlie winces and I know he knows I mean Finn. That I met Zane the same day I met Finn. "Zane was making kissing noises and patting his legs."

Charlie raises his eyebrows.

"It was adorable, actually. Eventually, Finn stopped playing with the other dogs and plopped down between us, Zane petting his little head. I got his butt and tail. Anyway, we started talking, mostly about how this was a thing we both did. It was incredibly endearing, that he had this same secret activity as me—showing up at adoption day just to play with the puppies . . . and not be so lonely on a Saturday morning." I practically wheeze when I say this last part. It's like I've sliced myself right down the middle and my guts are pouring out of me, spreading toward the toe of his gray flip-flop like a spill of oil. Admitting loneliness feels like the ultimate vulnerability.

Something changes in Charlie's face. A slight recoil or release of its tight hold.

"He stayed while I signed all the paperwork for the dog I had no plan to leave with. He helped me pick out supplies for Finn. We went and had lunch after, just like that, covered in dog hair, Finn in my lap at one of the sidewalk tables at Marv's. When I told Zane I was naming him after a *Buffy the Vampire Slayer* character, he said it made him think of a game. *Finn the Bird Hero*. I learned then he was a gamer too. I called Tess when I got home and told her I thought I'd met The One." I force out a breath, shake my head at my own idiocy.

"He sounds like a good guy," Charlie offers.

"He was, until he wasn't."

Charlie straightens in preparation for the blow that's coming.

"On Christmas Eve last year, he was supposed to come to my family's house for dinner. He was running late, had to stop at UPS to send a last-minute package to his parents, which is so stupid because who waits until the twenty-fourth to send Christmas presents—"

Charlie wraps his hand around my wrist and it grounds me. His grip says it all. *You're safe.*

"So when I got the text, I assumed it would be him saying he was on his way." My voice creaks. I take a breath in an attempt to control it.

"What did it say?" he asks.

"It said, 'Sorry I can't see you until later tonight.' Then some silly excuse about trying to leave his 'idiotic' office holiday party as soon as possible."

Charlie squeezes my wrist.

"It wasn't even a good lie. What company has a holiday party on Christmas Eve, anyway?" I mutter.

"Who was she?"

I picture perky, shiny Jenna doing squats, wearing a sports bra and those leggings that bunch just above the butt crack. "The cliché of it kills me more than anything. He cheated with a girl from the *gym*." I can't help but emphasize *gym* as if that place is somehow responsible for turning Zane unfaithful. "The worst part is, I took him back. Even after he had cheated on me, broke our trust, I took him back. We stayed together four more months after that. Until a day in late April when he asked me to meet at his apartment to tell me he was leaving me. For her. The same girl he cheated on me with. And had continued to cheat on me with for those additional four months."

Charlie releases a sharp breath, hand still cupped around my wrist, grounding me.

"And now they're engaged. I don't know if that makes it better or worse. That he left me for someone he really cared about rather than cheating with some random girl."

Charlie's face hangs like a picture frame on a loose nail. I know he can empathize all too well. "Which would have been worse?" he says, his voice suddenly hoarse.

I will my eyes to meet his. "It doesn't matter. The betrayal is still the same."

He nods with a gentle motion.

"I used to think that Zane and I were good," I continue. "That him cheating was what broke our otherwise solid relationship. The thing I've been realizing, though, over time, but also from watching you struggle through your feelings about Brooke, is that we weren't good. Not ever, really. I was never comfortable, never myself. I was always trying to live up to the expectation of who I thought someone as put together as Zane was meant to be with. And that last part, that's on me. Not him."

Charlie lowers his hand, interlaces his fingers once more with mine and squeezes. Something inside me cracks, sharp and precise, like the snap of a tendon or ribcage pried open.

"Some days, it feels like Zane owns me," I say, my eyes filling. "Like he took control and there's no way for me to break free of his hold. It was death by a thousand give-ins with him, losing myself a little each time."

"I'm sorry," Charlie says, and I know he gets it. How Zane forever changed my insides. It's a little less pristine in there, like he forced in a smoker's lung or a metastasizing tumor.

"Which is why it's been so difficult watching you try to win Brooke back. You deserve so much more than someone who would do that to you."

He looks up at the concrete ceiling and his lips part. Then he looks back at me, his blue eyes glowing. "So do you," he says.

I nod. "So I've been thinking since we've been here, far away from our former captors, that I kind of want there to be a part of me that Zane doesn't get to know. Something new, something changed. Something to show he doesn't own me. Not anymore."

Charlie squeezes my hand. "Thank you for letting me in." And then, moving his face close to mine, "I'm not Zane."

My throat tightens. And I'm not Brooke.

He looks around the shop again, his eyes resting on each of the photos of tattoos on the walls. Finally, he shifts his eyes back to me, and they are slightly bloodshot but alert. For the moment, he is sober. And a little somber.

"Would this be your first?"

I nod. He doesn't have to tell me it would be his too.

"What are you gonna get?" he asks, his voice gravelly.

"I'm not sure yet. Does that mean you're in?"

His eyes roam the shop once more. "I'm in."

I encircle my arms around his neck and press into him. He wraps his arms around my waist and squeezes me back. For a fleeting moment, I think we might kiss. He seems to be contemplating it too, his eyes taking on that searching quality that calls to my lips like a gravitational force. It doesn't matter whether we do or don't, though—the connection here, in this moment, is the same as if we did.

"Are the lovebirds ready?" asks the tattoo artist, who has reemerged.

I release our embrace and lead Charlie to the books on the counter with design ideas.

"You're sure you want this?" I ask him. "I don't want to be responsible for a permanent drunken mistake."

"I want this," he says with a fierceness that makes me want to grab onto him again and not let go.

We both flip through the pages of individual books as Harry, one of the tattoo artists, joins us after finishing with his other client. Harry stands across the counter thumbing through a worn magazine, patiently awaiting our decisions. I scan the countless options, wondering if there will be anything that strikes me enough to brand myself with permanently. The possibilities range from intricate floral patterns to animals to celebrity portraits. I contemplate a few. A video game controller, a Labrador's face, a pair of palm trees that fall perfectly together, reminiscent of the view from our terrace. I always thought if I got a tattoo, it would be something from one of my own games, a character or graphic that I hold dear. But now that I'm here, I'm compelled to choose something new.

On the second to last page, I know immediately I've found The One.

"This one," Charlie says at the same time I affirm, "Got it!"

We hold up our respective books, each pointing to our chosen design, staring at each other in disbelief.

"Oh my goodness! These lovebirds are real soulmates!" exclaims Harry. I think to correct him, that we are not lovebirds or soulmates, just two people trying to get over our exes. But I can't formulate the words, because I can't get over the fact that Charlie and I are pointing to the same exact image. Of the hundreds, maybe thousands, of ideas in these books, we've both decided on the same one.

"Dino!" Harry exclaims. "This calls for a side-by-side!"

Charlie and I continue to stare at each other, both of our mouths slightly ajar.

It's clear to me now there's something consequential between us, and it's far more than lust or mutual heartbreak.

We are positioned in the last two chairs in the line. Harry slowly lowers the needle to Charlie's wrist and just as it makes fleeting contact, Charlie jerks.

I grab his free hand, spanning the distance between our chairs. "If you need a safe word—"

"Kumquat," he whispers. "Kumquat, kumquat, kumquat." His smile gives him away—this isn't as torturous as he thought.

He sneaks a peek at the inside of his wrist as the needle makes contact. "I feel like Mrs. Crandall should be here for this," he says.

"Maybe we can take her to get one when we get back."

"This is so not something I ever thought I would do," he says. I think about his shirtless torso—that perfect, unblemished skin—and I almost want to tell Harry to stop.

"It makes sense for you though."

"How's that? This is my first and only tattoo." I'm propped on my side facing him, the waistline of my jean shorts folded down to reveal the tender skin just above my right hip.

"Because it fits you. It's got definite end-of-the-world vibes."

I look down at my hip. He's right, I think as the small needle buzzes against me. It does suit me.

When we've finished, Charlie and I stand side by side in front of the full-length mirror, admiring our new, matching ink.

I run a gentle thumb over the tender skin, slightly raised from its branding. The tattoo is small and will remain covered unless I'm at the beach, just mine. And a little bit Charlie's . . .

I can't take my eyes off the design.

A knife striking against flint, casting sparks.

A symbol of burning down the past, brightly lighting the future.

Flint, the long-term play when matches burn out.

"Okay," I say, recognizing that it does indeed fit me well. "What about you then? Why'd you pick it?"

He eyes his wrist. "Because—" he says, then halts. His face changes, like something is pulling it inward. He looks down at his wrist again. "It reminds me of Mrs. Crandall."

I keep watching him as he examines his wrist, unable to evade the nagging thought I can't escape.

Charlie and I are now branded together.

This might be exactly the opposite of distancing myself from him.

33.

POST-TATTOOS, WHETHER DUE TO THE ENTERTAINMENT WE ARE providing or his general lack of responsibilities for the afternoon, Andres decides to take us on an impromptu tour of the island. We stop at the Cheshire Hall Plantation, now mostly in ruins, where Andres regales us with its Loyalist history. We meet his friend Alec, the beer maker at Turk's Head Brewery, who leads us through a tour of the facility, showing us the steel casks that are nearly two stories tall. We even stop in at a storefront in the Saltmills Plaza, which turns out to be a non-profit rescue organization for potcakes, a unique breed of island dog.

Watching Charlie roll around on the ground with playfully nipping puppies, I try to commit the moment to memory. Charlie, without realizing it, has given me a gift. He has helped take that first meeting with Zane and push it out of its lodged spot in my brain, replaced by this one.

As we stumble off the shuttle back at the resort, we are in a post-tattoo, mid-intoxication euphoria. We laugh when Charlie catches the front edge of his flip-flop on the rug in the lobby and nearly falls on his face. We find Mr. and Mrs. Mustache exiting the elevator and run over to hug them. And we nearly miss our floor because we're doubled over in laughter when we see our reflections in the mirrored elevator wall, our hair ratted and matted (mostly mine), the waist of my shorts rolled down to allow my tattoo to breathe. His wrist is covered in plastic wrap.

When we are alone in the suite, he leans against the back of the door, lips parted, chest rising and falling from the exertion of breathing after so many cocktails and so much laughter. From a few feet away, next to the couch, I stare at him, my bliss quickly morphing into something else. It's as though there's a wasp trapped in my rib cage. The whole scene is entirely reminiscent of two nights ago. Of him rushing the room service delivery so we could be alone again. I can practically smell the burnt sugar of the soufflé, feel the crackly condom wrapper pressed between my thumb and forefinger. My face must give me away, because the playful smile that has adorned his face for the last several hours has dulled, replaced with a clenched jaw and hands he's rubbing in small circles in front of him. Back in our suite, alone for the first time since this morning, it's as though anything is possible. And the excitement of that anythingness is surging through my veins.

I told myself just one night.

Just one.

But why? Why, when we still have today, what remains of it? How does one more time change anything? Either way, we leave tomorrow and this beautiful bubble of time with Charlie ends. This little world of our creation—this period of fun and joy, indulgence and ease, all the complications of life so very far off—I feel it slipping away. And I desperately want to hold on to it for just a little while longer.

Fuck it, I think, shutting all opposing thoughts behind a mental door. We are still here, on this island, the fantasy of us still very much in play.

Fuck it.

I thought I only said those words in my head, but he heard them, because just like the other night, he is pushing himself off the door and is against me in an instant. I'm not sure where we connect first, his arm pressed around my back or our lips meshed urgently together. He lifts me from the waist with one wrapped arm, the other hand to the back of my head, ensuring our mouths remain connected. He lifts me so easily, barely off the ground so that my toes still sweep the floor as he walks us out to the terrace in two, maybe three long steps. There, he lowers me onto one of the chaises—the one that still carries the slight scent of cherry lube—and flattens the chair, then stands, towering over me, removing his shirt with one hand. God, it's sexy when he does things with one arm, one hand, as if there are so few things that require two-handed effort for a man built like him. I take in the bulge below his jeans and I'm instantly wet, knowing how satisfyingly he can maneuver it.

I scurry to undress, my jean shorts rubbing against the tender skin of my right hip as I slide them down, pain searing through me in a way I find rousing. When I'm down to my underwear (a matching black set this time, because my subconscious had my back this morning), he is already naked, pulling a condom from his discarded jeans pocket. "I hoped," he says in response to my pleased but questioning look.

He stands above me and I watch his cock rise, as though I'm the magnet it's charged to. He grins, his hair falling forward, cheeks and nose rosy from arousal and rum punch. He looks like a sculpture of what a man should be. Long and lean, built for use. Hands meant for grabbing and massaging, thighs built for stamina, eyes made to see all of me.

This time, he doesn't await my orders. He lowers himself to me. His arm presses on my lower back, lifting me slightly from the chaise so he can unclasp my bra, then tosses it to the ground. The light breeze catches us and my goosebumps are immediate.

There is no foreplay and I'm so very happy about it—I don't

need any more buildup, the want is already there, bursting from me like the flickers of a sparkler. This whole magnificent day has been more than enough to escalate my need for him. He enters me and it's not necessarily pure pleasure I feel, rather it's a long-grown discomfort finally ended. Relief. The first itch of an arm freshly out of a cast. The initial gulp of breath above the waterline after a deep dive.

While we are blocked from the sight of neighboring suites, there is indeed the added thrill of fucking outside like animals, and the intensity inside me grows more quickly than it ever has.

He slides into me again and again, relentless. He's not holding back and I don't want him to. The chaise creaks and rasps beneath us as it rocks with our unyielding motion.

There's an urgency, a need, that surpasses any need I've ever felt, an added intensity because I'm fucking him for what has to be the last time. There's pleasure, yes. So much of it. But also the agony of a fast-approaching, unmerciful end. He feels it now too. I know from the change in his movements. His full-force, unsparing thrusts change to slow and methodical slides, as if to memorize each millimeter of movement and the sensation it creates. He doesn't want it to end, but also desperately wants to feel the escalation. We are united in the same torturous dilemma.

"Charlie," I whisper into his neck, then run my tongue along his skin. He is salty and damp. I savor the taste of him, the sturdiness of his neck under my tongue. He stops, rises slightly, looks down at me. He brings his hand to the side of my face, then pins his lips to mine. It's the only soft thing about this interaction. It's the kiss of more than a lover, it's that of a boyfriend, a partner. Of someone who cares so much it scares them. It breaks me, that kiss. He doesn't see the single tear slide from the outer corner of my eye and disappear into my hairline, just above my ear.

He comes first, my fingertips pressed into his flexing backside. When it's my turn, he pays close attention as I close my eyes, tilt my chin in the balmy air toward the sky. When I come, just a moment later, his eyes are open, glued to mine as though he can't bear to miss it.

34.

AFTER A FEW MOMENTS' REST, WE SHOWER TOGETHER IN THE DARK, his hands serving as my loofah, sliding over every inch of my skin with great care.

We collapse into the lounge chairs on our terrace. I purposefully choose the one we just had sex on.

"This is my favorite place in all the world," I tell him, looking up at the now twinkling evening sky.

"Turks?"

"No, well, yes, but I mean here, specifically. These lounge chairs on this terrace." I turn toward him and he's grinning. "We should take a boat out tomorrow and find some remote island to live on so we can stay here forever," I say, wanting to extend this delirious enchantment as long as possible.

Charlie doesn't miss a beat. "Sounds good. We can build our own commune, completely shut off from the outside world."

"Like North Sentinel Island or that Leonardo DiCaprio movie *The Beach*."

He smiles. "Both of those end very badly for new arrivals. No new arrivals. That's key." He flicks his chin at me.

"Agreed. So do we bring others during the settlement, or is it just us?" I have a flash of an alternate life, Charlie and me alone on a remote island, covered in only loincloths and using rocks as hammers, Finn somehow with us. A perfect world of our creation, just like a video game.

"We'd probably need reinforcements. Andres. He's resourceful."

"Agreed. We'll definitely bring Andres. And maybe Mrs. Mustache and CrossFit Girl."

"Who?"

I shake my head. "Nothing. Never mind."

The sky is an early deep blue, full of stars, unobstructed and magnificent. It is wholly resemblant of our last intimate night together. As I sit here, next to Charlie, staring up at the endless void, I can't help but think wistfully about the equal grandness and quaintness of stargazing.

"Wasn't that Leo beach movie filmed somewhere around here?" he asks.

"No. Thailand."

"You are a wealth of a diverse range of information," he says with a loose grin, then leans in toward me. "It's a great plan. One problem though."

"What's that?"

"There is no tomorrow."

I exhale sharply. He's right. Tomorrow we'll be on a plane back to LA.

I can't think about that right now. Instead, I take note of his hand, which is now on my thigh. He has found a way to remain touching me since we sat down.

I abruptly turn to face Charlie again. "Tell me your baby name."

He shakes his head. "I knew you were dying to know."

I slap his arm. "Of course I am. Tell me."

He presses his lips together in almost a pucker, sinking his dimple deep into his cheek. "Was this entire day built around getting me wasted so you could get this out of me?"

I curve my body toward him. "No, but in hindsight, it should have been."

He rolls onto his back, clasps his hands behind his head, and stares up again. "Fine." He speaks to the sky. "It's Loki."

"What? Wait—you want to name your kid after one of the bad guys in the Avengers films?"

"He's complex," Charlie says matter-of-factly. "And he had a redemption arc."

"Don't you have some family obligation to name your kid the next in the row? Alpha, Bravo, Charlie . . ."

"Delta," he finishes, then smiles. "I like to break the rules."

Just when I think I've figured him out. Charlie—who's unnerved by airplane turbulence and centipedes and needles. Who painted Mrs. Crandall's kitchen. Who sings the wrong lyrics and dances to Taylor Swift. Who played Gomez Addams in multiple high school productions. Who has a seemingly endless collection of punny T-shirts. Who in the dark of the shower mere minutes ago felt like a tower I wanted to climb. Who wants to name his yet-to-be-created child *Loki*. Who has endured heartbreak and is somewhere on the other side of it. He is none of the things I would have expected from the guy who showed up at my apartment door with the offer of this trip.

"There's a shooting star!" Charlie points to a moving light in the sky, slightly brighter than the others.

"That's a plane, Charlie."

He turns to face me with an expression that I can only describe as Kix. "Just pretend," he says gently, and his voice tugs at my belly like a magnet.

We sit just that way, silent, watching the sky, looking for shooting stars that might be airplanes. It's one of those scarce moments when I try with all my might to stop time. And when I fail, I grasp at the bits of it to tuck away, so I can remember it just so when it's all gone. The balmy breeze. The euphoric glaze of several rum punches. The comfort of Charlie beside me. And most of all, the thing that makes memories truly stick, the feeling inside me—one of unabridged contentment. It's a feeling so foreign to me over the last several months, I feared I'd lost it forever. But I'm pleased to now know, the body remembers.

When I believe I've stored the moment away adequately, I turn to face Charlie. "Tell me about Brooke. About your relationship." My request doesn't carry the same unease as before when mentioning Brooke. Not for me, and I don't believe for Charlie any longer either. Now I want to know because I want to know him—this significant part of him that brought us here. And how his views have changed over this past week and even the last few days since we last spoke about her.

He rolls to face me, and we lie on our sides, heads propped facing each other with an elbow against the head of our chairs, a sky of stars and airplanes overhead.

"Like you and Zane, it was incredible. Until it wasn't. I think back to those first few months and how surreal it was. How everything was better, brighter. She was like this tour guide into how life was supposed to be, how it was supposed to feel."

I pay attention to the way he speaks and his expression, but don't hear or see the nostalgia I expect. Instead, it's a factual recount.

"When she started working more closely with Spencer at their PR firm, things changed. That was a year in." He picks at a loose thread at the chair's edge. "It was like I was her favorite pair of jeans that somehow didn't fit anymore," he continues, and I imagine the ache inside of him. "I chased that feeling more than I actually had it."

It's a complicated sensation, I know, devaluing yourself in a desperate attempt to hang on to the thing that once made you more alive than you've ever been.

His jaw tightens and I imagine his insides are passing through a shredder.

"It'll pass," I tell him softly. "It will. You'll get over it—her—eventually."

He looks up at me with impossibly big eyes. "I already have."

"Charlie, it's only been a few days."

"Yeah, but being here, with you, has made time move at warp speed. It seems like things with Brooke ended months ago. Years, even."

I turn onto my back, stare up at the stars. I see one move, though I don't point it out to him. "You need more time," I tell him softly.

He shakes his head but doesn't speak further. I quickly become consumed by my own thoughts. This trip has included some of the best days I've had in a long while, maybe ever. Perhaps it's the location. Perhaps it's Charlie. Perhaps it's that, bit by bit, I am finding my shine again.

"I have an idea," he says eventually, a strike of energy taking him on. He stumbles up from the chaise, disappears into the suite, and returns with my laptop and two Turk's Head beers from our minifridge. He sets the laptop on my thighs and hands me a beer.

"You should send Catapult the game. Here. Now." His unwieldy grin reminds me of his post-coital one.

"What? No, I haven't written the email to go along with it. And I need to review the game one more time—"

Charlie leans in even closer, ensuring my attention remains on him. "You are incredibly talented, Sloane," he says to stop me.

"I know I am," I tell him. Because I do know it. And with Charlie, I don't have to pretend I don't. He smiles. A wide, closed-mouth smile as he gives me a slight nod. There's baffling solidarity in his gesture.

"Sloane, it's done. You said so yourself earlier today. So why not just send it from here, your favorite place in the world? Can you think of a better way to cap off this trip?"

I raise my eyebrows. He's got a point. I feel good about my game design. No, I feel *great* about it. During this implausible week, I've managed to build a prototype I'm proud of. One Zane shouldn't be able to beat.

But just one more review and round of tweaks could give it the edge it needs . . .

I'm still looking at Charlie when I open my laptop. Next to him, I feel the urge to take a chance, more strongly than I ever have.

He looks on as I copy the link to the game, type out an email to Jack Palmer and team, and, before I can talk myself out of it, I hit send.

And exhale.

To my surprise, Charlie leans over, pulls my chaise closer to his, then throws his arms around me. He inhales sharply through his nose.

"Are you crying again, you drunken sap?"

"No, of course not," he says, pulling away quickly, forearm to his eyes.

"C'mon, lemme buy you dinner," I say, pulling on the sleeve of his sweatshirt.

"It's an all-inclusive," he reminds me, though he knows I know.

"Well then, let's go get your money's worth."

He tilts his beer bottle toward me. "You don't think we have yet?"

"Not quite yet." I jump to my feet and grab his elbows to pull him up. As he stands, the space between our chairs is barely there and means that we are pressed against each other. I think about him on top of me just two nights before, again just an hour ago, the sound of his whispering voice in my ear. The skin at the nape of my neck chills.

He's thinking about it too. I know he is. Everything in this moment gives him away. The blush of his cheeks evident across his tan face. The blue of his eyes almost completely taken over by the black of his pupils. The slight twitch at the outer corner of his right eye. We stand like that, pressed together between the two chairs, and we might as well be naked, the way the breeze hits me at all points.

Our shirts graze and retreat as our chests rise and release in unison. Each time the fabrics make contact, it's like a knife striking against flint, orange glints of flame leaping out at each swipe. Just like our matching tattoos.

There's a lot I want to say to him, even more I want to do, my desire for him insatiable.

I bring my hand up to cup his wrist and our eyes catch. On the other side, I feel his hand graze mine, then his pinkie clasps onto mine, and it's the strongest handhold imaginable.

We stand like this, pinkie curled around pinkie on one side, my fingers wrapped around his wrist on the other, and I don't want to move. Not closer, not farther away, not at all. I want to stay here, just like this, in our spot on this terrace—to remain in this bubble with him forever, drinking and laughing and exploring each other like nothing else exists or matters.

A dull ache builds in my chest, knowing our time together is coming to an end. I'm desperate to hold on to him a bit longer, but also afraid that if I do, it will be that much harder to let him go.

"Let's go to dinner," I say eventually, releasing his wrist. "I'm starving."

35.

THE MOOD AT DINNER IS AKIN TO WHAT I IMAGINE THE LAST NIGHT OF a honeymoon to be like. We laugh, tease each other, drink, and are so merry it's like there really is no tomorrow. And certainly not a tomorrow where we go back to all the things we've tried to leave behind this week.

We both order jerk chicken and rum punch as a celebration and goodbye, and all the while Charlie eyes me from across the table with a discerning look, as if studying the mechanisms that make me run. Just as our food arrives, we're greeted by CrossFit Guy and CrossFit Girl, who are wandering back from a beach stroll.

"Hang on to this one," CrossFit Girl says, her Australian accent thick in the evening air. She squeezes my arm but looks at Charlie. "She's special."

Charlie nods sheepishly before saying, "She is."

Halfway through our meal, Charlie raises his almost empty glass. "To you, Sloane. To the incredible job and future that awaits you back home." He clinks my glass.

When the server comes to clear our plates and I can't possibly consume anything else, I contemplate ordering another drink just to have an excuse to stay a little longer.

"Do you want anything else?" I ask him. We've somehow inched closer as the evening has pressed on, the arms of our chairs touching. He's looking at me like he definitely wants something else, his jaw clenched, eyes narrowed, hands circling under the table. The moment is so intense that I clear my throat and push back in my chair. In need of an activity away from the table, I head to the bathroom for the seventeenth time today (so many drinks) and stare at my reflection in the mirror. My hair is frizzy, my cheeks are tinged pink, and my eyes have that hazy quality I've seen in Charlie's all day.

I try to lie to her, the woman staring back at me, though she won't allow it.

I want Charlie. And not just tonight, but all of him. For as long as he might have me.

I grip the sides of the porcelain sink and bend forward, the weight of the realization pressing into my shoulder blades.

"Oh, hi," a voice behind me says, echoing against the terracotta tiles. I rise to find Maddie's face in the mirror. I muster a smile then turn to face her.

"Are you with Charlie?" she asks.

Does she mean here at dinner? With him, as in dating? "I am, yes."

She nods, and I step aside so she can wash her hands. I stand awkwardly as she washes, having pressed myself into the corner of the narrow space, not wanting to ram past her to leave. "He's really into you, you know," she says as she shakes off the excess water.

I want to say, *No, I don't think so* or *He's just caught up in this trip*, but instead what comes out is, "Really?"

She smiles as she pulls a thick, napkin-like folded paper towel from the stack on the counter. "Yeah. He talked about you a lot at dinner."

I want to know what he said, specifically, but thankfully, she continues without my having to ask.

"He told me that you're about to land your dream job. How hard you've been working to get it. Congrats."

"Oh, thank you. It's not a guarantee I'll get it. I'm still in the interview process . . ."

She tosses her paper towel into the waste bin and faces herself in the mirror, plumping her curls at the sides of her face. "Well, the way he talked, there's no way you won't get it. He's pretty in awe of you, you know." She pulls a lip gloss from her cross-body bag and puckers, then applies it with precision—a bubblegum pink. Satisfied, she pops her lips together twice. Replacing the cap, she turns to face me. "I doubt any guy has ever talked about me that way." She walks to the door and grasps the handle, then turns to me before she walks out. "Enjoy the rest of your trip. I know I would, if I was here with him."

When she's gone, I take her spot in front of the mirror. I think, perhaps there is a way to have it all. To have Charlie and also the job. We live across the hall from each other. Perhaps if we never go out and stay in our apartment building, sneak between our apartments, we could make it work. It could be kind of exhilarating, a secret affair. I'll be working crazy hours with no time for much else anyway. Late-night trysts are all I could likely manage. Though I realize it wouldn't necessarily be the foundation of a real, healthy relationship, it would mean I get Charlie.

And since it's the last night, I want nothing more than to give in. As I make my way back to the table, I begin imagining how hot our sex could be this evening, knowing it's the last time. The way it was earlier. Or, if there is another time, it will look very different than the here and now.

When I take my seat beside him again, I'm going to tell him we should go. Now. I want to race back to the suite, undressing as we go. I want to grab onto his flexed biceps as he hovers over me. Feel his hot breath against the side of my neck as he thrusts against me.

He rests his hand on the arm of my chair and angles toward me, seeming to know what I want.

"Charlie," I say, leaning in so close I can smell the sweet punch on his breath.

"Sloane," he responds, so playfully I don't need him to say anything else. I know he's in.

Before I can officially offer myself up on a cherry lube and condom-filled platter, a choir of voices interrupts from the far corner of the restaurant. Every diner turns to watch as a group of waiters assembles, whooping and cheering and whistling.

There are six waiters in total, two holding the sides of a platter (not the kind I had intended) with a cake, sparklers shooting off the top of it. They are headed in our direction. *Wow, this is quite the send-off*, I think. *I'll be leaving a five-star review for sure.*

It's not until they set the platter between us that I begin to comprehend what is happening. There, on a tall, round cake, coated in white icing with delicate pink chocolate strips lining the rim, written in bright yellow icing: WERE ENGAGED.

Were engaged? Who was engaged? Were Charlie and I engaged?

The waiter quiets the others and clears his throat, then bellows his announcement to the other patrons. "Congratulations to our newly engaged couple!" he says, arms outstretched.

Then the applause begins. Everyone's eyes are upon us, beaming as they clap. Why wouldn't they? Love loves love, and all of them are in love. The Bacon Bits have risen from their seats at a table a few feet away.

Finally, it clicks. *WE'RE* ENGAGED. A simple case of a missing apostrophe. Had I consumed fewer cocktails today, the recognition likely would have hit me much sooner.

I want to laugh at the absurdity. Somehow, Charlie and I have played loving couple so well on this trip that we've convinced everyone we are newly engaged. Perhaps there is a real, visible connection between us.

I'm about to give Charlie a good-natured elbow to the ribs

or play along and plant one on him in front of everyone, making a big show of it. We will most certainly laugh about this for some time. But then I see the tears welling in his eyes as he stares down at the cake, and I know instantly—they are not for me. I realize it all in this moment, in the expression on his face.

It's the grand gesture I've always wanted; it's just not for me.

I've been playing house in a picture frame that holds someone else's photo. I sat here at this final dinner, wondering if Charlie and I could somehow make it outside this bubble in paradise, and all the while, he was meant to propose to his ex at this restaurant, at this table, on this moonlit night on this white sand beach. Despite all the signals that he is not over *her*, I've misread the situation completely.

"You were going to propose. To Brooke." In my head, I meant to pose it as a question, but my words come out an unwavering statement.

Charlie looks up from the cake and in his big eyes, the slack of his jaw, I receive confirmation of the truth I already understand.

"I'm not feeling well. I'm gonna head up to the room," I tell him in a voice so soft I hardly recognize it as my own. By the time I've finished the sentence, I'm already halfway to the exit.

"Sloane," I hear him call after me, and it's reminiscent of that first night at the bar, him calling after me. Perhaps I should have kept running then.

I get to the suite and Charlie is half a step behind me when I enter. "Sloane, would you wait," he says as I instinctively head to my seat on the terrace.

"It's fine, Charlie. I'm nobody, right?" I look at him, really look, for some kind of recognition of his words.

"Of course you're not nobody. Why would you even say that?"

"That's what you told your friend. On the plane. I saw your text."

His shoulders round. "Sloane, I wasn't calling you nobody. I just didn't want to get into it, having to explain all the details of—"

"Of our *arrangement*? Of how you've been using me to get Brooke back?" I'm defensive now, bent forward like a cat about to pounce. My face is burning hot. I imagine placing a hand across his cheek, likely ice-cold like his hands.

"I'm sorry I ever put you in that position. Really, I am. It was wrong. But you have to know things have changed . . ." He's holding his hands out in front of him as if he's carrying a large load, and my eyes track to the plastic still covering his new tattoo. Just a few short hours ago, we were inexplicably connected. Now I don't know what we are. I silently curse myself for letting him in.

"Yeah, you got laid. Just like you wanted, actually. Just like you had originally planned for this trip. I guess everything really did go according to plan."

A big part of me wants to console Charlie, because I know seeing that cake hurt him. I know he's trying to figure out his evolving feelings for Brooke, for me. But I'm also furious that I've allowed myself to develop a desire for someone who was never available.

His lips part a bit and his eyes fall to the ground, but then they rise again, this time filled with fiery anguish.

"Do you really think I kissed you back on that first night at the bar, banged on your door during a fire alarm to make sure you got out safe, invited you on this trip, kissed you, had the intimate moments we had, got *matching tattoos* . . . are you honestly telling me you think all of that was for show?"

"I don't know what to think."

"Then you don't know me at all," he says, turning on his heel and heading for the bathroom, closing the door behind him.

"You're right," I mutter to the empty space. "I don't."

36.

NEARLY TWENTY MINUTES LATER, I'M STILL STATIONED IN THE CHAISE on the terrace looking out at the stars. I see one move and think of our conversation just a few hours earlier. I tell myself that this time it's just an airplane.

Charlie emerges from the bathroom and pops his head around the corner of the open terrace door. "I'm gonna take a walk," he says. His cheeks and the tip of his nose are red. On the surface, he looks like any vacationer after a week's worth of sun exposure and all-inclusive cocktails. But in his eyes, I see the weight. Before I can say anything, he ducks back into the suite and I hear the front door close behind him.

I want to go and find him. Being alone in this suite we've shared all week suddenly feels wrong. A few minutes after he's left, I grab a hoodie and head downstairs. I go straight to the beach, knowing there are only so many private places around here. He sits in a yellow beach chair facing the water, the row of identical loungers beside him empty at this late hour.

The wind gusts around me and I zip my sweatshirt closed. I cautiously take the seat beside him.

"Hi," he says, and I'm immediately relieved that he's said *something*.

I feel the time slipping away. Tomorrow, we will be back in LA. "Look, I'm sorry . . ." I say, struggling to find the right words. But I have to try. "That must have been hard for you."

He turns to face me. "Not for the reasons you think. These past few days . . ." He runs his hand down his face. "They've been some of the best I've ever had. Being here, with you, made me realize not only that I don't want or need Brooke back, but that also . . . perhaps there's a better match out there for me." He holds my gaze. "Someone who aligns with me in every way."

The first thing I think is, *He is so brave. Braver than me.* His heartbreak just happened, but it clearly didn't fracture him the way mine did me. He is capable of and willing to be vulnerable and honest, no matter the outcome.

Brave.

I want to tell him that I'm falling for him. I want to salvage this night, hold out hope that it still somehow ends with us disrobed together in that palatial resort bed. But I can't. There are so many reasons I just can't go there with him. He was ready to *propose* to someone else just a little over a week ago. More than just the job at Catapult, this truth keeps me from giving in.

"It's a bit unrealistic, isn't it? To think someone can be the perfect fit. A week ago, you thought that perfect fit was Brooke."

"Maybe . . . maybe you're right," he says, and it feels as though he's calling my bluff. He lets out a heavy sigh and puts his head in his hands.

"Do you want my emotional support hoodie?" I ask.

He lifts his head and faces me, the right corner of his mouth twitching upward in a half smile, though it doesn't reach his eyes.

"C'mon." I stand and offer a hand to help pull him up, still debating whether to give in to my feelings. Even though there's only a matter of hours left on this trip, I'm unsure if I can last mere minutes without laying it all on the line—without being brave like him.

My phone vibrates in my pocket, a reprieve from whatever this thing is that's happening between Charlie and me. "Get it," he says, voicing his permission to break our tension as though it's a welcome opportunity to regroup.

I don't want to focus on anything other than him, but I pull my phone out because I don't know how to solve for all the complications of us. Checking my phone is a much easier task.

"It's an email from Jack Palmer at Catapult," I say, frantically clicking at the screen.

I fall back into the chair and Charlie leans in close so he can see the screen. "What's it say?"

"Miss Cooper, thank you for your game concept submission. I've reviewed it briefly, and I must say, it was unexpected. A final decision will be made next week. Also, the attached photo was sent to me in an anonymous email this afternoon. Is this you?"

I open the attachment and there, filling the screen of my phone, is the picture of Charlie and me at dinner the first night of the trip. Holding hands across the table, smiling like a couple on a romantic getaway. The picture Charlie posted to win back his ex. I cannot believe I didn't adequately consider that Charlie's posts would get back to the team at Catapult. I let myself trust that being three thousand miles away would somehow keep my secret. That Charlie not tagging me and turning his account private was enough.

I knew this trip was a bad idea. And all my fears have been confirmed in this one-paragraph email from Jack Palmer. The one person I wanted to impress more than anyone, ever.

Charlie furrows his brow. "What does he mean that your game was *unexpected*?"

I have to reread the email. So consumed by the photo, my brain skipped over registering that part completely. I toggle over to my sent emails and pull up the message I sent a few hours earlier. "Oh my god."

"What?" Charlie's scanning the screen, but doesn't get it until I click on the link I sent Catapult. "Oh. Shit."

Now he gets it.

I did not send the team at the top gaming company in the world the link to the well-developed prototype of *Arsonist Betty*, which would have fit perfectly into their existing portfolio, and possesses undeniable commercial potential. No. Instead, in my drunken haze, I sent Jack Palmer the revenge cheese-throwing game I built for Charlie in a day to make him feel better about Brooke.

A tide of shame and embarrassment rushes over me, rendering me unable to move.

"Don't worry, Sloane, you can fix this. Respond now with the link to the real game and an explanation about the picture."

"And say what exactly? Sorry, king of the gaming industry Jack Palmer, but I decided to take a romantic trip out of the country while I was supposed to be preparing for my final interview, even though I told you I was solemnly single, and after seventy-five rum punches, I accidentally sent you a game where you *throw cheese at someone's face*!"

"You don't have to say all that. Just say it was a mistake. People make mistakes."

"It's too late. They'll forever think of me as the cheese girl who lied about being single."

"It's not too late, Sloane."

"I knew I should have waited to send the email. I never should have come on this trip in the first place." The rage and disappointment in me bubbles over, Charlie the only available target in my path.

"Do you really believe that?" When I don't respond, he continues, "Funny. Here I thought . . ."

I push a wisp of hair from my face as the wind gusts around us. "You thought what? I know your type, Charlie."

"My type." He crosses his arms and raises his chin, daring me to go on.

"Yes, your *type*. LA actor with a dimple." I'm grasping, but I've lived in LA my whole adult life. I can't imagine that who he has presented himself to be could actually be true. It's just too . . . good.

He leans forward, his volume rising a bit. "You're judging me because of my dimple?"

"Oh yeah, I most definitely am. That dimple is unfair. It should be considered a weapon. A panty penetrator."

"A *what*? What is that, a character from one of your games? The Panty Penetrator? Be serious, Sloane."

"Oh, I am. This is the most serious thing ever." I point to the phone in my hand. "And it's all ruined now."

"It's ridiculous they care if you're on a romantic getaway! They shouldn't care about your personal life at all. It's not fair." His face has hardened with a quality of impenetrability.

My emotions are a runaway train and the final collision is in sight. "You don't get it!" I say, looking in his general direction but unable to make eye contact. "There's nothing fair about what I have to do to get a job like this. Not only do I have to prove my game development skills, but I also have to prove that it wouldn't be a mistake to hire a girl." Charlie stands there slack-jawed as I throw it all onto him. "Everything is stacked against me and I have to work that much harder. I can't make mistakes. It's not easy for me the way it is for Zane. Or for you."

"Easy for me?" he says, pressing his fingers into his chest. "What part of my life makes you presume it's easy? I spent money I didn't have on a trip to propose to the girl I now know I had no business proposing to, and I've been pursuing a dream that nobody believes in for *years*, just to be a joke in a spray-on abs commercial. And I've been trying and failing to fight my feelings for you all week, because I don't want to stand in the way of your dreams."

I shake my head, wondering if I've imagined his words. I put my phone back in my pocket and look back at Charlie. I can't address the last part of what he's just said, not yet, so instead I say, pathetically, "You're not a joke, Charlie."

"Sloane," he says pleadingly, though he can't seem to find words beyond the one.

When it's evident neither of us have the words to resolve anything in this moment, I say, "Let's just get packed and back to reality. I can't play house anymore. I'm sorry, Charlie. I really am."

37.

CHARLIE AND I BARELY SPEAK THE REST OF THE NIGHT AND SUBSEquent morning. We move robotically through the suite, gathering our things. When it's time to leave for the airport, we head to the shuttle together in silence.

Three different couples stop to congratulate us on our engagement and we both mutter thank-yous because it's easier than explaining the truth. I'm not sure I could if I tried.

CrossFit Girl is the last to find us before we step onto the shuttle and she wraps her powerful arms around my neck in either a choke hold or a hug.

"Congrats," she says when she releases me. "I'd team up with you again anytime. And my name's Sienna, love." She winks, then waves from the sidewalk as the shuttle pulls away.

I did as Charlie suggested last night and sent a follow-up email to the team at Catapult, explaining my mistake and sharing the correct link. I even told them the picture, which I'm assuming Zane somehow managed to find and send anonymously to Jack Palmer, is of me and a friend. Though after last night, I don't even know if I get to call Charlie a friend. I doubt my efforts will matter much anyway. I picture Zane's pompous face when he gets the offer and it makes me want to retch.

Charlie and I keep our interactions to a minimum on the flight home. When the plane lurches mid-flight, I hand him a mini Jack Daniel's bottle I snagged from the resort. A little later, he finishes the second romance novel and hands it back to me. Closer to home, I give his forearm a supportive squeeze as the plane bumps down through the cloud layer. Somehow, my hand slides down to his. We both watch as he releases the armrest and turns his hand to greet mine. Our fingers interlace. We hold tight to each other in silence, our final goodbye, until the plane touches down far too quickly and it's time to deboard.

Beads of rain pelt the plane's windows as we exit. It's a dreary return to LA.

Tess picks me up at baggage claim and I practically knock her over with my embrace. She is the only good thing about leaving paradise. Her and Finn. I feel Charlie watching us embrace, standing a few feet off to the side, and I can't help the bit of sadness that creeps in that he doesn't have someone here for him. Tess must sense the heaviness between Charlie and me, because she refrains from asking invasive but typical Tess questions like "So how many times did you two . . . ?" or "Why no obscene PDA?"

When my bag arrives, Charlie lifts it from the conveyor and sets it in front of me, then turns to look for his duffel.

"Need a ride?" I ask as he scans the circling luggage.

"No, I've got it," he says, decidedly too upbeat.

"We're going to the exact same building, Charlie."

He turns and looks at me. "Really, it's okay." He gives me a lukewarm smile, and the look in his eyes is clear. *I need you to go.* So, I do. It's a painfully unceremonious end to seven incomparable days I already miss.

"What was that about?" Tess asks as soon as we're out of earshot.

I shake my head, because how can I possibly explain this last week in a way that does it justice? "Don't worry about it." She starts to give me the Tess stare, so I shut it down the best way I know how. "Are you going to tell me about Loafers Guy?"

She grabs the handle of my bag and starts in the direction of the parking garage. "Don't worry about it," she calls over her shoulder.

When I arrive home, there's a sheet of paper pinned to the door. A tiny thrill runs through me, hopeful for a fleeting moment it might somehow be a letter from Charlie.

Upon closer inspection, it's definitely not. And it's most certainly not a love letter of any kind. It's a final notice about my overdue rent. I think of Jeffrey and the nine more calls I ignored during the remainder of the trip, and I crumple the paper and toss it to Finn. He's as excited as if I'd brought him a gift all the way from Providenciales.

In the two days since we returned home, I've largely confined myself to my apartment, counting down the minutes to the final decision from Catapult, watching my bank account dwindle to single digits. I know there's little chance of an offer now. I mostly just want to receive the rejection so I can accept it and move on. I'm resigned to the notion that I will call my mom by the end of the week, ask her if Jaya's mom's engineering position might still be available.

I'm terrified of running into Charlie each time I open my apartment door, but there's also a charge that whirls inside me, hoping I do. There's been no sign of him, though, and I can't help but think he's avoiding me too.

When there's a rap at my door that afternoon, my heart crashes against its cage, as I immediately picture Charlie's face on the other side of it.

Instead, I find the last person I expect.

"Lo, hi." He speaks with a bit of wonder, as if he's surprised to find me opening the door of my own apartment. "I'm glad you're home. I didn't know if you were back."

I take note of his prominent nose.

Finn pokes his head between my knees to see who our visitor is and yelps in glee when he recognizes Zane. He pushes through my legs, practically knocking me over to get to him.

"Finn the Vampire Slayer, hey, bud," Zane says, giving him a scratch on his head. The effort is lackluster at best, and I wonder if he even likes dogs or if that was just another lie in his bottomless pit of untruths.

I glare at Finn, conveying my dismay at his lack of loyalty, and he hangs his head as he makes his walk of shame back into the apartment before turning back and settling at my feet.

Zane is wearing a button-down black-and-gray-checkered shirt, dark jeans, and black leather cap-toe dress shoes. He never used to wear anything but Vans. It's a reminder that the person standing before me is someone I used to know, past tense. This version of him is someone else entirely. A doppelgänger. A parallel-universe Zane who has traded Vans for cap-toe dress shoes.

"Zane. What are you doing here?" I finally manage.

"Can I come in?"

Can he come in? An answer doesn't come easily. Instead, the question pelts me like the cascade of a hailstorm. Do I let him in? Or force this conversation to occur in the hallway of my apartment? Can I handle him inside my walls again? Eventually, I relent and open the door wider, watch him brush past me, straight to his old spot on my couch, as if the indent of him still remains.

I close the door and lean against it, fingers curled tightly around the doorknob behind me.

"It's just the same in here," he says. Is my apartment supposed to look different? Perhaps he's expecting a parallel-universe me too. He stands and wanders, runs a finger along one of the lanterns lining the console table behind my couch with a bit of sentimentality in his eyes. I fight the urge to snap at him to not touch my stuff.

"What are you doing here?" I repeat.

He makes his way over to me, stands several steps away, but it's still too close. "I needed to see you."

"Why?"

He shrugs, as if his shoulders each weigh a metric ton. "I miss you."

It feels as though there's a block of dry ice wedged in my throat. I've imagined this moment, tried to visualize it into existence for six months. I abandoned the idea early on that I wanted him back, but I never stopped fantasizing about some kind of reckoning. And now that it's happening, it's not how I imagined.

"How's Jenna?" I ask.

He opens his mouth, releases a sharp breath. "We're not together anymore. That was . . . I don't know what that was."

"She dumped you?"

He shoves his hands into the front pockets of his jeans and there's something truly unappealing about his awshucksness. "We were never really together."

"That rock on her finger said otherwise."

His internal struggle spills across his face as he attempts to muster a response that won't make him sound like a dick.

"Look, I made a mistake. A big one. I ruined what we had. I realize that now. I'm ready to correct that mistake and be with you."

I let out a shrewd laugh that surprises us both. It's ironic: after all that effort to get Brooke's attention so she'd come crawling back to Charlie, it's my ghost who reappeared instead.

I was afraid that if and when I did get my reprisal with Zane, the good would all come flooding back. Because there was good. He couldn't have hurt me so badly had there not been good. The way he would play with my hair watching movies on the couch or while driving. The way he'd show up at my door with a bag of what he called "sad groceries" whenever I had a bad day: a bottle of cabernet, mint chocolate chip ice cream, and sheet masks. The fact that he knew what sheet masks are and where to buy them. The way he used to kiss the tip of my nose when I said or did something he found endearing. This last one he hadn't done in a long while. I do feel these memories playing back as he stands in my apartment again—a spool of memories uncoiling like ribbon. But they play like what they are—a highlight reel. One that is blurred and dulled by his indiscretion, his lies. His lack of belief in me. After Charlie, I can't unsee that. Even if he'd never cheated, he didn't give me enough.

I open the door. "I think you should leave."

"Sloane, please," he says, and it's slightly pathetic, the begging drawl in his voice.

His words from earlier slice my thoughts. *I didn't know if you were back*. "Actually, I do have one question before you go," I say, pressing myself against the doorframe. "Did you send a picture of me to Jack Palmer?"

Zane's face remains perfectly still, but I see it. The slight twitch, just once, of his right eyebrow. I picture him sitting with Jack Palmer and Kenji and Ross, laughing about how the other candidate is a girl who probably has relationship issues, the idea implanting into Zane's mind. I imagine the dozens, perhaps hundreds, of ways Charlie and Zane might be indirectly connected to where he could have come across the two photos Charlie posted early in our trip. Besides, who else could have possibly had anything to gain by sending that picture? I don't bother to ask for details. How he found it. If any part of him hesitated before ruining this opportunity for me. Because the details don't matter. He continues to show me who he is, and I don't need to know any more than I already do.

"Zane, we are never, ever getting back together." I realize I've just quoted Taylor Swift and, thinking of Charlie, have to fight the smile edging its way to my lips.

Because despite everything, I know he'd be proud of me in this moment.

38.

I CONTINUE BEFORE HE CAN DARE TO RESPOND. "YOU NEVER SAW ME as anything other than your girlfriend. You never saw my talent, my drive, my dreams. I was never good enough. It was exhausting, always trying to prove myself to you. And for what? Believe it or not, there's a guy out there who thinks I'm Kix."

Zane furrows his brow, and I know he thinks I sound insane. All the more reason he should leave. He walks to the door, stops, and turns toward me one step into the hallway. As he looks at me, I see a stranger. It's remarkable to stand here across from him and feel nothing. My anger that mutated to hurt has now turned into indifference. It's joyous, the indifference.

He lingers for a moment, then lifts his arms, takes a step forward, and throws his weight around me in an awkward embrace. I am rigid at first, but eventually, I close my eyes and soften, feeling something like release.

That's when I know, without a doubt, without any trace of regret or what-if, I'm over Zane. One hundred percent, absolutely over Zane. Because after six months of secretly, pathetically yearning for this opportunity at my lowest points, the instant Zane wraps himself around me, I think of Charlie.

I pull back and am about to tell him again to leave and not look back. But when we part, as if my realization summoned him, Charlie stands in his own doorway, trash bag in hand.

He's wearing a '93 TULSA, OK, SALSA DANCE COMPETITION tee and the sight of it makes my heart pinch.

The rest happens in slow motion, though somehow still too fast for me to intervene. Zane turns to follow my gaze, and now Zane and Charlie are face-to-face, between Charlie's door and mine, in a narrow hallway standoff.

Finn lifts from his position in the doorway, joins us in the hall. He shifts his face to Zane, then Charlie, then Zane again. We all watch as he then steps next to Charlie and lies down at his feet.

If only it were that easy.

After acknowledging Finn with a head scratch, Charlie turns his attention to me.

Zane clears his throat and extends his hand to Charlie. "Hey, man, Zane."

"Zane," Charlie repeats, shaking my ex's hand but still looking at me. "He's shorter than I expected."

"What?" Zane mutters.

We stand in this charged triangle for what feels like a year, Zane staring at Charlie, Charlie staring at me, me staring back at Charlie.

"You look familiar," Zane says, clearly not reading the hallway.

Don't say it, is all I can think. *Please don't say it.*

Zane points his finger at Charlie. "Aren't you the guy from that commercial? The fake abs guy?"

I clench my jaw as Charlie does the same. If Zane recognizes Charlie from the photo he sent to Catapult, he's certainly disguising it well.

Charlie still doesn't look at Zane. "Right, well, I'm gonna take out the trash." He raises the bag into the air. "Any garbage you'd like me to take out for you, neighbor?" His tone is steely, and I feel it rub against my skin like a Brillo pad.

I want to say yes. I want to announce, in front of both of

them, that I am officially, unequivocally over Zane, and the only person I care about in this hallway is Charlie. But when I open my mouth to speak, there's nothing except a sharp intake of air. Charlie gives me the slightest of nods, then heads off down the hall, garbage bag slung over his shoulder. He strides past our floor's trash chute and into the stairwell. I feel as though I may shatter from the center like a puzzle picked up from its edges.

Zane turns back to me, shrugs, leans in to embrace me again. I don't know how I overlooked his inability to read social cues for as long as I did.

"Zane, don't." I put my hand out to stop his motion, but it ends up more like a shove.

He narrows his eyes. "I don't get it, Sloane. I said I was sorry. I came back here, tail between my legs. What more do you want from me?"

"Nothing," I say. "I don't want anything from you anymore." I can practically see the ghost of him exit my body, viscous white matter floating up and away, disappearing into the dingy ceiling grate.

Zane scrunches his face in a look of dismissal. I saw this look throughout our relationship. He dismissed my design talent and interest in gaming. He dismissed me as a whole when he slept with Jenna, and he's dismissing me now. It's evident he assumed I'd be here waiting, when he eventually found Jenna's likely well-manicured bush wasn't in fact greener.

"Goodbye, Zane." I take a step backward and begin closing the door.

He stops it with his arm. "Wait. I at least want to say congratulations on the job. You earned it, fair and square." He looks down at the ground then back at me, his face neutral. "You're really talented, Sloane. I'm sorry I could never get out of my own way long enough to see it."

"You didn't get the job?"

He shakes his head. "They 'best of luck in your future endeavors'-ed me."

"The middle finger of corporate-speak," I mutter. Zane didn't get the job. And he was the other final candidate, or so Jack Palmer's email implied. But I didn't get an offer. After Zane sent that picture and my game debacle, perhaps they decided to scrap us both and start over.

He nods. His face remains even and I can't read him, but I choose, for me, to accept his apology.

"Thank you," I say.

When he steps back, I call Finn in and close the door, then watch through the peephole as he stands there for a moment, seemingly unsure what to do next. Finally, he makes his way down the hall. As soon as he's out of sight, I know I need to find Charlie. Explain to him the epiphany I've had. Tell him I was wrong to be so closed off. Wrong for not allowing myself to give in to what I felt—am feeling—for him. And mostly, wrong for not expressing how much he's affected me in a matter of days. As my hand curls around the knob, I hear the familiar soft ding from my phone on the table beside the door. I'm inclined to ignore it—Charlie is far more important than anyone trying to get ahold of me—but then I see the notification. An email from Catapult Games.

Ms. Cooper,

I'm pleased to inform you that, with HR's approval and strong input, we would like to offer you the game designer position at Catapult, assuming you can keep the promises you made in the interview. If so, see you Monday.

Best,
Jack Palmer

I stare at the screen, reread the email several times. What Zane said just now was true. Him congratulating me on getting the job was *real*. I *did* get the job. Over him. Over everyone else who has dreamt about this their whole lives, and they chose . . . me.

It occurs to me that they let him know of their decision before they even offered me the job, confident I will accept. The truth is . . . who wouldn't? They are the number one game design company in the world.

My back slides down the door until my butt hits the floor, knees pressed up to my chin. Finn sits beside me and scrapes his tongue along my cheek in a congratulatory lick.

Everything I've ever worked for—I just got. I'm vindicated at this moment. Quitting my previous job with no plan, risking losing my apartment, hedging my bet against Jaya's mom's engineering job, disappointing my mom—the risks were all worth it.

There's a satisfaction in me, yes. A feeling of validation I wasn't sure I'd ever get—someone recognizing what I already knew to be true. That I am a damn good game designer. But it's not the pure, blissful joy I thought I'd have, either. Because I know saying yes to this offer means proving myself in ways outside of just game design. That I'll have to be perfect in my efforts to "keep my interview promises." It also means saying goodbye to whatever small hope still existed for Charlie and me. By accepting this job, I'll be confirming that we are nothing more than those seven days on a tropical island.

39.

"I GOT THE JOB," I TELL TESS AS SOON AS SHE ANSWERS MY CALL LATER that day.

"Congrats?" she says, and I know her tone has several layers of underlying subtext. She's happy for me but doesn't condone the sexist details of my arrangement. She supports me in any choice I make but knows it means Charlie and I cannot continue.

"It's a dream come true," I tell her.

Before she can reply, Tess giggles distantly and it's clearly not intended for me. Tess giggling is, in and of itself, rare behavior.

"Teesss . . ." I say, long and drawn out.

"Sloane, I've gotta run. Keep me posted on the job, okay? I'm here for you," she says before hanging up.

I stare at my phone. Tess obviously has some semblance of a new relationship she's unwilling to divulge to me. And it's nagging at me that she hasn't told me she's finally found someone. Someone she spends sleep-in mornings with and who joins her for Runyon Canyon hikes. Someone who makes her *giggle*. Someone who has made her willing to take a chance, despite her uninspired days wading through client divorces, seeing the fallout of love.

Is she holding back on this big, momentous turn of events in her life because she's afraid of what it might do to me? Does she think it would send me backward into the breakup spiral I just recently crawled out of—the one she held me up through? She couldn't be more wrong. I want to call her back and tell her as much, but I don't. She's with this mystery man right now, and we should talk in person anyway.

Monday morning, I arrive at the Catapult Games office fifteen minutes early, dressed in slacks, a plain gray blouse, and black flats, my hair pulled back in a low, tight ponytail. It's the outfit I deemed most subdued but professional in my closet. When I arrive, I'm greeted by Anita.

"Welcome, Sloane. Nice to see you again," she says brightly, and I'm struck by her gorgeous magenta lipstick. Anita, Jack made sure to tell me when I called to accept the offer, is the only other woman who works regularly in the office. "We're lucky to have you. I saw your final interview game design of *Arsonist Betty*. Excellent concept," she says as we walk the long hallway to her office.

"Thank you," I tell her as we pass the *Zelda* conference room where my interview took place. Inside are all three of my interviewers: Jack Palmer, Kenji Sugano, Ross Feldman. Jack is facing me, and though we make eye contact, there's no smile or acknowledgment on his face. His lack of response makes me question if he remembers who I am and that I now work here.

Anita's office sits in the far back corner, though it's not *that* kind of corner office. It's stark and unexpectedly bare for someone who's been here almost four years. There is no artwork on the eggshell-painted walls, no framed family photos on the desk. Not even a nameplate or business card holder or sticky note stuck to the edge of her computer screen.

She catches me sizing up her space. "Never know when you'll need to make a quick escape," she says with a wink, and I'm pretty sure she's joking.

I sign the usual new hire paperwork and as we wrap up, I

wonder more and more about Anita's personal life. I take note of the bare ring finger on her left hand and wonder if she too promised her life away to Catapult in exchange for her continued employment.

I'm not comfortable asking Anita this within my first hour of employment, but something else has been gnawing at me since receiving the offer.

"Anita, can I ask you something?" I say as I hand her back the Catapult logo'd pen. She waves me off in a motion that says keep it, so I drop it into my purse, far too excited. The pen is a tangible reminder that I, *Sloane Cooper*, work at Catapult Games.

"What is it?" Anita asks.

"Did they—Jack and team—did they want me for this job?" I pitch my head in the vague direction of the *Zelda* conference room. *Or did you insist they hire the girl?* I want to add, but can't manage.

Anita clears her throat, clasps her hands atop the bare desk. Her nails, perfectly oval, are an impressive shade match to her magenta lipstick.

"You were the best person for the job," she says after a moment.

I understand her perfectly. I was—am—the best person for this job but they—Jack and team—wanted Zane anyway.

The burn of embarrassment rises to the tips of my ears.

"You'll prove yourself. You've got it in you. I can see it," she continues.

"How did you prove yourself? It seems like they respect you. Enough to take your hiring recommendations."

She smiles conspiratorially, leans farther in. "Off the record?"

I nod.

She glances at her office door, then centers her attention back on me. "I play the game when I have to. I smile. Laugh.

Nod. Excitedly agree when they come up with ideas I've already presented. But when I just can't anymore, when it becomes too much, I threaten legal action. Gets their panties in a wad every time." She winks again, and again I'm pretty sure she's joking.

Pretty sure.

I nod, my suspicions seemingly confirmed, but my resolve strong. It doesn't matter how or why. The fact is, I'm here. And I'm not afraid of proving myself.

I spend most of my first day with Anita. She gives me a tour, makes general introductions. She settles me in at my desk toward the end of the day, which is in the far corner of the main workspace where every employee other than the executives and Anita sits. All the desks around me are empty and I'm as far away from the others as possible, just outside Anita's office.

I ask her what I should do next.

"Read through all the policies and procedures and play the games."

I can't hide my smile. "Really?"

"Yes. You should get to know the products. Jack will get in touch when he needs you."

This particular "perk" of the job, getting to game at the office, is one I intend to take full advantage of. Once again, I feel like I should pinch myself. Whatever the exact circumstances that got me here, it's still my dream. And for that, I can't stop smiling.

When I arrive home in the early evening, Finn is equally excited and upset to see me. It's been a while since I've been away from him all day at work.

"I'm sorry, boy," I tell him, crouching down and holding his snout up to my nose. After an "it's okay" lick of my face, he pulls his leash from the hook by the door and walks it over to me. "Yeah, I bet you gotta go." I attach his leash and we head out.

When I open the door, Finn pulls me hard into the hallway and I stumble directly into Charlie. He drops three bags of groceries on the floor to catch me. There we stand, between our two doors, entwined in our first touch since Turks. Our first anything since Turks except for that unfortunate interaction with Zane.

It all blazes back with the feel of his arm wrapped around my waist, our faces inches apart. The hot coil at my base in reaction to his touch. The confidence I have when I am with him. The desire to be more like him—open, vulnerable, resilient. The ease that existed between us. The certainty that he is my biggest fan.

He clears his throat and gently steps backward over his groceries, lowering his arms from my waist. I can now see he's wearing the FREE HUGS cactus shirt from the night we met. I want, more than anything, to hug him, even if I get pricked. I want to grab his face, kiss him, pull him into my apartment for another couch romp. I want to sit on our terrace in Provo and watch the stars. I want to eat jerk chicken, sip rum punch, and dance to Taylor Swift. But I can't do these things. Whatever Charlie and I had needs to stay in that expensive suite in paradise.

"Sorry," I say, our eyes catching. We stay locked for a beat too long. I miss him, though he's right here in front of me. I miss everything about him. Those eyes. That dimple. The bar soap smell. The way his face lights up to match my insides when I talk about gaming.

Finn grabs a baguette from one of Charlie's grocery bags and holds it up, wagging his tail as if he's found the perfect stick.

"Finn!" I yell, pulling the baguette from his mouth, though it rips in half and Finn promptly chews and swallows his half. I look to Charlie. "I'm so sorry. I'll buy you another."

Charlie shakes his head. "Don't worry about it. I probably don't need the carbs anyway," he says, patting his stomach. Now I'm thinking about his abs. Another addition to The List.

"Hey, Finny!" he exclaims, bending down then rubbing his hands frantically all over Finn, who jumps and yelps excitedly.

When Charlie rises to his feet, he dusts his hands off on his jeans and looks at me again. I miss his board shorts too, I think, mentally adding them to my growing list of Things I Miss About Charlie.

"Did you get the job, then?" he asks, scanning my outfit.

"I did. Though I think I'm just filling some girl quota imposed by HR."

"Congrats, Sloane. I'm sure that's not the case. How could there be anyone better, when your game was so mind-blowing?"

As mind-blowing as our Turquoise Point Resort suite sex? I want to say, but don't have the nerve. "Thank you" is all I muster.

There's so much more I want to say. I want to thank him for believing in me. I want to tell him I care about him, far more than I've let on. I want to tell him those seven days with him are some of the happiest I've ever had. That I've never felt so connected to someone, yet so disconnected at the same time. I want to tell him I think *he* is Kix. Or Fruity Pebbles, more accurately, for me.

I also know I need to keep my distance. Sharing these things with Charlie could lead me down a path that ends with me losing everything I've worked so hard for.

But there is one thing I most certainly need to say.

"Look, Charlie, I owe you an apology. A big one. I never should have implied it was your fault that I sent the wrong game to Jack Palmer or that he got that picture of us. That was all me, my decisions. You're not responsible for any of it. And I'm sorry I blamed you for my own . . . stuff." I am about to say mistakes, but I can't in good faith refer to any moment of our seven days in paradise as a mistake.

They were too good.

"For what it's worth, I'm sorry too. I never should have

asked you to go on that trip, smile for pictures, and pretend to be with me. I didn't mean to use you, but I did. It was unfair to you. And I'm relieved to know that those things that happened didn't cost you the job. I know it means everything to you."

Not everything.

I don't know Charlie fully, I remind myself. You can't really know someone after just a few days together. But then I think about what I do know. I know I find his punny T-shirts oddly endearing—they make my heartbeat quicken a little each time I know I'm going to see him, in anticipation of what amusing statement his next one might make. I know he's barely flappable—consistently calm, happy, forgiving—except when he's on a plane. I know he wakes up with scrunched eyes that are vulnerable and sexy. I know he sees me. That there is no need to try to be a more perfect version of myself to impress him. That he is already impressed. I know that at first pass, I'd be inclined to say he changed me. But if I really look, I know that's not true. He didn't change me. He made me more deeply who I am and have been afraid to be.

I clear my throat. "Right, well, I'd better go. Finn needs to pee," I say. Charlie presses his lips together into a thin line and nods, then gives Finn one last head scratch before lifting his groceries from the floor. I feel his eyes on me as I head down the hall to the elevator. When I press the button, I turn back and find Charlie still standing at his door, bags in hand, watching. "Bye!" I call. "I didn't want the last thing I said to you to be, 'Finn needs to pee!'"

My raised voice causes 6F's goldendoodle to bark violently behind his apartment door. Finn grunts. He hates that uptight goldendoodle as much as I do.

Charlie looks down, shakes his head, and then back in my direction. "Yet, you just said it again as the last thing!" he calls back.

"Shit, you're right!"

"That's a much better way to end things! In acknowledgment of me being right!"

The elevator doors open. "Goodbye, Charlie," I say, too softly for him to hear. I smile before stepping into the elevator with Finn. When the door closes, sadness overtakes me. The gamer in me wants to give up on this life and start over, apply the lessons I've learned from this flawed one in the next. Avoid the potholes and dead ends, the shiny paths that wasted too much time. If I could start over with a second life, I'd pursue the path that leads straight to him.

I can't bear the thought of Charlie becoming someone I used to know.

40.

MY FIRST WEEK AT CATAPULT IS ELECTRIFYING. I SPEND MOST OF my time in the game room playing every release Catapult has produced in the last ten years (and some from their competitors). While I don't interact much with anyone besides Anita during her brief daily check-ins, I might even convince myself that getting paid to game all day is fulfilling enough.

On Friday, I come home to find a small wicker basket at my front door, filled with mangoes and kumquats. There's an immediate thunderstorm in my gut as I instinctively look to Charlie's door. I take the envelope lying atop the fruit and tear it open to find a card with the image of a night sky full of shooting stars. Inside it—two printed photos. The only two pictures we took on the trip. The first, our heads pressed together on the plane, the blue of his eyes popping out like it's a 3D image, and the other—us holding hands across the table at that first dinner. I fan the two photos in my hand so I can regard both at once. We really do look happy. Like a punch-drunk couple basking in a romantic getaway.

When I can't stare at the photos any longer, I move on to the card. On the otherwise blank inside, he has scrawled in surprisingly neat handwriting:

Sloane,

Congrats on making your dreams come true. I know you are going to do big things there. Your dedication to getting what you want is inspiring. You deserve it all.

Charlie

PS—I may have initially thought these photos were for Brooke. They never were. They are ours.

PPS—I would have gotten this to you sooner, but kumquats are surprisingly hard to find.

I stare at the card. At his handwriting, small and non-aggressive. The wide curves of his *d*'s and *b*'s. My eyes catch on his words. *I know you are going to do big things there.*

Like I have so many times since we have been home, I contemplate knocking on his door. Even if I don't have the words to say thank you, to commemorate what existed—and still does—between us, I'd settle for just staring at his face when he opens the door. But, as sweet as this gesture is, it also proves Charlie knows the importance of this job. That he wants to see me succeed in it and respects why we can't be together. I pick up the basket and head inside to greet Finn.

Later that night, I leave a note at his front door that simply says thank you, one kumquat set atop it.

By the following Monday afternoon, my enthusiasm for my new job has worn thin. If I'm not in the game room (alone), I'm at my desk staring at the eggshell wall (alone), wondering when I'll actually get to do something, even if it means fetching coffee or taking meeting notes. At least then someone might acknowledge me. Jack and Kenji spend virtually all their time in the *Zelda* conference room, which has a constant revolving door of activity. I've clocked every other person in the office has at least three meetings a day. Even Anita has a daily check-in with the partners.

To cozy up my little nook, I'd planned on bringing in the lucky bamboo Tess gifted me when I got the job and a picture of Finn, but after seeing Anita's office, I thought better of it. So instead, my area is as cold and impersonal as hers. Each day when she stops by my desk, I give her a brave smile.

It would be one thing if I were in training—watching videos about Catapult or building some sort of work plan. But I've been given zero direction except for Anita's advisement to play games and insisting Jack Palmer will include me in projects soon.

It's not until the Friday of my second week that I am actually invited to a meeting. And by invited, I mean self-invited. When Jack Palmer walks by my desk around ten that morning, I take his venture to my far corner of the Catapult galaxy as a sign.

I leap out of my chair to greet him. "Mr. Palmer!"

He halts mid-step. "Jack," he says, then goes quiet. He pulls a chocolate chip cookie from the breast pocket of his maroon tee and takes a bite.

"Right, Jack. I just wanted to say hello. I wasn't sure you remembered me. We haven't had a chance to interact since I started working here. Sloane Cooper, your new game designer." I hold out my hand.

"I know who you are," he says through a second and final bite, with a barely there handshake.

I rub the crumbs from my hand against my pants. "Right, well, over the last two weeks I've read every policy and played every game, and I wanted to see if perhaps I can start learning the business in other ways. Join some of the design meetings, perhaps? Or whatever you think is relevant or important. I'd love to learn and start contributing to the team." Other than as the token broad.

He eyes me for a moment, then releases his breath. "I suppose you should. *Zelda* in ten," he calls over his shoulder, already making his escape from my lonely corner.

When I enter the conference room nine and a half minutes later, I try to hide my delight.

I take the last seat at the far end of the long glass table. The level of adrenaline pulsing through me is equivalent to when I was competing against Charlie during Andres's field day. Maybe higher.

As man after man trickles in for the meeting, I shift awkwardly, waiting to be acknowledged, though no one seems to notice the lone female in the room adjusting the height of her chair up and down and up again. They're all chatting one-on-one or in small groups, and I'm decidedly the odd woman out, as if there were any question.

Ross Feldman leans over to the guy seated next to him, holding up his phone, and they share a chuckle at whatever is on the screen. The two guys at the far end of the table laugh extravagantly at a joke about truffle butter.

I cringe. I'm in the proverbial locker room, this one made up of twentysomething gamers whose most exercised body parts are likely their thumbs.

Jack is already stationed at the head of the table, the cookie earlier apparently an appetizer to the platter of BBQ he now has in front of him. He picks up a slathered rib and holds it before him. "Please welcome our new designer, Sloane Cooper," he says, and the room quiets. He doesn't point or nod or motion in any way in my direction. He doesn't have to.

I straighten in my chair, smile as confidently as possible. I'm met with a few mediocre smiles, a half wave, and one slow clap. Oh, and one glance at my chest from the one who made the joke about truffle butter.

It doesn't matter, I tell myself. *I'll win them over with my work ethic and design skills.*

The meeting begins with a recap of numbers for the company's newest release, *Shelf Life*, for which sales have been good, though lower than projected.

"Yeah, but the TTP was on point," Ross says, nudging the guy beside him with a pointy elbow.

I lean forward, clear my throat. "Sorry, what is TTP?"

There's a collective chuckle. "TTP. Time to Penis," he answers. "It's a metric for how long it takes players to build a penis using available materials in a game. Our games have the shortest TTP on the market." Ross proclaims this last part as if he has personally just won the Nobel Prize for this achievement, and I immediately regret the question.

The meeting moves on, and as Jack Palmer speaks, I quickly divine that this is a strategic planning session focused on gaining market share outside of the genre Catapult already dominates.

"So, what, you want us to start developing puzzles?" Ross says merrily, his round belly jiggling, and the room bursts into laughter again.

Jack Palmer doesn't seem to mind the comment. "No, that's not what I'm saying, guys. There's no *Words with Friends* in our future. But we need to develop some new concepts besides just apocalypse games. We can't become a one-trick pony." He takes multiple bites from a new rib as he rotates it in his fingers, like it's an ear of corn.

Kenji shakes his head. "Yeah, right, people clamor to buy whatever we put out. We could build a game *about* a one-trick pony, slap the Catapult logo on it, and sell the hell out of it."

Jack licks sauce from his bottom lip. "You may be right," he says, pointing the now impressively bare rib at Kenji. "But

I want to see what else we can come up with. What genre can we take over next?"

Everyone looks at one another, and I'm unsure whether Jack's question is rhetorical.

"New genres. Got it," Ross says with a salute, and once again, the room erupts into laughter.

Anything anyone says is hysterically funny to everyone else. It's as though I've walked into some gnarly, bro'd-out version of *The Stepford Wives*.

"I've got something. Should be ready to share next week," Kenji says.

"Great. Anyone else got anything on this topic before we move on?" Jack asks, raising a fresh rib into the air.

As I tentatively raise my hand, Kenji smirks. Right, raising my hand has likely made me look both too formal and childish at once.

"Sloane?" Jack Palmer says, giving me the floor.

I clear my throat. "First and foremost, I just wanted to say how excited I am to be here. To be part of this team." I attempt to avoid being deterred when Ross pulls his phone from his pants pocket and busies himself with it. "I've followed the gaming space closely the last several years, and I did quite a bit of research during the interview process here, including a deep dive into the competitive landscape."

"And," Jack says, leaning forward.

"And I'd be happy to take a deeper dive into researching market share, competitors . . . whatever might be helpful to the team."

All eyes in the room shift from me to Jack Palmer.

"Hon," he begins, and I know whatever comes next doesn't end with me feeling particularly good about myself. "We've been in business for over thirty years. I think we have a pulse on what our consumers want. We've got that covered."

"I thought this was a meeting to collaborate on expansion ideas," I say in a wimpy manner that reminds me of who I was with Zane. Jack Palmer's severe jaw and narrowed eyes across the table make it all clear. Yes, that is what this meeting is for. For everyone but me.

Ross Feldman and Truffle Butter snicker. I stare at my feet through the glass table, wishing I had stayed at my desk.

Entering my apartment lobby that evening, I'm completely exhausted in a "trying to look casual at a party where I know nobody for eight hours" sort of way. It's Friday, I remind myself, and I'm about to have two days off from staring at my strip of eggshell-colored wall while desperately attempting to avoid further embarrassment. Come Monday, I'm inclined to use my Catapult-branded pen to dig a little nick into that space of wall by my desk, just to give myself something new to look at.

When I return downstairs a few minutes later with Finn, I immediately spot Charlie. He's returning from a run, sweaty and red-faced. His breath is heavy and I can't avoid the sense memory of it against my ear. At least he's in a shirt . . . nope, wait, he's removed that, and now he's toweling himself off with it, wearing only a pair of black running shorts.

It's not just lust I feel seeing him in this state. It's longing. It's a rigid awareness of the void he briefly filled, now empty again. With him, I was my best version. Fun, carefree, creative, and most of all, true to myself. But I've ruined it all with this job, by not being able to be as vulnerable with him as he was with me.

He starts in my direction, toward the elevators, his tennis shoes squeaking against the linoleum like an alert siren, and I duck behind a column on the far side of the lobby. Finn looks up at me with disapproval. He needs to pee. I stand there, shoved up against a column, pulling Finn to my side, hiding from the one person I want to talk to more than anyone.

As soon as he passes, I rush Finn out the lobby doors, tears welling. I can't admit to Charlie that the dream job I wanted more than anything, the one he cheered me on for with more backing than anyone has ever provided me, is actually a Freddy Krueger–level nightmare. I may have to move out of my apartment—running into Charlie and having to keep my distance is a greater burden than I may be able to manage.

I put everything on the line for this job, this new start on the career path I've always wanted, and two weeks in, I'm miserable, wishing I could share it all with Charlie, knowing he'd know exactly what to say. That he'd take this massive, complicated thing and simplify it to a sharp point that makes perfect sense.

But I've already lost him.

And I can't go back.

41.

COME MONDAY, I DO WHAT I SHOULD HAVE DONE ALL ALONG. I VACILlate between keeping my head down and staring at the eggshell wall, reminding myself I'm lucky to be here. I eat my homemade salads at my bare desk, wishing it were jerk chicken and rum punch on a terrace overlooking shooting stars, Charlie by my side.

The week creeps, and by Friday, when Anita arrives at my workstation, I perk up at having a visitor in solitary confinement.

She holds out an envelope. "For you," she says as I close my Tupperware and place it back in my tote. Today, I made it to eleven a.m. before tearing into my lunch for something to do.

"Thank you," I declare, tearing into the envelope. A paystub for my first full paycheck from Catapult—my first in a long while. I breathe a sigh of relief, for myself and my credit cards.

"You've earned it," she says with a smile, before heading back to her office.

When she's gone, I examine the stub. After taxes and withholding, it's barely enough. But it *is* enough. Enough to cover my past due rent and late fees, and to ease the worry that's been mushrooming in my stomach. I don't know that I agree with Anita that I've earned it, but I'll certainly take it.

I've been avoiding my mom's calls since returning from the trip, too guilty and downtrodden to face her. I was waiting for this check, so I could prove to her that this job is valid. I'll call her tonight, show her this stub. Perhaps she'll even be happy for me. Happy enough to overlook the fact that I, once again, do not have a date for the upcoming vow renewal.

At noon, there's a faint ding from somewhere in my workspace. I inspect, attempting to determine the source. Finally, the realization hits: it's a message notification from my computer. Someone has messaged me!

Zelda. New game design.

Jack Palmer is a man of few words.

I gather my things and rush toward *Zelda*. Perhaps now that I've taken my hazing, they're ready to accept me.

I sit across from Jack, who is unwrapping the foil from a burrito. Kenji enters and takes the seat next to Jack. He's in a black GALAGA FIGHTER TRAINING T-shirt that immediately makes me think of Charlie. Charlie's tees are much cooler though.

The room fills quickly, a handful of people leaning against the conference room's glass walls when no empty seats remain, and my adrenaline surges. It's the largest meeting I've observed since I started working here.

"So, first order of business," Jack says, wheeling his chair to the switchboard on the wall and dimming the lights. "Kenji's got an update on his team's new game that's in early development." He nods across the table to Kenji and all heads turn toward the projector wall.

I lean forward. This is great. I'm in a standing-room-only meeting with the most important, influential, talented group of game designers in the world, and I'm about to learn something nobody else knows—what Catapult is developing next. There's been quite a bit of speculation on gamer Reddit and in various other online forums about whether Catapult would, in fact, branch out into a new genre or stick with apocalyptic action-adventure. But I, here, get to be one of the few who know the big secret, months, maybe even years, before its release. I feel like Dorothy in Oz as I grip the edge of the table in anticipation.

"Thanks, man." Kenji stands and pats Jack's shoulder. "As Jack mentioned the other day, and we all know, when we look at market data on what Catapult does well, it's pretty much everything." They all look around at one another, smile, and murmur their approval. "But there's one area where those bastards at Triton Media have been taking a percentage of market share, albeit a tiny one." Kenji hovers his pointer finger just above his thumb, a sliver of light between the two.

"Yeah, tiny like the size of James Cobb's dick," the guy seated next to me says, and a wave of laughter rolls through the room.

Kenji continues, "But that little corn on the Cobb-sized market share can be squashed."

Is this what happens when the brightest minds in the industry get together? Jokes about the penis size of their competitors' CEOs? And, the joke doesn't even make sense. Corn on the cob is quite girthy, if you think about it.

Jack takes a large bite from his burrito, sprinkling rice bits onto the table, bringing my attention back to the room.

Kenji goes on. "We can blow Triton out of the water with the thing no one else is doing. Not well at least. The new thing we can burst into the marketplace with." Kenji waits a moment, building anticipation, before he clicks his image onto the screen. "Arson," he says with a flame of provocation in his eyes.

Projected on the far wall is a game character. A large, tatted guy with biceps the size of truck tires poking out of the ripped fabric of a denim shirt. He's holding a massive assault rifle, which I don't particularly understand because Kenji referenced arson, not guns. Actually, now that I think about it, the character projected on the wall looks a lot like Cannon Jack. And a lot like every other character from every other game they have in their portfolio, just with a different shirt.

"Meet Arsonist Joe," Kenji says, grinning proudly at the character projection.

The room claps and whistles in rowdy approval.

I stare at the screen, the frustration inside me on slow boil.

Kenji continues, "You see, Arsonist Joe is an unassuming financier by day, but he has a secret life. He sneaks out of his apartment building in the middle of the night to set fires all around the city." Kenji holds his arms out wide, twisting his body from side to side like an oscillating fan, as though he is king of said city. He clicks to the next slide, where there's now a slew of items surrounding Joe. A gas can, matches, lighters.

"Joe here has more than his fair share of fire starter materials. He can strike a match to a brick building, smother newspaper in gasoline. He even gets creative—uses chocolate and a soda can to reflect sunlight." There's an impressed response from the others, all of whom are looking at Kenji like he's a genius. "But the best part is that just when you think the police are about to catch him, that they have extinguished all his fires, just when you think he's emptied his arsonist tool kit and you've lost the game, he pulls out—"

"Flint," I murmur under my breath as Kenji says it out loud. No one hears me, of course, because I'm a ghost. An HR-approved, completely disregarded ghost. Instinctively, I press my fingertips to my hip, where my tattoo sits just beneath my gray trousers.

Not only has Kenji built this new concept from my interview game, but he's also flipped the player position from proactive citizen working to stop an arsonist (arson = bad) to the player being the one setting the fires (arson = good).

I stare across the table at Jack, who takes another bite of his burrito, a smattering of salsa on his chin. I can't tell if he's avoiding my gaze or just not looking at me, though we both know *Arsonist Joe* is based on my design. Instead, he evaluates the images on the screen as he chews, open-mouthed. Charlie would be appalled.

Kenji hands the clicker to Ross to go over the marketing plan for *Arsonist Joe*, which I find incredibly premature given the game isn't even built yet. Better yet, I wonder why Ross is even dealing with marketing, when he has a team under him that handles it. Ross clicks to the next slide, and the room erupts in whistles and applause as the screen fills with shots of attractive, lightly clothed women gaming. I think I now get why Ross is involved.

"I've hand selected the hottest, grade-A female gamers from YouTube, who'll live stream themselves playing *Arsonist Joe*, prerelease, to build buzz." Ross licks his lips and runs a catcher's mitt of a hand through his thinning hair. "I'm thinking we send 'em little flame bikinis to wear."

More applause.

I can't seem to do much besides stare at Ross. Then Kenji. Then Jack. None of whom makes eye contact with me. I imagine sitting in that isolated corner of this building for months, perhaps years, on end, my only reprieve being meetings like this one where I'll hear about them putting out game after similar game, based on my designs. Designs they won't give me credit for and will take pride in obscuring from their original vision. The realization hits me at once. Jack invited me to this meeting to ensure I'll play ball. That I'll accept the proverbial game. Provide game ideas the team can leverage, all while not putting up a fuss.

I envision myself as their quota-filling female who mutely smiles and nods forevermore. Perhaps I would have been content with who they want me to be in my Zane era. Perhaps my expectations are too high. There are far worse circumstances out there, and I'm fortunate to have this job and its salary. But after Zane, after seeing myself through Charlie's eyes, I know I'm not the person they want me to be here at Catapult.

I quietly dig my thumbnail into my palm under the table as Ross and Kenji accept their accolades from the room.

I sit in silence for the rest of the meeting, willing myself to believe things will get better with time. It's only been three weeks, and I will earn my spot here. But, there's a nagging uncertainty that eats at my insides like termites on a log. I think about twelve-year-old me. How much I relied on video games to get me through difficult days. How working here, putting out games like Kenji's, would not have served her. This version of gaming doesn't feel like the dream I've held close for so long.

The thing I've learned recently, though, is that a few days can change the course of your life. I have to believe I'm still meant for game design. As I drive home after work, the dreary LA November evening quickly shifting dark, all I can seem to think about is Charlie.

42.

"HOW LONG ARE YOU GONNA MOPE AROUND?" TESS ASKS. SHE THROWS a punch and I shift to the left to avoid her gloved fist.

"I'm not moping. I'm just trying to figure out how to make this job work."

"And how will you do that?"

"I said figuring out, not *have* figured out." I dance around the ring, shifting my weight from one foot to the other.

Tess mimics my movements. "That means you've done nothing but mope."

I want to push back, but one, she's right, and two, it's challenging to argue while wearing a mouth guard. I remove it as I lean against the ropes of the ring in defeat. It's one of the first times I've seen Tess since being back from the trip. We've blamed our distance on mutual busyness, that I am time-constrained and exhausted from my new job. That she has been dealing with a particularly ugly divorce at work, a twenty-six yearer. Both of these justifications are true. But packed calendars have never stopped us from seeing each other before.

"I think I've found my sport," Tess says, shadowboxing in the middle of the ring. Her too large gloves against her tiny frame and long ponytail bouncing against her back make her look like a cross between Princess Peach and a miniature pinscher. She removes her own mouth guard, though because of the gloves she spits it to the ground outside the ring, which she takes great pleasure in doing. "Are you really this upset about the job?" she says, moving closer.

"Of course I am. Why would you ask that? This was . . . is my dream."

"If it's your dream, you wouldn't be miserable." She presses both her gloves forward and then spins in a circle in what I'm certain is not an actual boxing move.

"It would be if they'd just take me seriously. But instead, they're taking the thing I love and turning it into something I hate. Even so, I have to stick it out. What's the alternative? Perhaps I can even help pave the way like Anita—"

"Look at the bright side," she says. "If you were to quit and were no longer working with the game designers from frat boy hell, you could date again. And Charlie's just across the hall . . ."

I shake my head, push myself off the ropes, and start bouncing, doing my best impression of a capable boxer. "I'm sure he wants nothing to do with me. Why would he? I blamed him for *my* mistakes with the Catapult interview. I can't offer myself up now without it seeming like he's some sort of consolation prize because the job has turned out to be miserable. Besides, even though Catapult is not what I expected, I still have to play by their rules to keep a paycheck. And if that's not reason enough, he also saw me with Zane."

"You were with Zane?" Tess punches me square in the jaw.

"Ow!"

"Sorry. Natural reaction. You should deliver all horrific news in a boxing ring from now on."

"I wasn't *with* Zane," I say, rubbing my jaw with my glove, likely looking as though I'm punching myself in the face. "He came by to try to get back together, and Charlie saw us . . . embracing."

"You were cuddling with Zane?" Tess throws another punch. More prepared this time, I duck.

"*Not cuddling.* It was a goodbye hug. To get him to leave faster."

"At least it wasn't a kiss. People who surprise kiss are the worst," she says with a devious smile.

"Yeah yeah, I get it. All roads lead back to Charlie."

"Well, it sounds like you're just giving up on having him again because you think you ruined it."

"I never had him to win him back."

"That's not true. You had him twice," she says, jabbing her glove into the space between us.

"Our time together was . . . incredible," I say, my thoughts going immediately back to Charlie and me side by side on the resort terrace. "But it's hard for me to believe that he was fully in it when he had plans to propose to his ex on the last night of the trip."

"Maybe it really did all change when he met you."

I press my chin into my neck and give her a look of dismay. "No, he's not available. There's no way he could go from ready to get engaged to ready for a new relationship in just a few weeks."

"Why? Just because you couldn't?"

"Yes, actually. It has been seven months since Zane and I split and I've barely been able to feel again. There's no way Charlie is ready for anything other than a fling."

"Are *you*?"

I shake my head again. "I don't know." As soon as the words leave my lips, I know they're untrue. A few weeks ago, I would have been perfectly content never dating again. But after Charlie, I know I want those feelings back. The attraction. The joyous ache of physical want. The safety net. The friendship. All of it.

Tess sighs, presses a glove against her hip. "All I know is, I haven't seen you as happy—as dreamy—as you are when you talk about him."

I bite at the inside of my cheek in a poor attempt at staving off tears.

The truth is, Charlie is the person I want to share everything about the Catapult situation with. I know he'd say the perfect thing, whittling down this overwhelmingly complicated thing to a simple, hopeful solution. That he'd sit in the silence with me, then force me to stop blithering when it was time to stop blithering. But most of all, no matter what, he'd be proud of me. After everything that has happened, though, I can't manage to knock on his door.

"I had someone too, in the time you were away." Tess doesn't make eye contact as she says it, and if I didn't know better, I'd swear there's a pale blush across her usually unbothered face.

I push myself off the ropes. "Loafers Guy!" I am equally thrilled for the distraction from my thoughts about Charlie as I am that Tess has finally brought up her mystery man. "Are you finally ready to share all the sordid details?"

She nods, smile so wide her cupid's bow gets lost under her nose. "We've been seeing each other a few weeks. He's a math teacher. Sixth grade."

"*You* are dating a sixth-grade math teacher," I say, then shake my head and exhale sharply. "I guess it makes sense though. I mean, he probably has the patience of a saint."

Tess throws her glove into my rib and I double over. She's small but obnoxiously mighty.

"It's early, obviously. But we've hung out almost every day," she says as I catch my breath and unfold.

"That's great, Tess. Honestly. How'd you meet?"

"Actually," she says, "it was at that bar the same night you first kissed Charlie."

My eyes narrow then widen in recognition. "You're dating Man Bun Guy?"

"Yes." She manages to cross her arms, though it's difficult with gloves. "And let me tell you, the fantasies I've had about that hair . . ." She rolls her eyes to the back of her head and thrusts her lower jaw forward.

"I'm *so* happy for you. And look at the positive."

"What's that?" Tess says, head pitched to one side, hip jutted, knowing a jab is coming, either verbal or gloved.

"You can rest assured that your best friend will never, *ever* fall for him. Not unless he cuts his hair," I say with a fake shudder, and she punches me square in the left boob in a vicious crossover.

I will not be boxing with Tess again.

She stands still for one of the first times since we entered the ring. "We'll see where it goes," she says, her eyes flicking upward.

"Why'd you wait so long to tell me?" I ask, afraid I already know the answer.

She bites at her lower lip. "I wasn't sure you could handle it. After everything you've been through."

I push off the ropes and make my way to her to grab her hand, having momentarily forgotten about the gloves. Instead, we end up in a gloved fist bump.

"I didn't realize the aftermath of Zane affected me for so long. And how it affected you. You were there for me through it all. And of course I want you to be happy."

She nods, presses her gloves into mine.

I shake my head. "Look at you, all grown up."

"Yeah, it's nice over here. You should join me." She starts bouncing again, her ponytail wagging behind her like a wild stallion's tail.

Tess, who has a strict "keep it light" rule, has met someone she actually likes and dove straight in with seemingly no hesitation. I've waited for this moment our entire adult lives, fantasizing about a time when we could go on double dates to picnic at the Getty or to Wednesday night trivia at the pub on her corner. And yet, now that she's found someone, I'm more alone than ever. I feel Charlie's phantom embrace.

"Okay, enough about me. I don't understand how you could have complicated things so much with this guy in such a short time," she says. She finally stops moving and leans against the ropes, out of breath.

Leaning next to her, I think again about Charlie. Yes, there's a lot to like. His eyes, his cheek dimple, his not-at-all sprayed-on abs. His wit, caring nature, belief, and, dare I say, awe of my talent and dreams.

"It's written all over your face, you know." Tess motions a glove up and down me.

"He made me feel like I don't have to apologize for who I am or what I want. Nobody outside of you has believed in me the way he has. Not my parents, certainly not Zane. I just keep thinking . . . maybe that's special, you know? And I want to be that for him too. I want him to know I support him the way he has supported me. It's like I look at everything differently after meeting him. Like knowing there's magic left in the world makes me unable to settle for less than magical." As soon as I say the words, I close my eyes.

Because I realize it just as Tess does.

"Oh my god, you love him! This is so much more than a vacation bone with the spray-on abs guy!"

I keep my eyes pressed shut. I can't even argue. Because as she says the words, a warmth spreads over me. I feel the crush of my cheek against the fabric of his T-shirt when he wraps his arms around me. I feel the safety of it.

I feel the love of it.

Perhaps I've made an irreparable mess of things. Perhaps he's not available yet, no matter how much he insists he is. Perhaps I will lose my dream job. But I have to try to make it up to him, to prove to him that what we had—have—is real. So real that in just over a week together, I managed to fall in love with him. I have to know if he feels the same. There's no amount of fear or embarrassment that can keep me from finding out.

"I need him to show up to my parents' vow renewal," I say.

"You're really still worried about showing your parents you have a boyfriend?"

"No, I don't want any more fakeness between us. But he thinks I'm back with Zane, that I chose the job. I want him to know I choose him above it all. He deserves that and so much more."

"More like meeting your parents?"

I shake my head. "Think about it, if I take him to the renewal and introduce him to my parents as exactly who he is, exactly as what we are, it'll show him I am serious. That I want something real with him. And that I'm not going to try to hide him away for a job or anything else."

"What about your job?"

I exhale sharply, a sliver of doubt worming in. "I don't know," I say. "But I have to at least *try* to make it all work."

Tess breaks a moment of contemplative silence. "I can only imagine your mom's reaction to learning that your date to her vow renewal is a part-time actor with whom your status is, it's complicated." She exhales. "I've never understood your mom. She desperately wants you wifed up but doesn't want you to ever rely on a man. She wants you to be successful but not in what you actually want to do. And she wants you with anyone who will take you, but if you bring someone like Charlie, she'll inevitably be disappointed?"

"Bingo."

Tess shrugs, having known the dichotomy that is my mother for most of her teenage and adult life.

"I just need him to show up. He said he would, but after

everything that happened . . ." I trail off because I can't manage to say the rest aloud. *But after everything that happened . . . I don't know why he* would *show up.* But if he does, I can lay it all on the line, knowing I've done everything I can.

I just have to get him to show up.

"Ladies, less gossip, more punching, *please*!" Our instructor grabs the towel from around his neck and throws it to the ground outside the ring to show his dismay. Now that I really look at him, all I can see is Kenji Sugano's rendering of Arsonist Joe, tatted and all biceps, in desperate need of calf raises to build some counterbalance. Another class we can't show our faces in again.

Just as I'm about to suggest we make our exit, Tess lands a powerfully backed glove into me at ovary level. Her diminutive height and general lack of interest in physical activity made me completely underestimate her as an opponent.

"I'm definitely coming back here," she says as she dances around with her gloved hands in the air in celebration of her perceived KO.

43.

NEARLY FOUR WEEKS LATER, I HAVEN'T ENGAGED WITH CHARLIE since our hallway run-in on my first day at Catapult and that brief glimpse of him in our apartment lobby the week after.

I wonder if he's okay.

Perhaps there's been a gas leak that's somehow confined to his apartment, or he was targeted by the possible arsonist next door. Maybe Brooke showed up the way Zane did, declaring it a mistake to have let him go. Perhaps he remembered how, just a few short weeks ago, he wanted nothing more than to get back together with her and they've been holed up in his apartment having all the sexxx and doing butt stuff. I cringe at the thought.

I ultimately decided to leave a letter at his door about the vow renewal. Cowardly, yes. But also, I feared I'd turn into a bumbling idiot if I tried to explain everything to him. How could I possibly, clearly tell him that I'm sorry for all the mistakes I've made with us. That I don't quite know how yet, but I'm going to make us *and* gaming work, if he'll have me.

That I love him.

No, I needed time to clearly outline a plan. So instead, I kept it simple.

There's so much I need to say to you. And, equally, I don't know how to say it all. So I'll start with the basics. Zane and I are NOT together. I'm sorry if it looked like we were. You made me realize I deserve so much more. Second, I invited you to my parents' vow renewal, and I would still really love if you would come. As my date. I know it might affect my job, but it's worth the risk for the opportunity to tell you all the things I owe it to you to say.

PS—If you are back together with Brooke, please disregard this note in its entirety and give it to Mrs. Crandall to burn in one of her many ashtrays.

PPS—Should you be willing to give me—us—another chance, here are the details for the vow renewal.

I slipped it under his door on my way to work nearly two weeks ago.

I'd like to say things at Catapult have gotten better over the last few weeks, but it would be a sky-size lie. There's been zero mention of *Arsonist Joe* being based on my interview game design as the team has progressed with production, and they've slaughtered every good bit of it, the worst offense being the complete removal of the love story.

I know it's part of the job, part of many jobs even outside of gaming. To offer ideas that may be taken and used without credit. To watch those ideas become something you wholeheartedly believe is less than. These truths don't make my situation any less disheartening.

When Charlie doesn't respond to my note, it's Tess who ends up as my date to my parents' vow renewal, though technically, I'm third-wheeling because her actual date is Man Bun, whose real name is Nate. Today, Nate wears a white dress shirt with rolled-up sleeves under a gray vest. His hair is pulled into a particularly tight ball at the top of his head. A fancy man bun for a fancy afternoon and evening.

My parents, married thirty years today, offer a perfectly mixed message. My mother cooks every meal and waits on my father and his every need. She also keeps that separate bank account and preaches independence. My green-eyed American father is served every meal, but also can't make a decision without my mother. Regardless of their household dynamic, she is still the neck that controls the head.

Their vow renewal, for which they've rented out a reception hall in Van Nuys, is the ultimate melding of cultures. The buffet is lined with tandoori chicken and pakora, next to the mac 'n' cheese and scalloped potatoes that signify my father's Midwest upbringing. My father wears a plain navy suit. My mother, a red sari with gold accents (identical to the one she provided me to wear today), several pieces of gold jewelry, including a stack of bangles on each wrist, henna across her hands, and a large red press-on bindi at the center point of her forehead. The hall is strung with amber marigolds, the tables adorned with roses and baby's breath centerpieces.

"Do you think he'll show?" I ask Tess when we enter the hall. I've avoided the question until now because I'm afraid she'll confirm that after more than a month of not seeing him and no response to my note, it's unlikely.

Tess looks at me with a rare gentleness in her expression. "I don't know." She cups her hand around my wrist. "But our plan is ready, just in case."

I give her a weak smile, just as my mother spots us.

"Tess! Lovely to see you again!" My mom throws her arms around my friend, making a great show of how long it's been since I've brought Tess around. Her bangles jingle, and I can't help but smile at the sound that reminds me of childhood.

"Mrs. Cooper, you look beautiful! Happy anniversary. This is my boyfriend, Nate," Tess says, placing a hand behind his elbow. She says the word *boyfriend* as if it's a new dress she's trying on for size. From where I stand, it definitely fits.

"Nate, lovely to meet you," my mom says, her head moving in a familiar slight figure eight as she tries to figure out the romantic situation.

"That's right, Mom. Tess has a boyfriend. And I do not." Something about my time with Charlie has made me never again want to hide who I am or what I want. Even to my mother, who always has disappointment at the ready in her arsenal of emotions.

My mother's face drops, and I wonder if announcing Tess, Nate, and I as a throuple would have been more acceptable to her.

"Oh, that's okay, dear," she says. "Zane will come to his senses."

"We're gonna grab some samosas, give you two a minute," Tess announces before pulling Nate toward the buffet.

"What're samosas?" I hear him ask as they skitter off.

"Mom. Zane and I, we broke up. Eight months ago."

"I know that," she says, flicking her wrist and circling her head at me, bangles clanging.

"Yes, but what you don't know is that he was cheating on me. He met this girl at the gym, and they were, you know . . ."

I can't manage to say "sleeping together" to my mother. I've never actually discussed sex with her. I learned about sex with Tess from watching her father's collection of porn DVDs. Mr. Hubbard was particularly fond of cuckolds and celebrity sex tapes. It took me until my early twenties to realize the three-thrust orgasm wasn't actually a thing. In some ancient part of her mind, my mother may even believe I'm still a virgin.

She pushes her chin forward and steels her face. "I never liked him." She places her arm around my shoulder and steers us toward the buffet as I try to keep my jaw off the floor.

Was it really this simple all along?

I've grown. I don't know why I didn't give my mom the consideration that she could also grow. The allowance for doing the same. I stop her mid-step, deciding to ride this wave, see where it might take me. "There's something else," I tell her, and she furrows her perfectly threaded eyebrows. "I want to be honest and tell you the new job isn't exactly what I thought it would be—"

She opens her mouth to speak, but I keep going.

"But that doesn't mean I've changed my mind about game design. This is very much what I want to do. And I'm willing to give up anything for it."

Almost anything.

She looks at me for a long moment before she says, "I'll tell Jaya's mom you're not interested in the job at her firm. It's probably filled by now anyway."

Perhaps it's because she doesn't want this celebration ruined or because she truly has become more accepting, but it's as supportive a sentiment as has ever come out of her mouth. "Thank you," I tell her.

She pats my back. "You know, an engineering background *could* help with video games."

I give her the look she's known since I was two—chin tucked, head cocked to one side, eyebrows raised.

"I'm just saying."

We join my father at the buffet and fill our plates together. I watch her grab one pakora at a time, picking each one up with the pair of serving tongs and inspecting it before placing it on her plate. Since I was a teenager, I've blamed her for so much. I've blamed her for the flood—this uncontrollable situation she couldn't have reasonably prepared for. I've blamed her for me not pursuing my own dreams for my own life. Tonight, she has accepted everything I've thrown at her without flinching.

I put my arm around her shoulders in a rare act of physical affection between us. She smiles, holds up a samosa, and aims the tongs in my direction. I insist, as I have since I started speaking, that I don't like samosas. She acts as though it's the first time she's hearing this, then places one on my plate anyway.

I can't expect a 180-degree change in one evening, for either of us.

When the time comes, I sit front row in a white Chiavari chair, as my parents stand in front of the massive stone fireplace, a lungi-clad priest between them. My father holds my mother's hands in his, hers lying on top as they face each other. He smiles at her with knowing ease.

My father tears up. My mother does not. The entire ceremony is consummately them. They recite things they love about each other: for my mom, my father's calmness and kind spirit. His love of Indian food and Bette Midler films. His being the voice of reason in unreasonable times. And my father speaks of my mother's capacity for acts of service and her untamable spirit. How he admires her ability to keep so many balls in the air and how she cooks a mean mac 'n' cheese that's just as delicious as her butter chicken. I tear up, reliving the lifetime of love between them. Between us three.

I've often told myself I want something better than what they have, despite everyone around me insisting their relationship is aspirational. I thought I wanted something more balanced. Less traditional. With more laughter and adventure. More romantic and unconventional. But as I watch them reavow their pledge to each other, I think: They're committed. And happy. And that makes their relationship perfect for them. For perhaps the first time, I see them as everyone else does.

I think about Charlie. What it would have meant had he come tonight. What it means that he hasn't. My plan to demonstrate to him that I'm worth the risk of getting hurt again, that even if he's not ready, I at least want to try because I care about him too much not to . . . None of it matters now.

Because he didn't show up.

When the dancing starts, I sneak outside to avoid being pulled onto the dance floor by my thirteen-year-old cousin, who will inevitably step on my feet no fewer than six times. The music from inside is muffled by the thick-paned windows, and I close my eyes and tilt my chin toward the late afternoon sky. When I open them, the first thing I see is a plane, moving slowly, methodically across the cloudless blue. It's a shooting star, I decide, despite it not yet being dark, because I desperately want to make a wish.

I used to think I'd never get over Zane. Now I'm afraid I'll never get over Charlie. The difference is, I don't want to get over Charlie. Not at all.

When I can't stare up anymore, the nostalgia of this big, familiar sky too much to bear, I bring my head forward, eyes out to the grass, the row of trees beyond.

There, several yards in front of me, is a well-dressed Charlie. No punny T-shirt to be found.

44.

HE WEARS A NAVY BLUE SUIT SIMILAR TO THE ONE MY FATHER DONS just inside, a solid navy silk tie over a crisp white dress shirt. Tan, unbruised dress shoes. Hair smoothed precisely. Dimple invisible in the filter of the golden hour. Today's version of him is so imposingly attractive he rivals backward-hat Charlie. He rubs his hands together unconsciously in front of him in methodical circles. I can't help the warmth at my base that the familiar gesture provides me.

"You came," I say softly into the chilled afternoon air. He takes a step toward me. I'm quite sure he hasn't heard me, my muted words evaporating into the space between us before they could possibly reach him. He answers anyway.

"I made you a promise weeks ago that I would come. You kept your promise to me by going on the trip. I wanted to keep mine. I'm sorry I'm late." He smiles, though it doesn't quite reach his eyes.

As he finishes his slow approach, I attach to his gaze, bright and delicate in the stream of velvety yellow light. He looks me up and down. He's never seen me this dressed up, let alone in anything that represents my Indian culture.

"Wow," he whispers when his eyes reach mine again.

"Thank you for coming," I say.

I want to reach for him, for a hug or handhold or pinkie embrace. But I don't do it. Not yet.

"I've missed you," he says. The desperation in the sputter of his voice is familiar. Going from 24/7 togetherness in Turks to not speaking left a painful void I wasn't prepared for. "I'm sorry I'm late."

"You said that already."

"I know. But I want you to know why. I debated whether to come up until the last minute."

My heart constricts as he takes another step forward.

"I know how much your job means to you. That getting it is your dream come true. I know how hard you worked for it." He takes another cautious step. "And I know that I could jeopardize all of that for you. I can't be the reason you don't get everything you ever wanted."

The draw I feel to him is intense, the gravitational pull of water up the shore at high tide.

But not yet.

"I'm going to need a minute," I tell him, turning on my nude peep-toe heels to rush inside. His face falls. He thinks he's made a mistake coming here. That he is right about the job and that I regret inviting him. That I still choose it over him. But that's not it.

I dash inside.

Tess finds me, my phone in hand, having been spying out the window.

"Here." She shoves my phone at me. "Go get your guy," she declares with a slap on my butt to send me on my way.

Nate lifts his fist for a bump of solidarity.

I observe Charlie through the glass for a moment, hands in his pockets, back turned as he looks out at the tree-lined property edge. I can't get back to him fast enough. I've missed you too, I attempt to tell him telepathically.

At the click of my heels against the patio tile, he turns to me with a pensive look.

His face. It's full of fear and longing and want, bursting with hope and things unsaid. Observing him, I know he feels it. The connection between us that demands exploration.

Stepping onto the grass, I take my place in front of him. "Hi."

His mouth twitches. "Hi."

I hit play on my phone, click the volume up to high, and toss it beside us where it sinks into the freshly cut grass.

Charlie looks down, then back at me with a sentimental smile as "Drift Away" begins to play from my phone. I can't help but smile back, knowing the lyrics will be "give me the Beach Boys" forevermore.

He takes another step toward me where there was no space to be had. "What are you doing?"

I clear my throat, move even closer, ignoring my heels sinking into the soft earth. "The grand gesture."

He comes closer still, taking my hands in his. He is cold to the touch, as I've come to expect. I bask in the way the feel of them awakens me.

"Look, I'm sorry for making you feel like you were just a cover. That what we had was fake. Because it wasn't. It was real. It *is* real. More real than anything I've ever had."

I press my palm to his shirt at stomach level, feeling the ridges beneath the thick cotton of his dress shirt. "This is supposed to be my grand gesture."

He gives me that sheepish grin, and I want to kiss the dimple that digs into his cheek.

"I met up with Brooke," he says.

The sound of her name makes my throat clench. Perhaps this isn't going to turn out as I hoped.

"I told her everything. About our trip, my intentions when I invited you. About what it was like to learn of her relationship with Spencer, so soon after we broke up. I told her how much it hurt me, but that ultimately, I now know we weren't meant to be together."

"How'd that go?"

"It was good. I feel . . . relieved. She's genuinely happy. Happier than she ever was with me."

"That must have been hard."

He's thoughtful for a moment, eyes flickering to the ground then back to me. "Somewhat. I also told her about you. About how I fell in love with you."

A flutter makes its way from my belly to my toes.

Love.

"Fell in love, as in past tense? As in, no longer?"

He shakes his head. "Still, very much in love. But I didn't want to get in the way of your job. And I didn't want to tell you until I knew I was truly over Brooke. That I could give you all of me. It's one of the reasons I've stayed away as long as I have. I needed to ensure I was fully over her. Ready to move on. Ready to dive in. With you, if you'll have me. I don't know what that would look like with your job or if it can even work, but I want to try."

I thrust myself forward and kiss him in similar fashion to our kiss that first night at the bar. This time, he kisses back immediately, no hesitation or surprise to be had. Only aching want—soft and tender, then firm, crescendoing back and forth between the two. It's whole, this kiss. It's filled with the passion of recovering something once lost.

The song ends and immediately starts again.

He pulls away slightly. "You put it on repeat?"

I nod. "I knew this might take a while. More than three minutes and forty-eight seconds."

There's a flicker of an appreciative grin across his lips and it's gone as quickly as it came. "What about your job, Sloane?

I don't want to get in the way of that." A seriousness flattens his eyebrow ridge.

"I don't know what's going to happen, but I'm not going to give you up for a job. And Charlie, I need you to know, you are not almost good enough. You are more important than Zane ever was. More than any job. You're so much more than good enough. You're Fruity Pebbles."

His smile grows slowly. I pay close attention to its expansion. "I told Brooke I was genuinely happy too. And your message was right. I really am *happlier* than I've ever been. Because of you. *You're* Kix."

My breath catches. "You're taking over my grand gesture. I had a whole speech planned," I tell him, my arms wrapped around his neck.

"Oh? Please then, I'd like to hear it."

"Well, for starters, I'm sorry. I'm sorry for blaming you for the game mistake, and for the picture."

"You've already apologized for those things."

"I know, but it bears repeating. And there's more."

"So much to be sorry for after such a short period of time," he teases, forehead creased playfully.

"Yeah, but our time together was like summer camp."

"What?"

"Didn't you ever go to summer camp as a kid? Those relationships you build in a week are deeper than most that take years. Like me and Tess."

He shakes his head as he smiles so lovingly it makes the longing roll across my body.

"But back to my apology list. I'm sorry for acting like our time together didn't mean anything to me, because it did. It meant more than you could possibly know."

He leans in and kisses me. It's light and airy, like bread rising. "Does that mean you forgive me?"

"It means I was never mad at you." Here we stand, covered in the scar tissue of past relationships, alongside the fresh cuts we've given each other. But the new ones are still just cuts, shallow, with a chance at healing. He leans in to kiss me again. "I know this is supposed to be your grand gesture, not mine," he says when he pulls away. "But there's something else." He sprints across the grass, bends down behind a bush that lines the space between the patio and grass. When he shoots back up, he has the field day goat trophy/makeshift necklace around his neck.

"Wait, you still have that?"

He shrugs when he makes his way back to me. "You left it in the suite when we were leaving. I packed it." I kiss him again, though with some difficulty because the plastic goat ear presses into my chest.

"You sentimental sap," I say, straightening the goat just as I had when I presented it to him. He places his palms under each of my elbows, curls his fingers around my arms.

He leans in for another kiss, but I interrupt before his lips can connect with mine. "Wait. There's one more thing."

This grand gesture has turned into a back-and-forth between us, and perhaps it's just as it should be.

I turn and nod toward the window where I know Tess is still watching. She leaps from her seat and bursts out the side door, then creeps behind a bush near the reception entrance, carrying a long-reach lighter. She crouch-runs across the grass in her A-line royal blue dress and five-inch nude heels, clicking the flame, all the while acting as though her stealth efforts are somehow keeping her hidden.

"Is this some kind of real-life reenactment of *Arsonist Betty*?" Charlie asks as we watch her scurry across the manicured lawn.

I place his face between my palms and turn him toward me so he can't see her shrink down and light the flame behind him. Then to another, and another. Four in all. She darts back inside and once again, it's just Charlie and me.

Then, the gunshot-like pops begin. Despite knowing they're coming, I jump at the first blasts and Charlie tightens his grip around me. Behind him, light sprints into the sky, yellow and blue and green. Fireworks. Not guns. And before you wonder how I managed to afford a real fireworks display, let me clarify these are four little round cylinders you find in a tent on the side of a road around the Fourth of July. It's perfect. Until—

One of the four cylinders falls over from its perch in the grass, with Charlie and me in its direct line of carnage. The flames shoot ferociously toward us, snapping and snarling their way across the grass.

"Run!" Charlie orders, placing an arm behind my back and pushing me toward the building as if we're soldiers under fire on the battlefield.

"Charlie." I tug on his arm to stop him after a few steps. He looks back and sees that the small display is shooting short, singular strands of colored fire that don't quite reach us.

Again, side-of-the-road fireworks, not the midnight Disneyland kind.

"Oh. Right," he says, running his fingers along his chin. We hold hands, looking on as the final firework putters out.

When it does, he turns to face me again. "This is exactly why if the world was ending, I'd choose you. And not just because you'd keep me alive. But because you make me feel safe."

"If the world was ending, I'd choose you too. And don't worry. I'd protect you. Not just from the zombies and gangs, but from the cold. From needles and weird bugs and bumpy plane rides too, if airplanes are still a thing."

"I don't know what I'd bring to the table in terms of help, but it sounds perfect."

"Don't underestimate yourself. Your fishing skills make

you a hot commodity for the end of days. And if that doesn't work out, we can always sell your body for gas and eggs."

He smiles. "You've thought about this."

"Of course I have."

I'm not sure how we got here, talking about apocalyptic survival strategies, but I love it. Because it's the perfect grand gesture. For me. For us.

"Do you want to go inside and meet everyone?" I ask, pointing a thumb over my shoulder. "There's plenty of cheese on the buffet."

"There's nothing I'd love more," he says, squeezing my hand.

When the celebration dwindles in the early evening, and Charlie has adequately charmed Nate and Tess, my extended family, my dad and, somehow, my *mom*, we escape to a quiet spot on the second-floor terrace of the venue. It feels like home. Our version of comfort—sitting on a terrace looking out at the stars.

"I severely overestimated your dance moves," I tell him as we sit on the weathered wood deck, backs pressed against the chilled sliding glass door. Charlie's suit jacket is slung across my shoulders, and I can't help but close my eyes each time I inhale his scent of silky bar soap. I've craved that smell these last weeks. "They are so much worse than what I originally thought."

He bumps my shoulder playfully with his. "Is it true what they say then? Bad dancer, bad in bed?"

I shake my head. "Definitely not true. Though, I'm gonna need a refresher, just to be sure. *Very*, very soon."

We kiss.

This kiss, one of several this evening, is once again different from all the others. It's tender, unhurried, deliberate, and the feeling that comes to mind more than any is that of thankfulness. This kiss is thankful. As his tongue gently finds mine, I wonder when a kiss from Charlie might feel like a plain old kiss from Charlie. I can't imagine that day coming anytime soon.

When we part, I rest my head on his shoulder. He presses his lips to the top of my head. Now that we are together, out in the open for the world to see, the affection is unrelenting.

"I still cannot believe you managed to win over my mother. I thought it an impossible feat."

Just a few hours before, I had announced I was single, then I was introducing Charlie as my boyfriend, a statement that had unintentionally fallen out of my mouth when presenting him to my cousin Layla. Without a missed beat, he smiled and nodded in agreement.

"You didn't think she'd like me?"

"I didn't think she'd like anyone."

I could practically see the mechanisms turning in her head. She wanted to hate him. Part of her wanted to pull me aside and insist Charlie is not the guy for me. That I should be with a doctor or an engineer. That *I* should be a doctor or an engineer. But, alas, my mother has grown. And after the revelation about Zane, I believe she's giving up, little by little, her plan for me. She looked down at our clasped hands and, finally, said, "Very handsome."

I pulled him away before things could go south.

While I still care what my parents think, I also know I'm now prepared to follow my own instincts for my own life.

Charlie looks up at the sky and I do the same.

"I decided I'm going to keep at it with acting. It may take years more, but I want it. You've taught me there's no shame in pursuing what you want in life, I've just gotta build the path and see it through. Stamina, right?"

"Stamina." I reflect on my own situation. "Catapult isn't exactly what I was hoping it would be," I tell him.

He turns to face me. "No?" he says, and his furrowed expression is one of deep concern. I warm in appreciation at his ardent care for my dreams.

"No, but I'm starting to think perhaps there's another way. I thought for so long Catapult was the one way to get what I want in my career. But now, I wonder if there's more opportunity out there than I first realized."

"Honestly, I'm so glad to hear that. I never wanted to stand in the way of your dreams. I'll support you in any way that I can."

"I know. And you'll get the same from me."

He raises my hand and presses his lips to the back of it. "I know."

We stare at the sky, dark and flecked.

"Do you think it will be the same? Here, in the real world? Not in paradise?" I ask.

He's quiet for a moment before responding, "Turks was real life. It was picturesque, yes, but, Sloane, you know nothing about it was fake. It *was* real life, just with a beach. And if we can make it through living together and Amazonian centipedes, Andres-level resort games and too much rum punch—"

"Then we are adequately prepared for LA?"

He smirks. "Yes. Exactly. Besides"—he leans in and kisses me again, this one sturdy, grounded—"here, we have tomorrow."

I look into his eyes and see the shimmer of the millions of stars overhead.

"Did you think about me? Over these last few weeks?" I ask, now staring at the quickly emerging twinkling lights we pretended were shooting stars, a thousand miles away from here.

The sky seems bigger than it ever has. Vast and unbothered and humbling, steeped in history and hope.

"Every day," he says.

I already know the answer. I just want to hear him say it.

Glinting city lights flicker in the distance and the last of the bloodred sunset disappears completely.

It's just pollution, I tell myself when my eyes begin to water.

"Sloane Cooper, are you actually crying, you sap?"

"Please," I say, dabbing quickly at my inner eye.

We watch for a long while, the lights from the city twinkling brighter as the sky softens to a deep plum. And then one light in particular catches my eye, moving across the sky, leaving a trail of white dust behind it. A shooting star. A real one—seeming as though it started as a light from one of those downtown buildings and took off like a rocket and then, ended its voyage with a brief final sparkle.

Or maybe it's a faraway plane and its contrail.

I can't know for certain, but tonight, I decide with all of myself, it's a shooting star.

In this moment, on this terrace, I can see it all with him. A life of adventure. A potential lifelong partner who supports me with unabashed strength. I even see two little blue-eyed, tan-skinned babies—Loki and Delta—running along a sandy beach, giggling and kicking water at their dad.

I squeeze Charlie's hand, knowing wherever life takes us from here, it must include a terrace for stargazing.

Epilogue

One Year Later, Minus Six Weeks

MY COMPANY, IF THE WORLD WAS ENDING—THAT'S RIGHT, *MY* company—is a video game design firm that in the next few years, will focus on STEM training for girls and women interested in the field. Though most of our original game concepts center around doomsday prep, our first upcoming release is a mobile game called *Revenge Cheese*, where players create an avatar that resembles their ex (or whomever they are seeking vengeance on), then chase them around the city until they successfully land a slice of cheese across their face. Turns out, it *was* a great idea, and Charlie and I weren't the only ones out there who could use some bit of closure after a bad breakup. Though cheese can't fix everything, it sure does fix a lot.

The second game, releasing late next year and generating more buzz than the first, is *Arsonist Betty*. It seems people also love the idea of hunting down an elderly arsonist setting fires all across the city. Early players have enjoyed the opportunity to outsmart the villain only to help her be reunited with her lost love, and it seems to sit on shelves as a nice alternative to all the shoot-'em-up games out there. Catapult making significant changes to my design, and the fact that Anita somehow missed having me sign a work product agreement during my new hire paperwork, allowed for me to build my version of it the way I originally envisioned, without fear of infringement. *Arsonist Betty* bears only a slight resemblance to Mrs. Crandall in 6D.

Speaking of Mrs. Crandall, she's become a bit of a mainstay in our lives. Our interactions with her mostly involve Charlie changing her light bulbs or carrying her groceries, but every once in a while, she surprises us with a plate of homemade apple oatmeal muffins that only carry the faintest scent of cigarettes.

Mrs. Crandall doesn't know it yet, but thanks to her unintended contributions to the game, there's a check coming her way on release day.

As for future game plans, I've decided to move away from arson and arsenals. There are enough bad things in the world. And as Charlie (and even Mrs. Crandall) have reminded me, there is more good than bad. Our third release is still just an idea and likely a few years away from release, but it'll be different from anything on the market. Something Catapult would never dream of putting out.

I'm rather proud of that.

It wasn't long after my parents' vow renewal that I resigned from Catapult. And not because of Charlie and my broken promise to my interviewing trio about staying single. It was because I knew, after several more meetings like the initial *Arsonist Joe* one, that the job would take the thing I loved and rob me of the opportunity to turn it into a career I could equally love.

The sly flicker of a grin across Jack Palmer's face when I delivered my resignation letter—straight to him, rather than Anita—told me he believed I was proving him right. That hiring the girl had been a mistake. I almost ripped the letter from his hand and changed my mind because of that smirk. But then Charlie's words came to me like a hand of support in that moment. I was so afraid of ruining what I loved by staying in the job I hated. The truth is, once I did it on my own terms, I realized there was nothing to ruin.

Charlie has been so supportive of my entrepreneurial pursuits that he even offered his apartment to me, should I, in fact, be evicted from my own as I worked to launch my company. It was way too soon to live together, but the fact that he would even offer deepened my adoration of him.

As it turns out, I wouldn't need a new place to live.

Soon after my departure from Catapult, I approached an angel investor in the gaming space who had somehow already heard about the version of *Arsonist Betty* I submitted to Catapult. I can't be certain, but I would bet the two hundred thousand dollars her firm invested to get my new company off the ground that Anita had something to do with it.

As for Anita, the pen she gave me on my first day at Catapult sits in my desk drawer as a reminder of what this company, *my* company, will never be. And though I tried to recruit her several times after she left Catapult, she decided to build her own thing too. A career-coaching firm where she helps empower female executives to hold their own in a room full of Jack Palmers and Kenji Suganos. She's booked solid for the next eight months.

I used to wonder why she stayed at Catapult as long as she did, and now realize she was slowly building her business on the side, stealthily planning her escape. I've got mad respect for her patience and diplomacy.

She ended up getting out just in time.

A slew of lawsuits have been filed against Catapult Games for their illegal hiring and employment practices, the first of which was by the woman who departed right before me who had "too many boyfriend issues." Soon after, I hired her as my COO, offering her a stake in the company in lieu of a salary, which she was able to accept thanks to her hefty settlement from Catapult.

There have been many naysayers, skeptical of a woman who went from being an engineering firm office assistant to starting her own gaming company within two years. I simply remind those people that Jack Palmer had a similar start to his own gaming career.

As for Charlie and me, we've found our happiness. He has read many of the romance novels on my shelf, though he stays away from anything he considers "too doomsday." His favorite is still *The Burning Locke*.

Tess and I have made him and Nate endure many evenings with *Thelma & Louise*. Charlie and Nate were fast friends over their love of everything competitive (sports, games, general life activities that they enjoy turning into competitions wherever possible).

We've found a favorite stargazing spot, a secluded corner of Griffith Park. Somehow, we only ever see shooting stars, no airplanes. With a flask of homemade rum punch, we lie there often, throwing out game ideas.

The video of Charlie "saving" that girl Maddie from the Caribbean bathwater went viral after Andres posted it to his shockingly large social media following. As a result, Charlie was offered a multi-commercial deal with the spray-on abs company. It's not his dream job, but it's a step in the right direction. And thanks to the six-figure paycheck, he's no longer embarrassed to be recognized as the spray-on abs guy. Besides, he's also now moonlighting as a romance novel cover model. It pays surprisingly well.

We still compete, in ways big and small. Whose game idea will sell the best. Which book cover featuring his abs will be the most popular. Who will catch the largest trout, as I've developed my own love of fishing. How many rum punches it will take for me to turn frisky. (Hint: not many.) Game nights mean

Charlie and I are always on the same team, because Tess and Nate refuse to participate otherwise, citing our competitive intensity as frightening.

I've finally gotten the thing I always wanted but Tess intended never to oblige, a weekly double date with our respective partners. And Charlie has become and remains my safe place. He knows my ugliest thoughts and not only loves me anyway but helps love them out of me.

I'm surprised when Charlie shows up at my door on a seemingly random Tuesday evening, wearing a button-down shirt and holding a bouquet of black roses.

Finn gives me a hello butt waggle and lick of my bare shin from the hallway, then pushes past me into my apartment. He now travels back and forth between Charlie's place and mine, assuming the space as one extensive doggy suite.

"What's all this?" I ask.

Charlie cups my elbow with his free hand, grazes my cheek with a kiss before entering. He goes to the kitchen and effortlessly grabs the vase from the top of the refrigerator, the one I have to climb onto the counter to reach.

"It's a special night," he says, smiling secretively.

"What're you up to?"

He shakes his head as he fills the vase at my kitchen sink, before removing the paper wrap from the bouquet and arranging the flowers in the vase.

"Table?" he asks.

I shake my head. "Nightstand." I want to see them as I drift off to sleep and as soon as I wake up.

He grins in acknowledgment and I watch him carry the vase into the bedroom. I'm tempted to follow him in there. I don't know our plans for this evening, but certainly a quickie wouldn't derail them too much.

He's back in the living room before I can attack, glancing at his watch. "We should head out," he says as he reaches the door and opens it for me.

"Can you tell me where we're going?"

He shakes his head. "Can't. Sorry."

"Am I at least dressed appropriately?" I look down at my cornflower-blue maxi dress and sandals. It's one of the only nights I haven't been pinned to my kitchen table working on *Revenge Cheese*. My team of three doesn't yet require an office, not when Marv's best table is consistently reserved for us on the occasions we meet in person.

"Perfectly," he affirms. "But grab a coat."

We say our goodbyes to Finn and step into the hallway.

In the elevator, I'm about to push the button for the subfloor parking garage, but he beats me to the pad and presses the one for the street.

"We're walking?"

He holds his hands together in front of him, rubbing in small circles. "Mm-hmm."

There are only so many places within walking distance of my apartment. Marv's. Tess's. My dry cleaners. All great spots, but hardly surprise-worthy locations.

We stroll for a few blocks. The early October weather is unseasonably balmy and it reminds me a bit of the sticky evenings in Turks. We're already planning our return to paradise, timed to the release of *Arsonist Betty* late next year. Just as I'm about to try and wheedle our destination out of him, he stops.

"We're here," he says, grabbing the door handle.

I look up at the bar where we first met. It only occurs to me now that, somehow, we haven't been back since that night.

He raises his eyebrows at me as if it's a dare to walk in and find out what awaits me inside.

I take the bait, of course. Every gamer knows you've gotta

see what's behind the gateway. He holds the door open and I enter, surprised by what I find.

Music plays from the ceiling speakers and a waiter holds a tray with two champagne glasses atop it as if he's been stationed there for however long it might take us to arrive. A bartender stands at attention behind the bar. But otherwise, the place is entirely empty. Not empty as in, there are a few people scattered throughout, but it will likely pick up as the evening goes on. Rather, we are the only two people, outside of the waiter and bartender, here.

I look to Charlie, who simply shrugs.

"Sloane!" The voice comes from the back room and out bounds Tess, arms outstretched, champagne in hand. She makes contact aggressively, her fingertips pressing into my shoulder blades as she embraces me.

"What's going on?" I ask when she pulls away.

"I have no idea. Nate wouldn't tell me anything." Man Bun (I still primarily refer to him this way, to his face and otherwise) joins her side, gives Charlie a shoulder pat in greeting.

"Did you know I was going to be here?" I ask her.

"No! Did you know? About me?"

I shake my head.

"Why's there no one else here?" Tess inquires to no one in particular.

Charlie's and Nate's faces, I notice, hold identical mischief.

"Somebody better tell me what's happening here," Tess demands.

Just when I think Tess will nut-punch one or both of them, a familiar song billows through the speakers. I stare at Charlie, whose smile has overtaken his whole face. "*Give me the* Beach Boys *and free my soul . . .*"

Is this what I think it is?

It's then I fully take in what is happening.

A proposal.

But it's not Charlie who's bending down on one knee before us. It's Nate. There, band secured between Nate's thumb and index finger, is the diamond Tess never wanted.

She squeals in delight—in such roaring joy—that if I mention it later, she will wholeheartedly deny it. It doesn't matter though, I'll always know the truth.

Tess has joined Nate on the ground, her hands sandwiching his face, foreheads pressed together. Nate's entire proposal is whispered into Tess's ear, intimate and just for them.

Charlie sniffs beside me.

"Are you crying, you sap?" I whisper.

"No," he says, though he doesn't turn away when he swipes at his eye with his index finger. Then, Charlie squeezes my hand and whispers in my ear, "Happy anniversary."

I look up at him after Nate has slid the ring onto Tess's finger, and the two members of the wait staff applaud. "Our anniversary isn't for another six weeks."

"This is the night we first met. Here," he says, his eyes circling the room.

It all clicks. The night we met is also the night Tess and Nate met . . . as I was kissing a then-stranger. The song that was playing—our song—is also the song that was playing when Tess and Nate met. Also *their* song.

I squeeze Charlie's hand.

Tess is mostly emitting high-pitched squeals now, ones that remind me of Finn when he's excited for a walk. She's the happiest I've ever seen her. My best friend, who denounced love, relationships, and anything remotely sappy, is the most electrified newly engaged woman I could ever imagine.

Love suits her.

I watch my best friend as she laughs, eyes closed and chin tilted to the ceiling, wrapping her arms around Nate's neck in a vulnerable embrace. This, my best friend who a year ago would have indeed nut-punched anyone who asserted she might be engaged soon. She was afraid too. Like me, guarded. Skeptical. But she dropped all that bulky casing for the guy who could help her set it down.

We spend the evening drinking and dancing in the bar that is all ours. It's a night I will never forget and a hell of a way for Charlie and me to spend our first anniversary, though we will probably argue indefinitely about what our real anniversary date actually is. The first night we met, or the night we made it official at my parents' vow renewal?

When Charlie and I collapse into my bed, it's nearly two a.m. I roll onto my side, his bouquet of black roses on the nightstand beside me. Charlie scoots closer, cuddles in behind me. He's so damn cold. It feels good against the blaring heat he insists on dialing my thermostat up to no matter the temperature outside.

"Did you have fun tonight?" he murmurs into my ear.

"An insane amount of fun. How long have you known about this?"

"Awhile. I went ring-shopping with Nate and helped him reserve the bar for tonight. It was *really* hard to keep it from you."

"It was perfect. I'm so happy for them."

"Are you disappointed it wasn't us?"

I turn to face him. "What?"

"I was afraid you'd think this was all for you tonight, that you'd be disappointed when you realized it wasn't. I debated not taking you, or telling you, but Nate insisted Tess would want you there and that it should be a surprise so you could share in her excitement."

"He was right," I say. "And no, I'm not disappointed. I'm happy, Charlie. Really happy. I don't want or need anything to change right now."

He smiles—not one of relief, but rather it looks like love. "That's good," he says, his voice low and grumbly. "I was afraid Satan Sloane was gonna make an appearance."

I shake my head and scoot my body farther into his. "She's reserved for just the bedroom now."

He circles his eyes around the room markedly. "Lucky for me, we seem to be in one."

I take him in as if for the first time, light from the streetlamp beyond my bedroom window curling in around the edges of the linen shade. The almost unnoticeable indent of skin that hugs the curve of the right side of his neck, the remnant of a dog bite when he was six. The muscle that presses out against the line of his jaw. The slightly uneven edges of his cheek dimple. The details of him that can only be seen this close. That can only be known by careful study. His eyes have a searching quality that mirrors mine. Then, he lifts his tattooed wrist to my hair, cups my chin with his other hand, and kisses me. He continues his kiss, slow and deliberate. As he does, he positions his hand around me and we roll together so he's now on top of me. His kiss grows stronger, hungrier, and I eagerly respond. His erection seems to come in an instant, as if he's been fighting it off all evening and is just finally giving in.

We are out of our matching pairs of men's boxers in an instant, and his hands slide up and down as he enters me with firm desire. We find our rhythm, one quickly burned into the memory of our muscles like fingers finding the keys to a song once mastered on the piano. Mostly we fuck, but tonight, we make love with the passion of a year and a night like this one.

I wrap my legs around his waist and lift my hips as a final reward.

After we've recovered, Charlie curls against me once more and envelops me tightly in his arms. When I hear the slight shift in his breathing that indicates sleep, I gently push him over to his half of the bed, because, who can really sleep like that all night? I close my eyes soon after, the black rose bouquet the last thing my eyes register before I do.

I'm fully aware this thing with Charlie may not work out. In fact, everything logical in me tells me it won't. We're technically each other's rebound. We might blaze fast and furious and eventually die out like a shooting star. I am, after all, someone who spends my life planning for an inevitable end.

I think about it far less than I used to though—how society tightropes on the most delicate balance imaginable. How so many things have to work in unison to keep us from slipping into anarchy. This newfound faith in the world, in humanity, in love—it's because of him. That in a not so perfect world, there are things that can still be profoundly right.

And maybe, just maybe, there doesn't have to be an end this time. I open my eyes groggily to admire his sleeping face. As we glide one sleep closer to a possible end, I know I could leave this whole world behind to be with him and it would be more than enough. It would be everything.

Acknowledgments

My husband and I traveled to Turks and Caicos in 2019, on what would become our last international trip before COVID-19. There, we enjoyed a suite on Grace Bay, ate incredible jerk chicken, dove for conch, and drank rum punch with our toes in the sand at Da Conch Shack. It was delightful to look back through pictures and relive this magical place for some of the location details included in these pages.

There were several resources for bringing the gaming components of this book to life. One of my favorites was the show *Mythic Quest* on Apple TV. This show rocks and taught me what TTP means, thus leading to my absolute need to include it in these pages.

The first person I must acknowledge is Micaela Carr. Though we didn't officially get to work together on this book, you acquired it and collaborated on ideas for it, and that makes you an integral member of the WORLD team. Thank you, more than anything, for a dear, unexpected friendship.

Thank you to my agent, Elisabeth Weed, and the team at The Book Group, especially DJ Kim. You, Elisabeth, are my bulldog, cheerleader, champion, and advocate. I still can't believe I get to call you my agent.

I am constantly in awe of the team at HarperCollins and Harper Perennial, and how they go to bat for me and swing big. Thank you, Heather Drucker, Lisa Erickson, Amy Baker, Laurie

McGee, Emi Battaglia, Ezra Kupor, Suzy Lam, Gill Heeley, and Milan Bozic, among many more. Truly the best team. And especially Emily Griffin, thank you for being the most positive, capable editor I could ask for. I still want to pinch myself that I got to work with you on this.

Thank you to my brilliant additional publicity team: Hanna Lindsley, Leilani Fitzpatrick, and Crystal Patriarche at BookSparks for all you did to get this book into reader's hands.

Thank you, Laura McCorry, Jill Beissel, and Grace Shim, some of my incredible early readers, for your notes, wisdom, and encouragement. Laura, for *Revenge Cheese* in particular.

Madhu and Teddi, you are such fantastic supporters, critique givers, and early readers. Grateful for you both, always.

Kate Brauning. Thank you for the early collaboration on plot. You are a brilliant partner for story development. Of all the programs and people and crafts books I've come across, you are the realest deal. Thank you.

Allie Gravitt. Thank you for being a never-ending well of weird ideas that were just what I need. I'm so lucky to have you to go to for random ideas. You get me and my weird sense of humor deeply. Lindsey Redd and Adrienne Schenck, you are such incredible hype women. I'm so grateful for our little group.

Christelle Lujan. I have no words, only all the love emojis. The Thelma to my Louise. The Tess to my Sloane. Although, in reality, you are Sloane and I am Tess. I love being on this ride with you.

There have been several book people who have championed me and my work; the earliest of supporters, the rooftop shouters: @reviewsbybee, @chelseahudsonreads, @miks_bookpicks, @katiereads.nj, @olivias.bookclub, @elizabethlyonsauthor, @mary.belle.books, @subakka.bookstuff, @overbookedmoms, @eat.pray.decorate to name a few. I hope you enjoy this one too.

Mom, Dad, Raj, Jane Alexander, Raelene Plant, Beth Lebowitz, Lindsie Davis, LaTrenda Lawson, and #pilotjeff—just, thank you.

Sawyer and Sienna. You care deeply about seeing your names in my books. Here they are. Thank you for rooting me on. You're the best cheering section imaginable.

To my husband, Kris. I cannot write a love story without pieces and parcels of you sprinkled in. From the FREE HUGS shirt to "give me the Beach Boys," you are present in every love interest I write. Including details of you is my way of shamelessly flirting. Is it working?

Finally, for all the Jack Palmers I have encountered in my career, of which there have been many—thank you for the inspo. I hope you are blessed with badass, capable daughters who make you see the error of your ways.

Finally, finally—to the readers. Thank you. However you found your way to this book, I'm so grateful you did.

About the Author

NEELY TUBATI ALEXANDER is originally from the Seattle area and resides in Arizona with her husband and children. Her debut novel, *Love Buzz*, won the Zibby Award for Best Beach Read and was hailed by *Good Morning America* as "the perfect escapist read . . . absolutely delightful," and *Booklist* declared her "an exciting new romance writer."